'Tis the season to be merry…

Even at Christmas there are some people who just won't or *can't* enjoy the holidays. In this special collection, we see three such Scrooges get a taste of seasonal magic and

CHRISTMAS LOVING

Come and watch the fun…

CHRISTMAS LOVING

TIFFANY WHITE
ALYSSA DEAN
LEANDRA LOGAN

DID YOU PURCHASE THIS BOOK WITHOUT A COVER?
If you did, you should be aware it is **stolen property** as it was reported *unsold and destroyed* by a retailer. Neither the author nor the publisher has received any payment for this book.

All the characters in this book have no existence outside the imagination of the author, and have no relation whatsoever to anyone bearing the same name or names. They are not even distantly inspired by any individual known or unknown to the author, and all the incidents are pure invention.

First published in Great Britain 2000
by Harlequin Mills & Boon Limited, Eton House,
18-24 Paradise Road, Richmond, Surrey, TW9 1SR

ISBN 0 263 82480 2

101-0900

Printed and bound in Spain
by Litografia Rosés S.A., Barcelona

CONTENTS

THE 6' 1" GRINCH

Tiffany White

To Lance and Millicent Thomure

Thanks to Nancy DuMeyer—
real-estate agent par excellence

* * *

Tiffany White says,

"I have always adored romantic comedies because the man who can make me laugh wins my heart. And when it comes to the season of Christmas, well what's not to like about a holiday that celebrates love and involves presents! Combining the two seemed natural.

As an extroverted, impractical, extravagant Leo, I, of course, married an introverted, practical and thrifty Capricorn. Also known as a grinch. So when my editor invited me to write a Christmas book, I was thrilled. I had plenty of personal research on the 6' 1" grinch.

On our first Christmas together my grinch gave me bake wear. I didn't say a word in front of his family, but later explained I wanted a personal gift in the future.

Our second Christmas my grinch presented me with a blender. I pitched a fit right in front of his family…only to belatedly discover the beautiful gold locket inside the blender. I'd forgotten my grinch's wry humour.

But beware of what you wish for because my reformed grinch has taken my desire for personal gifts to heart, and while I'm longing for the newest laptop computer on the market, he's happily browsing through Victoria's Secret."

Prologue

December 15

IT WAS SNOWING.

Again.

Claudia Claus just adored her hubby, and even after all their years of marriage, and even with his ever-growing love handles, just the tickle of his white whiskers against her face still sent shivers—and not those of cold—right down to her toes. And she loved their life together, but for some peculiar reason, this Christmas she had cabin fever in the *worst* way. The howling December wind, the blowing snow and deserted isolation of the North Pole were really getting to her. She'd had enough of the ice, snow, blizzards and subzero temperatures, and being ignored by Santa while he obsessively prepared for his annual gift run. Jeez, you would have thought that he could practically do it in his sleep. But, no. He was as nervous and persnickety as if this was the first time he'd taken the sled and reindeers out.

What she needed was a distraction—a little Christmas project of her own. Why, Santa probably wouldn't even miss her, he was so busy breathing down the necks of the elves, if she did take a small vacation. Last night when she'd breathed on his neck, hoping to lure him into the bedroom, he'd had the audacity to suggest that she might be out of shape!

She walked around aimlessly from room to room. Then, recalling Santa's crack, she searched for an aerobics tape and tried working out with Claudia Schiffer for a while. That didn't hold her attention for long. It was too discouraging. No amount of prancing and dancing was ever going to make her thighs as firm as Claudia's. For that, she'd require the magic of David Copperfield.

Ejecting the tape, she picked up one of the glossy women's magazines she'd taken to reading. She sat down in a wing chair in the bedroom, her attention riveted by an article encouraging women to do their own things. Escape convention. Shape their own lives.

It was just the encouragement she needed to rationalize her escape from frostbite temperatures and frigid boredom. And to keep her out of the Christmas cookies!

She went to pull her dusty suitcase from beneath the giant four-timber bed. A mischievous smile played at her lips as she planned her trip south. True, St. Louis wasn't that far south, but somehow she knew it wouldn't be wise to come back to the North Pole with a tan.

As it was, she was going to have to bring one heck of an extraspecial souvenir for Santa as a peace offering.

1

December 16

EVERY YEAR Hollie Winslow put up her Christmas tree at Thanksgiving, and every year her friend Sarah Smith came over on Valentine's Day to make her take it down. Hollie knew Sarah considered her a holiday freak, but Hollie didn't agree. She didn't think you could overdo such a bright, magical season.

The strings of colorful Christmas lights in combination with the dusting of snow on the cupolas and gables and cornices of the turn-of-the-century houses on Wisteria Avenue made the street appear shimmering with Christmas magic and spirit, Hollie thought as she drove along it. She was en route to the Premiere Homes real estate office for her last turn at manning the telephones before she began her annual vacation.

Suddenly she slammed on the brakes. The Victorian gingerbread house she'd had her eye on had a sign outside. She'd tried to list the vacant house herself, but had been unable to locate the owner. Darn! It now appeared another real estate agent had beaten her to the listing.

Curious about which agent had gotten the jump on her, she backed up her four-door sedan and pulled over to park in front of the house, skidding to a stop on a slick patch of road. Unsquinching her eyes after not hearing the crumple of fender, she breathed a sigh of relief at the sight of the still-intact red sports car jutting out of the driveway adjoining the house. By squinting just a bit, she could make out the sign posted in the long front yard.

It read:

Ms. Claudia
VISIONARY
Special Holiday Rates

Hmm…this was curiouser and curiouser.

Hollie decided to see who had rented the property and from whom. If it was on a short-term lease, maybe it would need to be listed after the holidays. She didn't want to work during the holidays anyway. The next ten days were carefully planned, filled with enough activities to make Martha Stewart look like a slacker!

She made the trip up the walk in her snow boots without event. On the front porch, she pressed the bell, expecting someone in gold hoop earrings and a fringed shawl to answer the door. Instead she was met by a stylishly white-haired woman wearing a red holiday sweater and green leggings.

''Come in, come in,'' the woman said, as if she'd been expecting Hollie. ''I'm Ms. Claudia.''

''Hollie Winslow,'' she replied, shaking Ms. Claudia's hand and smiling as she read the slogan on the woman's red top: "You ain't seen cute till you've seen St. Louis." Hollie recognized the whimsical artwork of a local artist, who was gaining a good measure of national fame.

"Would you like me to do a reading? The special holiday rate is only fifty dollars."

"Uh..." Hollie glanced down at her favorite yuletide watch with the Christmas tree on its face. "I don't have much time before I have to be at my real estate office."

"Well, we could do a minireading for, say, twenty-five dollars. I'll just hit the high points."

"High points?"

Ms. Claudia's laugh was merry. "You know, like what Santa's bringing you for Christmas if you've been a good girl. And of course you've always been a good girl."

Ms. Claudia had that much right. Orphaned at seven when her parents had been killed in an automobile accident, she'd first been placed in a series of orphanages, then had grown up in foster care when she wasn't adopted. Trying to please and be good hadn't gotten her love, but it had gotten her by. In foster care they hadn't wanted her to get used to any family, so they'd changed families every couple of years. Foster care was meant to be temporary care.

All that uprooting and loneliness had made her hunger for a home of her own. And she supposed it was the reason she had chosen to become a real estate agent—it was her way of finding just the right houses to become homes for her clients. And she found it immensely rewarding when she succeeded. She smiled to herself.

Since childhood she'd had this fanciful affinity for houses. They were as real to her as people. And each time she'd leave a house she'd say goodbye.

She looked around the hallway, taken by the oak staircase and paneling and the whimsy of the decoration. Something about this house was calling out to her. Hollie supposed it would be rude not to let Ms. Claudia do her reading—especially if she wanted to see more of the gingerbread house and to learn the name of the owner.

''The abbreviated reading would be all right, I guess.''

Ms. Claudia nodded and took Hollie's red swing coat. After hanging it up on the brass coat tree, she led Hollie into the parlor, which was dominated by a huge, gloriously splendid Christmas tree, hung with balls, lights and Victorian-style ornaments. Perhaps Ms. Claudia had inherited the house. The place did suit her; both were cozy, familiar and inviting, Hollie thought, as she sat down in one of the green velvet wing chairs facing the blazing fire in the hearth.

''Now, what would you like to know?'' Ms. Claudia asked, settling into the chair across from her.

''Who the owner of this house is,'' Hollie said with a smile.

Ms. Claudia laughed. ''That's right, you're in real estate. Well, it isn't me. I've just leased it for the holidays. I answered an ad in the newspaper. Before you leave, I'll look up the number. I understand someone inherited the house, who isn't scheduled to take possession until after the holidays."

Hollie slumped at the news. It was such a darling house and she would have loved showing it. Oh, well, it wasn't meant to be.

"Surely there must be something else you want to know," Ms. Claudia said.

Hollie brightened. "Okay, what *is* Santa bringing me for Christmas?"

"Santa's got a great big package for you this year."

"How big?"

"Six feet one inch."

"What?"

"Santa's not bringing you a great big package with a bow on it—he's bringing you a beau." Ms. Claudia settled back in her wing chair, obviously delighted with her news.

"Wait a minute. Are you trying to tell me I should expect to find a man under my tree Christmas morning?" Hollie asked, laughing nervously.

"That's what I'm telling you. Anything else you'd like to know?"

"But…but there's not a man on my Christmas wish list. I wanted a bread maker—you know, one of those cool bread-and-butter makers." It really was what she wanted and she felt compelled to explain. "I sampled the bread from one of them in a housewares store a few weeks back. It smelled and tasted so-o-o good."

Ms. Claudia's eyes twinkled as she insisted, "So can a man."

Hollie felt herself blush. And she knew Ms. Claudia could tell. It was the fate of having a pale complexion—she lit up like a Christmas tree when she blushed.

''Are you sure about this? I'm not certain I want—I mean, I'm not ready for...''

''Love? How can anyone not be ready for love?'' Ms. Claudia asked, sounding amazed.

''It's not that I'm not ready for love. I'd like to fall in love, but with the right man.''

''And you haven't had much luck with men?'' Ms. Claudia guessed.

''They tend to disappoint me.''

''This one won't.''

''That's what I tell myself every time. Oh, well, at least I'll get my holidays in before he shows up to disrupt my life on Christmas Day.''

''You know, Hollie, peace and quiet can be way overrated.''

''So can men,'' Hollie grumbled a few hours later as she neared the end of her shift at the real estate office. In only five minutes she'd be off on vacation and could begin enjoying the holiday season she adored. Thank goodness the real estate business was slow at this time of year and she had a lenient boss. She glanced down at her watch. In mere minutes she'd be out of here, and she began to gather her purse and things to leave. Then the phone rang.

''Premiere Homes,'' she answered, mouthing ''go away'' beneath her breath.

''I need an agent to help me—''

Hollie interrupted the client before he got too involved. Through the front window, she caught sight of Sandy Martin, the receptionist, who was just pulling into the parking lot. If she could hold this guy off, Sandy could take a message.

"If you'll just wait, I'll have the receptionist make an appointment for you—"

"No, that won't do. You don't understand. I need an agent right now. I've found a house I want to see today."

"But—"

He was better at getting his way than she was. "I need to find a house by Christmas. I've just transferred in from another town," he said, his deep voice firm and insistent.

She found herself weakening, despite her vacation plans. Of course anyone would want his family settled for the holidays. No man would want his family to spend Christmas in a motel.

He pushed his case.

"Look, I'll make it easy on you," he said, softening his voice. "I'll waive all rights to any inspection—and I'll pay cash."

A cash buyer was an agent's dream, and waiving all rights to an inspection was the icing on the cake. Only a fool would pass on a lucrative client with such potential. And a woman whose old car was having such an intimate relationship with the repair garage would have to be plain nuts. With the down payment for a new car dancing in her head, she felt herself caving in.

''Where is the house you want to see? Do you have an address for me?''

''Yes,'' he replied. ''I stopped and jotted it down when I saw the For Sale sign in the yard.''

He gave her the address and she logged on to the computer to look up the specs on the house in the MLS network of listings. She found the place easily enough. It was listed at three hundred thousand dollars, making her commission—if she closed the sale—nine thousand dollars!

''What time would you be available to look at it if I can schedule an appointment?'' Hollie asked, trying to sound casual.

''As soon as possible. I want to buy a place by Christmas,'' he stressed.

''Okay, let me call the agent and see if I can set up a time for us to go through it. It's difficult during the holidays, so don't get your hopes up. Give me your number and I'll phone you as soon as I can.''

He gave her the name of his hotel and she repeated it to him. ''And your name?'' she inquired.

''Noel.''

''Did you say 'Noel'?''

''Is there a problem?'' he asked with an edge to his voice.

''No, no. It's just that it's Christmastime and your name is Noel and my name is Hollie, Hollie Winslow.''

''I'll be waiting for your call, Ms. Winslow.'' He replied so briskly that she felt foolish for bringing up the Christmasy associations of their names. She put down the receiver. Oh, well, she didn't have to like the man to sell him a house, and he most certainly didn't have to like her to buy the house. So why did it matter to her what kind of impression she'd made on him?

IT HADN'T BEEN an auspicious start to her holiday vacation, Hollie thought that evening at Leo's Garage, where she had been waiting for the past hour to have a new muffler installed in her car. Her old one had fallen off her car in the middle of the street, in the middle of rush hour, and she'd driven to Leo's making more noise than a freight train. Sandy had paged her that a Mr. Noel Hawksley was at the real estate office demanding to see her, more than a tad upset she wasn't there, demanding to know why she hadn't called back with an appointment to show him the house he wanted to see. Demanding to know if Ms. Winslow was always so inefficient. No doubt all his demands had fallen within earshot of the agency's owner. Hollie made a mental note to phone the owner the next morning and explain that she'd spent the afternoon driving by available stock in Mr. Hawksley's price range so she'd have something to show him if she couldn't get ahold of the agent who'd listed the house he wanted to see. That so far, she'd been unsuccessful in reaching the agent. Then her damn muffler had fallen off.

Aggravated, Hollie finished writing out a check for the new muffler. At least there hadn't been any more urgent pages from the real estate office while she was impatiently pacing at the garage.

As she ripped off the check from her checkbook to hand to the mechanic, she glanced at her cellular phone, which was lying beside her purse on the counter. She hoped it was working. It hadn't rung once. It was so frustrating trying to reach an agent during the holidays.

She'd wanted to get together with her anxious client, but it didn't look as if that was going to happen until tomorrow.

She glanced down at her watch again. Her godchild, Elena, was four years old, but had the patience of a two-year-old. Elena's mother, Sarah, Hollie's best friend, wasn't going to appreciate Hollie being late for their annual cookie-baking marathon. Most likely, Sarah had already started baking.

Hollie remembered the white chocolate Sarah had asked her to pick up. She'd have to make a stop for that and be even later. If she wasn't waiting for the agent to call, she'd call Sarah.

''Ring, damn it,'' she muttered, glaring at the silent phone.

She hoped this wasn't a foreshadowing of how her holidays were going to go.

Her vacation wouldn't swing into full gear until she'd settled her new client and his family in a new home for the holidays. With any luck at all, in the morning they'd get in to see the house he'd called her about.

She smiled as she handed Matt, who was new at the garage, her check. ''Tell Leo thanks for fitting me in.''

''Uncle Leo said any time you had trouble to take care of you right away.''

Hollie laughed. ''That's because I'm financing his holiday cruise with the repairs to my old clunker.''

''I think it's because of your great smile.''

Hollie blushed and he turned to ring up her check.

A woman in a holiday sweater came in looking for someone to repair a flat tire. The sweater made Hollie remember Ms. Claudia's promise of a six-foot-one-inch beau for Christmas. Leo's nephew Matt had a nice butt and he was kinda tall.

''How tall are you?'' she surprised him and herself by asking when he turned to hand her the receipt for the work on her car.

''How tall?'' he repeated.

She nodded.

''About five foot eleven,'' he answered, picking up the ringing wall phone.

Well, that left out Matt. Growing two inches by Christmas day wasn't within the realm of possibility. Neither was, Hollie smiled to herself, getting a tall, dark and handsome beau for Christmas. But it didn't stop a girl from hoping, did it?

On the drive home from the garage, she slipped in Kenny G's holiday tape and felt her stress melt as fast as last night's snowfall while the soothing notes of ''Silver Bells'' filled the car.

The cellular phone that had been annoyingly quiet rang, breaking into a soaring tenor sax solo.

''Hello,'' Hollie said, expectant.

''Where are you? You're supposed to be here already,'' Sarah said, her annoyance coming in loud and clear.

''And you're supposed to be the real estate agent I've been calling. What's up, Sarah?''

''Elena's insisting that I stop baking cookies and French-braid her hair like Auntie Hollie's. Did you remember the white chocolate?''

''Yeah, yeah. Tell Elena to find a ribbon for her braid and take a chill pill till I get there.''

''Which will be...?''

''Tonight, definitely tonight.''

''Hollie—''

''Okay, okay. Fifteen minutes. Unless six foot one inch shows, and then don't wait up.''

''What?''

''I'll tell you about it when I get there.''

''Whatever, just get here. No, Elena, you can't feed the dog chocolate chips....''

Elena answered the door when Hollie arrived. At four Elena had a mind of her own, a creative fashion sense and an advanced interest in makeup and hairstyles. At the moment she was dressed in a denim empire dress, hiking boots and her big, soft brown teddy bear backpack. ''You're late,'' she announced.

''Where are you going?'' Hollie asked Elena as Sarah peeked around the kitchen doorway, flour dusted on her nose and her hair in a haphazard ponytail.

''She isn't going anywhere,'' Sarah said. ''She just refuses to take her teddy bear backpack off. Even sleeps with it.''

''Should stand her in good stead as a Girl Scout—always be prepared, you know.''

''Yeah, right. I'm wrist deep in big boy brownies. You said you remembered the white chocolate....''

''Got it.'' Hollie produced it. ''And a new muffler—that's why I'm late. I swear every time I build up my fund for plastic surgery, I have to use it on my car.''

''What's 'lastic surgery, Mom?'' Elena wanted to know.

''Auntie Hollie wants bigger 'bumpies,''' Sarah explained, refusing as she had since she'd adopted Elena to shield her from any information.

''Me, too,'' Elena agreed.

Sarah just shook her head. ''You know, Hollie, I'm sending her to live with you when she turns thirteen.''

Unrepentant, Hollie replied, ''Good, then I'll have a whole new wardrobe to borrow from.''

''I don't know which of you is the bad influence.'' Sarah took the white chocolate and nodded for Hollie to follow her to the kitchen. ''You can drizzle the melted white chocolate and butter over the brownies when they come out of the oven.''

''What about my French braid?'' Elena pleaded, her ''licksticked'' pink pout evidence she had already been into her mom's makeup.

''I'll just be a sec,'' Hollie promised, taking Elena's tugging hand.

''I'm setting a timer,'' Sarah called out after them.

Hollie waved her hand over her head. ''Yeah, yeah.''

''Do you want to hear the Christmas song I learned

at day school?'' Elena asked, climbing up on the chintz bench in front of Sarah's makeup table.

Without waiting for an answer, Elena launched into ''Santa Claus Is Coming to Town,'' while Hollie braided her hair in a reverse French braid. By the time Elena had finished her rendition Hollie had tied the pink ribbon in a bow to anchor the braid.

''Now, let's go help your mom with the cookies.''

''Okay,'' Elena agreed, scampering ahead of her. ''Mom said I could ice the angel cookies.''

Hollie could smell the rich brownies baking in the oven as she watched Sarah expertly roll out an eighth-inch-thick circle of dough.

''Hand me the angel cookie cutter, Elena,'' Sarah instructed, then showed Elena how to use it.

While Elena was busy pressing the white plastic angel cookie cutter into the soft circle of yellow cookie dough, Hollie began giving Sarah the third degree about her love life. ''So, are you getting a diamond for Christmas?''

''If I buy one for myself.''

''What happened?''

''It didn't work out. He was great with Elena, but—''

''But you didn't need a man to get Elena and so you certainly don't need to marry one just for Elena, right?''

''Do you think I'm wrong, Hollie?''

''No. I think if you're happy, Elena's happy. You adopted her because you have a lot of love to give. When you find the guy you can both love, then you won't hesitate. There's no reason to settle. Besides, if I don't like the guy Santa leaves under my tree, I'll send him over to you."

"What guy? What are you talking about? Did I miss a meeting?" Sarah asked, trying to keep up with the conversation and bake at the same time. Sarah had been running her own catering business from home since she'd adopted Elena. It provided a good living and gave her time to enjoy Elena's years before she started school. She was thinking of expanding her business once the little girl was in grade one. On sleepless nights, Sarah worked on plans for her new venture.

"Well, Ms. Claudia said—promised, actually—that I was going to find a *beau* under my Christmas tree."

"And Ms. Claudia is...?"

"She's the psychic who's rented the Victorian gingerbread house I told you about. For a small fee she'll tell you what the near future holds. Maybe you should give her a try. She's something else." Hollie thought Sarah could use the bit of fun, at the very least.

"I think I'll pass. I already know what the near future holds—parties. I've got a party booked nearly every night from now until New Year's Day."

"That's what you get for being Martha Stewart's clone."

"Hey, no mocking my idol," Sarah warned with a teasing grin as she put cookies in the oven.

"Perky Martha exhausts me. Her so-called simple projects take more skills than I could muster in a lifetime of lessons. Still, I have been thinking of doing one of those gingerbread houses she claims are a piece of cake to make.''

''A gingerbread house! Oh, Auntie Hollie, can I help you?'' Elena said, jumping up and down beside Hollie.

''You sure can, sugarpie. I'm on vacation—well, sort of, if I can get rid of Noel.''

''Who's Noel?'' Sarah asked.

''A client. I've got to find a house for him and his family by Christmas. Hopefully he'll like the one I show him tomorrow, if I can get hold of the listing agent. He's a cash buyer who could make my Christmas very merry, as in a down payment for a new car.''

''Can I spend the night when we make the gingerbread house, Auntie Hollie?''

''Sure, sugarpie. Your mom can use a break while she gets ready to cater all the parties she has lined up. We'll rent *The Little Princess,* take bubble baths, do our toenails bright cherry red and eat cookies in bed.''

''Can we go now?'' Elena stopped jumping and wrapped her arms around Hollie.

''No, tonight we have to bake the cookies we're going to eat in bed. You're icing the angel cookies, remember,'' she said, looking down fondly at Elena, who nodded, her eyes bright with excitement. She stroked Elena's silky hair. Hollie wondered if she'd have a daughter someday. First, though, she would need a husband, since she was nowhere near as brave as Sarah to raise a daughter on her own. Growing up never having been part of a family, she didn't have the heart to deprive her own child of what she herself had been so painfully deprived of. Her longing to create a home and a traditional family life hadn't gone down well with the commitment-phobic men she dated. She was beginning to fear that the family man had gone the way of the dodo and dinosaur.

NOEL HAWKSLEY STARED at the phone that didn't ring in his hotel room.

Early in the morning he was going back to Premiere Homes and make sure Hollie Winslow got his message. The one the receptionist had apparently forgotten to give her. He wanted a deal closed on the house he'd seen as soon as possible. He'd taken vacation until the first of the year to get the house business settled. No way did he want to spend Christmas in the States. He could sum up his feelings about the holidays in two words—bah, humbug.

He began peeling off his clothes, then hung up his suit in the tiny closet. His designer suits fit him to perfection because they were custom-tailored and because he worked out regularly. While he was stuck here, he would have to find a local gym to join to work off stress and keep his body honed. He would be in great shape when he started his job in the new year.

He wasn't the sort of man who plumbed the depths of his soul. Better not to swim in those murky waters. Instead he focused on his career in business—it gave him an edge as well as an escape.

Talk about escape. Last Christmas he'd narrowly escaped Marcy, his overly possessive ex-fiancée, though it hadn't seemed like a good thing at the time.

Escape.

That was what he wanted to do right now, but he had to find a house first. He picked up the remote on the night table beside the king-size bed and clicked on the television.

At least Hollie Winslow appeared not to like the season any more than he did. That was some consolation, he thought, stretching out naked on the bed.

The last thing he wanted was some perky, happy-holiday lover.

Meanwhile, back at the North Pole…

CLAUDIA'S NOTE was irritatingly vague, Santa noted suspiciously. She hadn't said exactly where the spa she'd gone to was. His wife just hadn't been the same since she'd started working out to those videotapes and reading those women's magazines she subscribed to. *New Woman,* indeed.

Not that he was complaining. He thought Claudia looked awfully sexy in the elf tights she'd taken to wearing with her funky holiday sweaters. His ho-ho-ho's had definitely gotten a lot jollier.

Still, he'd be a lot happier if he knew where this spa was…and just where she'd hidden the Christmas cookies when she'd left.

2

December 17

NOEL HAWKSLEY PULLED his black Lexus sedan up in front of Premiere Homes. After his morning cup of coffee he'd decided to pay his visit to Ms. Winslow early before he missed her again.

He groaned as yet another Christmas song came on the radio. He turned off the ignition and the song a lot easier than he could his dislike of the season. Born on Christmas Day, he'd never received a separate birthday present as a kid. That had given him a head start on hating the day. And then he'd gone into retail—scouting out new locations and administratively orchestrating the openings of Bon Marché's national chain of upscale department stores. Everyone in retail eventually grew to dread the month of December. Overworked and stressed to the max, Noel found little joy by the end of the month and escaped every Christmas Eve to St. Bart in the Caribbean. Lots of shapely women in bikinis and white pristine beaches were his reward for not committing murder most jolly.

The one time he'd been inclined to change his mind about the holidays had been a disaster. A year ago, the woman he'd thought he was in love with had sealed his hatred for the season by breaking their engagement on Christmas Eve. He'd never forgiven Marcy for that.

He got out of the car and went inside the real estate office, determined to have his way.

''Noel Hawksley to see Ms. Winslow,'' he announced to Sandy, who looked up as she took a call.

''First door on your right,'' she mouthed, her hand covering the receiver.

Noel followed her direction, and found a lush brunette sitting at a cluttered desk, muttering as she searched through the pile of papers in front of her for something. ''Elena, you little squirrel, if you've taken my telephone book to color in...''

As she continued muttering and searching, he took a moment to glance around her office before announcing his presence.

At the sight of the framed poster on her right, he laughed outright, alerting Hollie. It was a picture of the famous Hearst Castle—San Simeon—and pasted across it was the banner ''Sold Fast.''

The woman blushed and tried to cover her embarrassment with a quick, businesslike ''Can I help you?''

He offered his hand. ''Noel Hawksley. You *do* remember talking with me?''

''Of course. I was just trying to find your number to call you. I've had trouble reaching the listing agent, but she finally returned my message this morning, and I've set up an appointment. The sellers are out of town for the holidays, but we can get in to see the house any time you like by using the agent's key."

"I'm ready whenever you are," he informed her, eyeing the pile of flotsam on her desk, which included a bottle of red nail polish, men's deodorant—she must subscribe to the never-let-them-see-you-sweat school of selling houses—pens, a cellular phone and sundry papers.

She swept the whole pile into her briefcase and flashed him a smile. "I'm ready."

She led him to her car, and he read the spec sheet on the house as she drove, restraining himself with difficulty from commenting on her propensity for changing lanes frequently. Usually erratic lane switchers drove him up the wall, but today, all things considered, a woman in a hurry was right up his alley. The sooner they found him a house, the happier he'd be.

"Were you thinking of private or public schools?" she asked as she waited at a stoplight.

"I'm out of school," he answered dryly.

"No, I meant—oh, you don't have children, then."

"No children."

"I see. Well, the taxes on this house are midrange. The neighborhood has a good tax base, what with it being close to the Galleria. Your wife will love the shopping there. It's where I'm going to do my Christmas shopping."

"No wife," he said, in a deadpan tone.

"Oh. Well, then *you'll* like the shopping there."

"No, I won't."

''Oh, you're like most men and don't like to shop.''

''It's not the shopping I mind. It's the time of year.''

''Don't you like the holidays?'' she asked, surprised.

''I loathe them.'' That appeared to shock her. It was as if he'd said he didn't believe in Santa Claus. Maybe he shouldn't be so hard on her. She seemed primed to do her holiday shopping—the back seat of her car was filled with rolls of gift wrapping, packages of bows and unwrapped gift boxes in every shape and size.

She would probably be astonished to learn he knew more about shopping than she did. It was his area of expertise. He knew just what configuration of merchandise would make a consumer turn loose her credit card. Knew what music would put her in the mood to spend a lot of cash. Knew what colors would induce her to linger in an area long enough to make a purchase.

And more than all the technology and science, he had something of even greater value to offer—his gut feelings about trends and the desires of the consumer mass. More than anything, that was what garnered him the high salary and the respectful attention of Bon Marché's money men.

But it wasn't money that drove or satisfied him. It was curiosity. He was always restless and easily bored.

''We're here,'' Hollie announced as they pulled up to a two-story house with a brick walkway that led to a wide front porch.

''So we are.'' He followed her up to the house. She walked slower than she drove, but that could be due to the ankle-length, black wool gabardine skirt with a back zip and kick pleat that she was wearing. Her trim ankles were hobbled in suede boots with two-inch heels. Her short black suede jacket covered the rest of her, hiding the more interesting details of her anatomy.

The house was decorated with only a simple wreath at the door, Noel noted, as Hollie rummaged about in her briefcase to get the key to the front door. Like many businesswomen he knew, Hollie evidently used her briefcase as her purse to avoid having to carry both.

''Elena, I'm going to throttle you,'' she muttered.

''Is there a problem?'' he asked as she grew more flustered, dropping to one knee for a closer look in her briefcase.

''I can't find the key. I'm sure it's in here somewhere. It has to be in here someplace. I'll have to pay a huge fine to replace it if it isn't. Please be in here,'' she begged, finally upending the briefcase in frustration.

''Sold Fast''? He couldn't imagine how. Ms. Winslow was about as professional and organized as a four-year-old.

He tried not to tap his foot as she sifted through the contents of her briefcase. He was certain the key wasn't there. This didn't bode well for seeing the house and making a buy anytime soon.

''It's not here,'' she finally announced.

To the surprise of no one.

''Now what?'' he asked, truly curious, as he watched her scoop up her stuff and toss it all back into the briefcase, about how she'd handle the situation.

''Ah, I really hate that we made the trip for nothing.''

She shoved her cloud of hair back and thought for a moment, while he waited, using the time to take in her lively green eyes.

''Okay, okay. I know, we can have a look in the windows since we're here.'' She walked over to the one on her left. The traditional-style house had tieback curtains, so one could easily see in through the multipaned glass.

She was actually serious, he realized, when she began describing the interior of the room, trying to sell him on the house from the outside.

''See, the dining room has a fireplace. That's a nice bonus, don't you think? It would be great for business dinners.''

He came to stand beside her and glanced in, then looked down at her. ''I don't have business dinners at home. I'm single, so I entertain in restaurants. I understand St. Louis has many fine such establishments.''

''That's true. St. Louis is known for its Italian cuisine in particular.''

Not giving up on her harebrained idea, Hollie moved to the window on her right. ''Look, the living room has a fireplace, too.''

She wasn't deterred when he didn't follow her to the window, just went on with her spiel about the room's selling points.

''Look at the big old rafters, and the pine floors are made of real tongue-and-groove boards. The French doors even have transoms.''

''I'm more interested in whether the kitchen has a built-in microwave and whether the family room is large enough to accommodate a big-screen TV and a regulation-size pool table. You know—is the place livable?''

''A pool table,'' she repeated, clearly taken aback.

Obviously she didn't think he was the type. His custom-tailored suit didn't suggest a taste for motorcycles and smoky rooms.

He shrugged. ''Some people relax with yoga or fly-fishing. I play pool to get mellow.''

''So let's see what's around back,'' she proposed. ''This house has the typical St. Louis floor plan, with the living room and dining room side by side in the front of the house and the kitchen and family room in back, forming a perfect square box.''

She was plucky; he'd give her that. And so, having nothing better to do, he trailed after her to the back of the house to see what the windows there yielded. If they could see in them.

The large cedar deck that ran across the back of the house afforded them an easy view of the rear rooms. He let her climb the steps to the deck first, enjoying the scenery...and not of the expansive backyard, either.

''Oh, it's plenty spacious for your needs,'' she cried out happily upon seeing the open-plan kitchen-family room. ''See, there's a built-in microwave in the center island and the kitchen even has white painted cabinets with glass fronts so you won't have to remember where you put the coffee when you wake up grouchy.''

He pretty much knew that was a dig. But peering inside, he had to admit the house met his requirements nicely.

''Okay, this is looking good, but what about the half story above? I'll need some room for a home office, with enough electricity for a fax, computer, copier and such.'' He glanced at the windows four feet above their heads, then back down at her. ''I suppose I could boost you up so you could stand on my shoulders and tell me....''

Hollie stared down at her long, narrow skirt and boots and then looked up at him again. ''Not a chance. You'll just have to use your imagination.''

Her reply got a flashy grin from the grinch. Clearly he was already doing just that—lasciviously.

Hollie knew they had gotten off to a bad start, with him thinking she was some incompetent fluff. But she knew better. And she was the one who would be smiling when she got the commission for selling him a house. Because she would sell it; she was very good at what she did.

As good as he figured he was.

HOLLIE'S RUSE of selling Noel the house from the outside hadn't worked. She couldn't believe she'd actually tried such a scheme. Every once in a while her Lucy Ricardo streak surfaced, despite her best efforts to keep it in check. And usually when she was confronted by someone stuffy like her tall broad-shouldered client. Noel Hawksley had perfect manners, and a peculiar effect on her. She was unaccountably nervous and self-conscious—as if they were on a first date instead of a first peek at a house.

She realized that her efforts to get inside were not just

professionally motivated. She wanted him to like her. Why? She wasn't even sure she liked him herself. One thing for sure—it appeared no one ever played fast with rules around him. *Play* wasn't a word she'd bet was in his vocabulary. He was all business and that was just fine with her, she thought, sitting across from him in her office, where they'd returned so she could do a computer search and printout of other similar-style and -size houses in the area for Noel to examine if he didn't like the inside of the house he'd first sighted.

"Did I hear you say 'rats'?" he asked.

She looked away from the screen. "No room for an office for you in that one."

She sighed and wished she were at home making pomanders, creating the fragrance of Christmas for her house. Instead she'd let her excitement at the possibility of earning a big commission—and doing a good deed for a family in dire need, or so she assumed wrongly, of a home for Christmas—interfere with her holiday preparations.

Not only had Noel Hawksley turned out to be single, he was a grinch. She just knew he was going to be one of those clients who took a tremendous amount of time to find that elusive something he wanted to make the purchase, despite his claim he had to be moved into a house by Christmas.

"Maybe your blood sugar is dropping and making you testy. Why don't I buy you lunch? Then we can swing by Elena's—whoever she is—house to check on the key and spend the rest of the afternoon looking at houses."

"Elena is my godchild. Her mother is my best friend, Sarah. But you're right about lunch." Hollie switched off her computer. She'd only breakfasted on an angel cookie she'd filched last night from Sarah with a conspiratorial wink to Elena.

"Okay, I'll let you buy me lunch, since you insist. But first I need to make a quick call to Sarah to make sure she'll be home."

As it happened, they went to Sarah's first because Elena had a dance class scheduled.

When Hollie rang the bell, she heard the patter of little tap shoes and a childlike "I'll get it, Mommy." Hollie quickly prayed that Elena didn't blurt out anything terribly embarrassing. Hollie wasn't at all sure about Sarah's permissive child-rearing practices.

The door eased open and Elena launched herself into Hollie's arms. "Can I spend the night with you, Auntie Hollie? Can I, huh?"

"Uh..."

"Who's he? Is he your new boyfriend?"

"Sorry," Sarah apologized.

She got to the door just as Hollie felt herself turning red.

"Elena's wound up tighter than a top because of the holidays. She takes after Hollie, I'm afraid. Elena get down. You've got tap shoes on and you'll ruin Hollie's pretty suit."

Elena unwound her arms from around Hollie's neck

and stretched them out to Noel, wriggling her fingers for him to take her.

Noel stepped back out of Elena's reach.

''Come on, sugarpie,'' Hollie said, setting the child down and taking her hand. ''Let's go look for my key and telephone book you borrowed from me last night. Do you remember where you stashed them?''

''Sarah Smith,'' Sarah said, holding out her hand and shaking her head. ''You'll have to forgive Hollie. She's a bit of a free spirit.''

''I've noticed. It's good, though, that Elena has a playmate.''

''Why don't you come out to the kitchen? I hear the dog scratching at the kitchen door to come in.''

Noel followed, leery about what might lurk in the topsy-turvy house. They passed a dining room table stacked high with enough Tupperware containers to start a franchise.

''I've been baking,'' Sarah explained. ''Since adopting Elena, I've been catering from my home, and this year the orders for Christmas cookies have been huge. No one seems to have time to bake anymore, thank goodness.''

Sarah's kitchen was as welcoming as she was. The white glass-front cabinets were filled with cheery Fiestaware, and a jumble of pots and pans danced on a rack above the center island.

Sarah opened the kitchen door as Noel took a seat at the round table by the bay window. A froufrou black-

and-white dog jumped into Noel's lap and put its little paws on his chest while it stood to lick his face.

''Midnight, get down,'' Sarah commanded.

Midnight was evidently hard-of-hearing.

''You aren't afraid of dogs, are you?'' Sarah asked, taking the animal and giving it a biscuit to distract it after she shooed it off Noel's lap.

''No. I'm just not used to them.''

''That's a shame. It must be hard moving around a lot the way you do for your career.''

So Sarah and Hollie had discussed him. Interesting.

''I like it. I like a challenge.''

''Then Hollie's the right woman for you. Although men always have a way of disappointing Hollie. Oops, I shouldn't have said that,'' Sarah said, caught up in her matchmaking.

Before Noel could ask why men disappointed Hollie, the subject of their conversation came into the kitchen, victorious in her search for her phone book.

''Found it in Elena's backpack. I had to trade her a tube of your magenta lipstick for it, Sarah. Alas, no key.''

''You didn't let her put the lipstick on—'' Sarah was headed for the bedroom before Hollie could tell her that she was only teasing and the tube she'd traded was jelly-bean pink.

''So what do you think?'' Hollie asked, taking the chair across from Noel.

''Think?'' he repeated, a puzzled expression on his face.

"About Sarah..." she coaxed.

"She's nice—"

"Nice. She's fabulous. Great legs, big blue eyes, and she's a great cook and a wonderful mother."

"I thought we were looking for a *house* for me."

"Of course. But you're single, and I thought that maybe you'd..."

"Make a great father for Elena?"

"That wasn't my first thought after you backed away from holding her."

"I don't know what to do with little kids," he dodged.

"Then you're wrong for Sarah. She wants to adopt another one."

"Do you always do drive-by matchmaking?" he asked, rubbing the wood-grained top of the table with his long fingers.

"Much to Sarah's chagrin. Sarah thinks it's just fine to raise children without a father. I'm not so sure. What do you think?"

"I spent my childhood at boarding school. Only saw my father at holidays."

"How awful."

"Is it?"

"You don't think so?" Hollie was astonished at his matter-of-fact acceptance of a lonely childhood.

She'd always missed having parents; he'd had them and apparently hadn't enjoyed the bond she'd assumed every child would crave.

''Are you close to your parents now?'' she asked, pushing.

''At holidays—except Christmas. That I don't celebrate anywhere but on a warm island away from all the madness.''

''How can you not love Christmas?'' She was serious. ''It's the most magical time of the year. Anything can happen. Anything at all.''

Midnight, done with her biscuit, jumped up into Hollie's lap, and she absentmindedly patted the animal's back.

''You're absolutely right.''

He didn't seem to want to discuss it. ''What time does your tree say?'' Noel asked.

He nodded at her Christmas watch, which he obviously disapproved of.

''Definitely time for lunch. You have anything we can grab a bite of while I keep looking for the key?'' Hollie asked Sarah as she joined them.

''Sorry, since Elena wouldn't take off the lipstick we had to find something that would match jelly-bean pink. How do peanut-butter-and-jelly sandwiches sound?''

''Like you've been around a four-year-old too long,'' Hollie said, wrinkling her nose. ''Don't you have any grown-up food?''

''How about grilled cheese?''

''Perfect. I'll help. You don't mind grabbing a bite here, do you, Noel? It will give us more time to look at houses.''

Noel shrugged, outnumbered and outmaneuvered.

Just when the kitchen was starting to smell buttery good, Elena wandered back in with a tape of *Cinderella* in her hand.

"Mommy, I can't reach the VCR. Will you put it in for me so I can watch like you said until it's time for dance class?"

Sarah was washing lettuce for a salad and Hollie was keeping an eye on the grilled cheese sandwiches so they didn't burn. Both women turned to Noel.

"I can handle the VCR," he assured them, and got up to give Elena a hand.

"You look like the handsome prince," they both heard Elena say as he followed her from the kitchen. The two friends broke up.

"Do you realize a four-year-old has better dating skills than either of us?" Hollie said.

"Yeah, I'm going to have to lock her in her room until she turns thirty. That's why I'm thinking of adopting an older brother for her."

"What did you think of Noel?" Hollie whispered so they wouldn't be overheard discussing their guest.

"What kind of man doesn't like kids or dogs?" Sarah replied. "It's like he's afraid of them."

"He grew up in boarding schools, so I don't think he's ever been around either."

"That's sad."

"He is kinda sad, don't you think?" Hollie slid the cheese sandwich onto a warm plate and began grilling another while Sarah mixed the salad.

''He said he likes a challenge, so I told him you were the perfect woman for him.''

Hollie dropped the spatula in her hand with a clatter. ''You didn't!''

''I did. Serves you right for matchmaking. Don't think I didn't know what you were up to.''

''But now he's going to think *I* want to jump his bones, Sarah.''

''Don't you?''

''Bury them, more like it.''

''Sell that to someone who'll buy it.''

''I'm not interested.'' Hollie emphasized her point by shaking her head. ''He's not my type.''

Sarah laughed. ''Yeah, too tall, too broad-shouldered, too good-looking.''

''He doesn't smile much,'' Hollie insisted.

''He will if he hangs around you for very long. You are a caution, girl.''

''I'm just going to sell him—oops—'' Hollie caught the grilled cheese that almost slid from her spatula to the floor ''—a house and that's all. And hopefully in record time so I can enjoy the holidays. With any luck at all we'll find something this afternoon, and Mr. Noel Hawksley, the grinch, will be history.''

''Grinch?''

''He hates Christmas.''

Sarah erupted into gales of laughter, just managing to blurt out that Hollie and Noel were meant for each other—perfect opposites.

''Be that way,'' Hollie sniffed, patting her riotous

curls. "And here I was going to tell you how much I liked your new haircut."

"Do you? It's a gum cut." Sarah carried the bowl of salad to the table.

"Gum cut?" Hollie added the plate of fragrant cheese sandwiches she'd grilled to a golden brown.

"Your sugarpie crawled into my bed when she had a bad dream last night and somehow her bubble gum got into my hair. So voilà, short haircut. I have to admit it's a lot easier to take care of than long hair. I don't know why I didn't try it sooner, since I'm always so pressed for time now."

"It makes you look like Demi Moore in *Ghost.*"

"Then I'm keeping it."

"Call the grinch and Elena while I get plates, napkins and some chips," Hollie said, not wanting to face Noel after Sarah's inept efforts at matchmaking. Hollie thought her own attempts had been at least semisubtle.

Sugarpie hadn't helped by reminding her that Noel did indeed look like the handsome prince.

Even she didn't believe there was a fairy godmother in existence who could turn Noel into a fun date. Even if Sarah did insist Hollie was a princess, intent on always getting things her way.

She had a plan: find a home for Noel fast, find a car for herself with her tidy commission, end of story. No magic slippers; no fancy ball; no handsome, brooding prince.

Now, that was what she called a happy ending.

NOEL LOOKED DOWN at the little princess who'd climbed up on his lap when he'd settled on the sofa after inserting the *Cinderella* tape in the VCR.

She seemed really comfortable, cuddling against him as she watched the fairy tale.

To his surprise, he felt really comfortable, as well.

Next thing he knew he'd be believing in fairy tales.

And happy holidays.

And happy endings.

He'd have to guard against that.

He'd especially have to guard against the foxy real estate agent starring in his fantasies. What was it about Hollie Winslow that tripped his switches? It was more than the body that wouldn't quit and the mind that eschewed logic in favor of magic.

Meanwhile, back at the North Pole…

SANTA SAT BACK in the recliner with his red stockinged feet up on the footrest. His tummy was stacked with women's magazines. The ones he'd found in Claudia's bathroom. If he was lucky, he might find the spa his wife had gone off to featured in one of them. She might have circled the name, giving herself away.

He hadn't had any luck yet finding the Christmas cookies she'd hidden. He'd looked and looked, even searching in the elves' quarters. They claimed not to have seen them. The reindeer shed hadn't turned up any cookies, either. He'd probably just imagined the crumbs on Rudolph's nose. Claudia wouldn't have fed his chocolate crinkles to the reindeer because she was miffed at him for ignoring her, would she?

He turned the page of the magazine he was holding and reached for the remote control, searching for the hockey game as he settled for some nonfat crackers he'd unearthed in the kitchen pantry.

Bah, humbug.

3

December 18

"SO WHAT HAPPENED to Mr. Smith?" Noel asked the following afternoon on their way to see the house he was interested in after Hollie had finally found the key in another purse of hers, not Elena's.

"There's no Mr. Smith. Never has been. Sarah adopted Elena as a single woman."

"And you think Elena needs a father? She seems happy, if not a little spoiled, to me."

"Having grown up in orphanages and foster homes, I guess I will always think having two parents is the way it should be."

"How'd you happen to grow up in orphanages?" Noel's voice changed to a shout. "Look out, that cigar-chomping idiot in the big boat is drifting over into our lane."

Hollie maneuvered to avoid the bald-headed driver she'd seen without Noel's back-seat driving. "My parents were killed in an accident when I was little."

"And you weren't adopted? I find that hard to believe, with your cute curls and all. You must have been more trouble than you were cute."

''I could never seem to remember when visiting day was,'' she hedged. ''When prospective parents came to look us over, I was always missing somehow.''

''More likely you'd shinnied up a neighborhood fruit tree to steal peaches while everyone was occupied, then sold the peaches to the other kids later.''

Hollie laughed. ''How'd you know?''

''I'm in sales.''

''So how did you happen to grow up in boarding school?'' she asked, as they drove down the street the house was located on.

''My father was ambassador to Holland. He fell in love with a Dutch girl. They traveled around quite a bit so I was sent to boarding school in The Hague.''

''That explains the slight accent.''

''Yeah,'' he agreed. ''Come on, Ms. Winslow, let's find out if you can sell me this house from the inside,'' Noel said, seeing he wasn't going to get a rise out of her.

A breeze lifted the bow on the holiday wreath on the door as Hollie inserted her key to get them inside the house.

''Sign in.'' Hollie slid the guest register on the table to him and handed him a pen.

Since she hadn't toured the house previously, they toured the place together. It had been professionally decorated, so it showed well. But the personal touches that give a house warmth were lacking. Anyone at all might have lived there. Hollie felt sad for the house. No pictures of loved ones anywhere. No children's drawings or funny cartoons or silly magnets on the refrigerator door in the kitchen.

With the exception of the clothes in the closets, the house looked as if it were a display home in one of the new developments nearby.

''What do you think?'' Hollie asked when they descended the stairs from the second floor.

''You're the saleslady—you tell me. Why should I buy this house?''

''It's in a good neighborhood, the price is reasonable, it's low maintenance and you can move in before Christmas,'' she said, checking the sheet in her hand about the availability to make sure.

''But—''

''But?''

''I hear a but in your voice. Tell me why I shouldn't buy this house.''

Hollie strolled to the expanse of windows in the kitchen and looked out over the large yard. The refrigerator kicked on and hummed in the silence between them. Finally she answered. ''I don't think this is the right house for you.'' There, it was out—and she was certifiable. She was supposed to be selling him the house, not trying to discourage him from buying it. ''This house is sad and deserves a happy family.''

''What?'' He looked at her, incredulous.

''Hey, I don't like it any more than you do, but you asked me, so I have to tell you. I don't think you and this house are a good match, no matter how much I'd like to sell it to you and get on with my vacation.''

"That's your only reason—this feeling you have about me and the house?"

She nodded.

"Then let's write up an offer," he insisted, going to sit down at the kitchen counter, where she'd left her briefcase. "You did remember to bring an offer form?"

"Of course."

She joined him at the counter and withdrew the necessary form from her briefcase.

"What do you want to offer on it?" she asked after filling out the standard information on the form.

"Let's make it twenty thousand under the asking price."

She didn't say anything as she jotted down the figure.

"You don't agree?" he asked.

"It's your money. I'm just surprised you're haggling when you're so anxious to get into a house and out of town before Christmas."

"No one expects you to offer the full price. I may be anxious, but I'm not foolish. Or sad," he insisted.

Hollie laughed. "You don't like being told anything, do you?"

"And you do?" he countered, signing the offer she slid across the counter to him.

He had her there. She didn't like being told much. Growing up alone had made her self-sufficient.

"Well, I'll present the offer for you and let you know as soon as I hear something." She folded the form and put it in her briefcase, then withdrew the cellular phone. "As soon as I put in a call on it, we can go."

Noel didn't walk around and inspect the house further while she made the call. He couldn't have appeared more uninterested. The house must just be a business investment for him, she decided. He'd probably grown tired of living out of hotel rooms. Sarah had mentioned something about him moving every year to set up new stores. What a terribly lonely life. No wonder he was sad.

She felt sorry for both him and the house.

HOLLIE HADN'T BELIEVED Noel was serious when he volunteered to go shopping with her while they waited to hear back on his offer. She had thought he'd be a wet blanket, complain nonstop about how long it took her to make up her mind, the holiday crowds, the long waits.

Instead he'd been a lot of help. With his assistance, she'd already gotten her business gifts out of the way, negotiated a great deal on some new lights for her Christmas mantel and found the Barbie Elena wanted for Christmas.

The last Barbie like it in the toy store.

Unfortunately, the Barbie had on the wrong color dress. Elena wanted the one with the pink dress, not the peach one. Noel even understood the distinction. She stood pondering the dilemma in the middle of the crowded toy store, her arms full of packages. He'd offered to carry, but she hadn't wanted to push her luck. The smart thing would be to return to the car and unload the packages into the trunk.

However, she didn't want to buy the Barbie in the

peach dress if the toy store at the other end of the mall had it in the pink dress. She knew that if she put down the Barbie she'd found, the chances were very good someone else would buy it before she returned to the store. Better a Barbie with the wrong color dress than no Barbie at all.

"Here, you hold this," Hollie said impulsively, shoving her packages and the Barbie into Noel's arms. Left with two small Barbie accessory packets, she slipped them into Noel's jacket pocket. "Whatever you do, hang on to the Barbie. I'll be right back."

"Where are you—" Noel started to ask, but she'd disappeared into the crowd.

The only thing he could do was wait—not his favorite thing.

And worse, clutching a Barbie the woman with the red hair was eyeing.

A four-year-old miniature of the woman was tugging her arm, yelling, "I want that Barbie, Mommy. I want it—I want it."

"There aren't any more," the woman tried saying patiently.

"But I want it," the child screamed.

Tired and cranky and just full of the holiday spirit, Noel thought, wanting to be somewhere else. He glanced around for Hollie, but she was nowhere in sight. If he moved she'd never find him, so he was stuck.

"I want that Barbie, Mommy. Why does that man have a Barbie?"

Oh, great. Now he felt like a pervert. And people were beginning to stare.

The woman approached him with her child in tow. ''Are you planning to buy that doll?'' she asked.

''Maybe,'' he answered honestly.

''Well, when will you know? Because if you don't plan to buy it, my daughter wants it.''

''I'm waiting for someone,'' Noel explained lamely.

''Can I hold it?'' the little girl asked, her tears making her eyes bright.

He knew better, but he was on the spot. Besides, what could it hurt to let the little girl hold the doll? Once her fascination was done with, she'd move on to wanting something else. Even children lost interest in things they'd wanted desperately, once they had them.

He relented and handed the doll to the little girl, who presented him with a smile. Noel wished Hollie would hurry up and return.

Another younger woman, perhaps twenty, felt the material of his jacket, distracting him.

''Where did you get your jacket? I need a present for my boyfriend and I really like yours. Was it terribly expensive?''

''It's ah...'' Noel couldn't remember who the designer was.

''Can I check the label...?'' the bold young woman asked, inching closer, reaching upward with her arm.

''It's Calvin Klein,'' Noel blurted, backing away.

He was getting warm, and the din of the shoppers was closing in on him.

Where was Hollie?

The young woman was incorrigible. And it was clear now that more than the jacket interested her.

''Was that doll you were looking at for your little girl?'' she asked.

It was plain to Noel she meant ''Are you married?''

''No. It's for—'' He glanced around and his stomach sank. The little girl and her mother were gone.

And so was the Barbie.

''Excuse me,'' he said, moving away from the woman flirting with him to search for the two who'd lifted the Barbie he was supposed to be holding for safekeeping. He didn't want to be there when Hollie got back if he'd lost the doll.

But the two weren't in the front of the store by the register. They'd checked out in record time, and now he'd never find them. Well, there was no use in waiting around in the store for Hollie to appear. He might as well find her and tell her he'd screwed up and get it over with.

He thought he'd heard Hollie mutter something about another toy store when she'd left. He asked the checkout clerk, who said there was one at the south entrance. Just as he was exiting the store to find it, loud beeping went off.

''Sir, sir. You have to wait,'' a young male clerk yelled after him.

While Noel stood where he was, the clerk called the manager to come to the front of the store. The manager still had pimples, and he had an attitude about having responsibility. He had something to prove to Noel.

''If you'll just step back inside the store and come with me,'' he instructed Noel.

''There's some mistake,'' Noel stated between clenched teeth.

''If you'll just come back to my office.''

Everyone had stopped to stare, making Noel feel like a criminal. He knew he hadn't stolen anything, but no one else did.

Hollie chose just that moment to return.

''Hey, John, how's the new house?'' She'd met John Pritchard a couple of months earlier when she'd helped him and his young wife find the ideal starter house—a cozy two-bedroom in the suburbs.

''Great. We love it. On another matter, do you know this man, Hollie?'' John asked.

''Yeah, he's shopping with me. Why?''

''The beepers went off when he tried to leave the store.''

''What? Are you trying to steal the Barbie, Noel?'' Hollie teased.

''I don't even have the Barbie,'' Noel said, fuming.

''What?'' The teasing note was gone from Hollie's voice. ''What do you mean, you don't have the Barbie?''

''I let a little kid hold it and she took off with it,'' Noel explained.

''There you have it, John. Some little kid set off the beepers.''

John glanced at the clerk by the door, who shook his head no.

"We'll need to look in your packages, sir," John insisted.

"Jo-ohn!" Hollie pleaded, embarrassed.

Noel could see the kid was determined, so he handed over the packages. He knew all about security systems and something had made this one go off. Unless it was malfunctioning. It didn't take much imagination to guess what had happened. Someone must have bumped something into one of his shopping bags. This could all be easily explained away as an accident if he just let the kid have his moment of glory.

John went through the shopping bags, while *everyone* looked on as though they were witnessing the climactic third act of a play. The moment was anticlimactic, however, because not a piece of merchandise from the store was in the shopping bags.

"See, I told you," Hollie stated triumphantly.

"We'll need you to empty your pockets," John said, ignoring Hollie.

"But, Jo-ohn!"

"It's store policy, Hollie."

So the system *had* malfunctioned. It was Noel's turn to be cocky. With an exasperated sigh, he reached into his pockets—and his face fell. Besides some change there *was* something in his left pocket. Reluctantly, he withdrew it for John to see.

"I don't know how these got here," Noel insisted, looking at the two small packets of Barbie accessories as if they were tiny alien spaceships that had somehow landed in his pocket.

''I do,'' Hollie interrupted.

''You do?'' both John and Noel said.

''I put them there when I gave you everything in my hands to hold.''

''Thanks for telling me.''

''So this is really all an innocent misunderstanding,'' John said, taking the two packets. ''You really didn't mean to, ah…''

''No, I can assure you I didn't mean to, ah…'' Noel informed him. ''Am I free to go?''

''Go,'' John said, handing the confiscated merchandise to the clerk. ''And you, Hollie. Next time be sure you don't—''

''I will, John. Promise.'' She hurried out of the store after Noel, whose long legs were carrying him to the nearest exit.

''Will you wait up for me?'' she said, finally catching up to Noel, struggling with her full shopping bags. ''Can't you see the funny side to this?'' she pleaded as they left the mall together.

He stopped and scowled down at her. ''There is nothing funny about almost being arrested for shoplifting,'' he declared. ''Nothing funny in the least.''

''Come on, weren't you just a little excited about the possibility of handcuffs?'' He looked sexy when he was angry. She liked making him lose his tight rein on his emotions.

''No.''

“Yeah, I keep forgetting how stuffy you are,” she said, as he picked up the shopping bags she’d set down and followed her to her car.

“I am not stuffy.” She made him nuts.

“Yeah, you’re just a real picnic in the park.” He made her nuts. “Okay, okay. Let’s just say we’re even.”

“‘Even’?” Clearly he didn’t believe what he was hearing.

She unlocked the trunk of her car and he piled the shopping bags inside. “Even. I might have nearly gotten you arrested, but you let a little girl rip off my Barbie doll. Do you know how hard that doll is going to be to find? And Elena has her heart set on it.”

“Well, I wasn’t about to try to take the Barbie away from that little girl once she had it. Can you imagine the scene that would have caused?”

Hollie laughed as the two of them got into the car. “Man, you sure don’t like to be embarrassed.”

“I don’t think anyone in his right mind wants to be handcuffed and carted off to jail. It’s not my idea of a real good time.” At least the “carted off to jail” part wasn’t.

“Oh, lighten up, Noel. *I’m* going to have to be fingerprinted for my job if the news media have their way. Some dumb study found there are more felons in real estate than any other profession. Since we have access to people’s homes…”

“Speaking of homes, your beeper didn’t go off signaling we had a deal on my offer, did it?”

“I’d have told you.” She exited the parking lot.

''Even in all the excitement?''

''I know you don't believe it, but I'm good at my job.''

''So you sold John a house?''

''Yeah, the cutest little starter house when he got promoted to store manager.''

They drove down Lindbergh through Kirkwood. Big red lanterns covered each streetlight and swags of greenery trailed down the poles.

Hollie loved it.

Noel just sulked, refusing to let Hollie cheer him up. Refusing to admit his attraction to Hollie.

But Hollie didn't need anyone to have fun. She could have fun all by herself. She had learned how to growing up alone more or less.

She began singing Madonna's saucy version of ''Santa Baby'' as they headed for Garvey's Restaurant on Telegraph. Their special onion blossom appetizer and an ice-cold St. Louis brewery product would put Noel in a much better mood; she just knew it.

Noel sat across from her feeling like Wile E. Coyote having run off a cliff, his body still in free-fall. Hollie Winslow could make him furious, laugh, shy—she could make him feel. She was a dangerous woman. The sooner he bought a house the better.

He'd only really just met her and he already knew.

He felt sexier all over.

He'd volunteered to go shopping with her.

He'd volunteer to do anything to be with her.

It was too fast. He didn't want it.

He wanted it desperately.

Most of all he didn't want to disappoint her.

Garvey's was a bistro cum sports bar. It was known for its delicious food, casual atmosphere, fifty-two-inch televisions you could see from every table and cold beer by the bucket at an economy price. Since two could eat a tasty meal for under twenty dollars, the place was always busy, even on a Wednesday night. Of course, Hollie being in real estate seven days a week, one day seemed much like any other.

When they were seated Hollie noticed *Miracle on 34th Street* was playing on every television screen. She grinned to herself, thinking how very much Noel would love to be able to escape the sentimental movie.

Hollie suggested she order since she knew the menu by heart, and Noel acquiesced. She ordered the onion blossom appetizer that Garvey's had built its reputation on. Unlike most fried onions, these weren't greasy. The batter was just sweet and crisp. The pretty young waitress brought them and two cold beers while they waited for their grilled chicken pastas.

"Are you sure your beeper's working?" Noel asked.

"It's working," she promised. "You've got to be patient. A lot of emotion is involved in letting go of a house, even if you've made the decision to sell. I've had people change their minds at the very last second."

"But you think I'll get the house?"

"I don't know. It hasn't been on the market that long. The probability is that they will at least counter your first offer."

''So this could drag out a while...''

''Yes. Try the onion blossom and quit worrying. That's my job. Have you seen this movie?'' she couldn't resist asking as Noel bit into the fragrant onion petals and made approving noises. ''I just love it.''

''I've managed to avoid it so far.'' He glanced up at the screen, then away quickly, as if the Christmas spirit might be catching.

''So how come you want to buy a house instead of renting, or just living in a hotel while you're opening a new store here?'' she asked. ''Not that I'm trying to talk you out of buying.''

''This might be my last store opening.''

''Have you been fired? Are you about to be laid off? Should I run a credit check?''

''Nothing like that. I told you it was a cash sale. I'm getting bored and ready for a new challenge. The worldwide market of the Internet interests me.''

Of course it did. He probably spoke more than one language. He'd had a European education. His background even showed in his appearance. His clothes had a European flair. He dressed very well. Better than most men. She'd chalked it up to his being in retail. But it was more than that. Noel Hawksley had style. She didn't want to think about how attractive he was. No self-respecting Christmas freak could find a grinch attractive. That would be nothing short of emotional suicide.

A tall young man approached their table and stopped. ''Hi, I'm Jake. Your waitress has been called away.

Her mom's car wouldn't start. I'll be taking care of the rest of your order. Would you like anything else?''

Jake had a great smile, and was distracted by the movie momentarily. ''Sorry, I just love this movie.''

''How tall are you, Jake?'' Hollie asked impulsively, looking for a path away from where her thoughts had been leading.

''Six-three. You're thinking I play basketball, aren't you? Well, you're right, and isn't it cool we're in the finals? Did you want my autograph?'' he joked.

''Just our food,'' Noel interjected.

''Right, let me check on that.''

''Why did you ask him how tall he was?''

''I was just curious, that's all,'' Hollie said evasively.

Moments later Jake returned with their pastas. He'd no sooner set them down than her beeper went off.

''It never fails. Cold food again,'' she said, checking the beeper. ''Looks like we've got an answer. I'll make this phone call and be right back. You go ahead and eat before the food gets cold.''

She returned a few minutes later with Noel's answer. ''Sorry. You lost the house. Someone else came in with a bid at the same time closer to the asking price. The owner took their offer, of course.''

Noel wasn't sure how to react to the news.

He should be disappointed, not oddly relieved because he found himself wanting to spend more time with Hollie.

He wasn't used to not getting his way.

And yet, somehow he knew this holiday was going to have its way with him.

Whether he liked it or not.

Meanwhile, back at the North Pole…

WELL, AT LEAST he was making the long-distance telephone companies have a Merry Christmas, Santa thought as he dialed yet another spa in the warmer climates. So far he hadn't had any luck tracking down Claudia.

''Hello, I'm trying to reach a Claudia Claus. Do you have anyone registered at your spa by that name?'' He waited while the person at the other end of the line checked.

''No, I'm sorry, sir. We have no one registered by that name.''

Santa hung up the phone glumly. What he was doing was useless anyway. Most likely Claudia had registered under an assumed name. If only he didn't miss her so much. This was the first time they'd ever been separated and it told him just how much he took her for granted. He hoped she was just teaching him a lesson and hadn't left for good.

To distract himself from that gloomy prospect, he put on his parka and trekked outside to the workshop. The elves were grumbling because he had them working overtime to make more Barbies in pink dresses.

It seemed every little girl in the world wanted one.

4

ON THE DRIVE over to her office to check out some more house listings on the computer so she could take Noel out looking again, Hollie passed the Victorian gingerbread. She stopped, backed up to pull into the driveway and parked. Perhaps this house would suit Noel. She'd left without getting the phone number Ms. Claudia had promised her.

She was about to ring the doorbell, when the door opened and two teenage girls came out. They were too busy comparing predictions to pay much attention to Hollie, who went on inside.

"Hello," she called out.

Ms. Claudia called back "Coming," and appeared a few moments later. "Why, hello—Hollie, isn't it?"

"Yes. I forgot to take the phone number from you for the owner of this house. I have a client who might be interested."

"Sure, let me just get it for you." She disappeared into one of the rooms and returned holding a card with the phone number written on it. "Here you are." She handed the card to Hollie. "How's your new beau?"

"You mean six foot one inch?" Hollie asked, tucking the card in her briefcase.

Ms. Claudia nodded.

"Haven't seen him. I think about the only way I'm going to find six foot one inch under my tree for Christmas is if I order in pizza Christmas morning and mug the delivery guy."

"I don't understand," Ms. Claudia said, looking puzzled. "I must have made some mistake in my calculations. He should have shown up by now."

"Not to worry. Maybe I'll get that bread-and-butter maker I was wanting. Well, I've got to run. Thanks for the phone number."

Outside, Hollie glanced down at her festive watch and saw that she did indeed have to hurry. She had agreed to meet Noel at the office and he freaked at tardiness. If she was going to spend the whole day with him looking at houses she didn't want him in a crabby mood.

At any rate, he was going to have to learn to lighten up.

With a quick peek in her rearview mirror, she backed out of the driveway.

And smack-dab into another car.

Now she was going to be late for sure and Noel would be furious. Her day had suddenly turned rotten.

When she checked her rearview mirror again and saw whose car she'd backed into, her day turned completely rotten.

Noel was already out of his luxury car, the back of

his wrists resting on his lean hips as he surveyed the damaged grille, then watched her approach.

"Are you all right?" he asked, concern in his voice.

"Of cour—" She began blinking to fight off a sudden bout of light-headedness. When she saw the damage to his car she, too, felt sick to her stomach. Choosing the coward's way out, she gave in to the light-headedness.

His strong arms caught her on the way down.

"Hollie, Hollie..."

At the alarm in his voice, she blinked away the fuzzies and opened her eyes. "I'm fine. Put me down. I only had a bottled water for breakfast. My blood sugar must have plummeted for a few seconds." She glanced at his car again. "Oh, no, look at your car. Where did you come from? I checked my rearview mirror before I began backing out."

"Your mirror must have a blind spot—or you do. But forget about the cars for now. I want to know how you are."

"If you'll please put me down you'll see that I'm fine," she instructed. She was happy that he was more concerned with her than his car. She'd dated men who weren't.

He set her down and she didn't faint.

"I think both cars are drivable. It's just a fender bender. Why don't I follow you to your house and we can do the insurance stuff there? You'll be a darn sight more comfortable than here in the street, and a lot safer.''

It started snowing as Noel and Hollie pulled up in their damaged cars in front of her little white frame house. The front door was a bright cheery red, Noel noticed while appreciating the symmetry of the green shutters decorating the small wood-paned windows. As he got out of his car, the sound of a holiday banner being whipped around by the wind caught his ear. It was definitely getting colder.

''Here, take my arm,'' Noel offered, helping Hollie out of her car.

When they reached the front door, he took her keys from her and opened the door, then followed her inside.

The first thing that hit him was the smell of pine. Her Christmas tree was announcing it was already up and probably decorated to the nines.

Everything sparkled—windows, mirrors, glass bowls of fruit and candy, he saw, when they entered the living area of the house from the tiny foyer. The layout was open kitchen and a greatroom-dining room. The twelve-foot windows that looked out over the backyard gave them a view of the falling snow, almost bringing it inside.

Hollie shook off a chill. ''I think I'll light a fire.''

''Just tell me where the woodpile is,'' Noel said. ''I'll get the fire going.''

''I'm afraid to disappoint you, Daniel Boone, but all it takes is a flick of the wrist. The fireplace is gas, though it looks real. And the house doesn't get as dirty. Come see.''

She was right. It did look real.

He helped her out of her red coat and she took both their coats to the hall closet. When she returned she was rotating her shoulders and moaning.

''I thought you said you were all right.'' He started to get up from the sofa by the fire.

''Just a little sore from the seat belt,'' she explained. ''I'll get us some hot chocolate and cookies and we can call the insurance companies.''

''Can I help?''

''No, just enjoy the fire.''

Noel did just that while taking in his surroundings. Candles of all sizes in holders of all descriptions, including hollowed-out apples on the coffee table, were everywhere. A garland of pine was draped over the mantel, which was also decorated with holly and clumps of baby's breath. A loop of fat yellow yarn held the holiday cards she'd already received from friends.

He smiled, delighted—despite his aversion to Christmas—by the festive beauty and homey warmth of her decorations.

Noel stared into the fire. The flames hypnotized him, making him sleepy. He'd stayed up late watching a movie on pay TV in his rented room. As soon as he got this house business settled and had relaxed on a tropical island over the holidays, he'd be ready to start work on opening the new store. Since he threw himself into his work, he didn't quite know what to do with himself when he wasn't working.

It was probably why he was crowding Hollie about finding a house. He should feel guilty, since she was supposed to be on her vacation. Maybe they would find a house later. When the snow stopped. Right now he just wanted to sit by the fire and relax. It was very comfortable in Hollie's house.

''Here we are,'' Hollie announced, bringing in two mugs of hot chocolate, which she placed on the coffee table. ''I put some butterscotch schnapps in the hot chocolate to calm our nerves—well, mine anyway. What do you think?'' she called back over her shoulder as she went to get the cookies she'd warmed in the microwave.

''Pretty smooth. Listen,'' he said when she came back with a plate of assorted cookies, ''do you have any board games we can play? I think we should wait till it stops snowing before we go look at houses.''

She picked up a chocolate crinkle cookie and bit into it while she thought. ''I've got a game of Monopoly. And, of course, Candyland, for when Elena stays over.''

''Monopoly,'' he decided.

''Why don't you call your insurance company while I find the game?'' she suggested after a sip of hot chocolate to wash down the cookie, and she handed him the portable phone.

He certainly looks comfortable, Hollie thought as she rummaged through a closet for the game. The accident hadn't caused him any ill effects. She was the one with a new bill to pay. Her insurance would total her car for any dent over three hundred dollars because that's all her car was worth. She'd be out a car or the money, since that was the amount of her deductible. Maybe she could just hang a wreath over the bumper until she sold Noel his house and got her commission. The car was still drivable; that much at least was good news.

She looked out the window of the bedroom Elena slept in when she stayed over. At least for part of the night. By morning Elena had usually finagled her way into Hollie's bed. It was still snowing. If it kept up she wasn't going to be able to track down that Barbie doll for Elena until tomorrow.

Her whole holiday was off kilter because of the man in her living room. And worse—she was off kilter. Noel Hawksley was a distracting man. He made her remember she was a woman. A sexual being.

She smiled as she picked up the game he wanted to play. Off kilter or not—she planned on winning that round with Noel.

She didn't win.

Noel played the game like Attila the Hun. Even knowing Noel's aggression was fueled by his need to be thought of in a certain light, Hollie wasn't a good loser. Not for the second time. He'd sent her straight to jail without passing go to collect her money one too many times.

''That's it. I don't want to play anymore,'' she announced when he gloated over his second win.

''But it's still snowing and I'm not playing Candyland,'' he said, and polished off the last cookie on the shiny red plate.

''I'm going to get some stuff done, like wrapping the presents I bought yesterday. Want to help?'' she asked, knowing he wouldn't.

''I'm all thumbs,'' he insisted. ''Mind if I take a nap here on the sofa by the fire until it stops snowing? You will wake me up when it does, won't you?''

''Sure, go ahead,'' she agreed as he toed off his loafers and—finally—loosened his tie. It didn't escape her notice that he was a perfect fit for her long sofa. She'd been torn between a love seat and a sofa, and had settled on the long, overstuffed sofa in yellow-and-navy chintz.

He didn't even look out of place on the chintz.

She decided not to notice and went to get her packages to wrap.

By the time Hollie had gathered up her packages, Noel was snoring softly in front of the fire. It was just as well he hadn't offered to help; he would have given her a lot of grief over how she wrapped her presents. Christmas brought her creativity to full bloom and every year she did something different in the way of wrapping.

This year she'd decided on white wrapping paper, which she tied with bright red yarn. Then, with the help of a glue gun, cotton, glitter, buttons and bows, she personalized each package with Santas and elves and reindeer, before using red marker pens to outline the recipient's name, which she then filled in with red glitter.

It wasn't an idea she expected ever to repeat because it was extremely time-consuming...over-the-top Martha Stewart. Still, when she had all the gifts personalized and stacked under the tree they did look awfully festive and special.

Noel had proved to be a deep sleeper. He hadn't moved once.

She watched him sleep and thought about her feelings for him. Instant annoyance had given way to a begrudging attraction of sorts. She could imagine him as the lonely boy at boarding school and forgive him much because of it. She'd had the same loneliness for a companion growing up. As she was making allowances for his broody behavior, his expression shifted. He moaned and a sexy smile crossed his lips.

She hoped he was dreaming of her. No, what was she thinking? She didn't want— Well, if she were smart she wouldn't allow her thoughts to linger over questions like how it would feel to have his lips linger over hers for real. Was he a good kisser? Would a kiss from him make her swoon? She wasn't the swooning sort, of course, but he was the tall, dark and handsome type who was likely given to making women swoon.

Lean and fit, he was probably a tireless lover.

Yes, but was he a selfish lover?

He didn't seem the type who was given to foreplay and sensitivity. He'd sweep her off her feet and have his way then leave. He wasn't the sort to fix breakfast in the morning as a show of tenderness.

Tender. Now that was funny. Noel was about as tender as a cheap cut of steak.

Just because he looked yummy when he was asleep didn't mean he was a dreamboat awake.

If she were the sort of woman who liked to make men over, who believed a man could change, then Noel might be a challenge. But she'd made enough bad choices to know that people seldom changed.

Noel was what he was. A grinch.

A sexy grinch, but a grinch nonetheless.

So any fancies she had about him—fancies about her being the woman who could tame him—were best left in her imagination. She could indulge herself with how it might feel to be kissed, caressed and more by the man asleep on her sofa, but to let down her guard and fall victim to Noel's charm was foolishness she couldn't afford.

He could bruise her heart, even break it.

Business.

That's what Noel was interested in. He wanted a house before Christmas. And it was what she had to remain focused on as well.

She would find Noel an irresistible house. She would close the deal and make both of them happy. He would have his house and she would have her new car and they both would have a Merry Christmas.

If Noel Hawksley was indeed capable of having a Merry Christmas.

She saw that now his eyes were moving beneath their lids. He was dreaming. Probably about killing Santa Claus, from the wicked smile that had shifted on his lips. She glanced to the window.

Rats. It was still snowing and business was going to have to wait despite her determination to get on with it. They weren't likely to see any more houses until tomorrow.

Deciding to make up her holiday Cherry Walnut bread for the neighbors, she went to the kitchen. Her refrigerator revealed she had all the necessary ingredients but eggs. Since there was a small market just two blocks away, she decided to walk over for the eggs while Noel slept peacefully.

She grabbed her red coat and headed out into the snowy afternoon. As she walked in the snow, her thoughts kept returning to the very complicated, the very sexy, the very exasperating man sleeping on her couch.

"YOU DO KNOW I'm planning to have my way with you, don't you?"

Noel decided he must be dreaming.

His real estate agent was behaving very unprofessionally. The look in her eyes was one of planned seduction. She twirled one of her sexy curls with her forefinger as she flirted with him. She had changed into a provocative outfit. The baby T-shirt clung to her soft breasts. He knew they'd bounce when she walked, because he'd seen them do just that. His agent, it seemed, didn't have the need or desire to wear a bra. The beige cotton drawstring pants were tied loosely, so they rode low to reveal a cute-as-a-button navel.

A navel he wanted to explore with his tongue.

''I'd be much obliged if you did just that,'' he heard himself say.

''Do you want to touch me?'' she asked, remaining just out of range.

''Desperately.'' He reached for her, but she evaded his grasp.

''First the rules,'' she explained.

''Rules?''

''Uh-huh. I can touch you, but you can't touch me.''

He thought a moment. It wasn't the best deal, but it was better than no touching at all. He lifted his hands in surrender. ''Okay, you're the boss. I'm your playground.''

''Why don't I trust you?'' She studied him a moment, then ordered, ''Put your hands behind your head.''

''Done,'' he said, following her rules.

She knelt before him. ''You're quite handsome, you know. Those clear blue eyes and dark lashes are a lethal combination.''

''You're just trying to flatter me so you'll get what you want, just like all the girls.''

''Lots of girls...''

''Legions,'' he bragged to annoy her.

''But none like me.'' She said it with such quiet confidence that he believed her. Believed her because when she stroked his cheeks, his eyes, his lips, her touch was gentle—a tender caress.

''No, none like you,'' he breathed.

She began unbuttoning his shirt. ''I can feel your warm skin through the cloth. Am I making you hot, Noel?''

''Ah, could you hurry up a little...'' he pleaded, just keeping himself from thrusting.

''Oh, no. We go slow, excruciatingly slow. I plan to make you suffer to get your reward. You aren't the only one who can play games, Mr. Hawksley.''

''I think under the circumstances you should call me 'Noel.'''

''But you don't like your first name, do you, Noel?''

''It's not a proper name.''

''I love it. Noel and Hollie—it's like we were meant to be together.'' She pushed back his shirt. ''Umm, smooth warm skin and rock-hard muscle. Very impressive for a businessman, Noel. Where'd you get this washboard belly?''

''Rock climbing. I find it's good for the gut and relieves stress. The danger makes you focus on the moment.''

She lowered her head and began kissing his flushed skin, starting at his flat brown nipples and working her way over the washboard stomach he was suddenly glad he had.

He was no longer able to keep himself from thrusting ever so slightly with his hips as her sweet lips moved inexorably downward to his belt.

He wanted like hell to bury his hands in her curly waves of light brown hair, but he knew he'd break the spell if he did. His hands remained captive beneath his head as he remained captive beneath her marauding lips.

She lifted her head and stared into his eyes, her pupils huge. ''Permission to proceed?'' she inquired, her hand on his belt buckle.

''As you may have guessed, the word *no* has left my vocabulary. Please,'' he urged.

She laughed, a throaty laugh full of girlish delight. It made him even harder, and the effect was almost painful.

She undid his belt buckle and pulled the belt from the loops of his trousers. Grinning down at him, she undid the button above the zipper of his fly. ''There, more comfy?'' she teased.

''Only slightly. If you could, ah, hurry the hell up.''

''I've noticed you have this problem with being impatient, Mr. Hawksley. Perhaps we should—''

''Now!'' he insisted.

Her answering laugh as she began easing down the zipper of his trousers was wicked with promise.

''You've been holding out on me, Noel. You've been pretending to be a grinch, and all the while you've had a present for me.'' Her hand closed over the smooth, satiny length of him. ''A very, very impressive present.''

''Glad you like it,'' he choked out as she began moving her hand up and down, squeezing and relaxing her grip.

''I like it so much I could kiss you!'' she declared. ''Right here.'' She punctuated her statement with a kiss to the head of his shaft, sending a delicious shock of pleasure through him.

And then a noise at the front door woke him.

Noel was disoriented at first. The dream had seemed so real.

So hot. He was still reeling from the effect. It certainly put the lie to any idea that everything between them was strictly business. He was very attracted to her, he admitted with some reluctance. And not just physically attracted. No, Hollie Winslow was reaching him on a level no one ever had.

And then he laughed, rueful that it was probably just business with Hollie. Her niceness was part of her professional image. He was more likely to buy a house from her if he liked her.

He needed to get a grip on reality.

Ah, but he wished she'd be as nice to him as she had been in his dream, he thought as the door swung open.

AS SHE INSERTED the key into the lock of her front door, Hollie shifted the bag on her hip, careful not to break the eggs. Her Christmas watch had told her she'd only been gone a half hour. The snowy day had kept most people at home with last-minute baking and wrapping and decorating. She'd checked out her eggs and a bottle of wine she'd gotten on impulse without having to wait in line.

When she entered the greatroom, Noel was sitting up on the sofa, stretching.

She grimaced, then hurried to the kitchen to set her small bag of groceries on the counter.

A large plastic sack of Tupperware sat there.

''Where did this come from?'' she asked Noel, who'd joined her in the kitchen.

''Sarah dropped it off. She said Elena was playing at a friend's house, so she was out running errands while she had the opportunity.''

Hollie looked at Noel's face. ''She didn't say anything?'' she asked.

''Oh, yeah—something about calling her. She needs you to take Elena to see Santa Claus at the mall because she got a big last-minute order.''

''That's all she said?'' Hollie asked, her head inside the refrigerator as she stowed the eggs and wine.

''Yeah, she mentioned you wanted to borrow the Tupperware and said to call her about Elena, that's all.''

Noel looked so sexy and sweet with sleep that Hollie couldn't resist going over to him and kissing him on the tip of his nose.

''What?'' Noel said, pleased yet taken aback.

Hollie shrugged. ''It's Christmas. You looked so...'' Hollie's voice trailed off. What had come over her? Kissing him on the nose? And her explanation would be worse. What was she going to say? That she'd done it because he looked sexy...and sweet?

''Do you always act on your impulses?'' Noel asked with a teasing glint in his eyes.

''Do you never have them?'' Hollie pouted, her teeth pulling at her full bottom lip, drawing Noel's attention.

He thought about the dream Sarah had interrupted with her Tupperware delivery. He'd been worried she would notice his arousal.

''I guess this wouldn't be a good time to ask you a favor, huh?'' Hollie ventured.

''I'm not taking Elena to see Santa Claus, if that's what you have in mind.''

''No, I haven't forgotten you're a grinch. What I need is for you to give me some help with the lights on my Christmas tree. There's a short somewhere and they keep going out. I thought perhaps you might be able to figure out what's wrong. I don't know which strand is shorting, and I hate to go out and buy all new lights.''

''Sure, I could check them out,'' he agreed. ''It seems we're not going to be busy seeing any houses this afternoon. This looks to be a half-foot-deep snowfall. I suppose you want me to shovel your driveway while I'm at it, too.''

''You'd do that?'' she asked on a hopeful note. It

wasn't as though she was suggesting he help build a snowman, not yet anyway.

''Why not? I might as well. That way I'll know whether this house requires a snow shovel. When it stops snowing I'll do the drive. Right now, let's have a look at the lights on your tree.'' He headed for the tree in the corner of the room.

''Wait a minute. What did you mean by you'll know whether this house requires a snow shovel?''

''Didn't I mention it? I've found the house I want to buy. *This one.*''

The news was as much a surprise to him as to Hollie. He hadn't known he wanted her house until he'd said it.

But once he'd said it, he knew it was true.

Hollie's house fit the fantasy of a home he'd never had. It was warm and inviting. So inviting he'd fallen asleep on her sofa. Spending time in the place had made him realize the strength of his long suppressed and denied fantasy and desire for a home.

What Hollie had made him realize was what he didn't have.

He'd realized his professional dreams, and maybe, just maybe, it was time he took a look at what his personal needs were.

He had a feeling Hollie could meet a lot of those, had certainly met one of them in his dreams!

She was sexy as all get out, but there was more to this hunger he had. He wanted a soul mate. For the first time in his life he considered that he might have found one…in Hollie.

He wanted to step into her dream. And that meant buying her house.

Meanwhile, back at the North Pole…

"I SURE HOPE Mrs. Claus comes back before we have to leave on Christmas Eve," Rudolph said to Prancer. "Santa's been a grouch ever since he found out she left on her little vacation."

Prancer danced around his stall. "I know one thing—it sure would be a help if he could find the Christmas cookies Mrs. Claus hid before she left."

"I wouldn't count on that…" Rudolph said, his nose turning red.

"Rudolph—you didn't! You didn't find Santa's cookies first and eat them?"

"Who, me?"

Prancer shook his head. "It's going to be a long sleigh ride Christmas Eve."

5

NOEL COULDN'T BELIEVE he was standing in a long line at the mall, waiting to see Santa Claus. But here he was, being pushed and shoved by impatient, restless, jumpy kids desperate to reach Santa and whisper their dream gift list in St. Nick's ear.

Hollie had insisted that he join her and Elena in the Santa line if he wanted to continue their discussion about her selling her house. And since he was as impatient, restless and jumpy to get the opportunity to try one more time to persuade Hollie to sell, he was on his way to Santa…and, hopefully, acquiring Hollie's house.

She'd already said no to him more than once, but for some reason it was important to him to buy her house. Where he lived had never been of consequence to him before. He had moved from one temporary residence to another. First with boarding school and then with his career.

For the first time, he desperately wanted a home. And Hollie's house was it.

Noel studied Hollie and Elena. Both were clearly girlie girls.

Hollie was kneeling to fasten the sparkly tiara

Elena had insisted on wearing. It had slipped sideways on the child's head. Fixing the tiara wasn't an easy task because Elena was so excited about seeing Santa she was chattering nonstop, her head moving the whole while.

"How many things can I ask Santa for?" Elena wanted to know. "Will he get mad if I ask for too many?"

"I think three would be a good number," Hollie said dryly. "That's the number that seems standard in any magical situation. Just remember to think about your wishes very carefully while we're waiting. You don't want to waste them on something silly like wishing Midnight would quit barking at airplanes when they fly over."

Elena giggled. "I know, she thinks she can catch them."

Hollie tickled Elena's tummy. Elena's fashion statement for meeting Santa was her tiara, of course. And, of all things, her neon sunglasses in the dead of winter with snow on the ground. The rest of her ensemble consisted of a white T-shirt beneath jeans overalls, black-and-white soccer shoes and all her jeweled necklaces.

Noel couldn't help but smile. Elena's style was utterly charming. She would make a great model for the children's department of the store he was opening.

At least, Noel thought, it was good to see that he wasn't the only male in line waiting with the children to see Santa. All around him fathers were standing patiently, while mothers combed children's hair and straightened their clothing—over and over again as the children continued hopping around. The din from the crowd was so loud he could barely make out Aaron Neville's ''Christmas Song'' on the mall's sound system.

If anyone had told him he'd willingly be at a mall five days before Christmas, he would have bet a considerable sum otherwise—and lost. He expected to see hives break out on his arm at any time. Last Christmas Marcy had insisted on him shopping with her while she selected the expensive gifts she wanted from him. She hadn't returned the pricey baubles when she'd broken their engagement and had even claimed possession of some of his things.

''I know one thing I'm going to ask Santa for,'' Elena said, as Noel winced in remembrance. ''I'm going to ask him to bring me the Barbie in the pink dress.''

Hollie shot Noel a look that told him he was in trouble. But hell, he already knew that. He was standing in a crowded mall with a woman who was something between a ballerina and a kick boxer and a child who would grow up under her influence. ''Under the influence'' gained a whole new meaning when he thought of Hollie. Under her influence he'd had a dream so sexy he'd woken up embarrassed.

''I'm sure Santa will bring you your Barbie,'' Noel assured Elena, to Hollie's raised eyebrow. ''What else are you going to wish for?''

‘‘I know, I want some rings like Hollie’s.’’

Hollie twisted the gold-and-gemstone stack rings on her ring finger of her right hand. Seeing Noel’s interest, she explained, ‘‘Elena’s coveted these since I bought them this past summer. I told her they don’t make them in her small size, so every time she comes over she asks me if they’re old yet.’’

‘‘Old?’’ Noel looked puzzled

‘‘It’s a scam of hers. When she spends the night she goes through my jewelry piece by piece and asks if each one is old. She gets to take anything that’s old home with her. You may have noticed she’s into jewelry in a big way.’’

‘‘Yeah. Some husband is going to be perpetually broke when she gets married—’’

‘‘What are you going to wish for?’’ Elena interrupted, looking at Noel.

‘‘That Hollie will sell me her house.’’

Elena appeared stricken. ‘‘No! You can’t move away, Auntie Hollie.’’ The child grabbed Hollie’s hand and clung to her, a tear trailing from her wide pale eyes.

‘‘Don’t worry, I’m *not* moving,’’ she assured the child.

‘‘But—’’

‘‘We’re going to find Noel a house he really, really likes. He was only teasing about wanting my house.’’

Noel didn’t want to push the matter in front of the upset child. After all, Hollie could move closer to Sarah and Elena. The child would love that. There was even room for Hollie to move in with Sarah and Elena until she found something.

He didn't have anywhere to go.

Unless you counted the impersonal hotel room he was staying in.

''And what are you going to wish for?'' Noel asked Hollie.

''That a grinch doesn't spoil my Christmas,'' she answered, frowning at him.

''What's a grinch, Auntie Hollie?''

''Someone who doesn't like Christmas.''

''Oh, you made that up. Everybody loves Christmas.'' The child didn't even wait for confirmation of her belief. She tugged on Hollie's hand to move them up in line as a flash went off when the child in front of them had his picture taken on Santa's lap.

Noel studied the Santa as the little boy climbed down off his lap and Elena moved to take his place, and thought Santa looked a little seedy, shabby. The whole thing commercial. But Hollie didn't see it that way. She saw the magic. She made the magic.

For herself.

For Elena.

For *him.*

For the first time in his life he wondered what it would be like to have a child. Wondered with his heart, not in an abstract way. The way he might have wondered when he'd become engaged last Christmas. He'd turned thirty and it had seemed time to marry.

He'd cared about the woman, but now saw he hadn't been in love.

Love was a much scarier proposition.

He hadn't been this disconcerted since the first time he'd arrived at boarding school. The school had been strict, and military. Emotions weren't encouraged; obedience was.

"Ho, ho, ho. And what do you want Santa to bring you, little girl?"

Elena smiled up at Santa. "I want a Barbie with a pink dress."

"And what else?"

"Some rings, a bunch of little bitty ones."

"Anything else?" Santa asked as the photographer snapped their picture.

Elena thought a minute, then was generous with her third wish. "I want you to bring a boyfriend for my mommy."

"Oh—" Santa said, caught off guard.

Then Elena cupped her hand and whispered something in Santa's ear.

"Of course you can have a fourth wish," Santa said magnanimously, obviously happy to be off the subject of granting the mother a boyfriend, not knowing how appropriate the wish was. "What else do you want?"

"I want you to make Auntie Hollie and him," she said loudly, pointing to Noel, "kiss each other so Auntie Hollie won't have to move away."

It wasn't an easier wish. Santa looked to Noel for help.

The crowd close around looked on in anticipation. The mothers looked hopeful. The fathers looked amused. The children giggled.

When Noel and Hollie remained frozen in place, a father in the crowd yelled out, ''Kiss her, for Pete's sake. I've got a hockey game to get my kid to.''

Hollie wouldn't look at him. She was sure she was as red as Santa's suit. Most of all because she wanted Noel to kiss her.

Since he'd clearly worried Elena, Noel found himself doing something out of character. Overt displays of public affection weren't his style. He stepped closer to Hollie.

She took a backward step, nervous and looking about to faint.

He handled that by taking her into his arms and dipping her back in a sweeping embrace. As he gazed into her startled eyes, he lowered his mouth and kissed her for the audience and Elena. His mouth moved tenderly over hers, then probed sexily, making her blush and break the kiss, flustered.

Upon hearing the applause, he came to his senses and quickly released Hollie, who appeared completely stunned.

''Thank you, Santa,'' Elena said, scampering off his lap and grinning widely.

''Are you satisfied now, you little minx?'' Hollie asked, taking the child's hand.

''Uh-huh. Noel was just tricking me about buying your house, huh?''

Hollie nodded.

Well, Elena might be satisfied, but Noel decidedly was not. He still wanted the house...and more of kissing Hollie. Was it possible he was falling in love?

Or was he just tired of being alone?

He couldn't trust his feelings at this time of year. That was why he always ran away during the holidays.

''Where are we going now?'' Elena asked as they left the mall.

''Noel and I are going to look at houses for him, right after I drop you off at home.''

''Can't I come with you?''

''No. Your mother says you have to clean your room if you want Santa to bring you any presents. Santa likes good little girls with clean rooms.''

''Aw right,'' Elena agreed reluctantly.

As they drove Elena home, Noel realized he hadn't seen Hollie's bedroom yet.

''MAYBE YOU'LL LIKE this one better,'' Hollie said as she parked her car and handed Noel the spec sheet to look at while they walked to the front door. So far they'd seen three houses, which he'd vetoed for what seemed to her one frivolous reason after another.

Clearly he was determined to have her house and was only humoring her by looking at others. She'd told him she'd think about selling her house. She'd lied.

Her mind was made up. She loved her house and her house loved her. They were a good match.

And she and Noel weren't, no matter how well he kissed.

She wanted to tell Noel that she couldn't help him any longer, wanted to bail out. What had started out to be a snap had grown complicated.

And now she was stuck. She had to deal with Noel. Her getting a new car was at risk. It didn't look great for a successful real estate agent to be driving around in a wreck. His commission would give her the down payment for a new car.

Her career was at risk. She had to be professional and maintain her reputation as a responsible agent. So there would be no quitting until she found Noel a house.

Her vacation was at risk. The longer it took, the less of the holidays she would be able to enjoy. And at this rate they'd still be looking for a new house for Noel in the New Year.

Her house was at risk.

All of the above could be solved by her selling him her house. But she couldn't and she wouldn't. It was hers. The only roots she had in the world. She felt safe there and happy.

Her heart was at risk.

There, she'd thought it. Of everything, that was the most worrisome. In Noel she recognized a kindred spirit. They didn't look at the world in the same way, but they had experienced loneliness in the same way. She'd determined to make her world a happy place.

He threatened that.

She didn't want to be disappointed, and as long as she was in control she knew how to prevent it.

It was only when she allowed herself to hope that someone might love her that she was vulnerable to misery.

Perhaps that was why she lived with one foot in the real world and one in the world of fantasy. The real world had a way of disappointing her.

''This looks like a place you might like,'' Noel said when they went inside the story-and-a-half house decorated to within an inch of its life in cluttered country.

''We're hunting for a house for you. I have one I like.''

''You aren't even trying to find another house,'' Noel complained.

''I told you—I don't want to move. Why won't you believe me and accept it? My house isn't that big. There isn't room for a big office or a pool table. This house, on the other hand, fits both those requirements. At least give it a chance.''

He walked through it with her, letting her try to sell him on its finer points, such as the study off the master bedroom, the fireplace in the hearth kitchen and the in-ground pool. While he agreed that all those things were pluses, he just didn't love the house.

Not the way he loved hers.

And so they closed the door and left once more, without his making an offer.

And closed the door on her having a long weekend. She was going to have to take Noel out the next day to look at houses again.

So much for her Friday. She'd have to battle the huge crowds on the weekend to get the rest of her holiday preparations done.

She had to find Noel a house.

Someone else's house.

''SO ELENA TELLS ME Noel kissed you at the mall,'' Sarah said later that evening as the two of them sat in front of the television they weren't watching. Elena was curled up asleep on the floor with Midnight. The child had drifted off watching *Pocahontas* and hadn't awoken when they'd slipped out the tape to turn on the news.

''Did she tell you it was her idea?'' Hollie blew on the nails of her left hand after giving them their first coat of polish.

''She left that out. What did she do now?'' Sarah was clearly delighted with her daughter's precocious ways.

''She pimped Santa at the mall into making us kiss as one of her wishes. For some reason she thought it would make me not sell my house to Noel.''

''When did you decide to sell your house to Noel—did I miss a meeting?'' Sarah asked, reaching for a bottle of top coat for her nails.

''I didn't. I'm not. But Noel isn't listening to me. He's got it into his head that he wants to buy it. He's positively fixated on the idea. I'm trying desperately to talk him out of it, to find the perfect house for him.''

''But you aren't having any luck...''

''None.''

''Hmm. So how does he kiss? You've completely avoided that—don't think I haven't noticed.''

''Like he's done it before.''

''Smooth, huh?''

''And sweet.''

''Sweet—now, that's something new. Sweet, huh?''

''Don't go making anything out of it. He was on the spot. It's not like it was his idea. Or mine,'' she added, seeing the speculative look in Sarah's eyes.

''Then maybe Elena's smarter than you. He's pretty hunky, Hollie.'' Sarah put the applicator back in the bottle and studied her manicure.

''Elena's smarter than you and I put together, Sarah. But I'm still not taking dating advice from a four-year-old. Besides, Santa's bringing me a beau for Christmas. All I have to do is get rid of Noel first.''

''So sell him your house.''

That was the practical answer, Hollie knew.

But she couldn't sell Noel her house. She just couldn't.

There had to be a house out there with his name

on it. She just hadn't found it yet. Maybe in the morning when she was fresh…

"Did Elena tell you she asked Santa to bring you a boyfriend?" Hollie inquired, changing the subject, as they waited for their nails to dry so they could carry Elena in to bed.

"So that's where he came from—"

"What? You've met someone. You've been holding out on me." Hollie settled back into the sofa, tucking her feet up beneath her.

"He's a fireman and really sweet. He came out this morning to rescue the kitten next door that got stuck up in a tree. He was really good with the kitten and the neighborhood kids. But I think he might be a bit young for me."

"How old is he?"

"I don't know for sure. I think late twenties, maybe."

"Old enough to vote," Hollie said, throwing a pillow at Sarah.

"You're bad."

"Moi?" The women collapsed in girlish giggles that woke up Elena.

"Is Santa here yet?" the child asked, rubbing her sleepy eyes.

"Not yet, sugarpie. You've still got a few days yet to wait for Santa to visit. Christmas isn't until Wednesday. Go back to sleep."

As Hollie lifted the child into her arms, Elena's eyes drifted closed again. Hollie walked with Sarah back to Elena's bedroom, where the two women tucked her in with kisses of good-night and sweet dreams.

"So, what's the fireman's name?" Hollie asked as they left the sleeping child and went back to watching the news, mainly interested in whether there would be more snow for Christmas.

"Rick Winzen."

"So are you going to see him?" Hollie persisted.

"He hasn't asked me out, if that's what you mean."

Hollie laughed. "Since when has that stopped you? So you ask him out."

"I think I might scare him off if I did."

Hollie looked more closely at her friend. Sarah was thirty-five, but appeared ten years younger. Sarah usually went after what she wanted, and usually got it. This hesitancy was new for her friend. There was almost a shyness in Sarah's demeanor.

"He's special, isn't he? You like this Rick Winzen a lot, don't you?"

"Maybe."

"I know, why don't you go see Ms. Claudia and ask her about Rick?"

"Really, Hollie. I've got a schedule that would panic Santa's elves from now to Christmas. Tomorrow I have to spend the whole day making a sit-down dinner for twenty-four to be delivered by seven o'clock. I don't have time for a visit to your favorite psychic. Besides, I'm sure Rick isn't interested in me. He's just a nice guy being polite.''

Sarah's disclaimer held a wistful note.

''I think—'' Hollie's thought was interrupted by the ringing of the telephone.

''Who could that be?'' Sarah said, glancing at the time on the VCR. ''It's after ten o'clock.''

Since Hollie was nearest the phone, she picked it up. ''Just a minute, she's here,'' she told the caller, and tossed the portable phone to Sarah.

Sarah caught the phone, her eyes questioning.

Hollie silently mouthed the words ''It's him.''

''Hello...'' Sarah said shyly. ''Hello, Rick,'' she added after the caller identified himself.

''Look, I may be being presumptuous here, Sarah, but I didn't see a wedding ring, so I thought maybe there wasn't a Mr. Smith and I was wondering if maybe you'd like to go out tomorrow.''

''Tomorrow night? You want to go out tomorrow night?'' Sarah grinned from ear to ear at Hollie, who encouraged her by nodding.

''No, not tomorrow night. I have an obligation for tomorrow night I can't get out of. I thought maybe you and Elena would like to have lunch and then go see the *Nutcracker* ballet. My sister can get us tickets.''

''Could you hold on a second, Rick.'' Sarah clutched the phone to her chest so he couldn't hear her. ''Hollie, he wants to take Elena and me to see the *Nutcracker* tomorrow!''

"So say yes."

"But I can't. I've got all that food to make for the dinner I'm catering tomorrow night."

"You two go. I'll make the food."

"But what about Noel?"

"I can handle Noel—don't you worry. You need a treat. So go. I'll handle making the food. And then you'll owe me big-time."

Sarah looked uncertain about Hollie's generous offer.

Hollie insisted.

"Rick, we'd love to go," Sarah finally said into the phone she'd returned to her ear. "What time?"

"Let's get an early start. I'll pick you up at eleven."

Sarah pushed the button to disconnect, tossed the phone to Hollie and let out a shriek. "He likes me!"

"Of course he likes you. And now I'm going home. I need a good night's sleep if I'm going to play Martha Stewart tomorrow."

"Oh, Hollie, are you sure about this?"

"Let me go before I come to my senses," Hollie teased, pulling on her coat.

"But what about Noel?"

"I'll tell him I had a little emergency and he'll adjust."

"But it's not going to endear you to him."

"Sarah, I don't think you can endear yourself to a grinch."

"Maybe he's not really such a grinch."

"Goodbye, Sarah."

"Bye."

Hollie hurried to her car, not wanting to remember that Noel certainly hadn't kissed like a grinch.

NOEL SAT ON THE BED in his room with the newspaper spread out around him. He was studying his competition. The papers were full of holiday ads and he could glean which store carried what merchandise and where each store focused their advertising for their market share.

He'd tried to distract himself at first with the television, but it was full of holiday specials, everything from old Bing Crosby repeats to a country gala. And the commercials were worse.

The newspaper ads were equally festive, but he could at least detach himself enough to study them with an eye to business.

But even the ads didn't hold his attention for very long. Soon his thoughts were back to the problem at hand.

He couldn't understand why Hollie was being so stubborn about selling him her house. She had even rejected his offer to pay her moving costs…rejected his second offer that was more than the fair market price.

How could anyone be such a bad businesswoman?

She needed the money to buy a new car; even he could see that.

He was beginning to think her refusal was personal.

He had the fanciful thought that she didn't want him living in her house. And he didn't ever have fanciful thoughts.

But what else could he think when she continued to refuse to sell her house to him?

Maybe what he needed to do was mount a campaign to make her like him better. Perhaps then she'd feel okay about selling him her house. He never would have thought he'd have to pass muster to buy something.

It was worth a try. Otherwise, he had the sinking feeling that he was going to be stuck in the States for the entire holiday season.

What, he wondered, would make Hollie approve of him buying her house?

He began drawing up a list of possibilities.

Having a plan made him confident that in a day or so he'd be relaxing in the islands, with a house to return to in the new year.

Meanwhile, back at the North Pole…

SANTA SAT AT HIS computer playing a game, one he'd invented with reindeer navigating an obstacle course. He'd been playing half the night.

His thumb was getting numb.

The mindless activity was his way of escaping the stress of having a missing wife.

He was going to have to get his act together and

take it on the road soon or a lot of little boys and girls were going to vote the Easter bunny top good guy.

6

December 21

HOLLIE HAD HOPED she'd have a day without Noel.

Just her luck, when she'd called to cancel looking at houses with him, he'd suggested he come over to Sarah's to help her so she would be done in half the time and there would still be a few hours for them to find a house for *her.* Like a tenacious dog with a bone, he wasn't giving up. He really believed he could convince her to sell him her place.

She saw his car pull up in Sarah's driveway as she began making an assembly line on the counter to put together the rolled breakfast steaks called rouladen. He was probably going to slow her down, since she imagined his primary contact with food had been in restaurants. She noted his car had been restored to its classic elegant line—all traces of the fender bender vanished. Her insurance had covered it.

He was as elegant as his car. Even casually dressed in slacks and a blue sweater beneath his bomber jacket, he appeared sleek and powerfully sexy.

Midnight set up a racket when she heard the doorbell, but went back to her usual spot by the picture window watching the birds at the feeder when Hollie shooed her away.

When Noel entered the house, he began to walk in the direction of the kitchen. ''The TV is in there, if you recall,'' Hollie said, pointing to the living room.

''But I came to help,'' Noel insisted.

''I thought you were kidding.''

He just stared at her. ''I never kid.''

''I should know that by now. What must I have been thinking? Okay, hang your jacket in the closet, push up your sleeves and I'll put you to work.''

Why hadn't she said no from the start? Hollie chastised herself. She hadn't liked how much she'd liked seeing him. Was used to seeing him every day. It occurred to her that she was going to miss him when he left...if he ever did. She had never had a client quite like him. And she had never gotten so involved with one.

''What do you want me to do?''

Noel's words filtered into her musing and she caught herself before she said, *Kiss me again the way you did at the mall.* What was wrong with her?

''Do the bacon strips in the microwave,'' she ordered. ''I'll get the other ingredients ready while you're doing that.''

Hollie took off her stack rings and laid them on the countertop out of the way. She focused on the task at hand, deliberately ignoring how good Noel smelled, and how disturbing and unnerving having him so close by was.

She got out the Italian bread crumbs and the Italian salad dressing and put both into deep bowls. She added a large package of shredded cheese to another bowl and then began shredding a dozen carrots.

When Noel had the bacon crisped, she showed him how to make the rouladens; demonstrating with one breakfast steak, she dipped it first in the Italian salad dressing, then in the Italian bread crumbs. Next she placed a piece of crisp bacon in the middle of the steak and added the shredded cheese and grated carrots by the heaping tablespoon. The finishing touch was rolling the stuffed strips up, jelly-roll fashion, and securing them with three toothpicks per rouladen.

"If you assemble the rouladens, I'll make a big pan of gravy to bake them in. Think you can manage—and aren't you sorry you offered to help?"

"I can manage," he assured her.

They worked in companionable silence, both lost in their own thoughts.

He finally interrupted her with a question.

"So how did you get into real estate?"

"I've always loved houses and I guess I just sort of drifted into it," Hollie answered, stirring the gravy continuously.

"It seems like a pretty tough way to make a living," he observed. "Don't you have to take a lot of grief from customers?"

"You may have noticed an agent learns to let the customer's frustration slide off—most of the time. It's tenacity that gets the sale. You have to be prepared to make sales calls and follow-up calls or face losing potential customers to another agent.''

He was quiet for a moment, as he absorbed her answer.

''Why? Are you thinking of taking it up?'' Hollie asked, turning up the gas flame beneath the pan of gravy.

''Not a chance. I don't enjoy working with the public.''

''Good choice, because you'd kill your clients when they changed their minds for the thirty-eighth time.''

''Is that a dig?''

''No, you've made up your mind. I'm working on changing it.''

''Why are you so stubborn?''

''Me?'' She frowned.

''Yes, you. I'm offering you more money than your house is worth.''

''You can't put a monetary value on some things. But I guess when you come from a wealthy background the way you do you wouldn't know that.''

UPS drove up at that moment, and the deliveryman ran up the walk and rang the doorbell. Midnight began barking and Hollie dropped the spoon she was stirring the gravy with into the pan of hot liquid. She swore beneath her breath, momentarily flustered.

''I'll get the door,'' Noel offered, washing off his hands and grabbing a towel as he headed for the front door. ''You deal with the dog.''

Midnight escaped Hollie's lunge and raced out the door between Noel's legs when Noel opened the door.

"Midnight!" Hollie yelled after the fleeing dog.

The dog had a taste of freedom and was scampering away across the muddy lawn as fast as its little feet would go. The ever changing St. Louis weather had turned warmer, melting the snow that had previously fallen.

"You sign for the package and I'll go get the dog," Noel ordered, taking charge.

"But—"

"I don't know what to do in the kitchen without you," Noel rationalized. "It shouldn't take me long to retrieve Midnight. She's just a little bit of a thing."

As Noel took off after Midnight, Hollie didn't have the heart to tell him that he'd met his match, little bitty or not.

"Ma'am?" The deliveryman was in a hurry. The pre-holiday schedule had him swinging double shifts.

Hollie signed for the package for Sarah and went back to the kitchen. She had mounds of spuds to peel for the mashed potatoes to go with the rouladens. Trust a man to disappear when the drudgery part of cooking arrived.

"DAMN IT," Noel swore as his loafers hit a slick patch of muddy lawn and he went sprawling.

Midnight barked at him and scampered beyond his reach.

Noel scowled at the little piece of fluff, then down at his ruined slacks. A large grass stain covered one knee and his hand hurt where it had landed on a rock, scraping off some skin.

''Come here, Midnight,'' he said in a tone that meant business.

No response.

''I said, come here.''

Midnight barked again and began walking away.

The stupid mutt thought they were playing a game, Noel soon realized. It would serve the animal right if he just left her outside until she got hungry enough to come home. But it might be a while. Midnight was well fed and used to being outside in the fenced yard. The delicious taste of freedom wasn't something she'd give up so easily.

Noel couldn't abandon the silly dog, because the animal was dumb enough to run out in front of a car. But it didn't keep him from feeling like a fool, he grumbled as he rose to chase the creature. It wasn't seemly. If the dog were a German shepherd or something, okay. But a wee little dog made him look ridiculous.

Still, Elena would be distraught if she returned home and her dog was missing, so he continued chasing Midnight.

''Come here, girl,'' Noel called, trying ever so discreetly to inch closer and closer to the dog without Midnight noticing what Noel was doing. How hard could it be to catch such a little bitty thing? He was certainly not about to be outsmarted by a piece of fluff.

Midnight sat down and waited, watching Noel's slow approach. She cocked her head and listened to him coax her to come to him.

''That's it, girl. Just sit very still until I reach you and pick you up ever so gently and wring your silly little neck.''

But just as soon as Noel got within lunging distance of Midnight, the dog would bounce away as though she were on tiny springs, then bark at him from a safe distance, as if Noel were some mean old dognapper.

Frustrated, Noel tried flat out running after the scampering dog and nearly knocked himself out when he ran smack into a low tree branch; he actually saw a burst of tiny stars momentarily. Feeling a little dizzy, he stayed put where he'd landed on the ground.

Which was what he should have done all along, because Midnight began whining and walked back over to him, jumping into Noel's lap and licking his face.

But a couple of neighborhood kids riding by on their bikes attracted Midnight's attention and the dog leaped from Noel's grasp to take off after the boys, yapping at their feet.

Noel held his head in his hands, wishing he were on a warm sunny island with his head hurting because he was hung over.

He had to get up and go after the dog.

Before he lost sight of it.

Sound of it, anyway.

Pushing himself up off the damp ground, he resumed the chase.

NOEL HAD BEEN GONE a long time, Hollie thought uneasily.

She prayed nothing had happened to Midnight. Elena

would be upset and her holiday would be completely ruined.

She emptied the boiling water from the large stockpot full of potatoes and shook them into a bowl for whipping.

By the time she'd finished making the mashed potatoes and checked on the rouladens in the oven, Noel and Midnight still had not returned.

Her worry increased as she worked to make the rest of the dishes for the dinner party Sarah was catering. Helping Sarah from time to time had taught her a lot about catering.

She checked her watch. ''Where are you, Noel?'' she asked aloud. Sarah and Elena weren't due back for a while, but that still didn't prevent Hollie from worrying.

To distract herself, she went to the stereo system and put on the radio, turning from a talk radio station to a station playing Christmas carols.

Returning to the refrigerator, she got out the endive bunches, red leaf lettuce and romaine to wash for the tub of salad. While her hands were busy with the idle task of rinsing the lettuce, she let herself itemize the holiday tasks she had yet to do. First on the list was finding the Barbie in the pink dress for Elena.

Then she wanted to try making sugared fruit. Oh, yes, she needed to get the makings for a gingerbread house because she'd promised Elena she could spend the night and they would make one together. And as of yet, she hadn't found the special ornament for this year to add to the tree, a custom she'd started when she'd bought the house.

She let out a little gasp, suddenly remembering she'd forgotten to kiss a pomegranate on December 15, which would have meant all her Christmas wishes would come true. Instead she'd kissed a grinch—it was impossible to know what that meant.

Noel could have easily spent the day doing something besides helping her cook and, now, chasing down Midnight. Was he trying to get into her good graces so she'd sell the house to him? He'd claimed he was helping so they could look at some houses later in the day. But she wondered if the real reason he'd offered was that he was lonely.

She'd just finished the lettuce and drained the water, when the doorbell rang. Wiping her hands dry on a dish towel, she went to get the door, hoping it was Noel with Midnight.

Her hopes were answered. Midnight was squirming, but safe and sound in Noel's arms. Noel, however, looked as though he'd been hit by a truck.

"What happened to you?" she cried, taking the dog as Noel came inside. "Are you all right?"

"I need to sit down."

She helped Noel to the sofa, while Midnight made her way to her water dish and lapped loudly.

Noel gingerly lowered himself to the sofa. "Can you turn off the music, please? And turn out the lights."

Hollie hurried to do as he requested. Midnight, tired from her adventure, headed for the bed in Elena's room.

''What happened to you?'' Hollie asked again when she returned to Noel's side.

''A low branch knocked me senseless when I was chasing that, that...dog! And then I had to crawl under a car to get her in the end.''

''I'm so sorry, Noel. Can I do anything for you?''

''As a matter of fact, you can. I'm prone to tension headaches and I've got a prescription to pick up.'' He reached in his pants pocket to withdraw his wallet. ''Here, take this. There's cash and my insurance card. Those pills should take care of this headache. I'll just wait here until you get back.''

''Will you be okay by yourself? You could have a concussion or something,'' she said with concern.

''No, I'm fine. I've got a goose egg on my forehead and a headache, but I'm not dizzy or nauseous. If you'll just fetch me my prescription from Walgreens on Lindbergh, I'll be fine.''

She took his wallet and jotted down her cell phone number on her business card, then placed the card on the table beside him. ''You can reach me on my cell phone if you need me,'' she said, retrieving the portable phone and setting it beside the business card.

''Thanks.''

Hollie checked the rouladens in the oven to make sure they were ready, then turned off the oven.

''Okay, I'm leaving now,'' she told him, heading for the front door.

''It smells good in here,'' he mumbled as she left.

Since it was the last Saturday before Christmas the

roads as well as the stores were packed. The drugstore was no exception. There was a long line and a long wait.

Standing in line, Hollie began looking through Noel's wallet for his insurance card. She sorted through a gas credit card, VISA, ATM card and an American Express card, before finding his insurance card. As she was putting the others back in their slots, his driver's license caught her eye.

No, it couldn't be. He was taller. Or shorter.

People lied on their driver's licenses, didn't they?

But in her heart she knew the driver's license wasn't a lie.

Knew it was true.

That Noel Hawksley was a six-foot-one-inch grinch.

''Next,'' the pharmacist called out, and she moved to the counter to be waited on.

THE WHOLE TRIP had taken Hollie an hour. When she returned to Sarah's, Noel was sleeping restfully on the sofa where she'd left him. She touched the bump that had risen on his forehead and winced at its size. Poor Noel! He must have taken quite a knock on the head.

After leaving the sack from the pharmacy on the coffee table, she returned to the kitchen to finish the catered meal for twenty-four. Midnight had come trotting out when she'd returned, recognized her and then lain in a corner of the kitchen, hoping for a bite or two of what smelled so good.

''You don't deserve a treat,'' she admonished the expectant dog.

Midnight barked and got her way, sort of.

Hollie rummaged around in the cabinets and found a dog treat to shut her up so she wouldn't wake Noel.

She wanted to think about things before she faced him again with her new knowledge that he was the beau Santa was bringing her for Christmas. She wasn't sure how she felt about it.

Taking several bunches of carrots from the refrigerator, she began peeling them, readying them for the food processor to make a vegetable dish of sliced carrots and snap peas.

Noel was certainly handsome. And he was tall. Six foot one inch. Smart. Successful. Heroic for rescuing Elena's mutt. He had a lot of admirable qualities.

But underneath he was a grinch.

And that just wouldn't do for her.

She insisted her life be sunny-side up. She didn't let her own unhappy past infringe on her present life. Instead she set about trying to make her life as filled with joy and love and good friends and good times as possible.

It was true, she didn't have a lot of money. But she was happy.

She hadn't allowed herself to have a pity party over life's disappointments. That was the road to Grinchville.

Well, at any rate, at least she knew Santa Claus had a major sense of humor. ''Ha, ha,'' she mumbled.

''What's so funny?''

She jumped, startled that Noel was up and about. He had the sack from the pharmacy in his hand.

''Can I get you something?'' she asked. ''Are you sure you should be up?''

He leaned against the counter. ''What smells so good?''

''The rouladens. Which reminds me, I've got to take them out of the oven.'' As she reached for the oven mitts to do just that, Noel ripped open the sack from the pharmacy and took out his prescription medicine for his headache.

''Where're the glasses?''

Hollie opened the cabinet and handed him one.

He ran the tap water while he opened the plastic bottle and shook out two pills. He tossed them in his mouth and washed them down with a glass of water, then set the empty glass down and rubbed the back of his neck. ''I think I'll pass on looking at any houses today. We can start fresh in the morning, if that's all right with you.''

''Do you want me to drive you back to the hotel?''

''No. I'm fine. All I need is a soak in a hot tub and some sleep. I'll call you in the morning.''

With a muttered expletive at Midnight, Noel donned his jacket and left.

Unperturbed, Midnight continued lying where she was, a ''who, me?'' look on her face.

Hollie laughed. ''Don't look so innocent. You're a very bad doggie.''

All her reprimand got Hollie was a wag of the unrepentant dog's tail.

Hollie shook her head at Midnight and went to turn

the music back on. Singing along with the Christmas carols, she finished the catered meal according to the notes Sarah had left for her. Finally she had everything ready for Sarah to deliver and thought that Noel's idea of a long soak in a hot tub had a lot of appeal.

While she waited for Sarah and Elena to return she called the number she remembered having put in her purse for the owner of the gingerbread house.

But there was no answer.

By the time Sarah and Elena returned, she had the kitchen cleaned up and was watching the evening news on television.

It was, Hollie decided, a toss-up over whose eyes held the most excitement over the afternoon outing, Sarah's or Elena's.

Finally she saw the reason she'd waited for Sarah's return.

Rick Winzen stepped into the kitchen. He had puppy-dog friendly brown eyes and muscles.

''Hi, I'm Rick,'' he offered without any prompting.

''I'm Hollie,'' she said, shaking his hand, which eclipsed hers.

''You're Auntie Hollie,'' Elena piped up.

''Only to you, sugarpie. So did you like the *Nutcracker?*'' Hollie asked.

''It was beautiful,'' Sarah enthused.

''I'm going to be a ballerina,'' Elena insisted, twirling in an arabesque pose.

''It's nice to meet you, Hollie, but I've got to run,'' Rick said. ''I didn't realize traffic would be this bad.

There's a charity event down at the firehouse for underprivileged kids.''

''Bye,'' Elena said, looking up from patting Midnight.

''Aren't you forgetting something?'' Sarah coached.

''Oh, yeah, I had a really good time, Rick. Thank you for inviting me.''

''You're welcome. I'll pick you up at seven tomorrow night, for our date,'' Rick reminded Sarah.

''You *are* still having Elena spend the night tomorrow?'' Sarah asked Hollie as Rick left. ''If not, I can try to get a baby-sitter.''

''Right on the last Sunday night before Christmas? No, I promised Elena we'd make a gingerbread house, though it's been so crazy that maybe we'll settle for gingerbread men.''

''Why is Midnight all muddy?'' Elena asked.

''She got out and she needs a bath,'' Hollie answered.

''She got out? How did you ever get her back?'' Sarah asked.

''We'll have to ask Noel that. But I don't think we'll ask him right away.''

Especially not when every time she thought of a long, hot soak, she thought of Noel relaxing in the tub—naked.

''Did you have any trouble with the food?'' Sarah peeked into the silver foil containers and tubs Hollie had packed the dinner in.

''Nope. Piece of cake. By the way, I do hope you weren't furnishing the dessert, because you didn't leave me any instructions for it.''

''Krausse is doing the cake. It will be beautiful. Her stuff is almost too beautiful to eat. You should have seen the chocolate statue she did for a wedding at the zoo.''

''Speaking of delicious,'' Hollie teased.

''What?'' Sarah blushed.

''You know what. Rick the cutiepie fireman what.''

''You think he's cute.''

''Very.''

''Yeah, me, too.''

''And you have a second date. Fast worker. He must be smitten.''

''What's 'smitten'?'' Elena piped up.

''Umm…it means when somebody likes you.''

''You mean like Noel likes you?''

''Who told you that?'' Hollie asked, probing.

''Nobody. I just know.''

''Everybody knows but you,'' Sarah said.

And Hollie threw the oven mitt at her.

''OH, AH, OHHHHH…'' Noel groaned as he lowered himself into a tub of hot bathwater to soak his achy bones. He felt as though he'd gone a full quarter with the Rams football team instead of a diminutive little dog.

At least his headache was fading.

He couldn't believe making Hollie like him was this painful. He hoped he'd scored enough points with her to make it worth his pain. And now he was hungry. Probably from smelling all the good food Hollie had been cooking. Perhaps if he leaned on her sympathy, he'd get an invitation out of this for a home-cooked meal.

Tomorrow night, after they looked at some houses, was going to be his time with Hollie. She owed him that much.

He'd earned it.

He settled back into the tub and smiled.

Yes, tomorrow night he and Hollie were going to follow up on that kiss they'd shared.

Meanwhile, back at the North Pole...

SANTA GROANED AS he lowered himself into the outdoor hot tub surrounded by snowdrifts.

He was tired and cranky. Nothing was the same without Claudia.

Especially not the hot tub.

He stretched out in the water and let his mind wander back to a particular starry night they'd shared that had started on the snowmobiles and ended in the hot tub.

The steam rose off the water into the frigid night air as he wondered where that infuriating woman of his was.

He'd gotten her point. It was past time for her to return home.

He missed her, damn it.

7

December 22

''THIS HOUSE IS perfect for you,'' Noel insisted. ''Look at the cathedral ceiling in the greatroom. You could put up as tall a Christmas tree as you want.''

''I have a house.'' She threw out her arms to indicate the expanse of the room. ''*You* could easily put a regulation-size pool table here.''

He ignored her. ''Look at this kitchen,'' he insisted. ''It's a custom-designed gourmet kitchen. You're a fabulous cook, if the aromas I smelled yesterday are any indication of your culinary skills. It's got a double oven, a convection oven and an oversize microwave. You can bake Christmas cookies to your heart's content. The range is a six-burner restaurant-style. It's lost on me because all I do is plug in the coffeemaker.''

''I have a house.'' She wasn't budging.

''Not if I buy it.'' He crossed his arms in front of his chest, indicating he wasn't budging one little inch, either.

''Come on, Noel. My feet hurt,'' she moaned, stepping out of her ivory silk heels with the classic bows. She'd paid too much for them, but since Elena kept asking her if they were old, she knew they were worth it. They made her feel confident. She had worn them for that very reason. She was determined to find Noel a house today—end of story.

"My head hurts," Noel countered. "And it's all your fault."

The rat was playing on her guilt over his misadventure with Midnight. Well, she wasn't going to let him get away with it.

"Okay, let's go. I've been saving the best for last. You're going to love this house," she insisted, slipping back into her shoes.

"Don't count your commission just yet," he grumbled, following her out the front door.

"If you want to get to the islands before Christmas you'd better get in a buying mood fast, because this is about it when it comes to available houses that fit your wish list," she warned. "In case you've lost track of time because you're having so much fun—there's only one day left until Christmas Eve."

"Only two shopping days left until Christmas. I know, I know." He grimaced. "You can't turn around without being bombarded by the date."

"Speaking of shopping, we have to make a stop at Julian's on the way to this last house."

"Your hairdresser?" he guessed.

"Shoe boutique. They finally got in the pair of shoes in my size that I want for Christmas."

"What, do they have little jingle bells on them?" he asked, grumpy and rubbing his sore head.

''No. They're white satin with ankle straps and tiny rosebuds.''

''I'll wait in the car.'' He slid down in the seat and closed his eyes.

She was glad he waited in the car. That way no one was there to raise an eyebrow at her when she impulsively added a pair of daring red sling-backs to her bill. ''Merry Christmas, Hollie,'' she said beneath her breath. Now she really had to get that commission by selling Noel a house. There was no incentive like a little indulgent shopping.

Stowing the shoe boxes in the trunk, she saw the little baskets she'd bought in which to pack the holiday bread she'd baked for the neighbors. She was way behind schedule on her Christmas preparations. Making a mental note to remember the baskets, she slammed the trunk with conviction. He was going to buy this house or else.

''Something wrong with the shoes?'' Noel slid her a questioning look as she got back in the car.

''No, why?''

''Well, the way you slammed the trunk, I figured maybe there was a problem.''

There was a problem and he was it. But she refrained from pointing that out to him, her discipline as a real estate agent coming to her aid—holding your tongue when you felt like screaming was one of the top ten requirements of a successful agent.

''By the way, you can cross one thing off your list,'' he said when she didn't answer. ''I located a Barbie doll with a pink dress.''

That got her attention. ''How? I've looked everywhere. It's *the* toy this season and there isn't one to be found,'' she insisted.

''I'm in retail, remember. I know where to shop, and how.''

''Yep, you just lift what you want and try not to get caught sneaking out of the store,'' she couldn't resist teasing.

''Don't remind me. I called in a favor, okay? So don't worry about the doll. It's on its way by courier and will be here in time for you to give it to Elena for Christmas.''

''You still have to buy this house.'' Pulling over to the exit ramp, Hollie navigated a few lefts and had them going up the secluded drive to the house on Mistletoe Lane. She hoped he didn't notice the name of the street. Noel Hawksley probably wouldn't enjoy living in a place that constantly reminded him of the holidays.

''It's secluded so no one will disturb you while you're working or destressing at the pool table,'' Hollie said, beginning her pitch as they got out of the car and made their way to the house.

''And I'm trapped if the snowplow doesn't show up,'' Noel countered.

''The grade of the drive isn't that steep that you'll need a snowplow to get out.'' Hollie took her key for the lock out of her briefcase as they reached the solid oak doors with etched-glass inserts. ''It's close to all the major arteries, so driving to the store you're opening won't take long. Neither will getting to a Rams game or the airport."

"Location, location, location—the real estate agent's creed, right?"

"Right. That means great resale value. And this house has just come on the market. You're going to have to snap it up before anyone else sees it. It's going to go fast. Right now we're in a seller's market. That's why you lost the first house you put in an offer on."

"We'll see."

His noncommittal attitude did not bode well, but Hollie chose to ignore it. She was going to sell him the house because it was right for him. And because if he got out of town before Christmas, it meant there was a more palatable six-foot-one-inch beau on his way from Santa.

She wished she'd never seen Noel's driver's license, because it only intensified her already too strong attraction to him. She didn't want to get involved with a great pair of broad shoulders, smoldering blue eyes, a rock-hard muscular body that would ruin her holiday. Even if he made her heart pound and made her daydream way too frequently about what it would be like to have those large, long-fingered hands of his roaming over her body, exploring and caressing. No matter how great the temptation. She wasn't about to allow his negativity to overwhelm her efforts to make the best of her life by being upbeat. Noel Hawksley just couldn't be Santa's idea of the perfect beau for her—even if he did have a sweet, heroic side to him. That side was only a *side,* she reminded herself.

They stood for a moment in the house. It had oversize natural clay tiles and was big enough to hold the statue of a wild horse pawing the air, which sat next to the stairs that led to the second floor.

"Isn't this spectacular?" Hollie said as they entered far enough into the foyer to see the two-story living room that offered a floor-to-ceiling view of the woods it overlooked.

"I like the horse," was all Noel would admit.

"Maybe we can get the owners to throw it in," Hollie said, not to be dissuaded as she stepped down the two steps to the sunken living room.

He followed her, dragging his feet. "It's awfully bright in here."

"Yes. Isn't it wonderful?"

She'd purposely taken his complaint as praise for the room. "And look over here. There's a screened-in sunroom. It's a perfect place for a picnic on a rainy day."

He grumbled something unintelligible.

"The kitchen's through here," Hollie called out to Noel, who stood staring out the screened sunroom into the dark woods at the edge of the sloping lawn.

"Noel?"

"Coming." He broke away from whatever called him in the darkness to join Hollie in the kitchen.

"While it isn't terribly large, it is efficient. And it has a built-in microwave. The counters are ceramic tile and all the appliances are top of the line and only two years old.''

He nodded noncommittally.

She couldn't get a read on him. He was purposely keeping her in the dark about his response to the house.

''The bedrooms are upstairs, I assume?''

''The master bedroom is on the first floor and the guest bedroom and additional bedrooms are on the second floor. There's also a loft that overlooks the living room. It's the perfect place for your pool table and big-screen television. Shall we have a look?''

Without waiting for his answer, she went through the foyer and began climbing the stairs. She heard his step on the stairs behind her.

When they reached the second floor they were standing directly in the large loft. It had the same view as the living room and from it they could see the pool.

''It's not bad,'' he conceded.

They did a quick tour of the second-floor bedrooms and baths, then headed back downstairs to check out the master bedroom.

It was oversize, with a walk-in closet as big as a normal bedroom.

''Is there an echo in here when I talk?'' Noel asked, commenting on the sheer expanse of space.

Wickedly, Hollie wondered if Noel fancied hearing the sound of his name echoing in the bedroom.

''What are you thinking?'' he asked, noticing the smile on her face.

Caught out, she made up a hasty lie. ''I wasn't going

to mention it, but it'll cost you a mint to mirror the ceiling.'' And then realized her lie was as bad as her thought.

''Why, Ms. Winslow!''

Wanting to distract him, she headed for the impressive bath with a double shower that looked too inviting. She focused on the oversize tub. ''This will accommodate your six-foot-one-inch frame,'' she informed him without thinking.

''What—did you measure me or something?''

''Oh…oh. Ah, I just happened to see your driver's license when I was looking for your insurance card.''

He let her hang for a few seconds and then made her embarrassment worse. ''So now you know all the intimate details about me,'' he teased.

Was it her, or had he moved closer?

They both looked at each other in one of those moments that could lead to loss of control; to acting on the simmering attraction between them.

He lifted his hand to her face and she stood stock-still, breathless.

''You've an eyelash on your cheek,'' he explained, brushing it away.

He stepped back then, diffusing the tension of the moment. But the attraction was still there…lurking.

''Um…would you like to see the garage?'' she asked, her voice cracking, giving her away.

''Yeah, why don't we do that?''

She forced herself not to run from the master bedroom as she turned away from him. She had been that close to doing something really foolish. If only Elena hadn't forced that kiss between them. It kept whispering suggestive ideas in her mind.

The garage was angled to the left side of the house and a basketball hoop hung above the garage door.

He picked up the basketball lying on the driveway and dribbled it, then shot a hoop. Then he turned to her with a grin and asked provocatively, ''Want to go one-on-one? You aren't afraid of me, are you?'' he challenged.

''I don't play basketball in heels, thank you.''

''So take them off.'' He dribbled around her and threw another hoop, sinking the ball.

''I'll ruin my hose.''

''So take them off.''

''I don't think so. I've played games with you before, Noel. You're ruthless about winning.''

He stopped dribbling and balanced the ball on his hip with his hand. ''Why else would you play?''

She shrugged. ''I admit I'm as competitive as the next person. I like to win. But I also really like the sheer joy of playing. Having a good time. Everything doesn't have to be about competition. Sometimes the fun is in the playing.''

''So you don't care if you sell me this house, then. Is that right?'' he asked, baiting her.

''No. I'm not playing a game here, Noel. This is what I do. It's my career. You wanted me to find you a house. I have. It's time you made a decision about it.''

Noel dropped the ball and let it roll to the side of the

driveway. "Boy, you're some closer. That's it? Take it or leave it?"

"I told you I don't have anything else to show you."

His eyes said that was debatable, but he knew better than to push any more of her buttons.

"Okay, I'll tell you what. I haven't really seen your house, just part of it. Why don't you take me home with you and I'll decide between the two houses."

It was certainly a step forward, Hollie had to admit, even if she wasn't crazy about showing him the rest of her house. But perhaps if she humored him and played along with his request, she'd be able to convince him to make an offer on this house and then she'd be done with Noel.

"I'll show you my place," she agreed. "But I'm not selling it." It wouldn't be fair to give him the wrong impression. Even though she knew he didn't pay the least heed to her refusal to sell. Evidently, he thought he could wear her down. Or maybe even charm her into doing what he wanted.

"I'd just like to look..."

And why did everything he say sound as though he were talking about sex?

Or was that just her?

"Speaking of looking... Do you want to see the basement or the grounds here before we leave? That way you won't have any unanswered questions later."

He let her finish showing him around, without further comment. He seemed to be planning something. She hoped it had to do with signing an offer on the house.

When they got in the car and headed down the long drive, he asked, ''Do you like it?''

''It doesn't matter if I like it.''

''It does to me.''

''Then I like it. I'd buy it myself if I could afford it, okay?''

''What was your favorite thing about the house?''

''The French doors leading from the master bedroom to the pool.''

''Umm...a romantic touch, I agree.''

Was he thinking the same thing she was? That it would be convenient for a late-night swim that would lead to skinny-dipping that would lead to—

''It's been a long day and neither of us had lunch. Why don't I take you out to dinner and then we'll go back to your place?''

It was her. She'd been thinking of seduction and he'd been thinking of food. ''We can't go out to dinner tonight, because I've got plans.''

He was very quiet, then he sighed. ''Oh, you've got a date, then.''

She nodded and pulled onto the service road to the highway. ''Yes, with a four-year-old. Elena's spending the night. I'm going to have to swing by now and pick her up because Sarah's got a date.''

''So I'll take you both out to dinner. I'll even let Elena choose.''

''No, you won't, unless you'd actually enjoy going to Honey Bear's Pizza Cave to watch the dancing costumed bears.''

"I'm thinking letting her choose is not cool."

Both had figured without the princess of whine. Elena had pestered them until they wound up at Honey Bear's. It worked out okay because they were hungry and the food was fast and tasty, if a tad juvenile. The pizzas were shaped in bear claws and beehives. They even had a dessert pizza, which made Noel look a little green when it passed by on its way to another table.

When they left, Elena shoved all her paper goodies into her teddy bear backpack. In the car on the ride back to Hollie's she was a chatterbox, happy at having gotten her way.

Hollie was going to be just as happy if she, too, got her way tonight and Noel made an offer on the house on Mistletoe Lane.

"Are we going to make a gingerbread house?" Elena asked when they were back at Hollie's.

Hollie ruffled Elena's hair. "There's been a little change in plans, sugarpie. We're going to make snowflakes, instead, because Noel and I spent too much time looking at houses."

"Snowflakes?"

"Yes, they're these pretty powdered-sugar, snowflake-shaped cookies. I've got a snowman tin we can put some in and you can give them to your mom for Christmas, okay?"

"Yeah." Elena scampered off to put her teddy bear on the bed.

Noel took Hollie's hand, tugging playfully. "Hi, remember me. You were going to show me the house."

''Right. But we have to be careful. I don't want Elena getting upset about me moving again. Why don't I let Elena show you the house?'' she suggested just as the little girl came down the hall.

''Elena, would you give Noel a tour of the house while I get everything ready to make the snowflakes?''

''Sure,'' Elena agreed, taking Noel's hand and leading him back to the room she'd just come from.

''This is my room when I stay over with Auntie Hollie.'' Elena went to the bed, sat on it and bounced up and down. ''I helped her paint it my favorite color. She said it's called straw color.''

Noel studied the pale yellow room. A full-length mirror leaned against one wall, and hats and purses and shoes with heels were scattered all around it.

''Those are Hollie's old things she lets me dress up in when I come over. Do you like my new dress?'' Elena tucked her fingers beneath the red-and-white gingham pinafore she wore with white long underwear. On her feet were hiking boots that lace-edged socks peeked over.

''I like your dress. Are those your favorite books?'' he asked, nodding to a stack beside the bed.

''Uh-huh, these two are my very favorites,'' she explained, handing him *Gilly, the Seasick Fish* by Susann Batson and *Snickerdoodle Is Not a Cookie* by Bonnie Jeanne Perry. ''Will you read them to me?''

''Why don't you show me the rest of the house and I'll read them to you later, after you've made the snowflake cookies with Hollie?'' He had to get this kid to sleep.

''Okay. Come on, I'll show you Hollie's bedroom.''

Good, Noel thought, relishing finally seeing Hollie's bedroom. Elena was a glitch in his plan for the evening, but the child had to go to sleep sometime. And then he'd have Auntie Hollie's undivided attention.

Elena tucked her hand in Noel's and tugged him along the hall until they reached Hollie's bedroom. ''It's really pretty,'' she declared.

The child was right. It was decorated in soft ice-cream shades. He chuckled when he saw the miniature Christmas tree with lights and tinsel on the night table by her bed.

Elena went over to it and plugged it in, her eyes lighting up. ''Auntie Hollie has her very own bedroom tree. I'm going to have one, too, when I get big.''

''I bet you are,'' Noel agreed.

There was a scurry on the roof and Elena's eyes got very big. ''Do you think it's Santa's reindeer already?''

Noel laughed. ''No, I don't think they make a practice run. Christmas Eve is pretty much it, as far as I know.''

''Oh.'' She went to bounce on Hollie's bed, seeming to find it impossible to pass a bed without bouncing on it.

''Auntie Hollie's bed is the softest bed ever.''

It looked it, he thought. It was covered with a pale pink comforter, and at the head of the bed were mounds of plump white pillows with pastel embroidered borders. The old-fashioned bed sat high off the floor. Elena had climbed up a little set of stairs beside the bed to reach it.

Done bouncing, Elena climbed back down and went to the big pine dresser. ''Auntie Hollie has lots of pretties. Want to see?'' The little girl pulled open the drawer and displayed a jumble of pastel satins, silks and lace dainties. ''She says I have to wait till I'm big to wear these.'' The child pulled out some of the lingerie and dreamily laid her head against the soft materials.

Noel wanted to do the same thing.

But Hollie chased such thoughts from his mind when she called out, ''It's not that big a house. Come on, you two. Time to make snowflakes.''

He was making snowflakes? He'd rather make love. Had plans along that line by morning if Elena ever went to bed.

He was, Hollie informed him when he and Elena returned to the kitchen.

''We'll get these in the oven and then we'll write up an offer, if you've made up your mind,'' she said, grating a lemon rind.

They spent the next hour making snowflakes, with Hollie frying the dough-covered iron in hot oil until the snowflakes were cooked, then Noel and Elena sprinkling the snowflakes with powdered sugar.

When they were finished, Noel and Elena were dusted with powdered sugar and looked like snowflakes themselves.

When at last the cookies had cooled it was time for Elena to go to bed. She cajoled Noel into reading her a story from one of her favorite books while Hollie cleaned up the mess.

Hollie was just hanging up a dish towel when Noel returned with the news that Elena was asleep. Finally they were alone.

"At least for now," Hollie acknowledged. "So what have you decided? Are you ready to make an offer on the house on Mistletoe Lane?"

"You sure you won't sell me this one?" he asked, taking a seat at the counter, where Hollie had brought out the papers to draw up the offer. "And I'm not certain about the street name now...."

"I'm sure."

"And you really liked the house we saw—you weren't just saying you liked it to make a sale?"

"I told you—I'd buy it myself. I don't know how to say I liked it any better than that. It's a great house at a fair price. If you want a house by Christmas, it's the one to buy."

"Okay, let's make an offer," he said. "I can even live with the street name." He frowned.

Hollie was relieved, excited and sad all at once. Relieved that Noel had given up on buying her house. Excited about the commission the sale would bring her. Sad that she would no longer be seeing Noel every day. Because as much as he drove her crazy, she'd grown used to the look of him, the smell of him, his company.

And there was still the matter of that kiss.

He could have given her a peck on the cheek. He

could have buzzed her lips briefly. He could even have refused.

But he hadn't. Instead he'd given her a real kiss. A very real, romantic kiss. The kind that led to… something. It hadn't been a perfunctory kiss between real estate agent and client, happily sealing a closed deal.

However, the kiss hadn't led to anything.

True, their relationship had grown more relaxed…less formal and more teasing…but it hadn't developed beyond that.

Now it was over as quickly as it had begun. She would show Noel's offer. The seller would haggle a little, maybe make one or two counteroffers before accepting Noel's price, and then Noel would be off to the islands for Christmas.

''How long do you think it's going to take to close the deal?'' Noel asked, interrupting her thoughts as she filled out the offer. His romantic plans didn't fit her plan to close the deal. He was hot and she was all business.

''Why? Did you want to use the phone to call the airline and make your reservations?'' He was really in a hurry to get away.

''There's that,'' he agreed, disappointed at his thwarted plans for the evening.

''Go ahead and call,'' she said, not looking at him. ''With any luck, we can settle everything tomorrow. And if need be, you can finish up by phone from your island.''

Without much effort, he'd managed to ruin her hope of a very Merry Christmas.

This time her daydreams had been way too fanciful.

The ones she hadn't even admitted to herself.

Till now.

Meanwhile, back at the North Pole…

"HOW COULD CLAUDIA GO away and leave me nothing to eat but a freezer full of Lean Cuisines," Santa muttered, pushing away his second empty container.

Santa hated how people who reformed their bad habits lost their senses of humor. Or was his workaholic schedule the reason Claudia didn't laugh anymore the way she used to?

He went back to the test in one of Claudia's glossy women's magazines he'd been checking for a hint to what spa she might be at. The test was to see if your marriage was in trouble.

He finished tallying his answers and found out what Claudia's absence had already told him.

He was going to have to make some changes.

A diamond tennis bracelet might be a good way to start. And an indoor tennis court.

Claudia would look sexy in one of those short white tennis skirts…if she came back.

8

December 23

"SO HOW WAS your date with the fireman last night?" Hollie asked, sitting on Sarah's striped sofa with her stocking feet up on the oak coffee table.

"He's coming over tomorrow night to celebrate Christmas Eve with us. Why don't you bring Noel?" Sarah hinted.

"Because Noel will be long gone."

"You didn't sell him your house, Hollie, did you?"

"No, but I finally found one he liked. We put in an offer early this morning and I'm waiting to hear," she said, patting the beeper she was never without. "It's weird. One minute he's gung ho for my house—the next minute he's buying another one. Not that I'm not thrilled to get a big commission and to keep my house…but still…"

Sarah took a sip of the honey-and-lemon tea she'd made them. "Here's some dime-store analysis—for what it's worth. Have you ever considered the fact that Noel was attracted to your house because he's attracted to you? Maybe it was his way of getting you in his life—symbolically, that is."

Hollie laughed nervously. ‘‘Thanks, Ms. Freud. *If* I believe your analysis, why has he decided to buy another house?’’

Sarah shrugged. ‘‘Got me there. Maybe...’’ She paused and gave Hollie a mischievous look. ‘‘Because he wants a house big enough for the both of you.’’

Hollie blushed. ‘‘Go on! I hardly know the man. He hardly knows me.’’

‘‘Yeah, right.’’ Sarah harrumphed. ‘‘You’ve spent day in and day out with him for over a week. What don’t you know about each other? And besides...let me tell you, there’s some heavy-duty intensity and spark-flying going on between the two of you. Why don’t you see where it can go? Maybe it you ask real nice Noel will stay for Christmas.’’

‘‘Not a chance. He’s a grinch, remember? And furthermore, he can’t wait to get away to a hot Caribbean island.’’

‘‘Come on, Hollie. Give it a chance. And give Noel a chance. Surely a Christmas freak like you can convert him. Make him want to celebrate with us. I know Elena would like him to be there. She came home all chirpy about how Noel read her stories from the books you’re constantly collecting for her.’’

‘‘Did he ever read her stories!’’ Hollie said, with a laugh. ‘‘She kept getting up when we thought she was asleep and begging Noel to read to her. We were both falling asleep by the time she did.’’

‘‘Aha, so there was *courting* going on. He lingered after you wrote up the offer. I’m sorry about Elena putting the damper on things for you two.'' Sarah's laugh was husky and girlish. ''Well, not that sorry. Otherwise Rick and I wouldn't have been necking—''

''Sarah! It was your second date!''

''Well, I had a child with me on the first one. I couldn't very well lock lips at the *Nutcracker*.''

''That's not what I meant and you know it, you hussy. You're not supposed to neck until the third date.''

''Midnight, get down,'' Sarah scolded as the little dog snitched a snowflake cookie from the open snowman tin on the coffee table. ''Tell me where it says you're not supposed to neck until the third date, Hollie.''

''I know I heard it somewhere.'' Hollie sniffed. ''Besides, Noel wasn't courting me. He was just lonely and didn't want to go back to his room. I think he gets a charge out of Elena's antics. He certainly did try to get her to sleep.''

''I'll bet,'' Sarah said beneath her breath. ''Well, I think you should at least ask him if he'll come Christmas Eve. Maybe if he has somewhere to go, he won't leave St. Louis at all.''

Hollie folded up her list of things to do and put on her shoes to head out and finish her last-minute errands. ''Think about it, Sarah. A sunny beach, warm sand, ocean breezes…he's not staying. And neither am I. As much as I'd like to laze away the day with you, I've places to go, crowds to shoulder through. Want me to pick up anything for you now that I'm finally officially on vacation and don't have to show Noel any more houses?''

''I'm all set. All the catering is done for now, and by the way, the Witmers were very complimentary about the dinner, thanks.''

As Hollie stood to leave, her beeper went off.

''So much for the best-laid plans. It's the offer. Can I use your phone?''

''Like you have to ask. Go, girl.''

SARAH RANG the doorbell on the Victorian gingerbread house. She felt Hollie could use all the help she could get, so she'd decided to pay Hollie's visionary a little visit as soon as Hollie left and while Miss Nosy Elena was still playing at a neighborhood chum's.

It had seemed like a good idea at the time, but now she felt a little foolish.

The woman who answered the door banished her reservations. Ms. Claudia was completely charming as she ushered Sarah into the living room, urging her to be seated near the fireplace.

''What is it you'd like to know?'' Ms. Claudia asked, taking Sarah's hand. ''Do you want to find out how your catering business is going to go, or if that sweet little Elena is going to have brothers and sisters?''

''Well, I ah—'' Sarah supposed she shouldn't be surprised Ms. Claudia knew so much…she was a psychic.

''Oh, you want to find out about that fireman of yours, I bet, from the way you're blushing.''

''He's not mine. I mean—''

''Oh, he's yours for the taking, honey.'' Ms. Claudia patted Sarah's hand.

''Really?''

Ms. Claudia nodded. ''You do like him, don't you?''

''Yes, but he's a little...''

''You need someone younger to keep up with you and Elena. Besides, with all his brothers and sisters, he's a very mature young man.''

''He does seem to be. But that's not really why I stopped by. I wanted to ask you about my friend Hollie. Hollie Winslow. She came to see you and you told her Santa was going to bring her a six-foot-one-inch beau for Christmas.''

''I know she doesn't believe it, does she?''

''I believe it. I think she's already met him, but she's too stubborn to act.''

Ms. Claudia leaned forward and smiled. ''They're both too stubborn.''

''Then how—''

''I know you want to help your friend, Sarah,'' Ms. Claudia interrupted. ''But they have to work it out for themselves. Hollie will have to come to understand that Noel needs what she has to offer.''

''There's nothing I can do?'' Sarah asked, wanting to bring her friend the happiness she deserved.

''They'll work it out,'' Ms. Claudia assured her.

Sarah smiled. ''In that case, how *is* my catering business going to do?''

''I think if your fireman has his way, you're going to be catering to him and...''

''More children!''

''If you want them.''

"Elena will be thrilled. She's been pestering me for a little sister. Oh, by the way, you wouldn't know where I could get a Barbie in a pink dress, would you?"

"It's on its way."

"You mean Santa is bringing it?"

"With a little help from a courier."

Sarah looked down at her watch. "Oops, I've got to run. Elena will wonder what's happened to me."

"Merry Christmas," Ms. Claudia said, walking Sarah to the door. She smiled, knowing that Sarah's unselfish act of adopting Elena was going to pay off in the dividend of twin boys. Elena had better enjoy being a spoiled princess while she could!

As Claudia went to the kitchen to warm up some soup, she wondered what Santa was doing.

Wondered if he missed her as much as she missed him.

"CONGRATULATIONS, you've got yourself a house," Hollie said, clinking her champagne glass with Noel's.

"And without any quibbling from the owners. They took my first offer."

"You got lucky," she said, pouring him some more champagne from the bottle he'd brought with him when he arrived at her house to celebrate closing the deal.

"You're pretty gussied up," she commented, taking in his double-breasted suit and his silk tie. "You sure you didn't already start work? You haven't changed your mind about leaving town for Christmas, have you?" She tried to keep the note of hope from her voice.

"I bought a ticket for a flight that leaves tomorrow afternoon at two. I'm dressed up because I thought maybe we could go to dinner to celebrate. I've given you a pretty hard time and you deserve a good meal on me."

"Dinner?"

He nodded. "Anywhere but Honey Bear's Pizza Cave."

"I'll have to shower and change...." She knew most men hated to wait for women.

"Go ahead—we've got time. Just tell me where you want to eat and I'll call and make reservations while you get ready."

Hollie took a sip of champagne, and felt giddy from the bubbly wine. It was the champagne, wasn't it, and not the man who looked as though he'd walked off the cover of *Gentlemen's Quarterly?* She remembered Sarah talking about an elegant restaurant in Clayton with a funny name. What was the name—Crazy something? "Crazy Fish," she said. "I've been wanting to try it."

"Crazy Fish, it is. Go ahead and get ready, then," he said, draining his champagne flute and setting it on the counter.

"The phone book is in the bread drawer," she informed him, heading off to her bedroom with a wave.

After he made the call and set the reservations for two, he settled on the sofa with a refilled flute of champagne to wait. He'd allotted an hour for her to get ready and a half hour for them to reach the restaurant.

Sitting on the sofa reminded him of the snowy day

he'd fallen asleep there and the sexy dream he'd had of Hollie. It had been a very vivid dream, romantic and sensual, and he was getting hot. He set down the champagne flute and walked down the hall to where he'd heard the shower running in Hollie's bathroom.

Another image came to mind.

The dresser drawer Elena had coveted and opened, much like Pandora's box. It tempted him into the bedroom.

The shower was still running, steam drifting out into the bedroom. He caught the scent of Hollie's perfumed soap. It smelled like honeysuckle and musk.

A bold desire overtook him as judgment left him. He slid open the lingerie drawer and began having a look through it. Merely professional curiosity, he told himself. After all, he was in retail.

He picked up a bra in lavish Venetian lace with dainty rosette trim, then discarded it and its matching stretch-mesh pantie in favor of a white teddy detailed with lovely eyelet embroidery and scalloped edging. It was pure and provocative, like Hollie.

Boldly, he laid it on the bed, then went to her closet and sorted through it, stopping first at a lemon pleated crepe suit. Its sunny color pleased him, but it wasn't exactly what he had in mind. Searching further, he came up with the perfect candidate for dinner at Crazy Fish: a sleek little white spandex top with a ballet neck and a midthigh-length black ribbed knit skirt.

He laid those out alongside the teddy. He looked at

the ensemble speculatively, then went back to the lingerie drawer for sheer nude panty hose.

The shower was still running, and the escaping steam lent a sultry atmosphere to the room and his clandestine behavior. He was taking a chance, risking blowing the evening.

Shoes! He'd almost forgotten. She had a thing for them, so choosing them would be a real treat. The top shelves of her closet were stacked high with shoe boxes. His task was made easy by her efficient system of taping a snapshot of each pair of shoes to the end of each box.

After a quick inventory, he settled on pretty black pumps with elasticized crisscross straps and about two-inch block heels.

He slipped the shoes from their box and hurried to the bed, where he placed them alongside his other selections for the evening.

His ears perked up at the sound of the shower being turned off and the shower door sliding open. She was getting out to towel off. He lingered a second to visualize her naked, with water droplets on her smooth skin and her curls damp against her neck.

And then he moved silently from the room to wait back in the living room.

How would she react when she saw the clothes laid out on her bed?

It was true he'd invaded her privacy. And what he'd done was very intimate.

Suggestive.

Possessive.

And maybe stupid.

But if she reacted the way he hoped, he'd be able to feast on the memory in the islands over Christmas. And just knowing he'd picked out every intimate detail of her clothing would excite him terribly as he sat across from her during dinner tonight.

He didn't know why he'd done it. He had certainly never done anything like it before. Never revealed himself so recklessly.

The wait seemed forever, although just seconds passed. Had she left the bathroom yet? Had she discovered the clothing?

When she did, what would she think?

What would she do?

It was so quiet he could hear the furnace kick on and the ping against the windows of a light sleet that had begun to fall.

He got up and began pacing absently, his nerves making him restless. There was a bowl of sugared fruit on the piano. He picked a grape and plopped it into his mouth before he knew what he was doing. The sweet-tart taste only heightened his senses.

Sitting down at the piano, he began doodling on the keys, picking out a favorite song by ear. He was no more than an adequate player, but the distraction relaxed him.

He didn't hear Hollie the first time she called his name. Or the next.

The third "Noel" caught his ear.

"Are you calling me?" he asked, leaving the piano and walking down the hall toward her bedroom, hoping like hell he wasn't hearing things. Afraid his overactive imagination had conjured the sound.

''Would you come in here, please?'' Hollie said as Noel walked by a framed handprint of Elena's on the wall, next to a picture of her in a ballerina outfit. He passed Elena's ''room,'' where he'd read her bedtime stories until midnight while Hollie had painted the little girl's toenails cherry red, as promised. She spoiled the child rotten.

He wouldn't mind being spoiled rotten by her, he thought, entering the bedroom…not knowing just what to expect.

She was dressed.

In the exact ensemble he'd picked out. And she was smiling, he saw with relief. A quirky little smile of acknowledgment.

''I thought you might like,'' she said, opening the velvet case on her dresser, ''to pick out my earrings, as well. Then all I have to do is my hair and we'll be ready to go.''

Hell, he was ready to go!

She looked like a sexy dream in the outfit he'd selected for her. Sweet and sexy at the same time.

Was it a trap? Was she ready to blast him for the liberties he'd taken? A little uncertain, he approached the velvet box and looked inside. Every piece of jewelry was whimsical, from angels to hearts to moons and stars.

He decided to give her what she wanted and picked up one of the red-and-green glitter holiday wreaths. He was close enough to see that her ears were pierced. Close enough to want to nibble on them. For starters.

Dinner was way down on the list of what he wanted at that moment.

She smiled at his selection.

"Do you want to put it in?" she asked.

He nearly swallowed his tongue, thinking she'd read his mind.

She turned her pierced ear toward him, waiting, and he realized she'd been talking about the earring in his hand.

Tongue-tied, he did just that, fumbling only a little with the delicate earring.

"Thanks," she said, handing him the other one. "I touched up my manicure and didn't want to wreck it," she explained, blowing on her nails.

He thought the gesture interesting. She could have been blowing on her nails to dry them, but it looked to him as if she was congratulating herself on accomplishing something.

He was afraid to think what.

Hell, he didn't want to think at all. And then, giving in to impulse, he didn't.

Running his forefinger from the shell of her ear along her jaw, he passed the pad of his thumb over her lips and then lowered his lips to hers in a moment of spontaneous passion. He coaxed a response from her as he buried his hands in her damp curls. His tongue explored her delicious mouth with a sense of urgency.

''We're going to be late,'' she said when he broke the kiss.

''Do you care?'' he asked.

She answered him by reaching up to kiss him back.

A kiss of invitation that made him lose control.

He swung her up into his arms without breaking the kiss and carried her across the room. She clung to his broad shoulders, breathless still from the deep, probing thrust of his tongue.

''What are you doing?'' she asked when they broke apart to gasp for air.

''Your bed has fascinated me since the first moment I saw it. It looks like a floating cloud, so high off the floor. I've wanted to see if it would possibly be as soft and inviting as it looks.''

Hollie squealed as he tossed her from his strong arms up on the bed.

She bounced once and then was enveloped in a tumble of plump white pillows.

Hurriedly he loosened his tie and shed it along with his suit jacket, then leaped to join her on the bed. Lying across her, he whispered in her ear, telling her about the dream he'd had about her, about what her lips had been up—er, down—to.

''Is that a request?'' she asked.

''Maybe later,'' he replied, pushing up her skirt as she arched her hips to assist him.

He cupped her bottom as he ground against her and moaned. His fingers flicked the snaps on the white teddy and he ripped the fabric of the sheer hose easily.

She let out a gasp of pleasure when he slid down on the bed to cover her pulsing sex with his warm mouth. While she squirmed beneath him, he sucked, then alternately raked his teeth against the tender flesh, until she was moaning his name. He upped the ante when he laved her with smooth, broad strokes of his tongue that didn't penetrate only tormented, teased.

And then her hands, which had been clutching the sheets, cupped his ears, guiding him, insisting, until he furled his tongue in swirls of pleasure inside her till she shuddered against him and then went limp beneath him with exhausted passion.

He took her hand and kissed her palm, then stretched out alongside her, listening to her breathing, shallow and fast, until it returned to normal.

"Where did that come from?" Hollie asked, turning on her side and facing him, trailing her fingers over his broad chest.

"Just being a gentleman," he answered.

"A gentleman? That's an interesting way of putting it, don't you think?"

"You know, returning the favor," he explained, referring to the dream he'd had about her.

She chuckled. "Yeah..."

He stacked his hands behind his head as he eased over onto his back. His sex was hard and saluting.

It drew her hand. "So what do you think?" she asked, stroking.

"At the moment I'm incapable of thought. All the blood has left my head and gone...elsewhere."

''I mean, what do you think—is the bed as soft as you imagined? Do you like it?''

''Um…'' was all he said as she squeezed the length of him with gentle command.

And then her lips replaced her hand.

''Wait, wait, wait a minute.'' He lifted her head. ''Why don't we eat dinner first and come back later for dessert?''

She laughed, knowing he didn't really want to wait. ''It's like I always tell Sarah—life is uncertain, have dessert first.''

He took control then, flipping her body beneath his and holding both her hands in his. His mouth was on hers as he thrust inside her core, authoritatively and then teasingly slow. The pattern soon broke, however, and they engaged in an escalating race, before crossing the finish line together.

When she opened her eyes moments later she saw that at some point he'd managed to shed every stitch of clothing he had on, while she was still completely dressed, was even wearing her shoes.

For the first time in her life a man had made love to her with her shoes on. It was thrilling.

And somehow she believed he knew it.

He'd picked one of her most favorite pairs of shoes and had scored a hit right out of the ballpark. This was not your average man. But, then, she'd known that from the first time he'd walked into the real estate office and into her life.

And tomorrow afternoon he was probably walking out.

But she wasn't going to think about that. She was going to enjoy her holiday. He hadn't said any sweet words to get her into bed. He hadn't had to.

She'd been ready ever since that kiss at the mall.

If she got her Christmas wish, he'd change his mind and stay. But it wouldn't do to let herself believe, only to wish.

She knew in her heart she could make him have a Merry Christmas.

"I don't know about you, but I'm famished," Noel said, breaking into her thoughts as he rolled over and nearly fell out of bed, stopping himself just in time.

"I could probably find something in the pantry to nibble on," Hollie suggested.

"Oh, no. I promised you a posh dinner and it's a posh dinner you'll have. Besides, you already cooked for me once tonight."

She hid her blush by looking at the clock on the bedside table. "I think we missed our reservation."

"Then I'll make another one. I'll tell them we were detained. But first I'm going to take a shower. Why don't you laze away a few minutes?"

She wasn't going to argue with him. The bed was too soft and inviting. In a few minutes she'd get up and look for something else to wear.

Or maybe she'd just let Noel pick something out. She'd liked that. How exciting to come out of the shower and find he'd laid out the clothing he wanted her to wear. The idea of him going through her intimate apparel was sexually intoxicating. What had he thought about her penchant for frilly things?

She heard the shower start up and imagined him with the water spraying down on him, sheeting his muscular body.

She was so blissed out that she didn't hear the shower turn off. Didn't hear anything until she heard Noel's pained ''Yeow!''

She shot out of bed and raced for the bathroom, thinking he'd slipped and fallen, broken something.

It was worse.

He was clutching the edge of the vanity, grimacing in pain, his face pale.

''What is it?''

''The curling iron,'' he gulped, his voice raspy. ''I burned myself when I leaned forward—didn't know it was on.''

Oh, Lord, no wonder he was pale. He'd nearly neutered himself. And then she had the wicked thought that she was glad she'd had dessert first, because it was going to be a while before…

Meanwhile, back at the North Pole…

''WE'VE GOT TO DO something,'' Terrell, the head elf, said to the elves he'd assembled for an emergency meeting the night before their biggest night of the year.

''But what?'' a redheaded elf named Sammy asked.

''Even Santa doesn't know where his wife disappeared to. She's the reason he's so glum.''

''I'm sure if we put our heads together we can come up with something. He can't go out with the reindeer and sleigh tomorrow night to make all his deliveries to the good little boys and girls. He's too depressed.''

''I know,'' Sammy said. ''Elf patrol.''

''Elf patrol!'' the rest of the elves chorused.

The last time it had been instigated was when Rudolph had refused to lead the way just before his fawn was born. They had tracked down Clarabell, the clown, to borrow her red nose for Prancer to wear to lead the reindeer.

They stacked their hands one on top of another and sang, ''All for one and one for all—everyone under four ft tall. We're on our way. It's off we go. For there is no Merry Christmas without Santa's ho, ho, ho.''

The oak chest was opened and elf patrol helmets dispatched. Magic was afoot.

9

December 24

HOLLIE HADN'T REALLY known what she'd wanted for Christmas until last night, when Christmas had come early, she decided with a wicked laugh as she lazed in bed. She should get up. There were all sorts of chores vying for her attention. But she wanted to linger longer. To enjoy reliving last night—well, right up until Noel had stepped out of the shower, reached for a towel on the vanity and leaned into pain.

That had ended dinner.

The evening.

Romance.

He'd limped out, to her profuse apologies.

She pulled the pillow next to her over and hugged it tight, inhaling the scent of him, all wood smoke and fresh citrus. She was naked beneath the covers save for one accessory: the earrings he'd selected. She'd left them on when she'd undressed after Noel had left. After unplugging the curling iron and putting it in a safe place to cool down, she'd showered and gone to bed, but not to sleep.

She'd been too keyed up. She'd been with a man

who'd known what he wanted and hadn't been shy about taking it and giving back. At that moment she'd bet her cheeks were as red as the glitter on her wreath ear-rings—or "ear bobs," as Elena called them. Lovemak-ing had never been so exciting as with Noel. He'd se-duced her without touching her by selecting what he wanted her to wear and laying it out for her on the bed as if she were some harem girl being prepared for a pasha.

It excited her to know he'd been going through her things while she'd been naked in the shower. To wonder if he'd watched her secretly while she'd showered.

From any other man that would have been an unfor-givable liberty, but Noel had done it in such a romantic way that she'd been pleased rather than angered.

A glance at the clock beside her told her she was going to have to get up no matter how delicious the lingering. But she was enjoying reliving each caress, the murmured words in a foreign language that had lent a fillip to the lovemaking, a fillip of mystery. What had he said to her? What had he said in the words that had been so full of emotion and desire?

Had he said "I love you"?

Could he have?

Her growling stomach rudely interrupted her girlish musings. They hadn't gotten to the restaurant last night, and she'd forgotten to eat. Her stomach was putting up a fuss. She stretched and sat up, and the comforter fell down to her waist, revealing her nudity.

She laughed. Noel couldn't have said anything that

sounded like a commitment, wouldn't have—he hadn't even seen her breasts. She couldn't imagine. They would not have escaped the notice of any other man she'd ever dated.

That made Noel special indeed. She slipped from the bed and searched out a long white shirt, closing it with the tie Noel had forgotten.

Padding barefoot to the kitchen, she checked her answering machine to see if he'd called.

A little moue of disappointment caused her lips to pucker downward.

Hunger pangs ruled and she searched the cabinet for something to eat. Since she felt celebratory, she fixed her favorite breakfast—Belgian waffles and ice cream. The combination of hot buttery waffles and cold smooth ice cream quieted her growling stomach.

''Come on, call,'' she said, wiping her mouth with a napkin as she stared at the telephone that didn't ring. That was one of the things she hated about being a woman in a society that let men make all the moves—all the choices. Waiting.

The doorbell rang and her heart jumped.

Noel!

This was even better than a phone call.

She hoped he'd come to tell her he had changed his mind about going away for Christmas, so she could invite him to Sarah's later.

When she looked out the window, however, she saw she'd leaped to the wrong conclusion. There was a deliveryman coming up the walk with a package and a clipboard.

She grabbed one of the extra-festive packages of homemade Christmas cookies for a tip and opened the door, wondering who'd sent her a present.

After signing the clipboard, she exchanged her cookies and "Merry Christmas" for the package the deliveryman had brought. Before he had made it back to his truck, she had the package open. Maybe patience wasn't her strong suit at this time of year any more than it was Elena's.

It was the Barbie in the pink dress, just as Noel had promised. He'd saved the day. Elena would have been really disappointed not to get her number-one request.

When Hollie went to get wrapping paper to wrap the gift, the phone rang.

Finally.

She went to answer it.

"Auntie Hollie, Auntie Hollie, Santa's coming *tonight!*"

It wasn't Noel, but it was the next best thing—the little girl who always made her smile. "Are you sure it's tonight?" she teased. "Maybe you counted wrong."

"Nope. Mommy says it's Christmas Eve tonight. And I have to go to bed early after we put out the milk and cookies for Santa. Rick's coming over tonight, too."

"I like Rick," Hollie said, hoping Elena did, also.

"He's gots a spotted puppy at the firehouse named Shana. And Mommy says he's the one who cooks for the fire guys."

''Shana cooks for the firemen?''

''No, Auntie Hollie, a dog can't cook. Rick cooks firehouse chili and stuff. He said he'd make some for me.''

''Well, I'll see you tonight, too, okay?''

''Uh-huh, and Mommy wants to talk to you.''

Sarah came on the phone with the question Hollie wished she could answer.

''Is Noel coming with you tonight?''

''I don't know.''

''What kind of RSVP is that? You did ask him, didn't you?''

''Uh…well, there wasn't a good time, and he had to leave early.''

''What do you mean?''

Hollie relayed what had happened with the curling iron and hung up on her best friend when she wouldn't stop laughing.

Having had enough of waiting, Hollie decided to act. With every house sale, she made up a special gift basket tailored to her client, as a thank-you. She'd make one up for Noel and deliver it to his hotel room, giving her an opportunity to invite him to Sarah's. At the very least it would let her check on Noel to make sure he was okay.

Since he was leaving at two, she had to hurry. Most of the fixings for the basket were on hand. She had the iridescent paper and ribbon for a bow to wrap around the basket. All she had to do was gather up the gift items. She quickly washed and dressed and headed out.

A good bottle of wine, crackers and cheese were all gleaned at the same market. The drugstore yielded a box of neon adhesive bandages she couldn't resist adding.

By noon she had the basket assembled and was on her way to Noel's hotel.

SHE WAS DETERMINED to get in his room.

She waited until the girl who was at the desk took a break and a man replaced her. The girl would have seen right through her lie, but the man, she knew from experience, would be susceptible to her flirting.

"Excuse me, I have a surprise for my boyfriend and he isn't answering my knock on his door. Do you think he's still in his room and has maybe fallen asleep?" She gave him her best smile, meant to make him feel like a stud muffin.

"Why don't I see if he's still registered?" the desk clerk asked, helpful as could be.

"Still registered," he reported. "But he's got a seat on the airport shuttle."

She checked her watch.

"I don't want to miss seeing him and I've got his Christmas present. Do you think I could just borrow the extra key long enough to deliver it?"

"I'm not supposed to—"

She didn't let him get his refusal out. She slid her hand over his, her eyes pleading. "But it's Christmas...and I'll only be a minute. Promise."

He gave in to her, no match for her wiles. "But hurry up," he warned, "before anyone notices the key is gone.'' Clearly he meant the woman who worked the front desk with him.

''Back in a wink,'' she said, taking the key and tossing him a wink.

SHE WAS NERVOUS as she stood outside the door of Noel's room with the gift basket.

Did she look dumb?

Worse, desperate?

Maybe she should just go.

Forget about it.

Forget about Noel.

No, she'd come this far. She wasn't a quitter when she wanted something. It was what made her such a good real estate agent. She saw things through to the end, no matter how difficult they were.

Taking a deep breath, she knocked on the door.

''Noel, I—''

The woman who'd opened the door to Noel's room clearly wasn't Noel, but clearly was expecting him. From the look of shock on her face, she was just as surprised to see Hollie as Hollie was to see her.

''Who are you?'' she demanded to know. ''Is that a parting gift from the hotel?''

Hollie looked down at the gift basket in her grip. ''No, I, ah—who are you?'' she blurted out, staring at the exquisite black lace lingerie peeking out from the cotton terry robe with the hotel's insignia on its breast pocket. ''Where's Noel?''

"Who wants to know?" the woman demanded in a very territorial tone.

"I'm Hollie. Hollie Winslow. I—I sold Noel his house," she found herself stammering.

"Oh, that explains the basket. You're Noel's real estate agent. That means he found a house for us!"

"'Us'?"

"I'm Marcy Walker, Noel's fiancée," the dark-haired woman explained, wriggling her huge square-cut diamond solitaire engagement ring in Hollie's face. "My flight just got in from Atlanta. Noel must have stepped out for a minute, but the maid let me in his room. I'll take that for him, if you like."

"You're going to the islands with Noel, for Christmas?"

"Yes. He can't wait to get away every December."

Of course. They were a perfect match.

She'd seen that when she'd opened the door.

She felt like a fool.

"Well, have a good trip," Hollie said, handing over the basket, suddenly wanting not to see or be seen by Noel. She couldn't get out of the hotel fast enough.

She wasn't going to cry.

She wasn't.

"All right, damn it, I am," she sobbed when she climbed inside her car.

How had this happened to her *again?*

Noel Hawksley couldn't disappoint her because she'd known he was going to disappoint her from the start. He hadn't hidden the fact that he already had one foot on a plane out of town. He hadn't hidden the fact that he hated her favorite holiday. He'd told her so up front and often.

She had a big fat commission check, a check that would buy her a new car.

She should be happy.

Noel Hawksley had done what she thought was impossible. He'd ruined Christmas for her.

And then through her tears she smiled.

She'd ruined Christmas for him, as well. She'd accidentally branded him with her curling iron last night.

He might be spending the holidays with his fiancée, but Hollie knew she herself wouldn't be far from Noel's thoughts the whole while. After the painful accident with her curling iron, he wouldn't be enjoying himself any more than she would be. And neither would Marcy, no matter her fancy lingerie.

Hollie took some comfort in that.

''AUNTIE HOLLIE, I thought you'd never get here,'' Elena said when she opened the door that evening. ''Are those presents all for me?''

''Have you been a good little girl?'' Hollie asked, taking off her coat and hanging it up.

''Yes.''

''Well, then put the presents under the tree, and no peeking who they're for. And no shaking, either,'' she said over her shoulder as she went to find Sarah.

''Not so much red pepper,'' Sarah instructed Rick, who was in the kitchen cooking.

''That doesn't smell like a Christmas ham to me,'' Hollie said.

''Elena insisted on Rick making his firehouse chili,'' Sarah explained. ''Christmas Eve is going to be a little unconventional.''

''What else would I expect at your house?'' Hollie said, and asked for an apron to help with the preparations.

''No, you're going to help me with the tree. Rick claims to have everything under control in here.'' Sarah steered Hollie to the boxes of lights and tree trimmings set out next to the bare tree. It was Sarah's custom to decorate her Christmas tree Christmas Eve—mainly because Midnight kept stealing the ornaments from the lower branches she could reach. And eating the tinsel. At the moment the dog was lying beneath the tree amid the presents, looking innocent.

When they were out of Rick's earshot and while Elena was peppering Rick with questions in the kitchen, Sarah whispered, ''What's wrong?''

''Nothing.'' Hollie picked up a string of lights. ''Have you tried these to make sure they're working?''

''Come on, Hollie, your eyes are puffy. You've been crying.''

''I watched *Miracle on 34th Street,* okay?''

''If you say so. But what about Noel—is he coming tonight?''

Hollie shook her head and plugged in the string of lights to make sure they worked. ''He's going away as planned.''

''I'm sorry.'' Sarah touched Hollie's arm.

''It's okay. He was just a client. I sold him a house and...and...'' Hollie started to sniffle.

''What is it?''

''He's engaged, Sarah.'' Hollie wiped her eyes and sniffed up her tears, gaining control of her emotions. She didn't want to ruin anyone's Christmas by being sad. Forcing a note of cheerfulness into her voice, she said, ''And she's beautiful.''

''What do you mean? How do you know?'' Sarah took the lights Hollie handed her around the tree, made a pass and handed the lights back to Hollie as they circled them around the tree.

''I saw her. She was in Noel's hotel room when I delivered the thank-you basket I made him for purchasing a house from me.'' Hollie picked up another strand of lights and checked them at the outlet.

''Maybe she was lying.''

Hollie shook her head. ''She showed me her engagement ring. It was huge.''

''I don't know what to say.''

The doorbell ringing prevented her from saying anything. She went to answer it, but Elena raced ahead before Sarah could get there. ''I'll get it,'' she yelled.

Hollie dropped the lights she was holding when she heard Elena squeal with delight, ''Noel!''

What was he doing here? How did he have the nerve to show up to face her? He must know she'd discovered his little secret.

She didn't want to see him. Didn't want him to see her. She rubbed her eyes.

Sarah came to fetch her.

"He wants to see you, Hollie," she said, knowing Hollie would have heard Elena.

"Tell him no."

Elena came running in with a small, gaily wrapped box. "Noel brought me a present!"

"Put it under the tree, honey," Sarah instructed, her eyes pleading with Hollie. "At least talk to him," she said.

Not wanting to make a scene and ruin the evening, Hollie agreed and went to the door, where Noel was waiting to see her.

"Can I come in?" he asked.

"No. I'll come out." She reached for her coat and slipped into it, going outside to join him.

"Hollie, you've got to let me explain."

She didn't answer him at first, biting her lower lip to keep from blurting out her hurt. Finally she said, "I don't think you can give me a satisfactory explanation, Noel. Anyway, it's your fiancée you owe the apology to, not me. She's the one with the claim on you, with your ring on her finger. I saw the ring, Noel. You aren't really going to stand there and tell me it's not your engagement ring she had on, are you?"

"It's my ring," he agreed. "But—"

"Goodbye, Noel." She turned to go back inside, but he grabbed her arm.

''Wait, Hollie, you have to listen. At least hear me out. You're wrong about—''

Rick, who had apparently been watching from the kitchen window, opened the door. ''Is everything all right out here, Hollie?'' he asked, concern and protection in his voice.

''Yes, I'm fine,'' she told him.

He went back inside, leaving them alone.

''What you don't understand is that Marcy Walker is my ex-fiancée.''

''So you had a little fight. I'm sure you'll patch it up. Meanwhile I have a life to get back to,'' Hollie said, looking at his hand on her arm.

He released his hand.

''No, you aren't listening to me, Hollie. I wouldn't have slept with you last night if I was still engaged to Marcy. She broke our engagement on Christmas Eve—last year. It seems that now she thinks she made a mistake and wants us to give it another try.''

''And I think you should,'' she lied, shaking off a gust of cold wind that made the pine tree by the mailbox shiver.

''Hollie, you're being unreasonable. Why won't you listen to what I'm trying to tell you?'' he pleaded, his hands shoved in his pockets so he wouldn't grab her again.

''I know what I saw, Noel. I came to your hotel to ask you here tonight, to try to convince you that running away wasn't the answer. But when I got to your room I saw that you weren't running away, but toward another woman. A half-dressed woman in *your* hotel room wearing *your* engagement ring. There isn't any spin you can put on that that I will believe. I think you should just go, please."

"Maybe you're right. I never did have much luck this time of year." He turned and walked away toward his car.

It took everything Hollie had not to run after him and stop him. But she didn't want just any man. She wanted a man who wouldn't disappoint her. A man she could believe in.

When Hollie went back inside, Sarah was setting the table and Elena was hanging tinsel on the tree as Midnight danced at her feet, trying to snag some.

"What can I do to help?" Hollie asked, forcing a note of brightness into her voice.

"Here, you can mix the salad," Rick offered. "On second thought, I'll do the salad and you chop the onions to go on top of the chili with the shredded cheese."

Hollie knew he'd offered her the onion job because there were tears in her eyes and chopping onions would help her hide the reason for them. Sarah had found herself a real catch. She hoped her friend realized it.

The rest of the evening went downhill from there.

Rick and Sarah were so smitten with each other that it was painful for Hollie to be around them. But she was a good friend, and complimented Rick on his cooking, made happy conversation with Elena and tried to assure Sarah with her eyes that she was fine.

She only had one second of doubt about her decision to send Noel away.

It was the moment Elena pestered her about when Noel was coming back and why he'd left without eating.

When Hollie explained that he'd only come by to say goodbye before he left on his vacation, Elena asked permission to open the present he'd left for her.

To defuse the situation, Sarah had agreed that Elena could open her present from Noel.

Hollie almost began crying again when she saw what the gift was. Somewhere he had managed to find a set of stack rings small enough for a child's finger. Elena was so excited she danced around showing everyone her jewels.

Right after that Hollie took her leave.

Setting up milk and cookies for Santa was something Rick and Sarah could share. She didn't belong.

For the first time Hollie felt really alone, even though she'd been alone all her life.

She didn't even bother to turn on her Christmas lights when she got home. Darkness welcomed her and she embraced it.

CLAUDIA CLAUS RUBBED her temples.

She had made a mess of things. She thought she'd read the manual that came with Santa's laptop, but somewhere along the line she must have done something wrong. After all, Santa used the computer to make children's Christmas dreams come true. All he did was type the wish into the computer and it was a done deal.

Perhaps she shouldn't have interfered in Hollie's life.

She had made Hollie miserable. She'd been so sure that Noel was the right one for her. Had been so sure that they were soul mates.

Both deserved their share of happiness.

Santa was not going to be happy with her when he found out she'd taken the special laptop and made a mess of things. She couldn't go back to the North Pole for Christmas having failed at her first project.

What had gone wrong? She'd spent years reading romance novels and dearly loved a happy ending.

Totally believed in them.

She should have started out smaller, worked on a first crush, an infatuation or something like that. It would have been like using training wheels to learn how to ride a bike.

True love was the big one and she was an amateur. Santa made it all look so easy, making everyone happy.

She'd found out it was easy to make someone cry.

Making them laugh—now that was the hard ticket. But she *would* do it. She still had time to make true love happen before Christmas was over.

She reread the manual.

And realized she'd forgotten to press Save.

She pressed the button to save Hollie's Christmas.

Meanwhile, back at the North Pole…

''TIME TO GO, Santa,'' Terrell said, checking his watch.

''I suppose.'' Santa sighed, taking his red suit from

the head elf.

When he was all dressed, down to his polished black boots, Terrell walked with Santa out to the sleigh, where the reindeer were stamping impatiently, excited to begin their long flight. They'd made bets as usual about the length of time it would take them to make the trip.

Prancer never won, but he always came back with the fullest tummy. He had a nose for sniffing out who put a bunch of fresh carrots on their doorstep for the reindeer.

When Santa was settled into his sleigh and the sacks of toys were secured—the magic, bottomless sacks—Terrell took a piece of paper from his pocket. ''This is for you, Santa,'' he said, handing it over.

''What is it—another name to add to the list of toy deliveries?''

''No, it's where Mrs. Claus is staying.''

''You found her!''

Terrell nodded. ''And, sir, there's a picnic basket in the back with a romantic dinner for two. I thought you might want to have a late-night snack with your wife....''

10

December 25

HOLLIE WAS DISAPPOINTED in herself when she woke up Christmas morning with raccoon eyes, having gone to bed and cried herself to sleep.

She shoved the covers off and went to take a shower, having had enough of feeling sorry for herself. It was self-indulgent and she was having none of it. She was taking her holiday back. Putting the Merry back in Christmas. Taking control.

Noel might have discombobulated her and derailed her and swept her off her feet and crashed her over a romantic cliff, but she was a survivor.

It was a day for fresh starts, believing in miracles and loving someone, even if it was only yourself.

After a breakfast of angel cookies and hot chocolate, she went out to get her mail, which she'd forgotten yesterday.

When she reached the mailbox, she found that it contained a surprise. Someone had left her a posy. A completely charming gesture. The arrangement was made up of apricot tulips, veronica, bouvardia and hypericum, and at this time of year had to have cost the earth.

Enchanted, she pulled the arrangement from the mailbox. Holding it where it was tied with a big red bow, she plucked the small white card and read: Merry Christmas.

The flowers hadn't been left that long ago. They weren't wilted from the cold. She looked around to see if a car was parked nearby, but there was none. Whoever had left them was gone.

And then she dropped the card, and when it fluttered to the ground it landed facedown. On the back Noel had scrawled his name.

He'd just been here.

She'd just missed him.

Why couldn't Ms. Claudia have left well enough alone? Why did she have to bring her a six-foot-one-inch grinch to break her heart?

She wouldn't think about him.

She wouldn't.

Once inside, she almost tossed the posy in the trash, but at the last second popped it in a small vase of water, instead.

It dawned on her suddenly what the fresh flowers meant.

Noel hadn't gone to the Caribbean with Marcy. Hadn't gone to the islands at all.

What did that mean?

She pushed the doubts from her mind, turned on the stereo system and put on her favorite CD of carols. Then she lost herself in work, cleaning out her briefcase.

When she had all her paperwork neat and tidy, she realized that her key was missing once again.

But this time it couldn't be Elena who'd lifted it. She must have left it at the house Noel had bought on Mistletoe Lane. It was the last time she remembered having it.

The owners would be back in the morning, so she needed to go to the house and hope she'd left something unlocked so she could retrieve the key.

She wanted to get out of the house anyway. There were too many memories of Noel being in her home. So she got dressed in warmer clothes and headed out.

Christmas was the quietest day of the year.

The streets were deserted as she drove to the house. She thought of Elena and wondered if she'd liked her Barbie in pink. She'd have to call her when she got home and share the excitement of Christmas morning with her over the phone.

Noel's luxury car parked outside the house when she pulled up the drive was a surprise.

She must have left the key with him.

Her first instinct was to leave. But she couldn't leave because she had to retrieve the key. So she got out of her car and walked up to the house.

She tried the door before knocking. It was open.

Should she go in? Maybe Noel was here with Marcy. Maybe he was showing her around the house he'd bought for her. She didn't know if she could handle seeing that.

But she needed the key. So she opened the door and went inside.

''Is anyone here?'' she called out.

No answer.

It was very quiet in the house. Maybe he was looking around outside. She twisted her hands together nervously.

She could do this, she promised herself.

Taking a deep breath, she headed for the kitchen, which was the most likely place Noel would have set down the key. However, she didn't make it to the kitchen.

Instead she stopped in her tracks when she saw Noel sitting on the floor in front of the empty fireplace. He was staring at the diamond ring he held in his fingers.

She cleared her throat. ''I came for the key,'' she said.

He looked up in surprise. ''It's on the kitchen counter.'' He nodded toward the kitchen, which adjoined the dining room.

''What do you do, buy a woman an engagement ring every Christmas? Is that how you get your kicks?'' she couldn't resist accusing.

''No, not this year. I told you this is last year's ring. I told Marcy to keep it, but when it became clear to her that I wasn't interested in having her back, she threw it at me and left.''

''I see.'' Could he be telling her the truth? She wanted desperately to believe him. Finding Marcy half-undressed in his room had been a shock, a terrible blow to her self-confidence.

''Did you know I bought this house for you?'' he asked, searching her face for some sign that he hadn't been wrong about them.

''What?''

''That was why I wanted to know, wanted to be sure you loved it. I wanted us to be happy in it. As happy as you are in the little house you now have. I wanted us to raise a family in it. You see, Hollie, I realized when I saw your house that I wasn't looking for a house at all.'' He hesitated. ''I was looking for a home.''

And she was crying again. ''Oh, No-oel—''

He got to his feet then and gathered her in his arms. ''Oh, Hollie. I thought I was done taking risks in my personal life. But once I met you I didn't have any choice. It was as if someone picked you out for me personally. Someone who knew who my fantasy soul mate was.''

Hollie let Noel wipe her tears away with the pads of his thumbs as he vowed, ''I want you. I need you. I love you, Hollie. Please put your magic in my life. I didn't know how alone I could feel until I thought I was losing you. We belong together, Hollie. Like apple pie and ice cream, like Hootie and the Blowfish, like Christmas and Santa Claus.''

She smiled at the last. ''There's never any mistletoe when you need it,'' she sniffed.

''Hell, we're on Mistletoe Lane, sweetheart,'' Noel said, laying on a kiss that made Ms. Claudia sigh.

Happy endings were the *best.*

Meanwhile, back at the North Pole…

"I'VE MISSED YOU terribly," Santa said, caressing Claudia's cheek.

"You mean you weren't too busy to notice I was gone?"

"You're my wife. How could you think I wouldn't miss you?" Santa asked, hugging her.

"Oh, my, is it me, or have you lost weight?" Claudia asked.

"I've been pining away for you."

"Then you didn't find where I hid the Christmas cookies…." Claudia Claus chuckled. She got up and promised to be right back with a surprise for him.

When she returned she had a big tin of homemade Christmas cookies and a six-pack of micro brewery beer.

"Where did you get them?" Santa asked when she sat back down beside him in front of the fire.

She handed him a cold bottle of "Santa's Suds," as the label on the long-necked beer bottle said, and took one for herself. "I had the beer made special for you at a small brewery in St. Louis. And the cookies were hidden in the box the treadmill came in. If you had set it up to use, as you promised, you would have found them."

Santa clinked his glass to Claudia's and toasted with a twinkle in his eye, "To my wife, I promise to set up the treadmill and never to take you for granted again."

"And to use the treadmill," Claudia added, as they both took a sip.

"Now I have a present for you," Santa said, slipping a small package from his pocket.

"What is it?" Claudia cried in delight.

"Open it and find out."

She unwrapped the package with a speed that rivaled Elena's. "Oh, Santa! It's beautiful."

"There's going to be a tennis court to go with it. That way we can exercise together."

"And have a love match," Claudia said with a sigh.

"Ho, ho, ho."

11

February 14

''BUT THE STORES are closed,'' Hollie said as Noel pulled into the parking lot of the posh mall where the new store he was opening was located.

''I know,'' Noel replied as they sat there outside the south end of the mall, the engine of his luxury car purring. ''But I have a key to the store.''

''You mean you have to work? I thought we were going to celebrate Valentine's Day.'' There was a hint of a sulk in her voice.

''I'm not working. Everything is ready for tomorrow's grand opening. But before the store opens in the morning, I thought the two of us could celebrate my favorite holiday here with plenty of privacy.''

''Not an easy thing to find at ten-thirty on a Friday night, I agree,'' Hollie said, warming to the idea.

''Well, you were the one who had to work late writing up a contract for a client. Tonight was one of my early nights. But that was okay, because it gave me time to set this up.''

''Set what up?''

"You'll see."

Hollie was giddy with excitement as Noel escorted her into the closed mall. There was something sexy and exciting about their clandestine entry into the upscale department store he was opening. He had overseen every detail of the store until it was perfect.

"Come on," he said, tugging her along when she would have lingered to look at every little thing. She and Sarah had been more likely to haunt flea markets and tag sales than do posh shopping. The only big purchase she'd made recently was the new car she'd bought using the commission check as a down payment.

Noel had been introducing her to a whole new world since they'd begun dating at Christmas. A world she'd known existed, of course, but one she'd not really had access to. It was sort of like a fairy tale. One with a happy ending. Noel had been talking about marriage, and although they were both scared, they were in love.

"You really did set this up," Hollie said when they stopped at the fine jewelry counter and a bottle of chilled champagne and two glasses were set out on a tray, waiting for them.

"I told you it was my favorite holiday," Noel said. The store was decorated with splashes of red to draw the eye to special displays and offers for the grand opening.

He went behind the counter and played host, pouring champagne into the two glasses after a showy pop of the cork and the bubbly flow of champagne, which he'd caught with a towel.

''To us,'' he said, offering her a glass.

She giggled at the bubbles that tickled her nose when she took a sip.

''Remember what happened the last time we had champagne,'' she warned.

''I was hoping you did. Only this time I've locked up all the curling irons,'' he teased.

''Noel!''

''It's okay. I'm as good as new, no permanent damage done. The doctor gave me the A-OK yesterday.''

''Good news,'' she toasted.

''See anything you like?'' he asked, grinning.

She leaned over the counter and pulled him toward her with his tie. ''Yeah, sweetie, you.''

''I meant in a solitaire....''

''Oh—'' She paused in her lean to kiss him, then looked down at the case. ''You mean?''

''You are going to make an honest man of me, aren't you?''

She let go of his tie and gave the case of diamond engagement rings some serious consideration.

''Pick any one you want,'' he said.

''For tonight or to keep?'' she asked, gazing up at him to see his true intention.

''If I give you an engagement ring, I mean for you never to take it off.'' She trusted the love she saw in his eyes.

Returning her attention to the rings, she pointed to a square-cut stone in a simple setting. He took it out and slipped it on her finger.

"It fits," she squealed with delight.

"Now, take your time, make sure. You can try on other rings."

"Not me," she assured him. "When something fits, I know it. This is the one."

"Come on," he said, grabbing her hand.

"Where to?"

"You'll see." He took her over to the escalator and they went upstairs to the bridal department.

"You don't expect me to pick out a wedding dress tonight, do you?"

"No. I have a surprise for you.

"Sit down here," he instructed, indicating a plush ottoman. "Close your eyes and I'll be right back with it."

As she sat there with her eyes closed, she wondered what Noel was up to. The past weeks had shown her that he was a true romantic beneath his dark, brooding looks.

"Keep your eyes closed," he said when he returned with her surprise.

She heard him kneel before her. Then heard the rustle of tissue as he opened a box.

"What is it?" she coaxed.

"Just put your foot here on my knee," he instructed, lifting it there. He then slipped off her pump and gently massaged her foot a moment.

''My surprise is a foot massage?'' she guessed. ''Not that I'm complaining—don't stop.''

But he did stop to slip on another shoe.

''You can open your eyes now.''

When she did, tears formed in the corners of her eyes. ''They're beautiful,'' she sniffed, staring at the wedding shoes he'd had made especially for her. They were white brocade, elaborately adorned with pearl beading and Austrian crystals.

''So you like them, then?''

''Like them? I love them. I'm going to have to keep them under lock and key when Elena comes over. They look like shoes made for a princess.''

''They were made for a princess,'' he said, slipping the other shoe on. ''While I'm on bended knee, there's something I want to ask you. Will you marry me, Hollie, and make all my Christmases merry?''

''Yes, I'll marry you, Noel. You may kiss your fiancée.''

He rose then from his kneeling position and made her very happy she'd said yes with a kiss fit for a princess wearing slippers that fit to perfection.

''Try walking to see if they feel okay,'' he suggested. ''That way if there is a problem I can have them—''

''No, it's bad luck to wear them before the wedding. They're fine. They feel wonderful.'' She slipped them off, put them back in the tissue paper and closed the white box.

''Now, I have one last surprise for you,'' Noel said,

tucking the box beneath his arm and motioning for her to follow him.

She tagged after him until he stopped one floor up in the sporting goods department.

"Why are we stopping here?" she asked, puzzled.

"I thought we'd go camping."

"Camping? I hate camping."

"You'll like this. Trust me. I'm doing pretty good so far, aren't I?"

A lot better than pretty good. He was making magic. He was magic. He'd put her under a spell. One she didn't want to break.

But *camping?*

He held out his hand for her.

And she said yes, unable to deny him.

He led her to an enclosed tent that was set up for display. It was the size of a large pup tent. Unzipping the flap, he motioned her inside.

She leaned forward and let out a gasp.

Inside the tent were red heart-shaped balloons blown up and floating. And a dish of chocolate-dipped strawberries on a little folding table. It was so romantic. She almost didn't hear the flap being closed when Noel ducked into the tent with her.

"Did you get any work done today?" she asked, reaching for a strawberry.

"I did this on the sly, just as the store closed. No one can ever find out. It's our little secret."

''I'm not telling,'' she said, savoring the chocolate-covered strawberry.

''Don't you think I deserve a little treat myself?'' he asked, pulling her into his arms, kissing her a seductive let's-make-love-right-now kiss.

''You mean here?''

He murmured that he did.

''Now?''

He murmured that he did.

''But—''

''We're alone and it's raining outside. Don't you hear the rain on the tent? Doesn't it make you feel romantic?''

She did. And it did.

''Can't go camping in a tie,'' she said, undoing the knot and removing the tie from around his neck.

''Or a jacket,'' he said, pushing hers off her shoulders and letting it fall to the floor of the tent.

''I've been waiting weeks for this,'' he said.

''You've been planning this for weeks?''

''Uh-huh. And waiting to heal.''

''You must be very frustrated.''

''Very.'' He began undoing the vest she'd worn alone under the jacket, kissing her temples as he did so. When he had it unbuttoned, he pushed it aside and reached to free her breast from the cup of her bra, taking it full into his mouth, his tongue swirling over her nipple, making it bud into a pearl.

"This feels so wicked," she said, her hands busy freeing the buckle of his belt.

"I know," he answered, undoing the clasp at the front of her sheer blush bra so that he had access to the full playground.

She pulled his belt from the loops and dropped it to the floor, moaning at the caress of his hands and mouth on her as he eased her to the floor.

"I want you naked beneath me," he said, earnestly undressing her, hurrying.

She was equally hot. Equally ready.

Equally frustrated.

Her hands moved to free him of his shirt, while he worked at his trousers, until they were both naked and entwined limb to limb, lips to lips, heart to heart.

She could feel him hard and insistent against her hip. His tongue was mimicking what he wanted, exploring her mouth with sweet promise.

"I can't wait any longer," he rasped.

"Now," she said, and he slid into her, just as they heard voices and froze.

"I think we'll set up right here, Jonathon. Is that all right with you, Mr. Baker?" said someone from outside.

"Damn."

"What is it? Who are they?"

"It's the store manager. I completely forgot that channel five television was doing a spot for the news tonight about the grand opening."

''You forgot!'' she whispered, feeling herself flush all over beneath him.

''I was busy with other things on my mind,'' he murmured, not moving a muscle.

Just then they heard another voice.

''This is Chriss Meyer with Channel Five at the new Bon Marché, which will open its doors in St. Louis tomorrow morning at ten o'clock. We're in the store now and—''

Hollie felt Noel begin moving inside her.

''What are you doing?'' she whispered into his ear, trying not to feel how good it felt. ''Are you crazy?''

''I have to, Hollie. *I have to.*''

''Noel!'' she persisted, trying to still him.

''Just don't yell out my name or anything,'' he said, as he ignored her efforts to stop him and began moving in full thrust. ''Don't scream, or we'll be on the news at eleven.''

Hollie had to use all her willpower not to.

And it was worth every terrifying, thrilling second, as she heard Chriss continue talking in the background, describing the store, while she herself prayed that no one would decide to demonstrate the size of the tent and open the flap.

Noel finally collapsed after one last deep thrust that took them both over the top, with both of them holding their hands over each other's mouths.

''Happy Valentine's Day, sweetheart,'' he murmured, breathless.

Hollie didn't answer. She was too busy planning to get even.

At Christmas.

MISTLETOE MISCHIEF

Alyssa Dean

For my mother, Phyllis and my Grandma King.
Two people who taught me
the real meaning of Christmas.

* * *

Alyssa Dean says,

"A lot of unexpected and funny things have happened to me while celebrating Christmas, but I fondly recall the year my boss went away for the holidays. (This was before my full-time writing career began.) While he was gone, we walled up the door to his office with nice wooden panelling. When we were finished, you couldn't tell there had ever been an office there. (I've got great pictures of this.) He was so surprised when he came back to work and discovered that his office was missing. I don't think it was the Christmas present he'd been expecting.

But it is just the sort of present my hero, Josh Larkland, would be receiving from his employees if he hadn't found his very own Christmas elf. I hope you enjoy *Mistletoe Mischief* and the holiday season!"

1

"CHRISTMAS ELVES!" Brandy snorted.

She indignantly marched into the vestibule of Amanda's apartment and stomped the snow off her boots onto the welcome mat. "Whose brilliant idea was it to advertise ourselves as Christmas elves?"

Amanda took a sip of coffee while considering the question. "Mine, I suppose. I thought it might attract attention." She picked up one of their flyers from the coffee table and read it out loud. "'Problems coping with Christmas? Call the Christmas Elves at A&B Executive Services. We provide everything the busy executive needs to have a Merry Christmas.'"

"I think it needs a disclaimer!" Brandy kicked off her boots, stormed into the living room, and flopped down onto the couch beside Amanda.

"What's wrong with it? It's lively and different, and...and we both do sort of look like elves." At least they were both on the short side, although Amanda thought Brandy's curly brown hair, green eyes and cuddly-looking figure was more elf-like than her own shoulder-length blond hair and slender build. She studied Brandy's face. "Although right now you look more like a wee cranky leprechaun. What's wrong?"

"Mr. Denton is what's wrong."

"Mr. Denton?" Amanda watched Brandy tug off

her jacket and toss it over a chair. "From Denton Accounting?"

"That's him." Brandy curled her legs under her. "You would not believe what that busy executive thought he needed to have a Merry Christmas!"

"Oh, no," said Amanda. "He didn't..."

"He did." Brandy shuddered. "Right there in his office. I asked him what I could do to make his Christmas merrier and he...lunged at me."

"Lunged at you?" Amanda looked over at her friend with concern. "Are you okay?"

"Yes. No." Brandy rubbed a hand across her forehead. "I don't know. Is there any more coffee?"

"Sure." Amanda stood and went into the kitchen to pour Brandy a mug and carried it into the living room. "Now tell me everything that happened."

"There's not much to tell." Brandy took a couple of sips and settled back into the cushiony back of the floral couch. "I arrived, Mr. Denton ushered me into his office, poured me a cup of coffee, and the next thing I knew, he had his hands all over me."

"That's...dreadful!"

"That's what I thought!" Brandy made a face. "I mean, at nine o'clock in the morning! If it had been an afternoon appointment I might have been expecting it, but in the morning? Most men are hardly awake, and this chunky little bald guy is all ready to rock and roll?"

Amanda almost giggled at Brandy's outraged expression. "That's peculiar, all right," she agreed. "Go on. What did you do?"

Brandy's lips twitched into a smile. "Well, actually it was kind of funny, Amanda. Mr. Denton is as short and chubby as I am. He touched, I shoved...it was sort of like being a participant in a midget sumo wrestling contest.''

Amanda smiled at the image, then almost immediately sobered. ''Who won?''

''I did, of course. I have three older brothers who are a lot tougher than Mr. Denton.'' Brandy raised one perfectly groomed eyebrow. ''Besides, as soon as I smacked him, he got the message and backed off.'' She sighed. ''I don't want to be pessimistic here, but I'd say we aren't going to get a whole lot of business from Denton Accounting—especially after Mr. Denton explains his bruise to Mrs. Denton...and all the little Dentonites.''

Amanda had almost forgotten what this meant to their business in her concern for Brandy. ''That's fine with me,'' she said firmly. ''We don't need *that* kind of business.''

''I suppose not,'' said Brandy. ''Although *some* business would be nice.'' She took another sip of coffee. ''You know the real scary thing, Amanda? For a moment I was actually tempted to go along with Mr. Denton.''

Amanda's jaw dropped. ''What?''

''I was.'' Brandy actually blushed. ''He lunged and this thought flashed through my mind that if that was what it was going to take to get our business off the ground, maybe I should do it.''

Amanda was horrified. ''Brandy!''

''Then I realized that if Mr. Denton touched me I'd throw up, and that wouldn't do one thing for our business, either. So I just smacked him and left.''

''Good,'' said Amanda. ''We aren't that desperate.''

Brandy raised an eyebrow. ''We're pretty close.

We've been in the executive services business for three months, and you can count our clients on my ring finger.''

Amanda squirmed. That was pretty close to true. Business hadn't been anywhere near what they'd projected. ''We've had more than that,'' she reminded them both. ''We did that thing for the Claire Foundation.''

''You didn't charge them anything more than cost!''

Amanda winced. ''They're a charitable organization. It didn't seem right...''

''We're *not* a charitable organization.'' Brandy took another gulp of coffee. ''And then there was that Bernard Trucking thing. You raced all over town lining up corporate gifts for him to hand out—and we ended up paying for them.''

Amanda winced again. ''He was such a nice man. And he really couldn't afford...''

''We couldn't afford it! And Mr. Bernard might have been a nice man but his son sure wasn't. You ended up dating Eddy Bernard! He borrowed a couple of hundred dollars from you and hasn't called you since.''

Amanda squirmed and bent her head. She didn't like thinking about Eddy. ''I'm sure he'll pay me back when he gets his feet on the ground,'' she murmured, although she'd be surprised if that happened.

''And what about that Higgins Stainless Steel thing?'' Brandy continued. ''They almost begged us to take their business and you refused.''

''I don't feel one bit guilty about that,'' Amanda announced, narrowing her eyes. ''Lenny Higgins was pond scum. Besides arranging the Higgins's Christmas party, he wanted me to buy his mistress a Christmas present so his wife wouldn't find out. That isn't right, Brandy. For one thing, he shouldn't have had a mistress. And for another, if he wanted to buy her a present he should have picked it out himself.''

''I suppose you've got a point,'' Brandy admitted. ''But you can't keep getting personally involved with the clients, or we'll never make any money.'' She sank even deeper into the cushions, then sighed. ''Maybe we aren't cut out for this business. You're too soft-hearted and I just seem to attract weirdos.''

''You don't...''

''Yes, I do. Look at the business I've brought in. First there was that fellow who wanted us to arrange the 'Welcome Winter' frolic in the park.'' She snorted. ''Remember how his little group wanted to welcome winter? If we hadn't caught on in time, we'd have ended up in jail!''

''True, but...''

''Then there was that group of insurance adjusters whose idea of a Christmas party was having me pop out of a Christmas cake. Me, for heaven's sake! Do you know how much icing it would take just to cover me up?''

Amanda pictured her partner covered in white gooey icing and giggled.

''Now I get Mr. Denton,'' Brandy continued. ''What is it about me, anyway? Aren't men supposed to prefer tall, leggy blondes, not short, dumpy brunettes?''

Amanda shook her head at that. Brandy might not be classically beautiful but there was a come-hither sparkle in her green eyes and her ample-bosomed figure had always attracted male attention. ''You might be short, but you aren't dumpy,'' Amanda decided. ''There's something kind of...earthy about you, I think. Men just look at you and think naughty thoughts.''

''That's for sure,'' Brandy groaned. ''Every man I meet wants to drag me into a bedroom.''

''And every man I meet thinks I'm a sucker,'' Amanda complained. That did seem to be the way her relationships went. She lent men money, did their laundry, got all involved in their problems...and then they'd decide they didn't need her.

Brandy was instantly sympathetic. ''You're not a sucker, Amanda. You just...pick the wrong men and get too involved with people. And it's a good thing for me you're like that. I don't know what I would have done without you after Charlie and I split up. Starting this business gave me something else to think about,'' she said, sighing sadly. ''I just wish it was going to work.''

''Of course it's going to work,'' Amanda insisted with a lot more confidence than she felt. ''It has to, Brandy. I don't have many other alternatives.''

''We could always go back to the temp agency.''

Amanda shuddered at the thought. ''No thanks. I've had enough of spending days at copy machines or filing papers—and so have you. We were both full-time secretaries before the world got into this downsizing kick. We're great at arranging things.''

''We could try to get permanent jobs.''

''I don't want to do that, either,'' Amanda objected. ''Even if we could find jobs, which is pretty doubtful these days, we'd just get terminated in the next downsizing. We're always the first to go.''

''It's because we're short,'' Brandy complained.

"When someone says down, people think of us. It always makes me feel like one of those ducks in the shooting gallery."

"I don't want to do it again! I don't want to work for anyone else. I want to work for myself."

"So do I, but I'd like an income while I do it." Brandy pushed aside a few strands of hair that were tickling her face. "I never thought we'd have this problem. After all, there aren't that many executive services companies in Calgary."

"It's probably because we aren't known," Amanda suggested. "When people want someone to handle office parties, and seminars, or to arrange a tasteful little business luncheon, they don't think of A&B Executive Services. If we could just get our foot in the door…"

"We'll find some weirdo or moocher on the other side?" Brandy guessed.

Amanda frowned at her. "No, we won't. There has to be some nice, normal, busy executive who is awful at dealing with Christmas. All we have to do is find him."

JOSH LARKLAND was dealing with Christmas in his own way—he was trying to ignore it.

Unfortunately, it wasn't ignoring him.

"Christmas!" he grunted.

He dropped the phone receiver into the cradle and gave it the scowl it deserved. That did it. If one more person said the C-word to him any time within the next ten years, he was going to scream.

He massaged his temples and looked longingly at his computer. That's what he should be doing today—working on the design for his voice response unit.

That's what his computer hardware company—Larkland Technology Development—did, and that's what Josh wanted to be doing. Instead, he'd spent a good portion of the morning talking to people about unimportant things that all had something to do with Christmas!

It had started with a phone call from his aunt Mimi at nine o'clock this morning. "It's not a Christmas party, Josh. We're just having a few people over tonight, under the umbrella of a Christmas theme. You will come, won't you? The whole family will be here, along with some of your uncle Reg's business friends and a few neighbors. Oh, and Marple Stevens is coming. She's got such a lovely daughter. You really should meet her."

That had been followed by a call from his stepsister, Charmaine. "It's my annual Universal Christmas Grandiola. You should come. My friend Stacey is going to be in from Detroit. You really should meet her."

Then there had been his aunt Louise. "We haven't seen you for such a long time. Do come. Frank's partner's friend's husband's cousin is going to be here. You really should meet her."

If it wasn't relatives calling, it was business acquaintances—potential investors who wanted him to make an appearance at their Christmas party, or to ensure that they were invited to his. Current investors who wanted much the same thing.

And to top it all off, his mother!

Now he really wanted to scream.

Josh thought for a second, then decided to do it. "Ma-aa-bb-bl-ee!" he bellowed.

He waited for a moment, and when no one showed up he did it again. ''Mable!''

There was silence, followed by a huge, dramatic sigh and the squeak of a chair. Finally Mable appeared in his doorway, her large, square figure blocking most of the light from the reception area. ''Do you want something or are you just trying to annoy me?''

''Yes, I want something. I want a one-way ticket to January.''

''Of course,'' said Mable. She took a few steps into the room. ''Would that be economy or first-class?''

''I'll go baggage if you can do it. And make sure no one else is on the plane. The rest of the world can stay in December, since they all seem to like it so much.''

''My, my!'' said Mable. She strolled closer and plunked her ample figure into the one visitor's chair Josh allowed in his office. ''We're really getting into the Christmas spirit this year, aren't we?''

''No, we aren't.'' Josh lowered his eyebrows. ''And it's not because there's something wrong with me. I like Christmas well enough. I just don't like it right now!''

Mable smiled. ''I'm afraid you're simply going to have to cope. Christmas isn't something I can reschedule.''

''Why not?'' Josh picked up a pencil and twirled it around his fingers. ''This happens every year. Christmas comes along and it's never convenient. If they have to have these sorts of holidays, why don't they do it some other time?''

''I don't know. I guess they just don't consider your schedule when they plan these things.''

"They certainly don't." Josh caught the twitch of her lips and his irritation increased. "Did you find that place yet, like I asked you to?"

"It was more like a royal command, and no, I didn't. It's almost impossible to find a place to have a Christmas party now! It's the first of December. Everything has been booked for months."

"That's just great." Josh tossed the pencil onto his desk. "According to Hank Turnbull, I have to host one of these Christmas things. He said it would be the perfect opportunity to show my hardware to potential investors. How can I do that if you won't find a place to have it?"

Mable stared right back at him. "Don't you blame this on me, Josh Larkland. I wouldn't have had any problem finding a place if *you* had thought about doing this a couple of months ago."

"I was busy a couple of months ago." Josh gestured at the papers littering his desk. "And I'm busy now, too. I've got networks to design, schematics to check...equipment to test. I don't have time for this Christmas stuff."

"It's not that bad. It just..."

"It's worse than that bad! It's a pain in the neck." Josh stretched back a hand to massage that part of his anatomy. "People have been phoning all day, suggesting we 'get together before Christmas.' A stack of invitations for me to go places came in the mail. Just thinking up reasons not to go is a full-time job!"

Mable's smile widened. "Why don't you just go to some of them? Most people enjoy..."

Josh shuddered at the thought. "Well, I don't. I hate those things. No one ever talks about interesting stuff like network throughput and voice response learning curves. They just sit around, laughing… talking…drinking. Sometimes they even…sing!''

Mable clamped her lips together, and her shoulders shook. ''How…uh…bizarre.''

''It sure is.'' Josh folded his arms and glowered at the world. ''Besides, most of these Christmas things are put on by *my* relatives.''

Mable rolled her eyes. ''There's nothing wrong with your relatives, Josh. Apart from the fact that you have an awful lot of them, they all seem like nice people.''

''They probably are.'' Josh got out of his chair and wandered over to look out the floor-to-ceiling windows behind his desk. There really wasn't anything wrong with his family, and it wasn't that Josh didn't like them. He was actually very fond of them, when he remembered they existed. However, none of them knew anything about electronics, telecommunications, robotics or remote voice activation, which was all Josh was interested in talking about. So he couldn't think of a single reason why he should leave his office early to drive across town just to spend an evening pretending to listen to them while he thought about something else.

Besides, they all had a bad habit of delivering little lectures to him about issues he didn't consider important. ''They just…don't approve of my life-style or something.''

Mable snorted. ''Of course they don't approve of your life-style! *I* don't approve of your life-style.'' She paused. ''Not that I consider the way you live much of a style.''

''Jeez!'' Josh turned to give her a warning glare,

and wondered how much trouble it would be to get a new secretary. ''Not you, too!''

''Yes, me, too.'' Mable held up a palm. ''Don't get me wrong. When you try, you can be a remarkably decent person. You just don't...pay much attention to your life.''

Josh furrowed his brow. ''What is that supposed to mean?''

''Well...you spend most of your waking hours either in the lab or this office.''

Josh took a quick look around. The room was exactly as he liked it—a sofa in a corner so he could catch a few hours' sleep when he worked all night, a computer on his desk, and another unit on the big table beside it. ''What's wrong with my office?'' he asked. ''It's just the way I like it. We're a high-tech—''

''I know, I know. And there's no question you're a supreme techo. But you really don't have much of a personal life.'' Mable sighed and shifted in the chair. ''For example, I've never known you to date the same woman any longer than a week—and that only happens if she keeps phoning you!''

''Yeah, well...'' Josh rubbed an eye. That seemed to be everyone's big complaint. If they weren't urging him to bring some woman home to meet them, they were dredging up women for him to meet. Sometimes they even hinted that he should be doing this himself.

Josh didn't grasp the logic of that. There were plenty of women in his family already. They didn't need any more. He certainly didn't need one. Oh, he liked women well enough, and when he was with one, he enjoyed himself. But they weren't as interesting or as important as the high-tech industry he was trying to develop.

"And then there's your family," Mable went on. "You don't spend much time with them, either."

"I spend lots of time with them," Josh insisted, although he had a funny feeling that wasn't really the case. "Besides, when I do see them, they take turns dragging me into a corner and telling me what's wrong with me. It's almost a tradition. If we could just eat turkey like everyone else, it might not be so bad." He returned to his chair and settled into it. "Now they've come up with this...this present thing!"

Mable looked bewildered. "What present thing?"

"You know. Christmas presents."

"Oh, that." Mable shrugged a shoulder. "You don't spend a lot of time on that, Josh. Every year you do the same thing. You buy a case of perfume and a case of brandy. Men get brandy. Women get perfume." She put her head to one side. "Which reminds me. Can I get on the brandy list this year? I've still got three bottles of perfume."

Josh rolled his eyes. "I'm not giving you perfume this year. Or brandy, either."

"Why not?"

"I don't know," Josh said irritably. "My mother just said that she didn't think it was appropriate."

"Your mother?" Mable glanced at the phone, then back at him. "That's right. She just called, didn't she?"

"Uh-huh."

Mable blinked twice. "She phoned to tell you that she doesn't think it's appropriate to give me perfume?"

''It's not just you. It's everyone. She suggested I do something a little more personal.''

Actually, it had been more than a suggestion. ''I want to talk to you about Christmas,'' she'd started. Then she'd gone into one of her unfathomable mother-type lectures about thoughtfulness and the real meaning of Christmas that had contained a whole bunch of ''not appropriates'' and ''It doesn't have to be expensive, dear. But something a little more personal would be better.'' And when he'd said he wasn't sure he could ''do'' personal, she'd said in that case it might be better if he didn't give them anything at all!

It had almost sounded good—except something in his mother's voice told Josh that if he said, ''Okay, fine, I won't,'' his mother would be really upset. And although she, along with the rest of his relatives, drove him crazy at times, he didn't like it when she was upset.

''She doesn't think giving everyone the same thing is very thoughtful.''

''Ah,'' said Mable. ''Well, she does have a point.''

''She does?'' Josh peered at her. ''What is it?''

''Well, it isn't very thoughtful. It's sort of like...Christmas shopping in bulk.''

Josh didn't see the problem. ''What's wrong with that?''

''It's just not done. If you're going to give someone a present, it should mean something. You don't just do it to get it over with.''

''Oh,'' said Josh. He studied her face for a moment. Mable was probably good at this sort of thing—certainly a lot better than he was. ''Well, since you understand it, how about if you...''

Mable shook her head. "There's no way I'm doing your Christmas shopping for you. For one thing, I don't have time, and for another, I don't do things like that."

"Jeez, Mabe!" Josh shoved an exasperated hand through his hair. "It's not as if I'm asking you to have my children. I just want you to pick up a few things."

"You want me to do more than pick up a few things. You want me to think up presents for—how many is it?—a couple of dozen of your relatives. I wouldn't have a clue how to do that."

"Neither do I," Josh muttered. That was the problem. He had no idea what his relatives would consider appropriately personal, and he didn't know how to find out, either. "Couldn't you just..."

"No, I couldn't."

Josh gave her his best I'm-totally-helpless-without-you look, accompanied by a smile. "Please? I really need some help and..."

"No." Mable pushed herself out of the chair. "There's no point in wasting all that charm on me, either. I'm not going to do it, and that's final. I'm your administrative assistant, not Santa Claus."

"Right about now I'd settle for one of his elves," Josh mumbled. He eyed Mable hopefully. "How about getting me one of them?"

"Sure, why not?" Mable turned to leave. "Right after I find a place for your Christmas party and arrange for a ticket to January." She chuckled. "Actually, getting you an elf might be a whole lot easier."

IF MABLE WAS GOING TO find that elf, she'd better do it soon, Josh decided a few hours later.

He sat at his desk and stared blindly at his computer screen. At least the afternoon had gone a little better than the morning. He'd given Mable firm instructions that he wasn't to be disturbed, and, for once, she'd actually carried them out. He'd had a good four hours without any interruptions.

But he hadn't accomplished anything. This whole present thing bothered him a lot more than he liked to admit. He had the distinct impression from his mother that it was important to her as well as to everyone else. It was one of those things the rest of the world seemed to understand, while he fumbled around, trying to figure out what was going on.

And, if he was going to be honest with himself, he'd have to admit that he didn't try very hard. He did care about his relatives, and he didn't like being the focus of their disapproval. But he had a business to run, inventions to invent, investors to line up. He didn't have time to worry about this sort of thing. What he needed was someone to handle all this Christmas stuff—the parties, the invitations, as well as producing a nice batch of personal Christmas presents, all gift-wrapped and labeled, without him having to do anything about it.

He'd just thought that when his office door opened and Mable stepped in. "I think I've found a solution to one of your problems," she said.

Josh eyed her warily. Her lips were stretched into a wide smile, and there was a definite twinkle in her eye. "Oh?" he said.

"Yes." Mable's smile grew. "I talked to a friend of mine who suggested I call an executive services agency. So I did."

"And?"

''And they sent someone right over.'' She turned toward the door. ''Come on in, dear. And don't let Mr. Larkland's manner put you off. He's horrible, but he's harmless.''

Josh opened his mouth to object, then closed it again and blinked with startled surprise at the woman entering his office. She stood about five-five, with shoulder-length, white-blond hair that curled around her face. She was wearing a dark green skirt, a long red jacket and high-laced black boots. ''This is Amanda Kringleton,'' Mable announced. She strode across the room and handed Josh a piece of red paper. ''Your Christmas elf.''

2

Terrific, thought Amanda. *This time I got the weirdo.*

She stood just inside the doorway of Josh Larkland's messy, high-tech office and wished Brandy was with her. However, Brandy had been out when Larkland Technical Development called. The woman on the other end of the phone had sounded perfectly normal. Amanda had been positive she could handle it by herself.

Now she wasn't so sure. It wasn't that the president of Larkland Technology Development had done anything to make her think he wasn't a nice, normal person. He hadn't said anything, either. All he had done was stare at her.

He wasn't even subtle about it. He leaned back against his desk, absently stroking his chin with one hand while he examined her from head to toe and back up again as if he'd never seen a woman before.

Since he was being so rude about it, Amanda didn't feel guilty scrutinizing him. She probably would have done it anyway, because Josh Larkland was one of the most attractive men she'd ever seen. He was just under six feet tall, with mussy curly brown hair, deliciously deep brown eyes framed with thick, dark lashes, and a high-cheekboned, square-jawed face that was almost classically handsome. The sleeves of his pink-and-gray striped white shirt were rolled up to his elbows, his tie was bundled up in a corner of his desk instead of tied neatly around his neck, and the blue suit jacket that matched his pants was thrown over the back of his chair in a manner that invited wrinkles.

Okay. He was a good-looking, well-dressed weirdo who didn't take care of his clothes, wasn't hung up on neatness and had never seen a woman before.

Amanda took a deep breath. She could handle this. All she had to do was act cool and professional and...

His gaze met hers. He blinked several times, then moved his lips into a slow smile that was so charming Amanda forgot all about acting cool and professional. "I'm staring, aren't I?" he asked.

"Well...uh...yes, I guess you are," said Amanda.

"I thought so." He shrugged. "It's a natural reaction, you know. After all, I've never seen an elf before." He looked a little puzzled by that, as if he couldn't understand why dozens of Santa's helpers weren't lurking about. Amanda glowered at the flyer in his hand. Darn those things. As soon as she left this office she was going to find them all and burn them. "I'm not really an elf, you know. I..."

"Oh, I know. They don't exist, right?" His eyes gleamed with admiration. "But if they did, they would look exactly like you."

Amanda's stomach fluttered. *Don't get involved with the clients,* she reminded herself. *Stick to a professional approach.* This guy was charming, but he could still be a creep on the make. She cleared her throat. "Look, Mr. Larkland..."

He waved that aside. "Josh. No one around here calls me Mr. Larkland, not even Mable. It's probably a sign of disrespect." He frowned. "So is her telling you I'm horrible. I'm not *that* horrible. Today was an exception. And now that you're here, I'm positive I'll be in a much better mood."

Amanda almost lost herself in his eyes and his smile. He might be on the make but he wasn't a creep. As a matter of fact...

"I guess we should get down to business, hmm?" Josh motioned her toward the single black leather visitor's chair in front of his desk and strolled around to the chair behind it. "What do you need to get started?"

Amanda struggled to remember what business she was in. "I, um..."

"I guess you'll require a list." He stretched back in his chair, blinked up at the ceiling, and started reciting names. "Let's see. There's my mother, of course. Edwina Davidson. She married Harold after my father died, which is why our last names aren't the same. Then there's my sisters, Shelby, Marilla, and Charmaine. They're actually my stepsisters, I suppose, since they're Harold's children. Oh, and my aunts—Judith, Francine, Sofia, Louise, and Mimi. Francine is my mother's sister. Sofia is my father's sister, and Louise and Mimi are Harold's sisters. Judith is their aunt. That makes her a stepsomething, but I can never remember..." He looked over at Amanda and stopped. "Shouldn't you be writing this down?"

Amanda had been listening in bewildered silence as he listed off his relatives. Now she snapped to attention. "I could but..." Was she missing something or was he simply not making any sense? "I was, um, under the impression that we were talking about a business function."

Josh looked puzzled. "A business function?"

"Yes. Your secretary said that you wanted to host a Christmas party…a *business* Christmas party."

"Oh, that." His eyes widened. "You can do that, *too?*"

"Of course." Amanda was starting to feel a little dizzy. "That's what A&B Executive Services does. We arrange office parties, organize business seminars…"

"And handle this Christmas present thing, too? That's…amazing."

"Christmas presents?" Amanda rubbed her forehead with a finger in a vain attempt to understand. "Well, um, we do handle a small line of corporate gifts. Coffee-table books. Business-card holders…"

"Don't you buy those in bulk?" asked Josh.

"Sometimes. But…"

"Then I don't think they'll work for my family."

"Your family?" Amanda stared at him in astonishment. Surely he wasn't suggesting… "You want me to get Christmas presents for your *family?*"

"Of course I do. Isn't that why you're here?"

Amanda was immensely disappointed in him. He was just like other executive types she'd run into—so absorbed in their work that they didn't have time to spend on the important things in life. "No, it isn't. I'm here to discuss your office Christmas party."

"But what about these Christmas presents? You can do that, too, can't you?"

There was a hint of desperation in his eyes. Amanda hesitated. He did look as if he needed help… She needed the business and it wouldn't hurt to…

It certainly would hurt. Brandy would be horrified. "No," said Amanda. "That's not really something A&B Executive Services does."

"It isn't?"

"No, it isn't," Amanda said firmly. "Besides, Christmas presents are something people should really handle themselves."

"Yeah?" He blinked a couple of times as if unclear on the concept. "What if they don't have time? Couldn't you just—" he made a vague, sweeping motion with one hand "—do it?"

Amanda hesitated. He looked so helpless… They desperately needed the business and…

And buying other people's Christmas presents had to be on Brandy's list of "getting too involved." Amanda gave him a small, cool smile. "I don't think so. Now, if we could get back to discussing your Christmas function…."

"My Christmas function." Josh stretched back in his chair and studied her. "Okay. Let's talk about that."

Amanda suddenly felt uneasy. There was something about the glint in his brown eyes that made her nervous. "Well, um, your secretary told me that you were having difficulty finding a place to host a Christmas party. She's right. I couldn't find a place, either, so I suggested you do it here. With a little work we could make the place look festive. Serve drinks…hors d'oeuvres. We could have a different theme for each floor…get in a string quartet…"

"That sounds interesting." Josh tapped his fingers together. "Tell me, Amanda… I can call you Amanda, can't I? Or do I have call you Ms. Kringleton?"

"Amanda is fine."

"Okay, Amanda. Exactly how many of these sorts of functions have you organized?"

"Me, personally? Quite a few actually. I…"

"I meant A&B Executive Services."

"Not a great deal," Amanda admitted after a pause. "We've only been in the business a few months, and..."

"Ah," said Josh. "I see."

Amanda looked into his face and got the distinct impression that he did see. He might not bear a strong resemblance to an efficient corporate executive, but she began to feel that he was not a man who should be underestimated.

Josh picked up a pencil and stroked it across his bottom lip. "It's a difficult business to break into, isn't it?"

Amanda watched the eraser end of the pencil move across his mouth and sucked in her own bottom lip. "It, uh, can be."

"Uh-huh. What you really need to get business is a track record, and to get a track record, you need business. Right?"

Amanda considered lying, caught the sparkle in his eye, and didn't. "Yes," she said.

"Arranging the Larkland Christmas party might be just the sort of thing you need, hmm?"

"It would certainly help."

"I would think so," said Josh. He was silent as he studied her. Then he spoke again in a silky smooth voice. "How about if we make a deal, Amanda?"

Amanda eyed him suspiciously. She was pretty sure she knew what was coming. "A deal?"

"Yeah." He dropped the pencil and leaned forward, forearms resting against the end of the desk. "You handle this Christmas present thing for me, and you can have the Larkland Christmas party business."

Amanda swallowed. ''That sounds a little like blackmail, Mr. Larkland.''

''Josh.'' He grinned. ''And it isn't blackmail at all. I believe it falls more under the heading of extortion. However, I'm desperate, I have a feeling you are, too, and this way we could help each other.'' He blinked in his deceptively innocent fashion. ''And I'm not suggesting you do it for free. I'll pay for your time.''

''Are you sure you can afford it?'' Amanda retorted. ''Considering how many relatives you have…''

''Oh, good,'' said Josh. ''You do have a sense of humor. I was starting to wonder.''

Amanda watched his lips move into that slow, sexy smile and felt herself melt. It was a bad sign. Josh Larkland was the epitome of the work-absorbed executive. He was twisting her arm to get her to do something she didn't want to do, and she still liked him.

''Don't worry about the money,'' Josh added. ''I can afford it. And this is an opportunity you can't afford to pass up. There'll be a lot of people at the Larkland Christmas thing—important people who I'm sure spend enormous sums on arranging… arrangements.'' He grinned. ''If you do a good job, you could end up with enough business to keep you going for a while.''

He was right about that. And maybe it wasn't such a big deal. All she had to do was handle his Christmas shopping. How hard could that be? Brandy might not like it, but she would be pleased that Amanda had landed a job that they'd get paid for—and that it didn't involve icing. ''All right,'' she said. ''I suppose I could pick up a few things.''

"And gift wrap them?"

"And gift wrap them."

"How about Christmas cards? Can you send those?"

Amanda felt as if she were sinking into quicksand. "I suppose I could..."

Josh gestured at a stack of envelopes on the corner of his desk. "And you'd have to go through all these invitations and send some sort of response. Something that says no without sounding as if it means 'There's no way in hell.'"

"Oh," said Amanda. She eyed the mound. "Well, um, okay, I guess I..."

"Good." Josh settled back into his chair with a satisfied smile. "You're hired."

"YOU CAN'T POSSIBLY be related to all these people," Amanda argued.

She stared at the list of sisters, aunts, uncles and cousins in stunned disbelief. "There are over twenty people on this list. You can't be related to all of them," she said, dropping the list onto her lap. She had been seated in the uncomfortable and only chair in his office for the past hour and would have given anything to get up and stretch her legs.

"Twenty?" Josh thought about it. "Did I mention Mable?"

"No."

"Well, make it twenty-one. And yes, I am related to most of them, except for Mable of course." He frowned. "It's my mother's fault. She married Harold without giving any consideration to the problems that was going to cause me at Christmas."

"I imagine she had other things on her mind at the

time,'' Amanda murmured, trying to surreptitiously stretch one leg, then the other. Ah, that felt better!

''I suppose,'' Josh agreed, and Amanda found herself wondering if he had the slightest idea what any of those things might have been. After an hour with him, she'd concluded that Josh Larkland was the most clued-out man she'd ever met...and perhaps the most irresistible. His aura of helplessness, along with his physical attractiveness and incredible charm, would stop any woman in her tracks.

So why didn't he have a woman around to handle his shopping for him?

That's none of your business, Amanda scolded herself. She was not getting personally involved with this guy. Still, she couldn't help wondering...

She focused her attention back on his list of relatives. ''At least most of these people are women. I can get them gift baskets filled with soap and perfume and...''

''Perfume?'' Josh shook his head. ''Perfume is out.''

''Why?''

He shrugged a shoulder. ''It just is, that's all. I want something more...personal.''

''Personal?'' That was the last thing Amanda had expected to hear. ''You want me to get these people something personal?''

''That's right,'' said Josh. ''I think it would be more...thoughtful.''

''Thoughtful.'' Amanda struggled to hold back a giggle. ''Thoughtful is not when you coerce someone else to do your shopping for you.''

Josh grinned right back at her. ''Hey, extortion

takes a lot of thought. Especially when you've never done it before.''

''Right.'' Darn, he was cute. It was almost a shame that he wasn't a creep on the make. Amanda shoved aside the thought and tried to concentrate on the task at hand. ''Personal thoughtful presents, hmm. Okay. Well, suppose you tell me something about these people.''

''Like what?''

''Something that would help,'' Amanda explained. ''What they do. What they like.'' Josh still looked blank. ''Why don't we start with your sisters? How old are they?''

''How old?'' Josh's forehead furrowed while he considered it. ''I don't know exactly. A lot older than me.''

Amanda wasn't certain if his idea of ''a lot'' was two or twenty-two. ''Would that make them over forty?''

''Not all of them.'' He stared into the space over her head. ''Marilla might be. There was some sort of party in the summer that had to do with forty. I think it was Marilla's birthday...unless it was for her husband. He's really old. Or was it was Frank and Louise's anniversary?''

At this rate she'd be over forty by the time Josh figured it out. Amanda decided to abandon the age angle. ''Let's forget that. How about what they do.''

''What they do?'' Josh looked as puzzled by that as he had been by their age.

''For a living,'' Amanda prompted. ''What do your sisters do for a living?''

''Well...um...Shelby does something with children.''

"A teacher?" Amanda guessed.

"Either that or a hairdresser," said Josh. "I can never remember. Charmaine works in a bank or a hospital, and Marilla has something to do with animals. She shows them or trains them or..." He shook his head. "I'm not positive. I just know she likes cats."

At last—a decent suggestion. Amanda wrote "cats" beside Marilla's name. It wasn't a bad hint. She could always find some kind of cat ornament. "How about Marilla's husband—" she scanned her list "—Tom?"

"Tom? Oh, he likes cats, too."

Amanda decided she'd heard enough about Marilla and Tom. "What about your other sisters—Shelby and Charmaine? What do they like?"

"I have no idea," said Josh.

No one could know this little about his family. "You must know," Amanda insisted. "Just think. When they get together, what do they talk about?"

Josh shrugged his shoulders. "Nothing in particular. Except for Marilla and Tom. They talk about cats."

Amanda was beginning to form a pretty weird picture of his family, all sitting mutely while this Tom and Marilla lectured on about felines. "Let's try someone else." She scanned her list again. "How about your aunts, Mimi and Louise. Tell me about them."

"There isn't anything to tell! They're my aunts, that's all. And I don't know how old they are!"

Of course he didn't. As a matter of fact, Amanda was starting to wonder if he even knew what his relatives looked like. "What about your mother? Do you know anything about her?"

Josh's cheekbones reddened. "Of course I know something about her! She's my mother. Her name is Edwina Davidson. She's been married twice—first to my father. Then to Harold."

Amanda frowned. "I need more than that." She sat up straighter in the uncomfortable chair.

"I don't know anything more than that!" Amanda rolled her eyes and Josh scowled. "Don't look so disapproving. I don't think people should know a whole bunch of personal information about their relatives. It's too..."

"Personal?" Amanda guessed.

"Exactly!"

Amanda looked down at the list resting on her lap, then back up at him. "I can't do this."

"What do you mean, you can't do it? You..."

"No, I can't! I don't think anyone could. It's utterly impossible."

"It can't be that impossible," Josh argued. "Lots of other people do it. And it's not as if I'm asking you to design a voice-response subrelay. I just want you to get a few presents..."

"Personal presents," Amanda corrected. "For people I haven't met and you don't know anything about."

They stared at each other. "Then I guess you'll just have to meet them," said Josh.

Amanda couldn't believe her ears. "Excuse me?"

"You're the one making the big fuss about knowing them," Josh observed. "I'd be perfectly happy if you'd get them something personal without ever meeting them. However, since you're going to be so difficult about it, I guess the only thing to do is to arrange for you to meet them."

Amanda didn't know what he had in mind, but she was positive she wasn't going to like it. "No," she said. "I am not going to do that. I absolutely refuse to walk up to over twenty strangers and ask them what they want for Christmas. For one thing, I doubt that they would tell me, and for another, they'd probably have me arrested."

"I wouldn't think so," said Josh. "Elves don't get sent to jail. It would just annoy Santa and no one wants to risk that." She scowled and he held up a hand. "But I'm not suggesting you do that. I don't want my relatives to know about you. I'm supposed to be doing this present thing myself."

"I guessed that," Amanda muttered under her breath.

Josh ignored her. "What you need to do is meet them...casually. Then you could ask them all kinds of personal questions without them getting suspicious. Sort of like a...a secret-agent elf." He drummed his fingers on his desktop. "Now, how can we arrange that?"

"We can't," said Amanda. "Maybe we should forget this. I—"

Josh interrupted her. "I've got it," he exclaimed. He got up out of his chair and began to pace in front of the windows. "Aunt Mimi."

"Aunt Mimi?"

"Yes. She's having the whole crowd. Everyone will be there. You can meet them all." He peered at Amanda. "You are free tonight, aren't you?"

Amanda nodded her head, wondering what she was getting herself into. ‘‘Great. Then you can go to Aunt Mimi’s party.’’

3

"AUNT MIMI'S PARTY?" Brandy repeated incredulously.

She put a hand over her mouth and giggled into it. "This guy actually expected you to go to a family party with him so you could find out personal things about his relatives?"

"That's right." Amanda sat in her kitchen, still a little stunned after her meeting with Josh. "He even hinted that I could go by myself. He said there would be so many people there that no one would notice that they didn't know me and that he wasn't there."

Brandy shook with laughter. "And I thought I'd met them all! What did you say?"

"I talked him out of it!" Amanda felt rather proud of this accomplishment. "After all, they are his relatives. If I have to go, he should have to go, as well."

Brandy's eyes widened. "You're not really going to do this, are you?"

Amanda shrugged. "I have to. If I'm going to get presents for these people, I have to meet them. It's the only way I'm going to find out anything about them." She checked her watch and rose out of her chair. If she hurried, she could have a quick shower. Then there was her hair... "Josh doesn't seem to know much more than their names."

"'Josh,'" Brandy repeated. She followed Amanda

down the hall. ''Listen, Amanda, I'm not so sure this is a good idea.''

''Why not?'' asked Amanda. She went into her bedroom, opened her closet and studied the contents. Josh hadn't been much help in the wardrobe department. ''I don't know what anyone wears,'' he'd said when she'd asked how formal this gathering was. ''They just look...clean.''

''I just don't,'' Brandy insisted. She plunked herself on the edge of Amanda's bed. ''For one thing, he doesn't sound like the kind of man any woman in her right mind would get near. And for another, he's a client. This morning you were horrified at the idea of me cozying up with a potential client just to improve business. Now you're going to do it.''

''I am not cozying up with him!'' Amanda objected. Not that she'd mind cozying up with Josh. He was certainly handsome and...

Amanda caught herself. Brandy was right. Josh wasn't the sort of man any woman in her right mind would date. Besides, she wasn't positive Josh would *know* how to cozy up with someone.

She giggled at the thought, then yanked a cherry red knit dress out of the closet. ''If anyone is cozying up, it's probably you.''

''Me?''

''Yes, you.'' Amanda turned around. ''There are a dozen roses on my kitchen table, along with a card addressed to you.''

''Oh, those.'' Brandy rolled her eyes. ''I got those for not cozying up with someone. Mr. Denton sent them.''

''Mr. Denton?''

''That character who attacked me this morning,''

Brandy explained. ‘‘He sent those along with a card that said ‘I’m terribly sorry.’ ’’

‘‘That was nice of him.’’

‘‘It was, wasn’t it?’’ Brandy considered it for a moment, then shrugged it off. ‘‘He’s probably just worried I’ll call the police…or his wife.’’

‘‘It was still a nice gesture.’’ Amanda held up the dress. ‘‘What do you think of this?’’

‘‘It’s fine.’’ Brandy’s forehead creased in concern. ‘‘Are you sure you want to go out with this guy? We don’t know much about him. He could be a psychopath or something.’’

‘‘Josh?’’ Amanda shook her head. ‘‘You don’t have to worry about that. And I’m not really going out with him. It’s more like I’m…I’m attending a business function.’’

‘‘Business?’’ Brandy snorted. ‘‘We’re in the executive services business, dear, not the executive *dating* services business.’’

‘‘It’s *not* a date!’’

‘‘I still don’t like it,’’ Brandy said stubbornly. ‘‘Maybe I should hang around so I can check him out.’’ She glanced at her watch. ‘‘What time is he picking you up?’’

‘‘He’s not. I’m meeting him there.’’

‘‘Ah,’’ Brandy drawled wisely. ‘‘Yet another gallant gentleman.’’

‘‘It’s not like that!’’ It wasn’t, either. Josh had volunteered to pick her up—after he’d agreed that he should attend, too. Amanda had decided against it. ‘‘It’s a business function, Brandy. People don’t pick up other people to attend a business function. Besides, this made more sense. We both had to change and…’’

''What's he changing into?'' Brandy interrupted. ''A human being?''

''Brandy!''

''We know this type, Amanda. We've both dated men like him. But even they knew something about their mother. This guy sounds like he hardly knows he's *got* a mother.''

''He does know he has a mother. He just doesn't know much about her,'' Brandy said dryly.

Amanda frowned at Brandy. ''Don't pick on me. I did what you said to do. I got the business, and I didn't give it away. He's paying full price.''

''For what?''

''Well, it's not for me. He's not at all interested in me.'' She thought about the way he'd looked at her when she'd first walked into this office. He had looked interested. But that was because he wanted her to do all his Christmas shopping for him. ''I'm just his...Christmas elf. He sees me as a solution to all his problems.''

''And the start of a bunch of yours,'' Brandy teased. ''Listen, Amanda, I do appreciate what you're trying to do, and I want the business as much as you do. But I don't want you to get hurt.''

''Don't worry, Brandy. I won't get hurt.''

''You will if you get involved with someone like this.''

''I'm *not* getting involved with him. I'm going to meet his family tonight, that's all. And we aren't staying long. I'm just supposed to pop in, ask them a whole bunch of personal questions, and pop out. I have to do it fast, because Josh hates those things.'' She paused. ''You know, I feel a little sorry for him.

He's so…clued out. And he sounds completely overwhelmed by his relatives."

"You feel sorry for him," Brandy repeated. She sighed. "Oh, dear, Amanda. What have you gotten yourself into?"

WHAT HAD HE GOTTEN himself into?

Josh leaned against the archway separating his aunt's living room from the dining room, and took a long swallow of the frothy eggnog punch that Mimi fondly imagined could replace a decent drink. As usual, his aunt had invited three times as many people as she could seat. There were people draped on the sofa, the chairs…even sprawled in front of the fireplace. More than over half were related to him, ninety percent were a good ten years older than he was, and the ones that didn't fall into either of those categories appeared to be women any one of his relatives was trying to set him up with—an intent, narrow-faced woman from Charmaine's cosmic connection class, a perky redhead whom Marilla had introduced as a cat groomer, and a dangerous-looking brunette who was to play the piano later. "So we can sing," Mimi had explained when she'd introduced them.

What in God's name was he doing here?

He took another sip of his drink and analyzed his own question. There were two reasons for his presence—one, so his Christmas elf could find out personal stuff about people, and two, because he was just a little bit uncomfortable with the conversation he'd had with Amanda.

He'd seen the look of disapproval on her face when he'd confessed that he didn't know a whole lot about his relations. He'd been surprised himself at how little he did know. There had been fewer lines of writing on her Christmas gift list than his first plan for his new company. He'd been around these people for most of his life. Granted, he didn't have much in common with them, but shouldn't he know basic details, like how old they were, and what they did for a living?

His musings were interrupted by a middle-aged angular woman wearing a dark blue dress. "Josh?"

"Hi, Mom." Josh bent to kiss her cheek with genuine affection. Come to think of it, he didn't know how old she was, either. He was thirty-two, so she'd have to be somewhere around...

"I'm surprised to see you here," she said. "Especially after our conversation this morning. I thought you might be a little...annoyed."

"Annoyed? Me?" Josh shook his head. "Of course not."

Her gaze searched his face, her blue eyes glimmering with uncertainty. "Then you did understand. About the presents, I mean?"

"Sure," said Josh, although he didn't. He patted her shoulder. "Don't worry. Everything's under control."

"It is?" Edwina looked puzzled, but before she could ask anything, Josh's aunt Mimi bustled up. "Oh, good, Josh, there you are. Marple Stevens has just arrived. She's got her daughter, Freeda, with her." She leaned closer. "Now I want you to be nice to this girl. She owns that little dress shop up on Fifty-ninth. She'd be such a help in your career."

Josh eyed the determined-looking woman entering the living room. "I design voice response systems, Aunt Mimi. It doesn't matter what they wear."

"Ah," said Mimi rather vacantly. "Well, I'm sure she has a nice voice. She sings in the choir, you know."

Before Josh could think of a suitable response, or even decide if there was one, Mimi trotted across the room toward her guests. "Marple, darling, how wonderful to see you. And this must be Freeda. I've got someone here who's anxious to meet you."

Josh groaned and turned, looking for some means of escape, and found himself face-to-face with his uncle Reggie. "Ah, there you are, Josh," Reggie rumbled. "I wanted to have a word with you."

"Did you?" Josh shook Reggie's hand without much enthusiasm. He didn't have anything against his uncle, but he had a strong suspicion that he knew what was coming.

"Yes, I do. Your aunt wanted me to speak to you. She's very concerned about you, you know. So is your mother. And I can understand..."

He went on talking about families and responsibilities and a bunch of other stuff that Josh wasn't interested in hearing. Josh took another sip from his glass. Now he remembered why he didn't spend a lot of time with these people—or know anything personal about them.

He abandoned all attempts to find out anything; his Christmas elf could handle it. She'd better show up soon, too, or he was going to announce that he had developed a sudden case of the plague and get out of here.

AT LEAST ONE of Josh's relatives had the Christmas spirit.

Amanda paid the cabbie, and walked toward the

sprawling bungalow, gaily decorated with an almost obscene number of Christmas lights. There was a large number of cars parked on the street and, as she approached the front door, she could hear music and laughter and the sound of many voices.

She raised a hand to press a finger against the doorbell and hesitated. What on earth had made her agree to do this? It had almost made sense when she was in Josh's office—pop in, ask a whole bunch of personal questions, then pop out. Now it seemed more like an episode of ''Mission Impossible.''

And, to be perfectly honest, she was a little apprehensive about meeting Josh's relatives. She wasn't sure what to expect—his various descriptions made them sound like either eccentric gargoyles or candidates for sainthood. Besides, in spite of his assurances that no one would notice they had an extra guest, or be upset about it, she felt a little uncomfortable about attending a party to which she hadn't been specifically invited.

She wasn't a party crasher, she reminded herself. She was attending a business function, that's all. Besides, if the noises in there and the number of cars parked on the street out here were any indication of the number of people in that house, there was a good chance no one would notice her. Even if they did, his relatives couldn't possibly be gargoyles, not if they had this many friends.

On the other hand, even gargoyles probably had friends.

Amanda took a deep breath and rang the doorbell. To her immense relief, it wasn't a gargoyle who opened the door. It was a tall, willowy woman with curly salt-and-pepper hair and a friendly smile. "Hello," said Amanda. "I'm Amanda..."

"Amanda! Of course!" The woman opened the door wider. "You must be Hemp's daughter. Do come in." She peered over Amanda's shoulder. "Is your husband not with you, or is he parking the car?"

"No. That is, um, I don't..."

"He couldn't make it? Such a shame. But how nice of you to come on your own. Hemp will be delighted. Come inside, dear. It's getting terribly cold out there, isn't it? Totally unpredicted, of course. Didn't they tell us we were going to have a few more days of warm weather before the cold set in?"

"I did hear something like..."

"They just never know, do they? Here, now, let me take your coat. And just leave your boots there. Finding your boots when you leave is something of a standard Christmas game, isn't it? Last year, I went home in someone else's." Her forehead furrowed. "They were men's size ten mukluks. I do wonder who ended up with my size sixes. I'm Mimi Saunders, by the way. Please just call me Mimi. Mrs. Saunders makes me feel quite old. Now you just come on in, and I'll see if I can find Hemp."

"No," Amanda said urgently. Mimi gave her a quizzical look and Amanda rushed on. "You see, Mrs. Saunders...uh, Mimi, I'm not Hemp's..."

"You're not Hemp's daughter?" Mimi peered into her face. "I must admit, I was wondering. You don't look at all like him or Margery, do you?"

"Probably not," Amanda agreed. "I..."

"Of course, you could always be the result of some wild fling." Mimi giggled and her face lit up with mirth. "But it's difficult to imagine Hemp having a wild fling—or anyone having a wild fling with Hemp.'' She turned as another woman wandered into the hall, this one slightly taller and more angularly built. ''Oh, here's Eeedee. Eeedee, this is...Amanda, isn't it? She's not Hemp's daughter.''

''Of course she isn't,'' Eeedee said briskly. ''Anyone looking at her can see that.'' She held out a hand. ''Hello, Amanda. Are you one of Charmaine's friends?''

''No,'' said Amanda, shaking hands. ''I'm...''

''Thank goodness for that.'' Eeedee leaned closer and lowered her voice. ''Not that there's anything wrong with Charmaine—or her friends. But they do tend to go and on about this cosmic connection thing. I think it's because most of them are from Detroit.''

''I've never been to Detroit,'' Amanda assured her. She looked curiously around the wide entranceway, admiring the pale green carpet and pastel walls. Not only were Josh's relatives not gargoyles but this one appeared to have good decorating sense.

''I've never been to Detroit, either,'' said Eeedee. ''I did spend a little time in Denver, though. I quite liked it there. I'm Edwina Davidson, by the way. Everyone calls me Eeedee. I don't really mind, although it does sound like they're reciting the alphabet backward.''

''Edwina,'' Amanda echoed. Then she made the connection. ''Edwina Davidson. You must be Josh's mother.''

''Why, yes, I...'' Edwina stopped talking and stared at Amanda out of two brown eyes that looked a lot like her son's. ''You know *Josh?*''

''Yes.'' Amanda felt herself flushing under Edwina's incredulous gaze. "He sort of...invited me here."

"Josh invited you here," Edwina repeated in a stunned-sounding voice. She turned to her stepsister. "Did you hear that, Mimi? Josh invited her here."

They both stared at Amanda as if she were the gargoyle. Amanda felt as if she'd made an enormous social blunder. "You see, he—I...that is...he asked me to..." She realized she was babbling and took a breath. "He said no one would mind."

"Mind?" Edwina beamed at her. "Of course we don't mind." She slipped her arm through Amanda's. "As a matter of fact, we're absolutely delighted."

"AND THESE ARE Josh's sisters," Edwina concluded. She gestured toward a group of three women, none of whom appeared to be "a lot older" than Josh. "This is Marilla, Shelby, and Charmaine. Darlings, this is Amanda." She paused for dramatic effect. "Josh's friend, Amanda."

There was a split second of silence that was broken by the women's excited chatter. "A girlfriend? Josh?"

"When did this all happen?" asked Shelby, her round, intelligent face alive with curiosity while the stunningly beautiful Charmaine shook Amanda's hand with outright enthusiasm. "I do hope you're considering a Christmas wedding. Christmas weddings are so...cosmic!"

"We're not considering any wedding," said Amanda. "As a matter of fact—"

"Honestly, Charmaine!" Marilla interrupted. "Can't you see things haven't got to that point yet? If you aren't careful, you'll scare her off." She gave

Charmaine a disgusted look and produced a friendly smile for Amanda. ''Don't worry about it, Amanda. Charmaine can find something cosmic in almost any date.''

''Every day is a cosmic day,'' Charmaine retorted, apparently not the least bit upset by her sister's attitude. ''Except the Ides of March. It has really bad connotations. I wouldn't get married on that date.''

Her smile was just as friendly as Marilla's. Amanda smiled back. Josh had misled her about his relatives, she decided. There wasn't anything wrong with them—except they all had a disturbing tendency to jump to conclusions. ''I'm not thinking about any date,'' she told Charmaine. ''But if I were, I wouldn't choose the Ides of March. Listen, I should explain...''

''Oh, please do,'' said Shelby. ''We're all agog with curiosity. How did you meet Josh?''

''I just walked into his office. I...''

''Ah,'' said Charmaine. ''Love at first sight.'' She dug an elbow into Marilla's side. ''Doesn't that sound like a cosmic connection?''

''Not really,'' said Marilla. ''It does sound romantic, though. What happened, Amanda? Did you just stare at each other and decide this was it?''

''I wouldn't exactly...''

''Amanda?'' called a male voice.

Amanda turned to see Josh maneuvering his way across the crowded room. He had on a pair of dark trousers, a white shirt, and a deep brown-and-green-patterned sweater that accented the hazel glints of his eyes. Amanda had never been so happy to see someone. That was just because she wanted him to clear up this misunderstanding, she told herself. It had nothing to do with how good he looked.

He stopped beside her and smiled down at her. "I didn't see you come in."

"I...uh...just got here," Amanda murmured, flustered by his nearness.

Josh glanced around the group. "I take it you've met my mother and my sisters?"

"Yes, I..."

"Yes, she has," Edwina interrupted. "And we're absolutely delighted, Josh." She gave him a little swat on the arm. "But you really should have told us sooner."

Josh's eyebrows gathered together, displaying his confusion. "Told you sooner about what?"

"About Amanda," explained Marilla. "Or, rather, you and Amanda."

"Me and Amanda," Josh echoed, his tone as blank as his expression.

"Why didn't you tell us?" asked Charmaine.

"Didn't you think we'd like her?" asked Marilla.

"Or did you want to surprise us?" asked Shelby.

Everyone looked at him expectantly. Josh's gaze met Amanda's, his expression still confused. Amanda cleared her throat. "I was just, um, trying to explain to your family about our...relationship."

"Ah. Our relationship."

"That's right." Amanda looked around the ensemble of faces. "You see, Josh and I aren't—"

"It's okay, darling," Josh interrupted. His eyes sparkled with merriment, his dimple flashed with his smile. He put an arm around Amanda and gave her a little hug. "They're my family. I want them to know." He smiled fondly into her eyes. His aunts, his mother and his stepsisters smiled fondly at them.

The only one who wasn't smiling was Amanda.

She was busy planning on the long, torturous method she was going to use to murder Josh Larkland.

"I PERSONALLY PREFER the short-haired varieties," Marilla explained earnestly. "Although I had an Angora once who was quite delightful." She raised an eyebrow in Amanda's direction. "What do you think?"

"I've, uh, actually never had much to do with cats," Amanda stuttered. "But...um, I do find them...intriguing."

"They certainly are. I just knew you'd feel that way," Marilla said, then gave Amanda a big smile. "Who knows? Maybe there is something to this cosmic connection stuff of Charmaine's."

Amanda couldn't do anything more than smile back. That was the worst part of all this. She liked these people—and they seemed to like her. The only person she didn't like was Josh. "Maybe there is," she said to Marilla. "Will you excuse me? I, uh, need to have a word with Josh."

Marilla nodded indulgently. "Ah, yes. Romance. Isn't it wonderful?"

"Just splendid," Amanda muttered. She maneuvered her way through the crowd to find Josh. He was standing with a couple of older men, cheerfully knocking back a glass of eggnog punch. "Ah, here she is now," he said as Amanda came up. He rested a casual arm across her shoulders. "Darling. Have you met Uncle Frank and Aunt Louise? Uncle Frank is an investment counselor."

"That's right," said Frank. He shook Amanda's hand enthusiastically. "Frank Bromwell. It's a pleasure to meet you. I was just telling Josh that he should get together with me in the New Year. Now that you're thinking of settling down, you should also be thinking about retirement."

"What a splendid idea," Amanda enthused before Josh could say anything. "You really should do that, honey. It sounds fascinating." She slipped her hand through Josh's arm. "Will you excuse us, please? I need to have a word with Josh."

"You two go right ahead." Louise gave them a misty look. "We remember how it is, don't we, Frank?" They wandered off, arm in arm.

As soon as they were out of earshot, Josh turned to Amanda. "Well?" he whispered. "How are you doing? Have you found out anything personal about them yet?"

"Only that Marilla likes cats. Josh, we have to do something about this. These people..."

Josh shook his head. "We can't do anything about them, Amanda. They've always been like this."

"Well, I haven't always been like this. Josh, they think you and I are...are...romantically involved."

"Do they?" he asked, and he took another sip of his drink. "I wonder why."

Amanda narrowed her eyes. "You know very well why they think that!"

Josh made a futile attempt to look philosophical. "I seldom know why they think anything."

"Well, in this case, I believe it's obvious. *You*..."

Josh put a finger over her lips. "Shh. Someone will hear you."

"I want them to hear me. I..."

"Shh!" Josh said again. He took her hand and led her through the dining room and into the kitchen.

''Now, what's the problem?'' he asked as soon as they were alone.

Amanda withdrew her hand and backed into a white kitchen counter. ''What do you think the problem is?'' she snapped. ''The problem is that these people think we are...involved.'' Her voice rose. ''And they think that because *you* told them...''

Josh shrugged. ''I had to tell them something.'' She frowned and he sighed. ''Well, what was I supposed to say? I couldn't very well tell them that you're my Christmas elf, now could I?''

''There's a big difference between elf and...and what those people are thinking.''

''Not really.'' He put a hand on one shoulder and guided her further into the kitchen. ''Your flyer did say that you'd provide everything I need to have a Merry Christmas.''

Amanda was starting to heartily regret that flyer. ''Yes, but...''

''Well, right now it looks like I need a girlfriend. Otherwise they'll force one on me.''

''Then maybe you should find a real one!'' Amanda flung.

''What? Between now and five minutes from now?'' Josh shook his head. ''Not only is that impossible, but I don't want to do it. Besides, this is your big chance to find out something personal about all these people. Did you see how they reacted out there? They're all dying to meet you...to talk to you.''

''Yes, but...''

''So you shouldn't have any problem finding out something personal about them.'' He grinned triumphantly.

At that very second Amanda could have cheerfully throttled him. ''It's not as if they just think we're dating, Josh! They think we're...we're serious.''

''So?''

''So, it isn't true.''

He shrugged. ''They don't need to know that.''

Amanda gaped at him. ''Josh Larkland, that is the worst thing I've ever heard anyone say. You can't go around lying to your relatives...especially at Christmas.''

''I didn't lie! They just jumped to a conclusion, that's all.''

''A conclusion you did nothing to correct.''

''No, I didn't,'' Josh said. ''And I'm not going to, either.'' He gestured toward the living room. ''You saw what it's like out there. They've got women lined up wall-to-wall to meet me.''

Amanda thought of the three predatory women she'd been introduced to. ''Some of them could be very nice,'' she said, lying through her teeth.

''Ha!''

''Josh!''

''Oh, come on, Amanda. I don't have anything to say to the owner of a dress shop, a cat groomer, or someone trying to cast cosmic spells!''

Amanda wrinkled her nose. ''They are a little...eccentric I suppose. But that's still no reason...''

''It's a very good reason! If I wasn't here with you, they'd all pounce on me. Then they'd phone, asking when we could get together. Marilla, Charmaine, Mimi, my mother, and God knows who else would call me, asking me when I'm going to see them again. I'd have to think up some excuse, or else spend a lot of time seeing women I'm not the least bit interested in seeing. This way, I don't have to do that.'' He shrugged.

''Yes, but...''

''And as for my relatives, well, it pretty much serves them right! They're the ones who leapt to the wrong conclusion.''

''They had a very good reason to leap to the wrong conclusion. You—''

Josh held up a hand. ''Okay. Maybe I did give them a little nudge. But they were all ready to do it. And it's not as if we're hurting anyone. They're happy! And they all seem to like you.''

They did, too. As a matter of fact, Amanda couldn't remember the last time she'd been in a room where everyone thought she was the most marvelous human being on the face of the earth. ''Yes, they're happy now. But how happy will they be when they find out the truth?''

Josh looked baffled. ''How would they find that out? I'm not going to tell them.''

Could he possibly be this dense? ''You'll have to tell them something,'' Amanda explained very slowly. ''The next time you come to one of these things...''

Josh shrugged that off. ''I have no intention of coming to another one of these things anytime in the near future. That's part of your job, remember? You are going to come up with reasons why I can't.''

''But...''

''And if they ask, I'll just say I'm not seeing you anymore. That won't be a lie.''

''No, it wouldn't, but...''

Josh sighed and leaned against the kitchen cabinet next to her. ''Oh, come on, Amanda, don't make a big deal out of this. It's just one evening. All you have to do is exactly what you're doing. And it's a perfect opportunity for you to find out personal stuff about all these people."

It almost made sense, in a weird, illogical sort of way. Almost.

"Besides, what else can you do?" Josh asked. "You'll never convince those people you aren't involved with me. They *want* to believe it."

"Well, uh..."

"And who knows," Josh added, "it might be kind of fun."

"In what way?"

He stroked a finger down her cheek, making her shiver. "Lots of ways."

Amanda stepped away. "You were a really bad child, weren't you?"

"The very worst," he said solemnly.

Mimi's booming voice could be heard coming from the living room. "They're in the kitchen, Edwina. And I think they're kissing!"

"There, see," said Josh. "You really don't have any choice, do you?"

"THAT WAS MORE FUN than I've had at one of those things in decades," Josh announced as they climbed into his car a few hours later.

He sprawled back in the seat, one of his arms stretched along the back, his right thigh just touching hers. "As soon as everyone saw you, they pretty much left me alone." He glanced over at her, grinning. "I should have gotten an elf years ago." He started the car and pulled out into traffic.

"You should have gotten a girlfriend years ago,"

Amanda scolded. "Haven't you ever introduced a date to your family before?"

Josh considered it, then shook his head. "I don't think so. At least, not recently."

"Why not?" She glanced sideways at him. "You do have dates, don't you?"

"Of course I have dates," said Josh, sounding a little defensive about it. "But I don't take them home to meet my family the first time we go out."

Amanda thought about the way she'd been received. "That's probably a good idea," she agreed. "However, after you've been together a couple of months, you could do it. Or don't you date the same person that long?"

"Well, not usually, no."

"Why not?" Amanda asked, still looking at him.

"I don't know." He was starting to sound really defensive now. "I just get busy and...and don't." He angled his head so he could see her. "What about you? Do you date a lot?"

Amanda thought about the last couple of men she'd been involved with. They hadn't really "dated." She'd spent more time cleaning Dwight's apartment than they had going anywhere. She had been out with Kyle quite often—but that was just to a doughnut shop. He'd fed her endless cups of coffee while he'd told her about his problems. "Off and on," she muttered.

"And do you introduce these 'on and off' dates to your family?"

"I would," said Amanda. "But my family doesn't live anywhere around here."

"Where do they live, then? The North Pole?"

"No," said Amanda. "My parents live in Yellowknife."

"Yellowknife? As in the Northwest Territories?" Josh snorted. "That's close enough to the North Pole for me."

"Sometimes it does feel like the North Pole," Amanda admitted. "It's so far away. I don't get back there to visit as often as I'd like." Amanda would love to have family like his around. But her relatives were scattered all over the country. Her parents were up north. Her brother was down east and her sister was in the States. They kept in touch with phone calls but it wasn't the same as living in the same city. It seemed rather ironic. She'd enjoy being closer to her family, and Josh seemed to wish he didn't have a family.

Josh patted her arm. "You can always hitch a ride on Santa's sleigh. I'm sure he wouldn't mind an elf perched among the toys. And speaking of elves, how did your elf business go tonight? Did you find out a whole lot of personal stuff about people?"

"Not a lot." Amanda leaned back and closed her eyes. "They all wanted to talk about me. Or you."

"Me?" Josh sounded alarmed. "What did they say about me?"

"Only that you spend too much time in your office and not enough time with them."

"Oh." He chuckled. "They're always saying stuff like that. I don't know why. I spend lot of time with them."

"Sure you do," Amanda said dryly. "That's why you know so many personal things about them."

"I found out something," Josh objected. "I now know that Uncle Frank is an investment counselor."

"How insightful," Amanda muttered.

"Hey, you spent a whole evening with them and the only thing you seemed to have found out is that they don't think I spend enough time with them. That doesn't sound very personal to me."

"It's hard to find out personal things about that many people in one evening," Amanda retorted. "They're your relatives. If anyone should be finding out personal things about them it should be you." She paused. "Besides, I did find out something. Your aunt Mimi collects Halsone's."

"Halsone's? What are those?"

"You can't have missed them, Josh. They're all over the house. Those little rabbit ornaments."

"Oh, those." He blinked. "Are they personal?"

"If you collect them, they are. Personal...and expensive."

"How do you know these things?"

"They're in all the stores." She considered it. "I didn't see the clown one there. That might be a good one to get her."

"Good," said Josh. "One down. What about the others?"

"I'll...give it some thought." Now that she had a face to connect with names, it should be a little easier.

Josh parked the car in the loading zone in front of her apartment building, and walked her to her door. Amanda took the key out of her pocket and turned to face Josh. "Well, good night. Thanks for taking me. I enjoyed it."

"So did I," said Josh.

"I just hope they aren't going to be too upset when they find out I'm not your girlfriend."

"But you were," said Josh. "At least for tonight,

anyway.'' He put his hands on her shoulders, turning her to face him. ''And since you are, it seems to me...''

He was going to kiss her. Amanda realized it as his head started to descend. She could easily have stopped it. She could have moved away, or pushed him away.

But she didn't. She stood very still as he touched his lips to hers, lightly, then deeply. A soft, unthreatening kiss, filled with charm and warmth, while one of his fingers brushed down her cheek and his tongue stroked her lips. When he moved away, she was hot and shaky and gasping for breath. ''Good night, Amanda,'' he said, and then he was gone.

Amanda watched the door close after him. A business relationship, she reminded herself. That's all this was.

She was going to have to concentrate hard on keeping it that way.

4

"YOU'RE IN A GOOD MOOD this morning," Mable accused.

She set a stack of technical manuals on Josh's desk, and studied him with a mixture of suspicion and astonishment. "You haven't yelled at me once, you even said thank-you, and just now I thought I heard you whistling 'Santa Claus is Coming to Town.' What's going on?"

"Nothing is going on," said Josh. He chose one of the manuals from the stack and began flipping through it.

"Oh." Mable's suspicious look increased in intensity. "In that case, I can only conclude that your body has been taken over by aliens."

Josh chuckled. "My body hasn't been taken over by anything. I'm just in a good mood. After all, it is Christmas. People are supposed to be in a good mood around Christmas."

"You aren't," said Mable. "Christmas brings out the worst in you. Why, just yesterday you were trying to get me to reschedule it...or buy you a ticket to January."

"Or find me a Christmas elf," Josh reminded her. "Since you did that, you don't have to do any of those other things."

"A Christmas elf?" For a second Mable looked

blank. Then she smiled. ''Ah, yes. The woman from that executive services company. The one who's doing the Christmas party for us.''

''Uh-huh,'' said Josh. ''Along with other things.''

''Other things? What other things?'' Her eyes widened. ''Oh, no. Don't tell me you talked that poor young woman into doing your Christmas shopping for you?''

''She's...helping me with it.'' Josh saw the look of disapproval on Mable's face and winced. ''Is there something wrong with that?''

''Of course there's something wrong with it! Your mother didn't ask you to get personal presents for people just so you could slough it off on a stranger!''

Josh felt a pang of guilt, which he immediately suppressed. ''I didn't have any choice. You wouldn't do it, and I don't have time.'' He bent his head to avoid seeing the censure in Mable's eyes. ''Besides, Amanda isn't a stranger. She met everybody last night.''

''Last night?''

''That's right,'' said Josh. ''I took her to Mimi's party.''

''You went to Mimi's party?'' Mable's eyes widened. ''I thought you didn't go to family gatherings of more than four people.''

''I don't,'' said Josh. ''But I had to go to that one so Amanda could meet everybody and find out personal stuff about them.''

''Oh, for heaven's sake, Josh!'' Mable exclaimed. She put her hands on her hips and positively glared at him. ''That is the tackiest thing I've ever heard of. They are *your* relatives, you know. If anyone is going to find out personal things about them, it should be you!''

Josh winced. ''Yeah, well, Amanda mentioned something like that herself.''

''Did she?'' said Mable.

''Yeah.'' Josh mulled it over, then shoved the small concern aside. ''But I'm sure she'll manage.''

''I think she just might,'' said Mable. She smiled. ''You know, I think I'm going to like Amanda.''

''Of course you'll like her. Everyone likes an elf.'' Josh looked up. ''But don't go spreading it around that that's what she is. I don't want anybody to know that I've got an elf.''

''You don't have to worry about that,'' Mable muttered. ''That's one secret that's safe with me.'' She walked out, shaking her head.

Josh watched her leave, then switched on his computer. This was working out wonderfully. His Christmas problems were solved. He could forget all about it and get back to concentrating on work.

''JUST A MINUTE,'' said Brandy. ''I'll see if she's in.'' She put a hand over the receiver and raised an eyebrow in Amanda's direction. ''It's someone named Charmaine,'' she announced in a stage whisper. Amanda shook her head. Brandy sighed and put the receiver to her ear again. ''I'm sorry, Charmaine, she can't come to phone right now. Yes...yes, I'll tell her you called.'' She hung up the phone and turned around. ''That was Charmaine,'' she said unnecessarily. ''Let me guess. She's related to Josh Larkland.''

''Uh-huh,'' said Amanda.

''I figured as much.'' Brandy dropped into a

kitchen chair. "At least it wasn't Harvy Denton again. He's called three times this morning to apologize. I'm starting to think he really is sorry."

"Maybe he is," said Amanda. "He did send you flowers. And didn't he say he got the wrong impression yesterday?"

"Uh-huh. He said he thought I was gorgeous and when I sat down and asked him how I could make his Christmas merrier, he thought I was making a pass at him."

Amanda pictured the sultry-looking Brandy saying those words. "It is possible that..."

"Maybe it is," Brandy interrupted. "But that still doesn't make it right. He should have *asked* before he lunged." She folded her arms. "I told him that, too."

"Oh? And what did he say?"

"He agreed with me." Brandy's lips twitched into a smile. "But he explained it by saying that he hadn't had much experience dating since his divorce and that he thought that might be the way it was done these days. Can you imagine?"

Amanda was starting to feel a little sorry for Harvy Denton. "Well," she said. "I suppose it is possible...."

"I suppose," said Brandy. "Now he wants me to come back to the office and give him another chance. I've told him no three times, but he just isn't getting the message."

"Maybe you should give him another chance," Amanda said tentatively. "Maybe he is a nice guy. If you want, we could go together and..."

"I've had enough wrestling matchcs for one month. Forget it, Amanda. I don't want to have anything to do with Harvy. He's a creep. Once a creep, always a creep."

"You never know," said Amanda. Her mind reverted to their most recent phone call. "What did Charmaine say?"

"The same thing as everyone else...she wants to get together with you." Brandy gave her a curious look. "These relatives of Josh Larkland's have been calling you all morning. So far we've had Judith, who wants to have tea with you. Shelby, who wanted to make sure you'd come to her party. And now Charmaine, who wanted you to go to some sort of cosmetology class."

"Not cosmetology," Amanda corrected. "Cosmicology."

"What's that?"

"It has something to do with being connected with the galaxy." She leaned back in the kitchen chair. "It's too bad I can't get together with Charmaine. It might be interesting." She wouldn't mind having tea with Aunt Judith, either, or going to Shelby's.

"So why don't you?"

"I can't, Brandy. The only reason these people want to get together with me is because they think I'm Josh's girlfriend. And I'm not." She frowned down at her list on the table, wishing that the business would really take off so they could start working out of an office, and finally get out of her kitchen.

Brandy ran her fingers through her hair. "We've had more phone calls this morning than we've had since we started this business. If they were about business, I'd be ecstatic. But they aren't. They're either Mr. Denton for me, or a bunch of Josh's relatives for you." She put her head to one side and stared at

Amanda. "What did you do to those people anyway?"

"I didn't do anything except walk into a room." Amanda picked up a cup of coffee from the table. As she drank it, she studied the list of Josh's relatives in front of her. "It was remarkable, Brandy. I have never been so socially accepted in my entire life. Everyone wanted to talk to me. It was almost like being back home."

"I don't suppose they wanted to talk about arranging some sort of business party?" Brandy said dryly.

"I'm afraid not." Amanda studied the list, then sighed loudly. "Unfortunately, they didn't want to talk about Christmas presents, either. All they wanted to talk about was me...or Josh."

"All you want to talk about is Josh," Brandy complained. "Since I've got here you've said his name about three hundred times."

"No, I haven't," Amanda objected, although she knew it wasn't true. Her mind did keep drifting off into happy little tangents about the sparkle in Josh's eyes, the feel of his cheek brushing against hers, the warmth of his lips... Amanda gave her head a slight shake. "I'm just trying to come up with suitable presents for these people."

"It's more than that," Brandy said disapprovingly as she leaned forward. "You're falling for Josh Larkland, aren't you?"

"No, I'm not," Amanda said firmly. "He is a sweet guy, though, Brandy. Charming when he wants to be. Good-looking." And a great kisser, too. She didn't think Brandy needed to know about that. "And he has a really nice family."

''Who he doesn't care about one little bit,'' Brandy reminded her.

''I'm not sure that's true,'' Amanda objected. ''I think he cares about them. He did spend most of the evening asking them how old they were and what they did for a living.''

''Something he already should have known,'' Brandy noted, sounding less than impressed.

''And he gets tired of them always criticizing him,'' Amanda said, ignoring her. ''They're always trying to line him up with someone. You should have seen the women they produced at Mimi's. I don't think they realize that some men just don't want to be lined up. As a matter of fact, I don't think they understand him at all.''

''That makes two of us,'' Brandy muttered. ''Or, in his case, twenty-two of us.''

''He's not that difficult to understand. He's just one of those people who's totally wrapped up in his work.'' Amanda stared off into space again. ''It's a simple lack of communication. He doesn't communicate with his family and they don't communicate with him. If they got together more often...''

''Don't do it, Amanda,'' Brandy warned.

''Don't do what?'' Amanda said, looking up with an innocent expression.

''Get involved in this. You're an executive services person, not a family therapist.''

''I know,'' Amanda said softly. ''But it *is* Christmas.''

''You can't reform people, even at Christmas. You certainly can't reform men. It's like getting something on sale. What you see is what you get—missing buttons and all.''

"I'm not..."

"You're thinking about it. We've both done this before. We date a guy whose an obvious loser, with the hopes of changing him. It never works. *Never.*" She raised an eyebrow. "Remember Kyle? You paid for all the dates, and spent hours listening to his problems. Then he dumped you and went off with some bimbo cocktail waitress from Vancouver."

"Actually she was from Victoria. And..."

"Then there was Dwight," Brandy said, warming to the topic. "You lent him money, helped him get a job, and as soon as he got a few bucks together, he announced he wasn't ready for any sort of commitment."

Amanda shifted in the chair, her face heating up. "All right," she said. "Maybe I do have lousy taste in men. But this time it's different."

"Yeah right! Not only are you getting involved with Josh Larkland, you're also getting involved with his entire extended family!"

"I'm not getting involved with any of them," Amanda said in an unconvincing tone.

Brandy threw up her hands. "That's not how it sounds," she said, sounding skeptical.

"Well, that's how it is. I doubt I'll see his family again—unless I happen to run into them on the street." Which she fervently hoped wouldn't happen. She couldn't imagine what she'd say to them. "And I won't be seeing Josh again, either," she added.

"You won't?"

"No, I won't. At least, not the way you mean. Oh, I'll probably run into him a few times while I'm organizing his officc party, although I suspect I'll be spending more time with his secretary than I will with him.''

Brandy didn't look persuaded. Not one bit. ''You're sure of that?''

''Absolutely positive.'' She was, too. In spite of the wonderful evening and terrific kiss, she knew very well that Josh wasn't interested in her. She was his Christmas elf, that's all—the person who was going to solve all his Christmas problems. She doubted he even remembered her name this morning.

IN TRUTH, Josh wasn't having any problems remembering Amanda's name—or a lot of other things about her.

She'd drifted across his mind more than once this morning—odd thought fragments about the silky feel of her blond hair, the way she'd looked in that red dress, and the tantalizing touch of her mouth against his. Memories of Amanda kept disturbing his concentration. So far this morning he had gotten nowhere on the network interface he was supposed to be redesigning.

And if he hadn't had his own unruly memories to remind him about Amanda, there was always his family.

A number of them had called this morning to wax enthusiastically about her. ''She's absolutely delightful, Josh.'' ''Such a charming girl, Josh.'' And, from his Aunt Judith, for some obscure reason, ''She's so intriguing, Josh. I understand she has a green bathroom.'' It seemed everyone approved of her—and wanted to see her again.

At first Josh had enjoyed their approval. However, when his mother called, he started to feel a tiny bit guilty. So when Edwina said, "I must say, there have been times when I wasn't sure if you were going to settle down—or what kind of girl you'd settle down with. It's such a relief to know that you've found someone like Amanda," he tried to tone things down. "We aren't exactly settled down, Mom."

"I know, dear," Edwina said in a wise-sounding voice. "But you are going to keep on seeing her, aren't you?"

"Of course I'm going to keep on seeing her," Josh muttered. Come to think of it, though, he didn't know *when* he'd see Amanda again. She'd be off doing elf-type stuff and he'd be working.

He gave his head a slight shake. Of course he was going to see her again. She was his elf. Apart from that, there was that kiss to consider. His mind reverted to the soft, luscious feel of her lips, only to be dragged back by Edwina's cheerful "In that case, I think I should get to know her better."

"Do you?" Josh was still enjoying the warm rush he was experiencing remembering Amanda's kiss.

"Yes. I'd like to have lunch with her sometime."

"Sure," Josh muttered absently.

"How about today?"

"Today?" Josh straightened in his chair. "I don't know about today."

"Then how about tomorrow?"

"I'm...uh...not sure," Josh mumbled. "I'll have to check with Amanda."

"Could you do that, dear? I've been trying to get her all morning but she wasn't available. Maybe when you're talking to her..."

Josh was almost positive he knew what Amanda's reaction would be, but before he could think of a way to put his mother off, she'd said goodbye and hung up.

Josh had just replaced the receiver when Mable buzzed through on the intercom. "Hank Turnbull on line one," she reported.

Josh studied the blinking light, then picked up the phone. "Hi, Hank. What's up?"

Hank's baritone, smooth and rich, eased out of the receiver. "To be perfectly honest, I'm calling to check out the gossip."

"Gossip?" Josh echoed. "What gossip?"

"About you." Hank chuckled. "I understand there's a new woman in your life."

Josh gave the phone a quizzical look. He'd been dealing with Hank for over a year now. Apart from mentioning his wife and kids, and once having to leave a meeting early to attend his son's hockey game, Hank had never made a personal remark about himself, or Josh. "Oh?" Josh said slowly. "How did you hear that?"

"Well..." Hank chuckled again. "Ed Baigly was talking to Jon Fieldman, who knows your uncle Reginald. He mentioned you brought a woman home to meet the family last night."

Josh had no idea why Hank would be interested in something as far away from business as this. "Uh-huh."

"So it's true, then?"

"Yeah, it's true." Josh was intrigued by Hank's interest. "Why are you..."

"It's not just idle curiosity," Hank assured him. "It's business."

Josh struggled to understand what Hank was talking about. "Business?"

"That's right. This might be exactly what we need to push some of those potential investors into current investors."

"Huh?"

"It's a question of reliability," Hank explained. "Everyone knows you're brilliant, but it's the other things that make people nervous. A married man does seem less risky. More solid. More mature."

"A married man?" Josh repeated, startled. "I'm not..."

"No, I know you're not, but from the way Reg was talking it sounds as if that's just around the corner." Hank chuckled. "Is she going to be at your office Christmas party?"

"I expect so, but..."

"Excellent. Excellent. Be sure to introduce her around. Oh, and why don't you bring her to our open house next week? Rhonda and I would like to meet her."

"I'll...uh...have to check with Amanda," Josh improvised. "I'm not sure of our schedule."

He hung up the phone and tapped his fingers thoughtfully on his desk. His Christmas elf was turning out to be more helpful—and more necessary—than he'd originally planned.

IT WAS JUST BEFORE ELEVEN when Josh phoned. Brandy was out trying to drum up more business so Amanda was forced to answer the phone. "People have been trying to get you all morning," he complained when Amanda said a tentative hello. "Where have you been?"

Amanda lost herself in the sound of his voice. She

could picture him sitting in his office, with papers strewn all over his desk. "In and out."

"Shopping?" he asked eagerly.

Of course. That's why he was calling. "I'm working on it," Amanda said.

"Good. Listen, are you free for lunch?"

Amanda's spirits rose. "Why, yes, I am."

"Great. My mother wants to have lunch with you."

Amanda bounced from dreamland back into reality. "Your mother?"

"Uh-huh. She wants to get to know you better."

"Wonderful," Amanda said sarcastically. This was some switch. Usually it was the mother who didn't like the girlfriend. This time, it was only the mother who liked the girlfriend—and she wasn't really a girlfriend. "I don't think that's a good idea."

"You don't?" Josh sounded as clued out as usual. "Why not?"

Honestly! "Because I don't." Amanda tapped her foot with irritation. "I told you last night that I didn't want to keep misleading your family."

"You also told me last night that you didn't find out a whole lot of personal things about everyone."

"True, but..."

"This would be a great opportunity to find out more. You could quiz my mother. I'm sure she knows a lot of personal stuff about people."

There were still a lot of question marks on her gift list. Edwina would undoubtedly be an excellent source of information. "I suppose it would, but..."

"Then why don't we have lunch with her and find out something?"

"I really don't..." Amanda paused. "Are you coming, too?"

"Sure. I can give you a hand with the personal stuff. Besides, there's something I need to discuss with you."

Amanda started to refuse again, then reconsidered. From what she'd heard last night, she'd say it had been a long time since Josh had lunched with his mother—or done anything else with her. Edwina would be so pleased if he did. It *would* give Amanda a chance to find out more about Josh's relatives—maybe enable her to fill in a few blanks on her Christmas shopping list.

And besides, she wouldn't mind seeing him again, either.

"All right," she said. "I suppose..."

"Good," said Josh. "Twelve o'clock at Charbais. And don't be late. Mom hates it when people are late."

Amanda hung up the phone and smiled. At least that was *one* thing Josh knew about his mother.

IT WAS TWO MINUTES PAST twelve when Amanda walked into Charbais. Edwina was already seated. Josh was nowhere in sight.

He'd better make an appearance, Amanda thought as she followed the maître d' to the table. Getting Josh together with his mother was the main reason she'd accepted this invitation. She also intended to find out as much as she could about Edwina as well as the other members of the family. Then she could erase all the question marks on her gift list. Furthermore, she was determined to convince Edwina that her relationship with Josh was extremely casual.

Actually, convincing Edwina probably wouldn't be the difficult part. The difficult part was that Amanda couldn't bring herself to do it. Edwina was so...delighted. Amanda realized that about six seconds after she was seated in the elegant upscale restaurant. "I'm so pleased you could come," Edwina said as the maître d' handed Amanda a menu. "I want to get to know you better." She reached across the table to squeeze Amanda's hand. "I want us to be friends."

Amanda doubted Josh's mother would feel that way if she knew the truth. "I'd like that, too," she said. She took a long swallow of water. "But I really should explain that Josh and I...that is, our relationship is very, uh, casual."

"Oh, dear," Edwina said faintly. She took a sip from her water glass. "I was afraid you were going to say something like that."

Amanda gaped at her. "You were?"

"Yes." Her lips turned down at the corners. "It's us, isn't it? We scared you off last night."

She looked so despondent that Amanda rushed to reassure her. "Oh, no. You were all wonderful. It's just that..."

"I know, dear." Edwina stretched forward to pat her hand. "You have to understand, Amanda. We've all been so concerned about Josh. We don't see much of him. He buries himself in his office and doesn't come out for weeks at a time. And he really doesn't have much of a life—or if he does, he doesn't share it with us."

"I do understand, but..."

"I blame myself, you know. After all, I did marry a man with three daughters. Not that there's anything wrong with them." Her forehead creased. "Charmaine can be a bit odd at times, and Marilla can be excessive about her cats. But Shelby is a darling. And they all mean well.''

''Of course they do,'' Amanda assured her. ''I liked all of them. And I'm sure your marriage...''

''It might have,'' said Edwina, sighing. ''Josh was seven when I remarried. The girls are much older and...well, they spoiled him. So did Mimi and Louise. They're Harold's sisters. Unfortunately, neither of them have children so they lavished all their attention on Josh. It was easy to do, even then. He's an easy person to like, don't you think?''

''He certainly is.''

''He's also a little self-centered, and he's much too fond of getting his own way. That's partly because he's very clever, and party because of us.''

''I don't think...''

''Yes, he is. But he can also be amazingly thoughtful, and exceedingly generous, when he gets around to thinking about it. The trouble is, he doesn't think about it very much anymore.'' She smiled sadly. ''Now that you're part of his life, I hope he'll think about it more often. And maybe we'll see a little more of him, too.''

Amanda would have loved to be able to tell this sweet woman that this was going to happen. Unfortunately, that wasn't the case. She took a deep breath. ''I'm not really part—'' She started.

What she was trying to say was interrupted by a commotion at the entrance. Amanda looked up to see Josh striding through the restaurant. He had on a pair of black jeans, his hair had obviously been combed by a hand, his running shoes were covered in snow, and every woman in the place was staring at him.

He stopped beside their table, and bent to kiss his mother on the cheek. ‘‘Hi, Mom. Sorry I'm late.’’

Edwina gaped at him. ‘‘I didn't realize you were joining us.’’

‘‘You didn't?’’ He settled into a chair beside Amanda and smiled into her eyes. ‘‘Didn't Amanda tell you?’’

Edwina shot Amanda a quizzical look. ‘‘She didn't mention it.’’

‘‘It must have slipped her mind.’’ He took Amanda's hand and slid his fingers through hers. ‘‘She left so early this morning I didn't have much of a chance to talk to her.’’

‘‘She left early?’’ Edwina looked from one to the other. ‘‘You two are…living together?’’

Amanda was still recovering from the sensation of his fingers closing around hers. ‘‘What?’’ she said. ‘‘Oh, no. No, we're…that is, I have my own place. I…’’

‘‘Yes, she does,’’ Josh interrupted. ‘‘She just doesn't seem to spend a lot of time there.’’

‘‘Ah,’’ said Edwina. ‘‘I see.’’

‘‘No, you don't,’’ Amanda said desperately. ‘‘It's not like that. I…’’

‘‘That's okay, dear,’’ Edwina soothed. ‘‘I understand completely…and I'm not at all prudish.’’ She beamed at both of them, emanating happiness and approval. Josh looked smug.

Amanda sighed and gave up.

5

"THAT WAS WONDERFUL," Edwina said as they left the restaurant. She turned to Amanda. "Thanks so much for coming, Amanda, dear. I hope I'll be seeing a lot more of you."

I wouldn't count on it, Amanda thought. She'd hardly heard a word that had been spoken at lunch, being too preoccupied trying to find a way out of the situation she'd found herself in. She'd even considered telling Edwina the truth, but couldn't bring herself to do it. It might be what Josh deserved, but it wasn't what Edwina deserved. She'd be very hurt. No matter how annoyed Amanda was with Josh, she didn't want to upset Edwina.

She didn't feel that way about Josh, though. The second they were alone, she planned on telling him what an utter jerk she thought he was. She was also going to tell him what he could do with his job. He could figure out what to tell his relations. She winced at that. He was quite capable of telling them Amanda had been bumped off in a plane crash or had accepted a job in Siberia.

Outside the restaurant, Edwina gave Josh an extra-long hug. "I can't remember the last time we had lunch together. We really should do it more often." Then she affectionately patted his cheek. "And I hope you fixed that stove of yours for Amanda. It seems to me the last time I was there you had to do something with the television to get the burners to come on.''

As Edwina walked away Amanda stared after her, then turned on Josh. ''All right, Josh Larkland, what was that all about?''

''Hmm?'' He glanced down at her. ''Actually it was about the microwave.''

''What?''

Josh put a hand on her back to guide her down the busy street. ''You had to talk to the microwave to turn on the television. It was a simple problem...and I fixed it months ago.''

''I wasn't talking about that. I was talking about what happened at lunch.''

''Lunch?'' Josh looked as if he'd forgotten he'd eaten it. ''Oh, yeah, lunch. How was it? Did you find out anything personal about...anyone?''

''Only about myself,'' Amanda complained. ''Just out of idle curiosity, how did we go from casual friends to living together in a little under twenty-four hours?''

Josh stopped beside a bell-ringing Santa Claus and dropped a handful of change into the collection box. ''I'm a fast worker when I make up my mind.'' He shoved his hands into his pockets, pulled out a couple of bills and dropped them in, as well, before starting down the street. ''I think I fixed that problem with the microwave sometime in the spring.''

''Good for you. Look, I...''

''Do you really think it's been that long since my mother was over at my place?''

''No. Maybe you should have her over a little more often.''

"That's a good idea," Josh said. "Why don't you arrange it?"

The suggestion caught Amanda off guard. Why didn't she arrange it? Maybe they could have more than his mother over. Maybe they could have his whole family. His family would certainly appreciate it. Of course Amanda had no idea how he lived. He probably had a downtown apartment ten seconds from his office, filled with ugly furniture and a truckload of high-tech equipment. It might not be a good place to entertain his family. On the other hand, they were his family. They had a right to know how he lived...

And that it wasn't with her. Amanda stopped walking and turned to face Josh. "Me? What do you mean, me?"

Josh stopped beside her and stared down at her with mild surprise. "You did say dinner parties were your specialty."

"*Business* dinner parties are my specialty," Amanda said from between clenched teeth.

"What's the difference? People eat and drink whether you work with them or are related to them."

"Yes, but..." Amanda gave her head a slight shake. She had to watch herself around this guy. He could use his weird logic to talk her into almost anything. "That is not the point! The point is that we can't go around deceiving people about our relationship."

"Why not?" he said nonchalantly. "You were perfectly willing to do it last night."

"I was not *willing* to do it last night! *You* talked me into it." Amanda realized she was raising her voice and lowered it a notch. "Besides, that was only supposed to be for one night. Now your mother thinks we're living together!''

''Yeah, well...uh.'' Josh cleared his throat. ''She's not the only one who thinks that.''

Amanda wasn't sure what he meant but she was positive she wasn't going to like it. ''She isn't?''

''No.'' Josh took a deep breath. ''Hank Turnbull called this morning. He's the guy who's lining up investors for me.''

''Oh?'' Amanda stared at him. ''Oh, no. Don't tell me you told him that we were living together, too?''

''Not exactly.'' Josh looked uncomfortable. ''He heard about us from Uncle Reggie.''

''Wonderful,'' Amanda muttered. She had a brief flash of all the people who'd been at Mimi's last night. If every one of them told a friend... ''Now the whole city thinks we're a couple.''

Josh gave her a bracing pat on the shoulder. ''Don't worry. They're all thrilled about it.''

''I'm not,'' Amanda muttered.

''Well, Hank is. It seems as if these investors aren't going to invest unless they think I'm mature and stable. Hank thinks I need some sort of...relationship to convince them of that.'' Josh looked as flummoxed by this as he did by everything else.

''I see,'' said Amanda. She had a strong suspicion she knew where this was leading. ''And I suppose you want me to pretend we have this...relationship.''

''Uh-huh,'' he said, nodding his head.

Amanda glanced up and down the street at the people hurrying by. ''Have you ever considered having a *real* relationship?''

''No,'' Josh admitted. ''But I would have if I'd known it was important.''

The helpless look in his brown eyes was enough to make the snow melt, much less Amanda's soft heart. Then he spoiled it by adding, "Besides, now I don't have to. I've got you."

"But..."

"It's too late to back out now, Amanda. My family thinks you're it, and apparently so does everyone else."

Amanda slumped back against the building. "Oh, no."

"What's wrong?" His eyes widened. "There isn't some guy hanging around you who is going to get mad about this, is there?"

"Well...no, but..."

"Good." He smiled in satisfaction. "I don't want some bozo in a leather jacket punching my face in."

"How about if a woman in a business suit does it?" Amanda asked, feeling very close to doing just that.

Josh chuckled. "I think I can handle an elf. Look, I'm not asking you to do anything unreasonable. I mean, you don't have to move in with me or anything."

"Good," said Amanda. "Because I wasn't planning on it. I am not going to do this, Josh. Deceiving your family for one night was bad enough. I..."

"It's for a good cause, Amanda."

"What cause? Getting your family off your back?" She shook her head. "I don't think..."

Josh took her arm. "Come on," he said. "There's something I want to show you."

AMANDA HAD BEEN in a number of high-tech offices but she'd never seen one quite like the room Josh had just ushered her into.

It was an enormous room, with wall-to-wall gray carpeting that went a foot up the side of the white walls. The ceiling was a continuous series of undulating ripples, and the walls were cut to match. The shelves at the back were filled with electronic equipment with hundreds of little blinking lights like an enormous, flat, wall-to-wall Christmas tree. The long counter was covered with computers, screens and stacks of paper.

The perimeter of the room was composed of six glassed-in compartments, each containing a desk, one or two computers, screens and equipment. All but one of these areas was occupied by one or two clever-looking individuals, some engaged in animated conversation. However, the place where Amanda was standing was so quiet and so still she could have heard a pin drop. "What on earth..." she said.

"They're soundproof rooms," Josh explained. "Come on." He took her arm and led her toward the one empty cubicle. "Open," he said. As they approached, the glass doors swung open.

Josh urged her through them. "Lights," he said. "Dim fifty percent." The lights dimmed.

"That's...uh...impressive," Amanda said inadequately.

"Hey, that's just the easy stuff." He gestured toward the desk, where a television, a VCR and a radio sat side by side. "Television," Josh said. "Channel Four. Mute sound."

Amanda stared in astonishment as the appliance followed orders.

"It's part of the smart house concept," Josh explained. ''I'm working with a builder now. Someday all this will be standard features in new houses.''

Amanda turned around the room, staring in awe at what she was seeing. ''It's remarkable,'' she said inadequately.

''They aren't just high-tech toys, Amanda, although that's how a lot of people see them,'' he said, brimming with excitement. ''There are other people who would see them as a great deal more. People who have problems with mobility, for example. Voice-controlled units would make life a lot easier for them.''

It struck Amanda how wonderful this would be for someone in that position.

''But I need a large capital investment to get this from the preliminary stages into full production. And to do that, I need you.''

''I don't know, Josh. I...''

''I wouldn't expect you to do it for nothing, Amanda.''

'Oh?'' Amanda's annoyance returned in full force. Brandy was right. This guy was a real creep. Next to him, Dwight and Kyle were saints! ''What are you suggesting? That you *pay* me to date you? Because if you are...''

Josh held up a hand. ''Not money, no. That would be a little...tacky, wouldn't it?''

''Yes, it would.''

''I thought so. But I do have something else.'' He put a hand in his pocket and pulled out a piece of paper. ''I made a few phone calls this morning. Friends of mine. Business acquaintances.''

Amanda eyed the list. ''Why? So you could tell them we were living together, too?''

Josh grinned. "No. I'll let them hear that on the street like everyone else. I just found out which ones were planning business functions in the near future—functions that would require an executive services company." He raised an eyebrow. "You help me. I'll help you."

Amanda stared at the list. This was more than a foot in the door. This was a whole body in the door. "This is more extortion, isn't it?"

He smiled. "Actually, I think it's more like a bribe."

"It's a pretty good one," Amanda admitted.

"It is, isn't it?" He looked pleased with himself. "And it wouldn't be all that difficult for you. You simply have to do what you agreed to in the first place. Handle this Christmas present stuff. Arrange my office Christmas party. Attend a couple of business things with me. And let people go on thinking you're my…significant other for a while."

Amanda hesitated, amazed at herself for even considering it. "How long would this go on?"

"Not all that long," Josh assured her. "Just up until after my office Christmas party."

"Your office Christmas party? But that's December twenty-third."

"Perfect," said Josh. "Then you'll be free to go back to the North Pole on Christmas Eve to give Santa a hand."

Amanda studied him. He was lounging against the wall, looking cool and confident and sure of himself. He's far too accustomed to getting his own way, Edwina had told her. And Edwina was right.

Still, it was an offer that was almost impossible to refuse. Not only would she be helping their business, she'd also be helping a lot of other people who really needed help. Plus there was his family to consider. Edwina already thought Amanda and Josh were living together—and she could very well be spreading that information to the rest of his family. Apart from telling them the entire story, there wasn't much Amanda could do about that. Besides, if everyone reacted the same way as Edwina, they'd all be thrilled that Josh had a relationship. Would it be so terrible if she let them go on being thrilled a little while longer?

She didn't really have to do that much more than she'd already agreed to do. All she had to do was play the part of his girlfriend for the rest of the month, attend a couple of business functions, organize an office Christmas party, and find out something personal about every one of his relatives…all without getting too involved with Josh or his family.

''Well,'' she said. ''I suppose…''

And then she stopped. Maybe it was the hint of triumph in Josh's eyes—or perhaps it was the fact that she'd been held hostage in her apartment all morning by his relatives. Or maybe it was simply because of her recent lunch with his mother. But it suddenly occurred to Amanda that she might just be able to use this situation to get Edwina—and the rest of Josh's family—what they all really wanted for Christmas. A little more time with him.

Don't get involved, Brandy had told her. Amanda decided to throw caution to the winds. ''If I'm going to do this, I'm going to need some help.''

Josh looked faintly alarmed. ''What sort of help?''

''I'm going to need to know a little more about your family if I'm going to get them decent Christmas presents. It seems to me that you could help me out in that area.''

Josh shoved a hand through his hair. ''How? I've already told you everything I know about them.''

Amanda pursed her lips. ''I'm sure if you spent a little more time with them, you could find out a little more.''

Josh's eyes widened. ''That sounds a lot like blackmail.''

''No,'' Amanda corrected. ''Actually I believe it comes more under the heading of extortion.''

Josh stared at her in outright surprise. Then he chuckled. ''You catch on fast, don't you?''

''Yes, I do,'' said Amanda, already a little appalled at her own audacity. ''Us elves are a pretty clever bunch.''

''I must remember that.'' He grinned. ''Yeah, okay. I guess I deserve it. Although you didn't have to resort to extortion to do it. I was thinking something along those lines myself.''

It was Amanda's turn to be surprised. ''You were?''

''Uh-huh. I do have an awful lot of relatives. It was unreasonable to expect you to find out something personal about them all by yourself, in one evening. And I'm sure I can find out a few things. I did figure out that Uncle Frank is an investment counselor.''

''Yes, you did,'' Amanda agreed, hiding her smile.

''Besides, they are my relatives. I suppose I should know something personal about them.''

''You certainly should,'' Amanda agreed.

Josh winced. ''Okay, I'll tell you what. How about if we go to a couple more of these family things?

That would give us both a chance to find out personal things about people.''

Amanda felt a surge of triumph that almost immediately faded. ''We? I didn't mean...''

''Hey, you're the elf around here. If I have to go, you have to go.'' He tugged on his bottom lip. ''Besides, I suppose if we want people to think we're a couple, we should go a few places as a couple.''

That's just what she needed...to go a few more places with him. ''I suppose so,'' she said. ''But...''

''Terrific,'' said Josh. ''I guess we're now officially living together.''

''Right,'' said Amanda. He started to move toward her and she took a tentative step back. ''But I want to make it perfectly clear that this is strictly a business relationship.''

''A business relationship,'' Josh repeated. He stopped where he was, his gaze met hers, he smiled his slow, sexy smile, and although there was an entire room between them, Amanda was positive she could feel the heat emanating from his body. ''Of course. What else would it be?''

''What else, indeed,'' Amanda murmured.

6

"I DON'T LIKE THIS," Brandy said.

She was sitting in one of the chairs in Amanda's living room, radiating disapproval. "It might have been better if you'd turned down the business, given the guy a good hard smack, and left."

"I couldn't do that," Amanda insisted, although she was already half wishing that she had. "There was that list of contacts...this room filled with the most wonderful equipment that would help thousands of people...and it was the perfect opportunity to get Josh to spend more time with his family. I just couldn't say no."

"Maybe you should have tried harder," Brandy suggested. "It sounds to me as if this guy just wants to get you into a bedroom! Conning you into pretending to live with him. Really!"

"Getting me into a bedroom is the farthest thing from Josh's mind," Amanda assured her. "And it's not as if I'm really going to be living with him. He told me quite specifically that I didn't have to move in." She felt a small burst of feminine pique at that. He hadn't even tried to talk her into moving in. Not that she would have done it, but...

"That was big of him," Brandy grunted. "Look, Amanda, I do understand why you're doing this. And I certainly appreciate what it could do for our business. But you didn't have to go to these lengths to do it. As it turns out, I managed to get a little business for us myself this afternoon.''

''Oh?''

''Yes, I...uh...'' Brandy looked a little sheepish. ''I agreed to do Harvy Denton's office party for him.''

Amanda was astonished by that. ''You *what?*''

''He called again while you were out, and I decided the only way to get rid of him was to see him again.''

''You should have waited for me, Brandy. I...''

''I was pretty sure I could handle Harvy. And nothing happened.'' Brandy's lips flickered into a smile. ''He had his receptionist stay in the room with us the whole time. I stood at the door. Harvy stood at the far end of his office, with his hands held up in front of his chest. It looked as if he was afraid I'd attack him!'' She shrugged. ''He apologized...again! Then he asked me if we'd consider handling the Denton Christmas party.''

''And you said yes?'' Amanda exclaimed. ''I thought you weren't going to have anything to do with the guy.''

''I wasn't.'' Brandy looked guilty. ''But he seemed so...pathetic, Amanda. And we do need the business.''

''See,'' Amanda said. ''You're doing the same thing I'm doing.''

''Am not,'' Brandy said. ''This is strictly a business deal. I'm not getting involved with the guy.''

''I'm not getting involved, either,'' said Amanda. She thought about Josh's slow, sexy smile and drew in a breath. Brandy was right. The last thing she wanted to do was get involved with Josh Larkland, in any way, shape or form. He was too attractive—and he seemed to be able to talk her into anything. He also had heartbreaker written all over him. From the sound of things, he hadn't had a serious relationship in his life, and Amanda wasn't dumb enough to think he'd start with her. The only reason he was going through this charade was because of his business. "This is strictly a business deal, too. We're just pretending to be involved. And it's only going to be until Christmas."

"Just be careful," Brandy warned. "You don't want to find a broken heart in your stocking Christmas morning."

IT WASN'T A BROKEN HEART Amanda was worried about a couple of days later.

It was a lump of coal.

She walked along between Marilla and her husband Tom, feeling worse and worse with each step. It wasn't because of the cat show they were attending, although she had discovered that an hour of looking at cats was more than enough. It was because she felt so immensely, immensely guilty.

It was a familiar feeling. Amanda had felt that way when she'd had lunch with Edwina, and yesterday when she'd had tea with Josh's aunt Judith. Today it was stronger than ever.

If she'd had any sense, she would have said no when Marilla called this morning and invited her attend the cat show with them. "I'm sure you'll enjoy it," Marilla had assured her. "Besides, it will give us a chance to get to know each other." Amanda hadn't been able to think of a reason to refuse.

Now she wished she'd tried harder.

They stopped beside a cage holding two fluffy silver animals. ''These are excellent Persians,'' Marilla advised. ''Aren't they lovely?''

''Spectacular,'' Amanda said. She glanced around the crowded auditorium. ''I had no idea there were this many different kinds of cats in the world.''

''There are hundreds of species,'' Marilla announced. She took Amanda's arm. ''I'm so pleased that Josh met someone like you, Amanda.''

''Are you?'' Amanda said. She wasn't. As a matter of fact, she was beginning to regret she'd ever laid eyes on the man.

''Yes. That's what we all want for Josh. For him to settle down—and raise a family.''

''A family?'' Amanda repeated. She closed her eyes and issued a fervent prayer that Marilla wouldn't suggest this to Josh. He might tell her that kids were on their way, just to make his relatives all happy. Then he'd expect Amanda to produce a few—all before Christmas! ''We aren't even close to the family stage,'' she said.

''I'm sure it will come up.'' Marilla squeezed Amanda's arm. ''You know, Amanda, there are times when Tom and I find Josh a little intimidating. Don't we, Tom?''

''We certainly do,'' Tom said.

Since Tom had spent the entire afternoon agreeing with Marilla, Amanda wasn't too surprised at his response. However, she was surprised by Marilla's comment. Amanda didn't consider Josh intimidating. Insensitive, yes. Intimidating, no.

''Intimidating?'' she asked.

''Sometimes. He's so...clever. Not that we're not

clever, but…well, he's clever in a different direction. Isn't he, Tom?''

''Sure is,'' Tom said.

''He's always been like that,'' Marilla confided. ''Not that I know him that well. There's quite a few years between us, so we didn't really grow up together. When Dad married Edwina, I was already away from home, taking my veterinary assistant course.''

''Oh.'' Amanda blinked. So that's what she did.

''I did used to take care of him sometimes, though. He used to come and stay with me when Dad and Edwina went off for a holiday.'' She chuckled. ''He was very fond of that Sphinx cat I had. His name was Fitzgerald, but for some reason Josh called him Fluffy.'' Her face curled into confusion. ''I never did understand it, because that particular breed is completely hairless.''

''Really?'' Amanda said, trying to repress a smile.

''We lost poor Fitzgerald last year. He contracted a serious case of pneumonia and we just couldn't save him.''

''Oh,'' Amanda said faintly. ''I'm…um…terribly sorry.''

''It was a tragedy,'' Marilla agreed. ''But now we have Algonquin. I'm not sure Josh has ever met him. We don't see much of him these days.'' She patted Amanda's arm. ''Of course, now that you're part of his life, I'm sure we'll see him a lot more.'' They paused beside another cage. ''Look at this Burmese. Doesn't it just take your breath away?''

''Definitely,'' Amanda said.

She'd never felt like such a low-life in her whole life.

JOSH WALKED into the lobby of his office the next afternoon to find Mable standing beside a fully decorated Christmas tree that seemed to have materialized in the corner opposite her desk.

''Has that always been here?'' Josh asked as he stopped to admire it.

''No,'' said Mable. She adjusted an ornament. ''We've never had one in here before. I have suggested putting one up a few times but you usually say something touching and Christmassy like 'Over my dead body.' ''

''Oh,'' Josh said. ''Well, I didn't know it would look this attractive.'' He glanced over at Mable. ''Did you put it up?''

''I helped,'' Mable said modestly. ''But Amanda did most of it.''

''Amanda?'' Of course, Amanda. He'd thought he'd caught a whiff of her perfume when he'd stepped off the elevator. He smiled. He should have known his Christmas elf would be behind a Christmas tree. He glanced down the hall. ''Where is she?''

''She just left.'' Mable returned to her desk. ''I must say, I'm glad I called that executive services company. Amanda is exactly what we need around here.'' She frowned up at Josh. ''That doesn't mean I like what you're doing with her.''

Josh grimaced. He'd told Mable about his arrangement with Amanda, on the off chance that his business acquaintances would ask her about it. Mable didn't approve, and she'd been very vocal about it. ''I'm not doing anything with her. As a matter of fact, I've hardly seen her.'' That was certainly true. He hadn't seen much of Amanda at all these past couple of days. He knew she'd been working with Mable on making arrangements for the office Christmas party, but she seemed to come and go when he wasn't around, or had been too busy to notice. He had spoken with her a few times on the phone, to pass on social arrangements, or to check on her Christmas present progress. That wasn't strictly necessary, since his family kept him up to date on her activities. "I just had tea with Amanda," Aunt Judith had enthused. "I do like her, Josh. And I love the towels she has in her bathroom."

"Amanda came to the cat show with me," Marilla had informed him this morning. "She's thinking of getting a Siamese."

It seems the only person who didn't see Amanda was him. "You don't think she's...avoiding me, do you?" he asked Mable.

"I have no idea," said Mable. "But I wouldn't blame her if she was. *I'd* avoid you if I were her."

"You would?" Josh didn't understand that. "Why?"

Mable gave him an impatient look. "Well, you haven't treated her very nicely, have you? First you con her into doing your Christmas shopping for you. Then you con her into pretending she's you're girlfriend. She's probably wondering what else you're going to try to con her into."

Josh stroked a hand around his chin. "What does that mean?"

"You're telling people that you two are living together. She might think that you're planning on...taking advantage of the situation."

"Taking advantage of the situation?" Josh blinked a few times. "Me?"

Mable smiled slightly. ''She doesn't know you very well.''

''That's for sure,'' Josh grumbled. And if she kept avoiding him, she'd never get to know him very well.

He wandered into his office and dropped into a chair. Come to think of it, Amanda had said something about this being a business relationship. At the time he hadn't been sure what she meant. Perhaps she had been warning him not to take advantage of the situation. Of course, he'd never do anything like that. A brief memory of that kiss they'd shared flashed through his mind. He wouldn't mind repeating that experience though.

Mable had made another good point. He had used a pretty underhanded technique to get Amanda to act as his girlfriend. He couldn't really blame her if she was annoyed with him about that. However, he could make up for that by giving her a hand with this personal stuff.

He picked up the phone. Hadn't Shelby mentioned something about a party tonight? They could go to that. He could get started on this personal business right away.

AMANDA WAS STILL FEELING depressed that afternoon when Brandy rushed into her apartment. ''You will never believe what just happened,'' Brandy exclaimed as she threw off her coat.

Amanda eyed her with some alarm. ''Oh, no. Don't tell me another guy tried to jump you?''

''No,'' said Brandy. ''No one tried to jump me. I've just met with Harvey McCormick's secretary's assistant.''

''Harvey McCormick's secretary's assistant,''

Amanda repeated. She smiled vacantly at Brandy, and returned to studying her gift list. "How...nice."

"It's not just nice, Amanda. It's fabulous!"

"Is it?" Amanda considered the names in front of her. "Do you think a tie is a personal gift for a man?"

"It depends on the man. Don't you know who Harvey McCormick is?"

"No," said Amanda. "How about if the man is an uncle?"

"Then a tie is fine," said Brandy. "Amanda, Harvey McCormick is the president of the NorthRim Oil and Gas Company."

"Is he?" Amanda wrote "tie" beside Frank's name. "That explains why his secretary has an assistant. I think Josh's uncle Frank needs a new tie. The one he was wearing the other night was really old-fashioned. And it was so...blue." She tapped her pencil thoughtfully against the paper. "On the other hand, maybe all investment counselors wear old-fashioned blue ties. Do you know any?"

"Not on purpose." Brandy reached over and pulled the pencil out of Amanda's hand. "Will you pay attention here? I just met with the assistant to the secretary of the president of the NorthRim Oil and Gas Company. She wants to arrange a little function they are having for some of their corporate pals."

"Ah," said Amanda, her mind still filled with gift ideas. "That's...great."

"Great?" Brandy gave her a look of total disgust. "It's...incredible. Amanda, Harvey McCormick's idea of a 'little function' is two hundred people."

Amanda eyed her warily. "Do we have to get them Christmas presents?"

"No, we don't! We just have to organize it." She

grinned practically from ear to ear. ''And they're not just any people. They're important people!''

''Are they?'' said Amanda. ''Well, that's...great.''

Brandy peered into her face. ''It could just be my imagination, but you don't seem to be sharing my enthusiasm here.''

''I'm enthusiastic,'' Amanda assured her. ''I'm happy we're getting the business, but—well, there's just so much to do. I've lined up the caterers for Josh's office party. I'm working on getting the entertainment. I've got the decorations ordered—along with a few Christmas trees and ornaments. I've phoned all over the city for that Halsone for Aunt Mimi and I've thought up a billion reasons why Josh can't go anywhere.'' She grimaced at the stack of invitations sitting on the sofa beside her. ''I think that's the hardest part. I mean, how many ways are there to say, 'He never leaves his office'?''

''I thought he was supposed to leave his office,'' Brandy complained. ''Isn't that the whole point of this?''

''He can't possibly go to everything.'' Even if he could, Amanda strongly doubted that he would. ''Besides, he is coming to Shelby's with me tonight.'' She'd been a little surprised when Josh had called and suggested they go, although she suspected he was just trying to finish off his obligation to ''give her a hand with the personal stuff.'' ''And before you say anything, I am not, repeat not, getting involved. It's simply a business function.''

''Sure,'' Brandy said.

''It is,'' Amanda insisted. She gave Brandy a hopeful look. ''Why don't you come with us? I'm sure

Shelby wouldn't mind. And I could use the moral support.''

''I can't,'' said Brandy. ''I'm busy this evening.'' She looked down at her hands. ''I'm...um...meeting Harvy for a drink.''

''Harvy?'' Amanda studied Brandy's rather sheepish demeanor. ''You mean...Harvy Denton?''

''Uh-huh.''

''I thought you weren't going to have anything to do with him.''

''I'm not,'' Brandy assured her. ''But I've talked to him a couple of times at his office...and so far he's behaved himself. So when he suggested we get together to have a drink, I said yes, just to see what he'd do.'' She raised an eyebrow. ''However, I plan on making it clear that I have no intention of crawling into bed with him.'' She sighed. ''That will probably convince him to leave me alone.''

''Sounds like a fun evening,'' said Amanda. ''At least a lot more fun than trying to force Josh Larkland to find out anything personal about his relatives.''

''What?''

''Let's be realistic here, Brandy. I might get Josh to one or two family get-togethers at the very most. And the possibility of him coming up with something personal about his relatives is slim to none. If he manages to discover their ages and occupations, I'll be surprised.''

''So will I, but I didn't think you felt that way.''

''I didn't,'' said Amanda. ''I thought all I had to do was get Josh together with his family a little more. Now I'm starting to wonder if I even should be doing it.''

"Oh?" Brandy blinked a few times. "What brought this on?"

"I was at a cat show with Marilla last night."

"Ah, a cat show." Brandy snapped her fingers. "Maybe I should have sent you to one of those before you went into Josh's office."

Amanda ignored her. "Marilla told me that she used to baby-sit Josh when he was younger. Now she hardly ever sees him." She gave Brandy an anguished look. "So far, every single one of his relatives has told me the same thing. They're all crazy about him, but they just don't see him anymore. And they're all so eager to meet me and they just hope that now he has a relationship he'll spend more time with them."

"So?"

"So he doesn't have a relationship! He's hired me, and I blackmailed him into spending a little time with his family. If this doesn't work, they are all going to be really disappointed, and I'm going to feel terrible." She sighed. "I don't know what possessed me to take a job as a Christmas elf in the first place."

AT FIVE O'CLOCK, Mable walked into Josh's office and came to a full stop in the doorway. "What happened in here?" she asked.

Josh took a look around. His computers were switched off, the test equipment was put away, and his papers were neatly stacked on his desk. "Nothing," he said. "I'm just leaving."

"You're leaving?" Mable checked her watch. "But it's just five o'clock."

"I know," said Josh. "I have to leave now. We're going to Shelby's tonight, and she lives miles away from the city. I have to go home, change, and pick up Amanda—and a map."

"Shelby?" Mable repeated. "You mean, your sister Shelby? The one who teaches at the university?"

"Uh-huh," he said, looking quizzically at Mable. So that's what Shelby did. He'd known it had something to do with children.

Mable's forehead furrowed. "You know, Josh, this is the second family thing you've gone to in a week. Is there something wrong that you haven't told me about, or are you just trying to set a world record?"

"No," said Josh. "I'm giving Amanda a hand—at finding out personal things about people."

"Oh." Mable's lips twitched slightly. "That's... uh...decent of you."

Josh put on his coat. "They are my relatives, Mable, and there are a lot of them. I can't expect Amanda to do it all by herself."

"Right," said Mable. "Well, it's...uh...nice of you to sacrifice yourself." She walked out of the office, shaking her head.

IT'S A BUSINESS FUNCTION, Amanda told herself.

However, when she opened her door and saw Josh standing on the other side, it was very difficult to remember that.

He stood in the entranceway and studied her from head to toe. "You look nice," he said. "Very elf-like."

Amanda flushed with pleasure at the compliment. "You look nice, too." He looked more than nice. He looked scrumptious, dressed in a long brown parka, which he hadn't buttoned up, a pair of dress pants, and a white-and-gray shirt under a dark blue sweater. "That's a great sweater."

"Is it?" He shrugged. "I think my mother gave it to me. Or one of my sisters. Or maybe an aunt." He glanced around her small place with outright curiosity. "You know what," he said. "This does look like an elf lives here, except the doors are normal size."

Amanda glanced over her shoulder, taking in the small, square living room with the odd bits of furniture her grandmother had given her—a small, dark-oak coffee table with matching end tables, a white-and-green-striped couch, the minuscule Christmas tree in the corner—their papers spread over the coffee table. "A messy elf," Amanda confessed. "We're using my entire apartment as an office until we can afford a real one."

Brandy came out of the kitchen while she was pulling on her coat. Amanda introduced them. "This is my partner, Brandy Bradford. Brandy, this is Josh Larkland."

"Hi," Josh said. He smiled his charming smile and shook Brandy's hand. "Mandy and Brandy. The Christmas elves. You even look like one, too."

Brandy scowled at him. "It's not polite to make remarks about people's height. And for your information, I am not short. I am vertically challenged." She turned to Amanda. "Remember, you can't reform them." She nodded at Josh, and stomped into the living room.

Josh stared after her. "Was it something I said?"

"Don't mind Brandy," Amanda advised as she took her coat out of the closet. "She's just having a...a bad elf day."

"Oh," Josh said. He helped Amanda on with her

coat, his breath warm against her neck. ''I hope it isn't contagious. Otherwise it could be a very long evening.''

IF THE DRIVE to Shelby's place was any indication, it was going to be an extremely long evening.

''Are you positive you know where she lives?'' Amanda asked as she peered out the window. The city was receding rapidly out the back window, there didn't seem to be very many lights out here, and Amanda was starting to wish she'd found another means of transportation.

That wasn't just because of the drive. Being alone with Josh in the dark intimacy of the car just reminded her of how attractive he was. She had to keep looking out the window to stop herself from admiring his profile, the way his hands curled around the steering wheel, or the movement of his thigh when he pressed on the brakes.

''Of course I know where she lives,'' said Josh. ''I have been here before, you know.''

''Really?'' Amanda studied him. ''When was that?''

''I'm...not sure. In the fall, I think. Or maybe it was spring.''

''More likely two years ago,'' Amanda muttered.

Josh glanced over at her and frowned. ''Don't worry. I'm not going to get you lost.'' He stretched out an arm to ruffle her hair. ''God knows what Santa would do to me if I lost one of his elves.''

If he didn't stop touching her, Amanda wasn't sure what she'd do to him. Just the feel of his hand on her hair made her dizzy.

''Is Brandy your roommate?'' he asked after a moment.

''Not anymore,'' said Amanda. ''She's been a friend for a long time. When she broke up with her boyfriend she moved in with me for a few months, but now she has a place of her own.''

''Oh,'' Josh said. ''Well, it was nice of you to help her out.''

''She's my friend,'' said Amanda. ''Naturally I wanted to help her out. That's what friends are for.'' She paused, then added pointedly, ''That's what families are for, too.''

''Of course they are,'' Josh said easily. ''And speaking of family, I hear you were at a cat show yesterday with Marilla.''

''Oh? How did you hear that?''

''The family grapevine keeps me informed.'' He glanced over at her. ''How did that go? Did you find out anything personal about her?''

''Only that she really, really likes cats, she used to have one named Fitzgerald, and that she finds you intimidating.''

''Intimidating? Me?'' He chuckled. ''I wouldn't call myself intimidating.'' He glanced over at her. ''What do you mean she *used* to have a cat named Fitzgerald?''

''He got pneumonia.''

''Fluffy got pneumonia?'' Josh's eyes widened. ''Poor Marilla. She must be really upset.''

''I think she's getting over it,'' said Amanda. ''After all, it did happen last year.''

''Oh,'' said Josh. ''I didn't know that.'' His forehead furrowed. ''I don't know why people don't tell me these things.'' He stopped the car in front of an enormous house that seemed to have appeared from out of nowhere. ''Oh, no,'' he said.

Amanda took a quick look around, but couldn't spot anything unusual. ''What's the matter?'' she asked. ''Isn't this the place?''

''No, this is the place, all right.'' Josh looked over at her and grimaced. ''I've just remembered a couple of personal things about Shelby.''

''What?'' asked Amanda.

''Well, for one thing she's a university professor.'' He switched off the engine and opened his door. ''And for another...she's a lousy cook.''

UNFORTUNATELY, Josh was right.

Amanda stood in Shelby's kitchen and eyed the tray Shelby was pulling out of the oven. ''They're crab canapés,'' Shelby explained. ''It's a variation of a recipe I got when I was in Tucson a few years ago. I discovered that the addition of a little Tabasco sauce and a few jalapeno peppers really spices it up.''

''They look...uh...interesting,'' Amanda said, then began to arrange the canapés on a platter. ''I really like your house, Shelby. It's beautiful. And it's the perfect place to raise a family.''

''We like it,'' said Shelby. ''Although the drive out here can get exhausting. I seem to spend half my life on that highway.'' She paused. ''You know, I'd almost forgotten that you hadn't been out here before. You seem to belong with us, if you know what I mean.''

Amanda shifted uncomfortably. ''Well...uh... thank you, but...um...I'm not exactly—''

''And I'm so pleased about it, too,'' Shelby went

on. ''It's so nice to see Josh out and about again. He seems to spend his entire life in his office—at least that's where I assume he is,'' she said dryly. ''My children have even suggested that their uncle Josh might be an agent.''

''An agent?''

''A secret agent,'' Shelby explained.

''You mean, a spy?'' Amanda bit down on her lip. In that profession he probably wouldn't last more than a day. On the other hand, when she'd left Josh in the living room a little while ago, he'd been pumping Shelby's husband Gordon for information. ''So, Gordon,'' he'd been saying. ''Tell me. What exactly is it that you do?''

Come to think of it, he was sort of acting like a cloak-and-dagger Christmas agent.

''Yes.'' Shelby shoved another cooking platter into the oven. ''On our side, of course.''

''Of course,'' said Amanda.

''I know it seems far-fetched. But he has all the signs. He's never around, no one understands what he does, and we don't see much of him.'' She waved around an oven-mitted hand. ''He does behave like he's a spy, doesn't he?''

Amanda focused on the platter she was creating. ''I suppose he does.''

''For a while I almost believed it myself,'' Shelby continued. ''I think I wanted to. It's much better than the truth.''

''The truth?''

''You know. That he just isn't very interested in us.''

Amanda looked over her shoulder at Shelby's earnest face. ''I'm sure he's interested in you, Shelby.''

''Not really,'' said Shelby. ''Months go by when no one hears from him, and we seldom see him anymore. I think the party at Mimi's was the first time I've seen him since the summer. And I can't remember the last time he was out here. Today he even had to ask me for directions.''

Amanda narrowed her eyes. ''Oh, he did, did he?''

''Of course, I can't remember the last time I was at his place, either. And I have no idea what he does. I have asked but he says something like 'network throughput factors.' I don't know what any of those words mean.''

''Neither do I,'' Amanda admitted.

''Of course, Josh has always been like that,'' Shelby continued. ''Even when he was young I couldn't follow what he was doing.''

Amanda found the idea of a little Josh incredibly interesting. ''Really?''

''Oh, yes. He was always wiring things up in the most amazing ways. At one point he had half the house wired up to the television remote control. The only way you could make toast was to turn the television to channel three.'' She busied herself doing something with salmon. ''Of course, that might have been because of his father.''

Amanda hadn't followed that. ''His father?''

''Yes. He was in some sort of car accident, you know.''

''No,'' Amanda said. ''No, I didn't know that.''

''Well, he was. Of course, I never met him. He passed away before Dad met Edwina. But I understand that he was pretty crippled by it. He found it difficult to get around.''

Amanda was just digesting that when Josh wandered into the room. ''Gordon's been showing me your computer,'' he confessed. ''I reconfigured your memory, fixed the lost clusters on your hard drive, and got your printer working.''

Shelby stared at him. ''You did? That hasn't been working for six months.''

''That's what Gordon said.'' Josh shook his head. ''You should have fixed it a long time ago, Shel. It wasn't that hard to do.''

''I certainly don't know how. And neither does Gordon.''

''Yeah, but I do.'' Josh washed the black toner off his hands at the sink. ''I don't know why you people don't call me when you have problems like this.''

''I...uh...just didn't want to bother you,'' Shelby stammered. ''You're busy and...''

''You're my sister, Shelby,'' Josh said patiently. ''I'm never too busy to help you out. After all, that is what families are for.'' His gaze met Amanda's over Shelby's head, and he gave her a smug smile before glancing down at the canapé tray in her hand. His eyes widened, and he cleared his throat. ''Well...uh...this has been great, Shelby, but I'm afraid we're going to have to leave now.''

''But it's only ten o'clock,'' Shelby objected. ''And you've hardly eaten anything. I...''

''I know,'' said Josh. ''But we have to get home. Amanda has a headache.''

''She does?'' Shelby glanced at Amanda. ''She didn't mention it to me.''

''She didn't mention it to me, either,'' said Josh. He put an arm around Amanda. ''But all I have to do is look at her and I know she isn't feeling well.''

"ALL YOU HAVE TO DO is look at me and you know I'm not feeling well?" Amanda repeated incredulously. She took a bite out of her hamburger and frowned at Josh. "I can't believe you actually said that."

Josh's eyes gleamed with amusement. "Hey, if we're going to go places as a couple there are some things we should know about each other. Besides, I was getting hungry...and I wasn't going to eat that. Was it my imagination, or was there fish in everything she served?"

"There was a lot of fish," Amanda admitted. "Shelby said it was brain food."

"My brain wasn't getting full on it." Josh set down his hamburger while he took a sip of his Coke. He'd stopped at the first fast-food place they'd come to, insisting that he was going to perish if he didn't have something to eat. "Let's give her a cookbook for Christmas."

"We can't do that!"

"Why not?" Josh asked. "Isn't it personal?"

Amanda hesitated. "Actually, it's a little too personal."

"Oh," he said. "Well, how about if we give it to Gordon, then?"

"No. In Gordon's case it wouldn't be personal enough."

"This is really complicated," Josh complained. "Ornaments are personal, cookbooks are too personal, or not personal enough. Who writes the rules on this stuff?"

"No one writes them," said Amanda. "Everybody just knows them."

"I don't," said Josh. He smiled into her eyes. "It's a good thing I've got you around."

Amanda averted her gaze. *Don't you dare come on to me, Josh Larkland,* she thought. *I just might go along with it.* She knew how that would end. She'd get too intense and he wouldn't even know it had happened.

"Shelby could sure use some new computer equipment," Josh said after a moment. "I don't know why she didn't call me to take a look at it before."

"Perhaps she didn't think you'd be interested in her problems," Amanda suggested.

Josh looked shocked. "Of course I'm interested! She's my sister. I'm interested in her."

"Maybe she doesn't know that. After all, it doesn't sound as if you spend much time with her."

Josh lowered his eyelids. "I spend time with her. Besides, I'm...busy." He was silent for a moment. "You know what I'd like to give Shelby? A ten-gig hard drive, some extra RAM memory and a fast data/fax modem. Would that be personal?"

"It depends what it is," said Amanda. "I didn't understand a word you said."

"It's what Shelby needs to bring that computer of theirs up to date." He leaned back in his chair. "Gordon told me that Shelby spends a lot of time driving back to the university at night to use the Internet. With some new equipment, she'd get better response time at home, and she wouldn't have to do that. I'd even volunteer to come out and install it—as long as it's after lunch and before dinner."

"You would?"

"Of course, I would. She's my sister, Amanda. I'd like to help her out."

"Oh," said Amanda. "Well, in that case, I'd say it's very personal. And very thoughtful."

"It is?" Josh looked both pleased and surprised. "Hey, maybe I'm getting the hang of this, after all."

Amanda watched him munch away on his hamburger. Maybe he was getting the hang of this.

When Josh stopped his car in front of her apartment building, switched off the engine, and started to get out, Amanda put a hand on his arm to hold him back. "Thank you for taking me," she said. "But there's no need for you to get out."

He turned his head toward her, with a quizzical expression on his face.

"This is a business arrangement, Josh," Amanda reminded him. "I think we should keep it that way."

JOSH WAS DEEP in thought when Mable walked into his office the next morning.

"So?" she asked. "How was the party last night?"

"Not too bad," Josh said.

"Did you…uh…find out anything personal about anyone?"

"Yup," Josh said. "Shelby serves a lot of fish, she doesn't know anything about computers, and Fluffy got pneumonia."

"Oh," said Mable. "Well, I suppose that's something."

She was on her way out the door when Josh called her back. "Tell me something, Mabe. Would you call me intimidating?"

"Intimidating?" Mable turned to face him and released a bark of laughter. "No, I certainly wouldn't. Obnoxious, maybe. Overbearing. Sometimes belligerent. Intelligent, of course, but…"

Josh scowled at her. "I wasn't asking for a personal critique. I was asking about intimidating."

"Oh," said Mable. "Well, in that case, no. I don't think you're particularly intimidating." She gave him a curious look. "Why?"

"Marilla told Amanda she thinks I'm intimidating."

"Oh," said Mable. "Well, I'd say Marilla doesn't know you very well."

"That's what I thought," Josh muttered. He watched Mable walk out of his office, then pushed himself out of his chair and wandered over to the window. He had found out a few more personal things last night, but they were mostly about himself.

For one thing, he hadn't expected Amanda to practically leap out of his car when he took her home, after coolly advising him that she thought they should keep their relationship strictly business. He hadn't realized how much he'd been anticipating another of those tantalizing kisses of hers.

However, now that he thought about it Amanda was probably right. They should keep their relationship strictly business. If they didn't, it could turn into a relationship sort of relationship, and Josh wanted no part of that. He'd been in enough of those to know how they turned out. As soon as he started dating a woman, she expected him to do things like go out every night, or show up someplace on time...and she'd get annoyed when he didn't do it. He didn't want that to happen with Amanda. She was his Christmas elf, and that's all he wanted her to be.

He shoved aside the niggling suspicion that he wasn't being completely honest about that and concentrated on his family.

For some time they had been telling him that they didn't see enough of him. He had thought they were exaggerating, but he was starting to wonder if maybe they were right. There sure seemed to be a lot of things he didn't know about them. He couldn't remember the last time he was at Shelby's. He hadn't even known she owned a computer, much less needed help with it. She hadn't called him to give her a hand, either. Marilla thought he was intimidating and she hadn't told him that cat of hers had gotten pneumonia.

Maybe he was a little out of touch with his relatives. There was a good reason for that, though, he thought furiously. He had a lot to do! It certainly wasn't that he wasn't interested in them or didn't care about them. He was just...busy.

Still, he wasn't busy tonight, was he?

He checked his calendar, then picked up the phone. Maybe he should go to another one of these family things. After all, he was getting the hang of this personal stuff. And he was curious to see what his family hadn't gotten around to telling him.

"HOW DID THINGS with Harvy go last night?" Amanda asked Brandy. They were stretched at either ends of the couch in Amanda's living room. "He didn't try to jump you, did he?"

"No, he didn't." Brandy said, sounding puzzled. "He actually behaved like a gentleman. I told him flat-out that I wasn't sleeping with him and he seemed...relieved." Brandy massaged the back of her neck like she had a major kink in it.

"Relieved?"

"Uh-huh," Brandy said. "Then we had a couple

of drinks...we talked...and he took me home. He didn't even try to *kiss* me!''

''See,'' Amanda said. ''Maybe you were wrong about him.''

''Maybe.'' Brandy didn't sound convinced. ''Or maybe he was trying out a new technique on me.'' Still rubbing her neck, she gave Amanda a penetrating look. ''How was your *date?*''

''It wasn't a date,'' Amanda said too quickly. ''It was a business function. And it went a lot better than I expected. Josh did find out something personal about Shelby.''

''Her age and occupation?'' Brandy teased.

''No. He already knew that.'' Amanda told her all about the computer equipment. ''It sounds like a great present. And it's exactly what Shelby needs.''

''I suppose that's something,'' Brandy admitted grudgingly.

''It's more than something,'' Amanda insisted. ''This just might work, Brandy. He found out something personal about one person.'' She leaned back. ''He seemed interested in Shelby, too. He seemed as if he cared about her. Not only that, but this morning he called and said he wanted to go to a few more family things—so he can find out more personal stuff about people.'' She smiled. ''However, he also added that he wants me to find out what they're serving before I say we'll come.''

''*We'll* come?'' Brandy stressed, raising an eyebrow. ''You mean, you're going to go out with him *again?*''

''I have to,'' said Amanda. ''After all, we are supposed to be a couple.'' She caught Brandy's frown and sighed. ''It's strictly a business arrangement, Brandy.''

''Does Josh know that?''

''Yes, he does,'' Amanda said, trying to sound cool and casual. ''I made it very clear to him last night.'' She felt a pang of regret at that. She would have enjoyed another one of his kisses.

''What about you?'' Brandy asked. ''Do you still remember it's strictly a business arrangement?''

''Of course. That's exactly what it is,'' she said, her voice quivering slightly. She snuck a glance in Brandy's direction. Brandy appeared unconvinced. Her relationship with Josh was strictly business, right? So why did her voice quiver every time she said his name, and why did the memory of his kiss keep replaying over and over again?

7

"LET'S SEE," Amanda said.

She sat in Josh's office, a calendar on her lap, along with her lists. "We've got Frank and Louise's party, Aunt Francine's open house, and your cousin Glenda's barbecue..." She paused. "Does your cousin really have a barbecue in December?"

Josh shrugged. "I guess we'll find out. Go on."

"Okay." Amanda referred back to her book. "Then your mother is having a few people over, and we've been invited to drop by Hemp's place for drinks. Oh, and we've also got Hank Turnbull's open house. You said you wanted to go to that."

"I do." Josh gave her a hopeful look. "I don't suppose you know what they're going to be..."

"No, I don't," Amanda interrupted. "I have not yet found a polite way of saying 'I'll come to your Christmas thing if you tell me what you're serving and it better not be fish.'"

"Too bad." Josh lounged back in his office chair. "I don't suppose you could just *ask?*"

"Absolutely not," Amanda said firmly. "It would be considered rude."

"What? Aren't there any rude elves in the world?"

"Not a single one," said Amanda. "We are all a very polite bunch."

"Darn," said Josh, and he looked so cute and disgruntled that Amanda completely lost track of the conversation and had to refer back to her notes.

It was a familiar problem. She had it frequently when she was with Josh, and she had only herself to blame. She'd wanted him to get involved with his family. Well, he was definitely doing that—and he was taking her along with him.

Josh had been pretty accurate when he'd said that he was a fast worker when he made up his mind. Apparently he'd made up his mind to find out personal things about his relatives. And he was now charging at it, full steam ahead.

Since Shelby's party, they'd been to a family dinner at his aunt Sofia's, where he'd discovered that Sofia liked Frank Sinatra records, an open house at Judith's, where they'd spent most of the evening looking at old family photographs and talking about bathrooms, and had even stopped by Marilla's for drinks. Josh had taken Marilla flowers. ''I was really sorry to hear about Fluffy,'' he'd said as he'd handed them over. Then he'd spent the rest of the evening trying not to act intimidating.

Amanda was doing everything she could to keep her dealings with Josh as businesslike as possible, but it was difficult. Josh was difficult. He phoned her three or four times a day to check their schedule, to throw in some brainstorm he'd had that might possibly be personal, or sometimes, it seemed, just to talk.

He'd insisted that she accompany him to every social event. ''We're supposed to be a couple,'' he'd reminded her. ''That means we go to these things together.'' Sometimes Amanda thought that might be because he wanted to be with her, although the more realistic part of her knew it was because he wanted them to be seen as a couple, and because he considered it part of her job to go. He also used her as an excuse to leave when he'd had enough. "We have to go now," he'd say. "Amanda has to be at work early." Then he'd add, in an undertone, "Elves need lots of sleep."

"We don't have to go to every single function, you know," she told him. "We could miss a few."

"Christmas isn't that far away...and we've still got a lot of people to go—including my mother." He drew his eyebrows together. "I don't suppose you've come up with any good ideas for her yet."

"I've come up with a lot of good ideas for her," Amanda objected. "*You* just don't like any of them."

"I just don't *understand* them. How can a watch be personal? Everyone in the world has one. It has to be as bad as giving everybody the same perfume."

"It isn't, but..."

"And a pasta maker?" He frowned at her. "I didn't even know what a pasta maker was until you told me. And even then, I don't see what's personal about it. Spaghetti just doesn't do it for me. If I built a voice-activated one, it might be, but..."

"Forget the pasta maker," Amanda said quickly. "I'm sure we can come up with something else." She paused. "There's no reason for us both to go to these things. You are getting really good at this. I'm sure if you went..."

"No." Josh folded his arms and looked stubborn. "You're the Christmas elf around here. If I have to go, you have to go." He paused, then added, "Besides, those things are more fun when you are there. I almost enjoy thcm."

He looked puzzled by that, as if he wasn't expecting it. Amanda's body tingled at the words, a tingle that faded when he added, ''And it gives me a good excuse to leave when I want.''

''Just make sure you tell me which excuse you use,'' Amanda warned. ''The other night you told everyone we had to leave because I wasn't feeling well. The next morning, when everyone called to see how I was, I had no idea what they were talking about.'' She'd been particularly flummoxed when Aunt Judith had called her to see if the rabbit had died. It had taken Amanda a good minute to realize Judith was hinting that she might be pregnant—a suggestion Amanda had vehemently denied. The last thing she needed was for Mimi to make that suggestion to Josh. She wouldn't be one bit surprised if Josh said she was, just to make his family happy! Then nine months from now, he'd probably demand that she produce an offspring.

She smiled at the image, then almost immediately sobered up. Nine months from now she wouldn't be seeing Josh or his family. As a matter of fact, in just under two weeks she wouldn't be seeing them. By Christmas Eve, their work was through.

The prospect made her suddenly feel cold. She flipped over a page in her notebook, and turned her attention back to business. ''All right. We both go. Now let's discuss your Christmas party. I've arranged for a string quartet and a piano player...''

''A piano player!'' Josh said in a mock horrified tone. ''Oh, no. Don't tell me we're going to have...singing?''

''THERE'S THE INTERNET trade show, the Vistech open house, and the corporate gifts for the Dawson building supply company,'' Brandy reported later that afternoon to Amanda as they quickly gobbled down a late lunch of take-out pizza. ''I have only one question. How do we clone ourselves?'' Brandy said, grinning with satisfaction.

''That's a good question,'' Amanda agreed. There were boxes of corporate gifts and stacks of papers strewn all around her apartment. ''Or I guess a better question is, how do we clone this apartment?'' She rested back against the chair. ''This is ridiculous. A few weeks ago we couldn't get any business. Now we almost have too much.''

''That's thanks to you, Amanda,'' Brandy said, wiping the grease off her fingers with a napkin before she picked up her To-Do list. ''Every person we contacted on that list Josh gave you has hired us to do something.'' She paused. ''You know, Amanda, I'm starting to think I was wrong about this character. He's brought us all this business. He's paying his bills on time. And he does seem to be getting involved with his family.''

''That's true,'' Amanda agreed. ''He's going to everything there is to go to. And has come up with some wonderful presents for people. The computer equipment he got for Shelby is exactly what she needs. Of course, he's insisted on giving her some kind of computer cookbook program, too.'' He'd also come up with fishing equipment for his uncle Reg after he'd remembered that Reg had taken him fishing a couple of times when he was a boy.

''He's suggested some pretty bizarre things, too. He wanted to give his aunt Sofia a can of spray paint because he didn't like the colors in her house.''

Amanda shuddered. "I didn't like the color, either. You should have seen it. Everything in it was cherry-red, including the toilet paper...although I think that's a gift from Aunt Judith." She paused, looking at all the work spread out in front of her. "I suppose the only down side of all this is that you're getting stuck with most of the work. I'm just...too busy."

"You sure are," Brandy agreed. "You're out with this guy almost every night."

"They're just business functions," Amanda reminded her.

"They're Larkland family functions," Brandy corrected. She furrowed her forehead. "And I must say they sure hold a lot of them. How can all the same people go to that many parties?"

"They aren't the same people," Amanda explained. "Shelby told me all about it. Everyone invites their friends over and includes their family. But no one goes to everything—although Josh is certainly giving it a good try." Amanda thought about his eyes and the feeling of his hand on her shoulder, and decided to change the subject. "How are things going with you and Harvy Denton? You seem to have been spending a lot of time with him."

"Well, yes," Brandy said with a smile. "He's really quite interesting when you get to know him." She screwed up her face. "Although I must say, I'm starting to really wonder about him."

"Why?"

"Well...it's just that all we seem to do is go out for dinner."

Amanda didn't see the significance of that. She'd been out for dinner with Josh—at his suggestion. "We both have to eat. And I'm not going to go to another one of those things on an empty stomach.'' They'd also gotten into the habit of stopping for coffee after they left a family party. At first that was just so they could compare notes about gift ideas—and also because Josh seldom liked what he'd been served. However the conversation usually digressed to discuss other things. Josh told her all about his work, and his plans for the future. Sometimes Amanda didn't understand what he was talking about, but she liked watching the sparkle in his eye when he explained it. He might be clued out about life, but when it came to his job, he was definitely clued in. ''That sounds pleasant,'' she said to Brandy.

''It is pleasant,'' Brandy said. ''But don't you think it's a little...peculiar?''

''Eating dinner isn't peculiar.''

''It is if it's all you do.''

''What do you mean?'' Amanda asked, still not getting it.

''I mean that Harvy hasn't made a pass at me. All we do is...talk.''

She looked so perplexed, Amanda had to smile. ''I thought you didn't want him to make a pass at you.''

''I didn't,'' Brandy assured her. ''But I'm starting to think that I wouldn't mind getting involved with him.'' A dreamy look crept across her face. ''He doesn't seem to be the creep I thought he was at all. He's polite and kind...and he treats me better than any man I've ever met. I'm just not sure he's interested.''

''I'm sure he is.''

''I'm not. It's a little weird. Last week he was jumping me in his office. Since then, he's taken me out three times, and he hasn't done anything more than take my arm when we're crossing the street.'' She paused. ''Actually, I take his arm when we cross the street. I thought he was just going out with me to soften me up for another encounter, but so far he hasn't made any moves in that direction.'' She sighed. ''What about you? Has Josh put any moves on you?''

''I don't think Josh *has* moves,'' Amanda said. She thought about that long-ago kiss and changed her mind. ''Okay, he might have a few. But I'm sure he wouldn't use them on me.'' He certainly hadn't made any move to do so. He treated her with the same casual affection he used toward Mable. Oh, he did seem to drop an arm around her shoulders, or take her hand, but he only did that when they were with other people. ''He treats me the same way he treats his secretary,'' she told Brandy.

Brandy snorted. ''I've seen his secretary, Amanda. I doubt he's dating her.''

''He's not dating me, either,'' Amanda reminded her.

''You go out with him practically every night.''

''They aren't dates,'' Amanda insisted. They did feel a lot like dates...except for the way they ended. Which was exactly how she wanted them to end. ''We're just...pretending to be involved.''

''Have you ever considered really getting involved with him?''

''Absolutely not,'' Amanda said firmly. She might be having a few lustful thoughts about Josh, but she had no intention of doing anything about it. ''I'm just trying to finish up our Christmas shopping list.'' Of course, when that was done, she wouldn't be seeing him anymore. It was far too depressing a thought.

"'Our Christmas shopping list'?" Brandy said, raising an eyebrow.

"I mean, Josh's Christmas shopping list," Amanda said. "As soon as that's finished, I won't be so busy. Then I'll have a lot more time." She glanced around her apartment again and gave herself a pep talk. "Which is a good thing considering how much work we have here."

"Right," said Brandy. "Well, in the meantime maybe we should call up the temp agency and see if we can get someone to give us a hand."

"That's a great idea," Amanda agreed. "Us Christmas elves need a lot of helpers, you know."

IF AMANDA WAS HARBORING any ideas about getting involved with Josh, she changed her mind after Hank Turnbull's open house.

It was the first affair she attended with Josh that didn't involve family, and Amanda was unusually nervous about it. She changed her clothes three times, finally settling for a dark green skirt, a matching blazer, and a ruffled white blouse. "Is this all right?" she asked Josh when he came to pick her up.

"It's fine," he assured her. "Very elflike."

"That's less than reassuring," Amanda complained as he helped her on with her coat. "You know, you really should pay more attention to what people wear at these things—just so you can tell your date."

Josh shrugged that off. "I don't usually take 'dates' to these things. And I'm sure it doesn't matter what you wear. These aren't my relatives, remember? They're just business acquaintances." He grinned happily. "We don't even have to find out personal things about them. We can just relax."

"Maybe you can," Amanda muttered. "But I imagine they'll be curious about me."

She was right. Hank Turnbull and his wife were charming people, and the rest of his business acquaintances were pleasant. However, it was obvious from their questions that they were indeed curious about her, and about her relationship with Josh. After answering a number of questions, Amanda managed to escape into a corner. She was sipping on a drink and enjoying a few moments of peace and quiet when a statuesque brunette named Susan Smyth wandered over to talk to her. "I've been really curious about you," Susan confided. "I wanted to meet the woman who finally captured Josh Larkland's attention." Her lips moved into a friendly, teasing smile. "What did you have to do? Hit him over the head with a sledgehammer?"

"Not exactly," Amanda murmured. She glanced across the room at Josh. "Although sometimes I've been tempted."

"I know what you mean." Susan eyed Josh over Amanda's shoulder. "I...uh...went out with him a few times, you know. He's a remarkably compelling man, isn't he?"

Amanda didn't want to think about how attractive Josh was. "Yes."

"Unfortunately he's the champion of all workaholics, isn't he?" Susan chatted on. "I pretty much had to force him to go out with me in the first place." She eyed Amanda with outright curiosity. "Is that how it happened with you?"

"Not exactly," Amanda murmured. She had blackmailed Josh into going out with her...but he was the one who kept forcing the issue.

''And he never called,'' said Susan. ''I mean...never. I was always calling him.''

''You were?'' Amanda seldom called Josh. He always seemed to be phoning her. Sometimes she wished he'd stop doing it. Every time she talked to him on the phone her mind went blank and it took her a good ten minutes to settle down after she hung up.

''He was always late for appointments, too...or else he'd forget about them.'' Susan sighed. ''After a while it just petered out. I got tired of chasing him, and he didn't seem interested and...'' She shrugged. ''Sometimes I felt as if he'd actually forgotten I existed.''

''Really?'' Amanda eyed Susan's perfectly put-together figure. Heavens, the woman even had a bustline. And Josh...forgot about her?

She took another swallow of her drink, more convinced than ever that getting involved with Josh Larkland would be a very bad idea.

ALTHOUGH SHE WAS JUST pretending to be involved with Josh, Amanda discovered at Josh's cousin Alaina's that the line between pretense and reality was becoming a little blurry.

Alaina was the only one of Josh's relations Amanda was having problems liking. She was a middle-aged woman with perfectly coiffed hair, piercing blue eyes and a manner that set Amanda's teeth on edge. When she first met Amanda, she said, ''I was so amazed to hear about you and Josh. Just astounded actually.'' She eyed Amanda up and down. ''It's actually like the tenth wonder of the world.'' Amanda wasn't sure what she was more surprised at—the fact that Josh could get a date, or that the date was Amanda.

Josh wasn't fond of her, either. ''I think I already know something personal about Alaina,'' he told Amanda. ''She's a pain in the neck.''

Unfortunately, he was right. Alaina had a professionally decorated house, which she insisted on showing to Amanda, and an extensive art collection, which she insisted on describing to Amanda.

Amanda was plotting her escape when she glanced over Alaina's shoulder and noticed Josh heavily involved in a conversation with a tall, well-proportioned redhead. Alaina's friend, Samantha, Amanda remembered. She did a quick mental run-through of her Christmas list. Sure enough, there weren't any well-built redheads on it.

''And this is a Sudcliff,'' Alaina advised, gesturing at one of the paintings hanging on the wall. ''Isn't it fabulous?''

''Fabulous,'' Amanda agreed. She kept her eye on the redhead. Josh had his hands in his pockets now. The redhead was leaning forward.

She gave her own head a shake, and tried to focus on what Alaina was saying.

''I just love its primeval qualities,'' Alaina continued. ''Don't you?''

''Yes,'' Amanda said in a distracted fashion. Was he smiling at that woman? He was…that slow, sexy smile that always made Amanda forget what they were talking about. She felt an overpowering and very un-Christmassy urge to smack both the redhead and Josh.

Believe it or not, Amanda was jealous, which was totally irrational. It wasn't as if she and Josh were really involved. She was here as a business associate, nothing more. So why was she consumed with jealousy by Josh's conversation with that, that...redheaded vixen?

"Is something the matter?" asked Alaina. "I thought you would be fascinated by Sudcliff's originality."

Amanda realized Alaina was eyeing her curiously, and pasted a fake smile on her face. "I'm...enthralled," she lied.

However, when they stopped at a coffee shop on the way home, she was still feeling a little put out with both Josh and his cousin. So when Josh asked, "Did you find out anything personal about Alaina?" Amanda snapped, "No, I did not, except that she's a pain in the neck."

"I told you that," Josh agreed. His eyes sparkled. "What do you say we get her a book on how the pretentious really live. Or would that be too personal?"

"I think it would." Amanda waited for a moment. "How about you? Do you have a brilliant gift idea for her?" She narrowed her eyes. "Or were you too busy finding out something personal about Samantha?"

"Samantha?" Josh looked blank. "Who is Samantha?"

Amanda's spirits lifted. At least she didn't stand out in his mind. "She's the woman you were talking with—you know, the redhead."

"Oh, her." Josh shrugged. "I was wondering who she was." He rolled his eyes. "The only thing personal I found out about her is that she is the most boring woman I have ever met. She's an artist of some sort. She kept talking about the surreal aspects of deep-sea diving or something of that nature. I wasn't really paying attention.''

''Good,'' Amanda murmured under her breath.

Josh leaned his elbows on the table and took a sip of his coffee. ''You know, I think she was the woman Alaina was trying to set me up with.''

''Really?''

''Uh-huh.'' He smiled across the table at Amanda. ''Thank goodness I've got a Christmas elf around, or I'd probably have had to go out with her.''

Amanda suddenly felt better. Then she was annoyed with herself for feeling better.

This Christmas elf stuff was starting to drive her crazy.

8

''DON'T TELL ME, let me guess,'' Mable said when Josh walked passed her desk a couple of days later. ''You are leaving early. Again.''

''Uh-huh,'' Josh said.

''Another family party?''

''Uh-huh.''

Mable eyed him thoughtfully. ''You know, for someone who hated going to family get-togethers, you're sure going to a lot of them.''

Josh shrugged. ''I'm just giving Amanda a hand.''

''Really?'' Mable's eyes twinkled. ''I don't know, Josh. It almost seems as if you're starting to enjoy them.''

''I think I might be,'' Josh said thoughtfully. He shoved his hands into his pockets and strode out the door. Mable was right. He was enjoying these parties a lot more than he used to. Of course, that was because he had Amanda. He had no idea how he'd ever coped without her.

Over the past weeks he'd discovered a lot of great things about having his very own Christmas elf. The ''I'll have to check with Amanda'' excuse was one of them. It was a wonderful way of getting out of things he didn't want to do without getting anyone mad at him.

He enjoyed using it, too. He liked the way it felt

to be part of a couple—that there was another person who was involved in his schedule outside of work. And it was the truth. He always checked with Amanda. She had easily and seemingly effortlessly taken over all the mundane details of his social life. She handled his relatives. She took care of the invitations, and thought up wonderful reasons for refusing.

They didn't refuse that many. In spite of his token objections, and the chance of being fed something he didn't like, Josh looked forward to attending family gatherings. For a long time, he'd felt as if his relatives lived in an alien world that he wasn't a part of. Now he felt like he was becoming part of it again. He'd forgotten how much he liked most of his family, and he was becoming increasingly fascinated by finding out personal things about them.

That wasn't the only reason he enjoyed those parties. Probably the biggest reason was Amanda. He looked forward to the time they spent together. It wasn't like being with other women, where he had to make an effort at conversation and usually pretend an interest he didn't feel in what they were saying. He never felt that way with Amanda. He enjoyed everything about her…except the way she scampered out of his car when he took her home. He was finding that increasingly frustrating.

He'd told himself that a business relationship with Amanda was fine with him. However, he was starting to think that an exclusively business relationship was the last thing he wanted with his Christmas elf.

''DO WE HAVE ANYTHING on that Christmas list for Tom yet?'' Josh asked Amanda as they drove to Louise and Franks's place later.

Amanda did a quick mental run-through of her list. ‘‘No, we don’t. Why?’’

‘‘Marilla gave me the title of a book he wants. It’s a Hungarian philosophy book. I don’t know if that’s personal, but…’’

‘‘It’ll do,’’ said Amanda. She waited for a moment. ‘‘You saw Marilla today?’’

‘‘Uh-huh. I dropped by her office to take her to lunch.’’

Amanda stared at him. ‘‘You did?’’

‘‘Yes, I did.’’ He slowed for a light. ‘‘She’s my sister, Amanda. I should know where she works.’’ He was silent for a moment. ‘‘She also asked me what I thought she should get you for Christmas.’’

‘‘Oh, no,’’ Amanda said. She hadn’t thought of his family wanting to exchange presents with her. ‘‘I don’t want…’’

‘‘You never told me you could do that,’’ Josh accused. ‘‘I thought you had to be subtle about this. I didn’t know you could just ask someone what they wanted!’’

‘‘You can’t just ask! However, it’s all right to ask one of the couple if they have any suggestions for the other.’’

‘‘Okay,’’ Josh said. ‘‘In that case you’d better tell me what you want so I can pass it on.’’

‘‘I don’t want anything,’’ Amanda said. ‘‘You can’t let your family get me presents, Josh. You just can’t.’’

‘‘Why not?’’ Josh asked, his familiar puzzled-looking expression on his face.

‘‘Because you can’t. The only reason they’d get me presents is because they think you and I are involved in a relationship and we aren’t!’’

"Sure we are," said Josh comfortably. "You're my elf. Isn't that a relationship?"

"It's not the one they have in mind," Amanda said. "I'm serious about this. I don't want presents from your family. I'd feel terribly guilty about it. Just tell them that I don't feel I know them well enough to exchange presents with them."

Josh started to argue, then, taking one look at her face, he held up a hand. "All right. I'll tell them. But what do you want, by the way?"

"Josh!"

"I'm just curious, that's all. What does an elf want for Christmas? Besides an office, I mean."

"An office?" Amanda repeated.

"Well, you could certainly use something," Josh explained. "Your apartment seems to get smaller and more cluttered every time I pick you up."

Amanda was touched that he'd noticed. "You're right, it does. My apartment was fine as a make-do office when we didn't have much business. But now that we have business, it's not big enough. We've also hired a couple of temps to help out, so there always seem to be people around. Sometimes I can't even find a private place to change my clothes."

"You can change your clothes at my place if you like." He glanced over, grinning. "After all, we are supposed to be living together."

Amanda imagined herself undressing in his place and shivered. *Steady Amanda, steady. You don't want to get involved, remember?* "Thank you, but I'll manage somehow."

"Why don't you just rent yourself an office?" Josh asked after a moment.

"We can't afford it right now. But someday we're

going to.'' Amanda closed her eyes and pictured it. ''Someday I'm going to have an office with my name on the door. Permanent. So you can't erase it.'' She chuckled. ''I've been downsized, and right-sized, and then I was a temp. It's no fun. You just get attached to something and they take it away. That's why I'm doing this. I want my very own office with my very own name carved on the door, so the only person who can kick me out is me.'' She hesitated. ''And it's not going to have the word elf anywhere on it, either.''

IT WAS JOSH'S IDEA to go to Charmaine's cosmic connection meeting. ''She's my sister,'' he'd explained. ''I think I should know what weird thing she's into.''

Charmaine was clearly delighted they'd come.

She led them around her beige and green living room, introducing her to the other guests, who, Amanda was amused to discover, mostly did seem to be from Detroit. Then she proudly showed them a large crystal pyramid that was sitting in the middle of the dark oak coffee table. ''For meditation later,'' she explained.

Josh's eyes widened and for a moment Amanda was afraid he was going to announce she had another headache. Instead he produced a heroic smile, said ''I'm looking forward to that,'' and wandered over to check out the buffet.

Charmaine turned to Amanda. ''I'm so thrilled about you and Josh,'' she confided. ''I can just feel the connection between you two.''

''Can you?'' Amanda glanced across the room, where Josh was heavily involved in studying the food. He caught her eye, grinned and mouthed ''No fish'' before turning away. She could almost feel the connection herself.

"Josh and I used to be connected, too," said Charmaine. "In a platonic way, of course. When we were younger, we were very close."

"You were?" Amanda had a hard time imagining that. There was something so otherworldly about Josh's gorgeous stepsister that she couldn't imagine her having much in common with Josh.

"Yes." Charmaine's dark eyes lit up with mirth. "I used to get into terrible trouble because of him. He could talk me into almost anything. It would be his idea, and I'd get the blame."

"I can believe that," Amanda murmured.

"Oh, and he was always doing the most dreadful things to my boyfriends. I don't think there was one he liked. He'd wire up their car so the horn wouldn't stop. And he once set up some kind of system so when my date walked me to the door, this deep voice said, 'Touch her and you will be liquidated' over and over." She rolled her eyes. "You can imagine what that did for my social life."

"Not a whole lot?" Amanda said, with a smile.

When Charmaine went to greet some guests who had just arrived, Amanda chatted with Edwina, Marilla and Shelby. There weren't many other relatives present. "Not many of us can understand Charmaine," Shelby explained tactfully. "However, Marilla and I always come. After all, Charmaine is our sister. If it's important to her, it's important to us. I hope you can persuade Josh to come to a few more...for moral support."

But I won't be here, Amanda thought. And it

wasn't just Josh she was going to miss. It was his entire family, as well.

She was just pondering this depressing thought when a smooth young man dressed entirely in beige came up to her. ''Hi,'' he said. ''Maurice. From Detroit.'' He rested an outstretched arm against the wall and looked down at her with obvious admiration. ''I don't believe I've seen you around here before.''

''I wouldn't think so,'' Amanda said. Was it her imagination or was this guy coming on to her? ''I'm Amanda,'' she said. ''From...the North Pole.''

''Perhaps I ran into you there, during one of my cosmic journeys,'' Maurice suggested. He looked deeply into her eyes. ''Don't you feel that we've met on another plane?'' He took her hand and squeezed it tight.

''Not really,'' Amanda said. ''Actually, I'm... uh...a little afraid of flying, so I usually take the bus.'' She tried to extract her hand and failed. She glanced over her shoulder. Josh was deeply involved in his discussion with Charmaine, and Shelby and Marilla had joined him. Amanda heaved a mental sigh. She'd wanted him to communicate with his family. She just wished right now he'd communicate with her.

She focused back on Maurice and gave him a tentative smile. ''Well, it's been great talking to you, but I really should...''

''It's wonderful talking to you, too,'' Maurice said. ''But words aren't necessary between connected individual minds. Don't you feel the same way?''

She was certainly feeling something. ''You're so right about that,'' said Amanda. ''Will you excuse me, please? I have to go check on Josh. I have a feeling he's getting a terrible headache."

"THAT WAS CERTAINLY an experience," Amanda said as they left Charmaine's party a few hours later.

"It was certainly something." Josh made a face. "And I seemed to have missed the point. Why were we sitting there in the dark, staring at that plastic pyramid?"

"I think it was a crystal pyramid," said Amanda, hiding her smile. "We were supposed to be getting in touch with our inner self to form a cosmic connection to the universe. You seemed to be getting right into it."

"I wasn't," Josh grumbled. "I was trying to figure out how I could wire up the thing."

"Wire it up?"

"So it would say something. Just imagine the expression on all those people's faces if that plastic pyramid had made a sudden announcement. Something like 'Josh Larkland, you left your lights on.'" He chuckled. "That would have cleared the room in a hurry and given us an excuse to leave."

Amanda laughed along with him. "I guess it was a rather bizarre experience."

"Bizarre isn't the word." He stepped on the gas a little too hard. "Some of those people were more than a little off-the-wall. One of them kept asking me how I was feeling."

"Oh, him." Amanda chuckled. "That's because I told him I felt you had a headache coming on. It was the only excuse I could think of to get away from him."

Josh scowled. "Get away from him?"

"Yes. He was trying to cosmically connect with me."

"He was, was he?" Josh's expression darkened. "Well, he can forget that." He stopped at a red light and locked gazes with her. "If anyone is going to cosmically connect with you, it's going to be me."

His strong, possessive tone and the expression in his dark eyes warmed Amanda from head to toe. Then he swiveled his head to face the front. "After all, you are my elf."

Right, thought Amanda. The elf you hired. For a second there she'd thought he might be a little jealous. "What did you think of Charmaine's boyfriend?" she asked after a moment.

Josh gave her a puzzled look. "Boyfriend? You mean Charmaine's *dating* one of those guys?"

"Well, yes, she is."

Josh looked totally flummoxed by that. "Which one?"

"Russell."

"Oh?" He blinked. "Which one was Russell? The one with Saturn tattooed on his cheek, or the one with the diamond in his left nostril?"

"I think it was the diamond."

"Oh." He scowled. "Well, I don't like it. I don't think Charmaine should be dating a forty-year-old guy who doesn't have a decent job."

Amanda stared at him. "How do you know so much about him?"

"I asked him," said Josh. "There wasn't anything else to talk about and I was getting tired of staring at that pyramid so I asked him how old he was and what he did for a living just to pass the time." He smiled fleetingly. "It's a great way to start a conversation."

"That's...true, I suppose," Amanda agreed, making a valiant attempt not to laugh.

"It wasn't a great conversation," Josh continued. "He said he thought gainful employment was for people who couldn't find contentment in their universe! It took me half the night to figure out that meant he doesn't have a job." He lowered his brow. "Of course, I shouldn't be all that surprised. Charmaine always attracts losers."

"Really?" Amanda said, surprised that he remembered.

"Uh-huh. Even when we were kids, I was always having to scare them off." He chuckled. "And you wouldn't believe some of the things I had to do." He was silent for a moment. When he looked over at her, his eyes glinted with mischief. "You know, Amanda. I think I've just thought up the perfect present for Charmaine."

Amanda eyed him suspiciously. "If it's got anything to do with wiring up her house so it *talks* to her dates, you can forget it." She paused. "Although I must admit, it would be extremely personal."

"YOU HAVE GOT TO DO something about this apartment," Josh complained a few days later.

He sat in her kitchen, his feet propped up on one of her chairs, and shook his head at the stacks of papers and boxes in the living room. "There isn't room to swing a cat, much less an elf."

"I know," said Amanda. "But it will soon be over." It would, too. There was just over a week before Christmas. Josh was picking her up to go to his mother's open house, and had come early so they could go through a status report.

"I hope I'm going to be ready on time." He stretched back and closed his eyes. "Okay. Let's go through this gift list."

Amanda obediently began reading from her notes. "We've got the Halsone for Mimi, fishing tackle for Reg, and a red toothbrush holder for your aunt Judith." She hesitated. "Are you sure your aunt Judith wants a toothbrush holder?"

"Uh-huh," Josh said without opening his eyes. "I broke hers when I was six. I think it's time I replaced it. But maybe we could get her some photograph albums, as well. She needs some new ones."

Amanda studied him. "How do you know?"

"I was over there the other day to set the time on her VCR and we were looking at some photographs." He rolled his eyes. "I'm telling you, Amanda, as soon as my prototype circuitry is in production, I'm going to install a voice-activated VCR in Judith's place. She doesn't have one clue how to do it." He gestured at the list. "Go on."

"Okay. You're giving Marilla an A-12 Pneumatic Door Activator—whatever that is."

"It's an automatic sensor so their cats can open the window themselves," Josh explained. "Marilla was so worried that her cats weren't going to be able to let themselves out while she was at work. With this, they should be able to do it themselves—assuming I can get it tuned to the correct 'meow.'"

"It sounds...perfect," Amanda said. She returned to reading her list. "Shelby's getting the computer equipment, but we don't have anything for Gordon. I..."

"Yeah, we do," Josh said. "I was out at the university to see Shelby and she mentioned Gordon is into building model boats.'' He opened one eye. ''I don't know if that's personal, but...''

''It'll be fine,'' Amanda assured him. ''You had lunch with Shelby?''

''Uh-huh. I had to go to the university to check up on the equipment out there. She showed me around.'' He grinned. ''I still don't understand what she teaches, but at least now I know where she does it. Go on.''

''We've got a tie for your uncle Frank. And a pasta maker...''

''A pasta maker?'' Josh's eyes widened. ''We're not giving my mother a pasta maker. I...''

''I know,'' said Amanda. ''I thought we'd give it to Alaina.''

Josh grinned. ''Perfect.''

Amanda referred back to her notes. ''I think that's about it. We still don't have anything for your mother yet, but I did find a crystal moon pendant for Charmaine.''

''I think my idea was much better.'' Josh stroked his finger across his bottom lip. ''You know, Amanda, I really don't like the idea of her dating weird men with tattoos on their cheek.''

''Don't you?'' Amanda watched his finger, then dragged her gaze back to her notes. She must have a serious problem if a man's finger turned her on.

Josh didn't seem to be suffering from the same problem. ''What I'd really like to get her is a decent man with a decent job. Every time I think of that Russell character I get cold shivers.''

''Do you?'' said Amanda. Every time she thought of him she got hot shivers—for an entirely different reason.

"You know who she should meet? She should meet Wendell."

"Wendell?" Amanda echoed absently.

"Wendell Philmore. He's one of the techs who works for me. He's a little peculiar, too—but he's not a bad guy. He's certainly much better than that Russell character. At least he's got a job in this universe."

Amanda gaped at him. "Are you actually thinking of setting up your own sister with somebody?"

"Why not?" said Josh. "Everyone does it to me. Besides, who knows? Maybe Charmaine and Wendell will cosmically connect."

It was possible, and Amanda was thrilled he was this interested in his sister's life. "Maybe they will."

"Good. Why don't you arrange it?"

"Arrange what?"

"Having them over," Josh prompted. "That's how everyone always sets me up."

"Having them over," Amanda repeated slowly. "You mean, to your place?"

"Uh-huh. Oh, and don't just have them. We might as well have everyone we don't have a present for. That way we can quiz them without having to go anywhere. Be sure to include my mother—she hasn't seen my place for a while." He tapped his fingers on his thigh, obviously taken with the idea. "Oh, and we might as well ask my other sisters, too. From the way they talk, I sometimes wonder if they have any idea about what I do."

"They don't, but..."

"They can see it at my place. I've got most of my prototype equipment there. Oh, I think Uncle Reg would be interested in that, as well, so we should ask him, too.'' He looked over at Amanda. ''You can do this, can't you?''

''Well…uh…I suppose, but…''

''Good,'' said Josh. ''How about tomorrow?''

9

JOSH WAS IN the process of packing up his things when Mable came into his office. ''I know,'' she said before he could say anything. ''You're leaving early.''

''Uh-huh,'' he said. ''I have to get right home. There's something wrong with my microwave.'' He liked the way that sounded. He'd often been around when other men had been summoned home to fix some emergency. They'd always rolled their eyes and looked exasperated, but they'd looked a little pleased, as well. Josh had never understood why, but now he did. He liked the feeling that someone not connected with work needed his help.

Mable looked down at the phone, then back at him. ''Your microwave *phoned* you?'' She shook her head. ''This high-tech stuff is getting so it's beyond me.''

''My microwave didn't phone me, although that's a great idea,'' Josh explained. ''Amanda phoned me. She's trying to get the microwave to work, but when she tries to turn it on, the oven cuts in.''

''Amanda's at your place?''

''Uh-huh.'' The image of her in his place gave him a pleasant thrill. ''We're having a few people over tonight.'' He liked saying that, too. It was exactly the sort of thing a couple did—have people over to their place. He was looking forward to it, too. He wanted to show his family what he did, and he was eager to see their reaction.

Mable's eyes widened considerably. "*You?*"

"Yeah, me." He frowned. "I wanted to do it last night, but Amanda insisted she needed more than one day's notice to organize it. She gets funny about things like that sometimes."

"How...peculiar." Mable eyed him suspiciously. "It's not a Christmas party, is it?"

"Not really," he said, although now that she'd mentioned it, it was sort of a Christmas party. "I guess you could say we're having a few people over under the umbrella of a Christmas theme."

"Good heavens," Mable said faintly. "Is there...uh...going to be singing?"

"There better not be," Josh said.

"Good," Mable said. "At least I know one thing hasn't changed."

JOSH HAD A CONDO in an upscale area of Calgary. He'd chosen it because of the location, had it professionally decorated, professionally cleaned, and, apart from sleeping there, he spent less than ten hours a week in the place. When he wasn't in it, he'd be hard-pressed to describe what his apartment looked like.

However, when he let himself in at six o'clock, he knew immediately that it didn't usually look or smell like this.

He noticed the scent as soon as he stepped inside—a Christmassy mixture of pine intermingled with delicious food odors wafting from the kitchen. "Amanda?" he called.

Amanda came out of the kitchen. She stopped in the doorway and stared at him with obvious surprise.

"Oh," she said. "I didn't expect you to be here this early."

Josh took one look at her and felt as if he'd just been hit in the solar plexus. She had on another one of her bright red dresses, her short blond hair curled damply around her ears, her face was flushed and she wasn't wearing any shoes. She looked sweet, and sexy, and desirable. Just seeing her looking like that, in his place, was an incredible turn-on.

"You didn't have to rush home just because I couldn't get the microwave to work," Amanda continued. "I could have coped for a little while."

Josh cleared his throat. "I…uh…thought I'd better," he explained. He kicked off his boots and hung his coat in the closet. "Besides, I was planning on coming home anyway to give you a hand."

"Really?" She smiled and her eyes sparkled with appreciation. "Well, that was very nice of you."

"Very nice" wasn't a good description for him right now, Josh thought. "Decidedly lustful" was. He gave his head a shake to clear it and took a look around, not all that surprised to see a fully decorated Christmas tree in one corner of the living room. There was a fire in the fireplace, the furniture had been polished to a shine, and everything looked clean and fresh and homey. "Not that it looks like you need a hand."

"Just with the oven," said Amanda. "And it is working. It just won't…mind its own business." She furrowed her brow. "I just hope I haven't broken something. I'm not used to working with such smart appliances."

"You can't break anything," Josh assured her. He

put an arm across her shoulders, getting another rush from touching her. ''Let's take a look.''

Amanda stood beside him as he checked the sensitivity circuitry on the microwave. Her scent surrounded him, making it difficult for him to concentrate, so it took him longer than it should have to make the adjustments. ''Now I know why there aren't a lot of elves in high-tech industries,'' he said as he turned to face her.

She tilted up her head, looking puzzled. ''Why?''

''It's too distracting.'' He took a step toward her. ''Dim lights,'' he said. The lights dimmed. The microwave didn't come on.

''I think you fixed it,'' said Amanda, and she looked impressed.

''It's because of the prototype circuit board,'' Josh said. ''I had to improvise here. When the new houses are built, they'll have things set up properly. Then we won't have these sorts of problems.''

''Oh,'' Amanda said. Her tongue flicked across her bottom lip. ''Are you going to move into one of those new homes?''

Josh seldom gave one second of thought to where he lived now, much less where he might live in the future, and right now he didn't care, as long as she was going to be in the kitchen. ''I might,'' he said.

''Oh,'' she said again.

Her gaze met his. Her eyes were a deeper shade of green than he'd seen them before, the blush on her cheeks a darker pink, and her breathing was faster than normal. Was that a reaction to him being so close? Josh's own breathing rate increased at the idea that it was. He toyed with the idea of pressing his lips against the smooth skin of her throat to see what her reaction would be to that. However, before he could do it, Amanda took a wary step backward. "We've got less than an hour before people start arriving," she said briskly. "If you're going to take a shower, you should probably do it now."

Maybe she'd like to join him. Josh considered inviting her, but something in her eyes told him now was not a good time. "Good idea," he said instead.

He wandered up the stairs and into the bathroom. Amanda's shampoo and perfume and hair-dryer were lying on the counter. The towels from her shower were damp, and held a lingering scent of her. The idea of her standing totally naked in his shower was even more arousing than her bare feet. Too bad his shower wasn't a smart appliance. He'd like to know what it had to say about her naked body. No, actually, he'd rather find out for himself.

There was no doubt about it. He wanted to do something with his Christmas elf that had nothing to do with business arrangements...or Christmas.

A BUSINESS FUNCTION, Amanda reminded herself as she studied the buffet. This was a business function; she was catering a business function and Josh Larkland was nothing more than her employer at a business function.

But when Josh came padding into the dining room a few minutes later, the term "business function" fled from her brain, along with almost everything else. He was wearing a pair of brown pants, his pale yellow shirt was unbuttoned and he was clutching his socks in his right hand. The man even had sexy toes, not to mention the great wide, muscular chest that went with everything else that was great about him. "This looks terrific,'' he approved as he surveyed the food. ''Did you do it all?''

Clean men, Amanda was thinking. There's something so appealing about a clean man. In all honesty, though, she'd probably find Josh appealing if he were covered with mud.

She grinned at the image and ordered her brain to clear. ''Just me, the caterers, the cleaners and almost everyone else in the city. You know, Josh, the next time you plan a party, you should do it with more than forty-eight hours' notice. It would be a lot easier—and a lot cheaper.''

''I don't plan on having another party,'' he said. ''I don't even think I planned this party.'' That familiar puzzled look crept over his face. ''As a matter of fact, I didn't even realize it *was* a party until Mable told me. I thought we were just having a few people over.''

Only Josh would be that clued out. ''When it's your entire family, it's a party! The amazing thing is that they're almost all coming, too, in spite of the short notice. Mimi canceled tickets to the theater, Francine and Wally are missing Wally's office party, and Charmaine is forgoing the New Moon Avizandum so she could come.''

''Great. We want Charmaine here so she can meet Wendell. Maybe she'll cosmically connect with him and forget the other bozos.'' He studied the buffet table. ''The good news is, there is enough food here for a few hundred people—and I know for sure none of it has anything to do with fish.'' He gave Amanda a warning look. ''It doesn't, does it?''

''No, of course not.''

''Good thing.'' He turned to face her. ''Now, what

can I do to help? It has to be something technical. I'm no good with knives, cutting things up, setting things out, cooking things or cleaning things up.'' He smiled his slow, sexy smile. ''But I've got lots of talent in other areas.''

Did he mean what she thought he meant? Probably not. ''Good,'' she said. ''Then how about demonstrating them by putting on some music? The stereo refuses to listen to me.''

Josh leaned against the wall while he pulled on his socks. ''That's because the stereo is not modified for voice input yet. All you have to do is press the On button.''

''I never thought of that,'' Amanda said, smiling. As Josh walked around with a loose, easy, yet sexy stride, she kept reminding herself that this party was business, strictly business. But it was near impossible to keep her mind on business when Josh was tantalizingly near, so she fled into the kitchen.

She was taking the vegetable tray out of the fridge when the sounds of Christmas music filled the condo. Josh came into the kitchen. ''How's that?''

''Good. Thank you.''

''You're welcome. Say, where did I get that collection of Christmas music? I didn't think I had any.''

''You didn't,'' Amanda said. ''I brought it with me.''

''What about the tree? Did you bring that with you, too?''

''No. That I had delivered.''

His forehead wrinkled. ''I didn't know you could have a tree delivered—complete with ornaments and strings of lights.''

''You can have almost anything delivered, as long

as you're willing to pay for it,'' Amanda informed him. ''This is not going to be a cheap party, Josh. There's the food, the cleaners, the caterers... Oh, and I also had to buy Christmas ornaments because you didn't have any.''

Josh shrugged. ''I never needed them before.'' He put his head to one side. ''You think of everything, don't you?''

''That's why us elves are paid the big bucks,'' Amanda quipped. ''We're supposed to think of everything.''

''Ah,'' said Josh. ''Well, you're very good at it.''

There was a gleam in his eye that hadn't been there before. Amanda's heart rate increased. She bent her head and busied herself with the vegetables. ''I like doing it. And it's fun working in your kitchen—when the appliances cooperate, that is.''

''Is it?'' Josh shrugged. ''I wouldn't know. I don't cook here much. As a matter of fact, no one cooks here much.''

''I gathered that from the dust in the oven.'' Amanda glanced over her shoulder at him. ''You must have had other women in here to cook you a meal?''

''Nope.'' He examined the bottles of wine sitting on the counter. ''Should I open these?''

''Yes. You mean...never?''

''No,'' said Josh. ''Never. At least, not that I can remember.''

''Why not?''

He shrugged as if it wasn't important. ''I don't know.'' He finished opening the wine, and rounded the corner to stand behind her.

''You must have people over sometime,'' Amanda persisted.

"Just some guys." He was so close she could feel his breath against her neck. "You know, a bunch of propeller-heads talking techy-byte stuff, drinking beer and eating pretzels."

The doorbell rang as Amanda was setting out the vegetable tray. She straightened her dress, whisked off her apron, and found her shoes. "How do I look?"

She expected him to say "elflike" or something of that nature. Instead he said, "I think you're missing something." Then he stepped forward, put his arms around her and before Amanda realized what was happening, he was kissing her—a hard, hot kiss that started with his mouth stroking over hers, then his tongue licking along her top lip, moving around to her bottom lip, then sliding inside her mouth. His body was hard against hers, her breasts crushed against his chest and Amanda couldn't think of anything except how good it felt, and how much she wished it would go on forever.

But it didn't. The doorbell rang again. "I suppose one of us better get that," Josh mumbled against her lips.

He released her, and stepped back. Amanda blinked up at him, her mind still numb from his kiss. "Just a minute," she said as he started to move toward the door. "You've got lipstick..."

"That's okay." He grinned. "Now we both look as if we live together."

IT WAS ONE O'CLOCK in the morning when Amanda and Josh bade goodbye to the last of their guests and collapsed onto the couch, with the enthusiastic comments from Josh's family still ringing in their ears.

"It was fabulous, Amanda. However, I would add a dash of cinnamon to the veggie dip. It gives it such flavor."

"A Siamese would be perfect here, Amanda. And it could even let itself out!"

"Wonderful gadgets, Josh. I had no idea they used these sorts of things on trains." And, obscurely, from Aunt Judith, "What an amazing bathroom, dear. The sink is so...white!"

Edwina and Harold were the last to leave. Edwina had given Amanda an extra-long hug just before she went out. "Thank you so much, Amanda," she'd said, and Amanda knew she wasn't just thanking her for the evening.

Josh rubbed an eye and yawned. "That's the problem with having your own party," he groaned. "You can't leave when you feel like it."

Which was probably a good thing, thought Amanda. If they'd been somewhere else, she probably would have dragged him out the door after that mind-numbing kiss in the kitchen. She'd spent half the evening trying not to think about it, and the other half thinking about it anyway. And every time she'd looked at him, she'd thought about it again.

She looked up at him. His head was back against the pillows, his eyes were half closed and a small smile of satisfaction played across his lips. "You don't look like someone who wanted to leave," she accused. "You look like someone who had a good time."

His lips curved upward. "Yeah, I guess I did. Except when Uncle Frank started reciting actuarial tables to me." He dropped a casual arm around her shoulders. ''He had on that same ugly blue tie, too. It's a good thing we got him a new one.''

''Uh-huh.'' Amanda rested her head against his shoulder. ''What about your mother? Did you have any brilliant ideas for her yet?''

''No.'' He sighed, then brightened. ''But I did come up with something for Aunt Francine.''

Amanda glanced up at him. ''You did?''

''Yup.'' Josh sounded smug. ''She wants a variable speed, battery-operated reversible drill.''

Amanda tried to imagine the proper-looking Francine with a variable-speed drill and failed completely. ''Are you sure?''

''Absolutely positive. She kept playing with mine.'' He chuckled. ''Although I'm not too sure she knew what it was. It didn't look as if Wendell and Charmaine hit it off, after all. They hardly said a word to each other all evening.''

''I think they were connecting,'' Amanda told him. ''And they did leave together.''

''Good.'' He stretched back, his lips widening into a smile. ''Did you see Aunt Mimi and Uncle Reg? They spent the entire evening wandering from room to room saying 'lights on, lights off.' ''

''They were impressed,'' Amanda said. ''Your whole family was impressed, Josh. You should have shown them all this years ago.''

''I never thought about it.'' He shifted sideways so he was facing her, and raised a hand to brush a strand of hair off her cheek. ''What I should have done is gotten a Christmas elf years ago.''

His palm moved across her face, and he ran his thumb along her bottom lip. Amanda could hear her own heartbeat, feel herself gasping with pleasure at his touch. Then his mouth was where his thumb used to be, hot and heavy against hers, while his tongue curled around hers and his hands pulled her closer. This was strictly a business function, Amanda reminded herself hazily, but it was impossible to think about business functions when his large palms were gently stroking down her back.

He slid back, taking her with him, so his head rested against the arm of the sofa, still kissing her, his arms wrapped around her. When they finally came up for air, Amanda was sprawled on top of him, her legs entwined with his, her hips pressed against his. The heat emanated from him, and the knowledge that he wanted her as much as she wanted him increased her desire.

She raised her head. His face was ruddy, his eyelids drooping sensuously, and his breathing was as rapid and uneven as her own. ''We shouldn't be doing this,'' she said, having trouble catching her breath. ''This is supposed to be a business relationship, remember? I'm just your Christmas elf and...''

''I know,'' Josh said. ''But I've never made love with an elf before.'' His hand moved up and down her back. ''Do you really think it's an experience I should miss?''

Amanda hesitated. If she refused, he wouldn't make a fuss about it. He'd just say something like ''Too bad'' and never mention it again.

But he was right underneath her. She could feel his hardness and she could see the passion in his eyes. She didn't want to refuse. Right now, she just wanted him. ''I don't think it's an experience you should miss, either,'' she whispered.

''Good,'' said Josh. He eased her head back down

to his. ‘‘Because that’s all I could think about all evening.’’

Then he was kissing her again, holding her hips against his so she could feel him against her, and even though they were dressed, the sensation was so erotic and so arousing that Amanda moaned and bit against his neck, squirming against him to get closer. He fumbled with the zipper on her dress, finally raising his head so he could see what he was doing. ‘‘That’s going to be my next invention,’’ he growled into her ear. ‘‘A voice-activated zipper.’’ The feel of his breath, the knowledge that he was as aroused as she was, excited Amanda even more.

He finally got it undone, and raised her up into a sitting position so he could work the dress off her shoulders and down to her waist. His hands trembled slightly and when he freed her breasts from her bra his eyes widened and his lips curled into his slow, sexy smile. He cupped a breast in each hand, and rubbed his thumb across her nipples. Amanda gasped with pleasure and his eyes darkened. ‘‘You like that?’’ he asked.

‘‘Yes,’’ Amanda breathed.

‘‘So do I.’’

He fondled her breasts while she undid his shirt. When she pressed her palms against his warm, bare chest, he closed his eyes and groaned and pulled her down so he could take a breast in his mouth. Amanda was so mindless with pleasure that she only half realized he was trying to remove the rest of her clothes until he raised her up a little. ‘‘We have to move, Amanda,’’ he mumbled against her skin. ‘‘I’m no good at undressing someone on a sofa.’’

He eased her up, but instead of taking her to his

bedroom, as she expected, he slid down to the floor, taking her with him. "I want to do this here, beside the Christmas tree," he explained. "It seems rather...fitting."

Amanda didn't care where they did it as long as it happened right now. She helped him get her clothes off, laughing as he complained about her panty hose—"I have no idea how you women get these things on"—then, seeing the expression on his face as he looked at her, she didn't feel like laughing anymore.

He knelt to remove his pants, then stretched down beside her, pulling her against his naked body, easing his thigh between her legs, then gently parting her and sliding a finger into her. Amanda arched against him. He took her breast in his mouth again, caressing a nipple with his tongue, while his fingers searched and found the sensitive place between her legs. He kept moving his fingers and touching her and licking her breasts as the pressure built inside Amanda, finally driving her over the edge into a shuddering climax.

Then Josh was rolling away from her to pull a condom out of his pants' pocket. "Just a little planning ahead," he explained, catching the surprised look on her face. He used his teeth to rip open the foil packet. "I told you. I've been thinking about this all evening."

Then he pulled her down onto him, parting her, easing himself up into her. "Oh, Amanda," he groaned into her ear, as he wrapped his arms around her. They moved together, at first slowly, then faster and harder and deeper, and Amanda moaned her pleasure into his ear.

Afterward, they cuddled together on his carpet, with the Christmas tree lights pulsing down on them. "I liked that," Josh announced in a satisfied-sounding voice.

"Me, too," Amanda murmured. She rested her head against his chest and closed her eyes.

"Good." He caressed a hand up and down her arm. "Let's go up to the bedroom and do it again there. And then we could try the kitchen..."

Amanda raised her head to look at his face. "Are you planning some sort of marathon here?"

"Why not?" Josh asked. He took her into his arms and smiled up at her. "After all, we've got all night."

We've got longer than that, Amanda thought. We've got until Christmas Eve.

10

"YES, I KNOW," Josh said to Mable as he walked into his office three days later. "I'm a little late, aren't I?"

"You're not just a little late," Mable scolded. "It's almost eleven." She frowned at him, although her eyes sparkled. "First you start leaving at five. Now you don't come in until eleven. What's next? Are you going to stop coming in at all?"

"I'm considering it," he said, chuckling at her expression. "It's Christmas, Mable. People have things to do at Christmas."

"Like what?"

Like spending most of the morning making love with Amanda. Josh almost blurted that out before he remembered it wasn't the sort of information Mable needed to know. "Just…things," he said. "And I'm going to be leaving early, too, so if I've got any appointments after three, you'll have to reschedule them. I'm going shopping."

"Shopping?" Mable looked more astonished than ever. "You're going shopping?"

"Uh-huh. I told Amanda I'd give her a hand." He grinned again as he recalled the way Amanda's eyes had sparkled when he'd offered to accompany her.

"Amanda, hmm?" Mable cleared her throat. "You

two sure seem to be spending a lot of time together these days.''

Josh nodded. He had been spending a lot of time with Amanda. She'd spent every night since their Christmas party at his place. When they weren't attending a family or a business function, they spent the evening together, watching television, reviewing their Christmas shopping list, talking and making love.

Josh was enjoying every second of it. It wasn't at all like any of his other brief relationships. He didn't feel obligated to spend time with Amanda. He wanted to do it. She never got annoyed with him because he forgot an appointment they'd made, because he never forgot an appointment. Most of the time he was early, because he was eager to see her. He liked going to his place and finding her there, and he liked not having to eat alone.

''With all this going on, it's a wonder we get any work done around here,'' said Mable.

Josh was already lining up his work for the day. ''Don't worry,'' he said absentmindedly. ''Soon it will be Christmas.''

Mable paused at the doorway. ''And then what?''

Josh shrugged. After Christmas he wouldn't be going to all these parties. He wouldn't be looking for presents, or trying to find out personal things about people. ''Then things will get back to normal.''

''And...uh...what about Amanda?'' Mable pursued.

''What about her?'' Josh hadn't thought that far ahead. Right now, he was enjoying having Amanda around. But somewhere in the back of his mind he knew that Amanda would drift out of his life, the same way other women had drifted away. The idea bothered him, so he pushed it to one side. Right now everything was perfect. They'd nearly completed his Christmas shopping list. His family was happy with him. And best of all, he had his evenings with Amanda.

Getting a Christmas elf was definitely the smartest thing he'd ever done.

''I'M STARTING TO FEEL as if we've got this under control,'' Brandy advised. ''I've got the exhibitors arranged for the Internet trade show we're doing next month. We sent out the invitations for VisTech's open house. And we've got the corporate gifts for Dawson's Building Supplies.'' She looked down at the boxes. ''Although I still don't understand why a building supply company wants to give their corporate pals books on horse breeding.''

''Neither do I,'' Amanda murmured. Her mind wasn't on horse breeding…or even work. It was busy thinking about Josh…the way he'd looked this morning after his shower. She smiled.

Brandy leaned back against the sofa and studied her. ''We've been so busy these past few days that it feels like I've hardly seen you.''

''I have been busy,'' Amanda said. She'd been busy organizing Josh's office party, finishing the last of the shopping, wrapping presents…and when she wasn't doing that, she was with Josh.

''You certainly have been working long hours,'' Brandy said, with an innocent expression on her face. ''Although I've been here before you just about every day.'' She paused. ''Which is rather startling, since *you* live here.''

Amanda flushed and averted her face. ''That's another problem with using your apartment as your office. There's just no privacy."

"I'm you're best friend. We aren't supposed to have privacy from each other." Brandy's eyes sparkled. "I gather you and Josh don't have a 'business relationship' anymore."

"Not exactly," Amanda admitted.

"How about that!" Brandy said, flushing. "You and me in the same weekend."

Amanda saw the color on Brandy's cheek and the sparkle in her eyes and wondered if she looked the same way. "You mean, you and Harvy..."

"Finally," Brandy said, with a satisfied sigh. "Oh, we talked about it first. Endlessly, as a matter of fact. He had all these deep thoughts about not offending me, and what we meant to each other... It was really sweet. And then it was...wonderful. Of course I knew it would be. Harvy is so...sexy."

"Harvy?" Amanda pictured the short, rotund Harvy Denton. "Harvy is sexy?"

"Well, he is when you get to know him." Brandy's flush deepened. "He's really getting serious, Amanda. He's even invited me to meet his mother."

"Really?" Amanda smiled. She'd already met Josh's mother.

"Yes." Brandy got a dreamy look on her face. "You know, I think this might be the real thing."

Amanda had been too busy and too happy to dwell on the faint, niggling worry at the back of her mind. However, Brandy's words brought them to the front of it. "I wish I was so sure," she murmured.

"What do you mean? This has to be something, Amanda. You and Josh are together all the time—and you have been for most of the month."

"I know," Amanda said. She was positive Josh felt something for her. He certainly had to be attracted to her, considering how much time they spent making love. And she was sure she saw genuinc affection in his eyes. "It's probably silly," she said. "But I think it's because Josh keeps referring to me as his Christmas elf."

"So?"

"I guess I started thinking of myself as that, too. All month I've been thinking that by Christmas Eve, I won't be shopping for Josh anymore, or going to parties with him anymore. That all will be ended by then. And now we're nearly at that point. Christmas is just a few days away," Amanda explained. "We've nearly finished Josh's shopping list. We've just got his mother left—and we'll see her at Francine's open house tonight. Then we have the Larkland Christmas party and then it will be Christmas Eve. And then what?"

"I think you're worried over nothing, Amanda," Brandy said in a reassuring tone. "You're not going to stop seeing Josh just because Christmas has arrived."

"I hope you're right," Amanda said, worried all the same.

"I NEVER KNEW shopping could be so exhausting," Josh complained as they were getting ready for Francine's party that evening.

He came out of the bathroom, buttoning up the collar on his shirt, and gave Amanda a kiss on the nose. "What were all those people doing there anyway?"

"Possibly Christmas shopping," Amanda teased. "Just like we were."

"Well, they should be more organized," Josh complained. "They should have finished their shopping a long time ago."

"You haven't finished your shopping yet," Amanda scolded. "And it wouldn't have taken us all day to find two things if you weren't so difficult! I told you. They don't *make* variable-speed reversible drills with *pink* handles."

"Aunt Francine needs a drill and she always wears pink."

"It doesn't matter," said Amanda. "People do not color coordinate their wardrobe to their work tools."

"Oh." He grinned, hugged her and then released her so they could finish dressing. "The good news is, we're nearly finished. We just have to think up something for my mother." He glanced over his shoulder at her. "You haven't had a brilliant idea, have you—besides a pasta maker, I mean?"

"No," Amanda admitted.

"Me, neither," Josh admitted. "I've talked to her, I've taken her for lunch, and I even asked Shelby and Charmaine for suggestions." He grimaced. "They weren't much help. Shelby thought I should get her a cookbook and Charmaine's idea was perfume. Obviously they're no better at this personal stuff than I am."

"We're running out of time," Amanda reminded him. "We'd better come up with some ideas tonight."

"I will." Josh's eyes sparkled at her. "We're getting down to the final stretch here. This is the last family party we have to go to. We're on the last present. Soon we'll just have the office Christmas party to get through."

A cold shiver traveled up Amanda's spine. Don't

be ridiculous, she scolded herself. So what if Christmas comes. You're going to stay right here and be with Josh... Still, she couldn't stop herself from asking. "What happens after that?"

Josh shrugged. "Things get back to normal." He expertly knotted his tie. "It's about time, too. The work is just piling up on my desk."

Amanda shivered again. The possibility of this wonderful thing with Josh ending seemed frighteningly possible.

It seemed even more possible when they were at Francine's that night.

"It's something of a family tradition," Edwina explained to Amanda. "Mimi has the first party of the season. Francine has the last one before Christmas. And then on Christmas Day, everyone comes to my place." She smiled at Amanda. "I never thought to ask before, but I assume you'll be joining us at Christmas. Or are you going to be with your own family?"

Amanda would have loved to be with her family, but they had so much business now, and it was so expensive to get there, that she had decided to stay here. She'd planned on spending the day with Brandy's family, although she had been expecting Edwina's invitation. She opened her mouth to accept, then changed her mind. "I'm not really sure what I'm doing," she said instead.

"You'll always be welcome with us," Edwina said. She gazed across the room, where Josh was involved in an animated discussion with his sisters. "Josh has been so different since you've become part of his life."

Everyone kept saying that. "It's so amazing to see the change in Josh since you're part of his life."

"Josh is so happy since you're part of his life."

"Josh is so cosmically aware since you're part of his life."

"I think Josh is starting to give serious consideration to getting a cat," Marilla said. "It's all because you've become part of his life."

Amanda watched Josh chat with his mother. She was part of his life, wasn't she? Or was she just his Christmas elf who was pretending to be part of his life?

Josh caught her eye and began moving through the crowd toward her, his face lit by a cheerful smile. "I've got it," he whispered into her ear. "A Christmas present for my mother."

"What?"

"A pearl necklace. She mentioned she broke the ones my father gave her. I'd like to replace it." He studied Amanda's face. "That is...personal, isn't it?"

"It's perfect," Amanda said, giving him a little hug. She was touched by his thoughtfulness.

"That's it, then," he said. "The last present." He grinned with pleasure. "We've done it, Amanda. Now we don't have to do this anymore."

He sounded happy about it. Amanda felt colder than ever.

"I THINK WE'VE GOT THIS organized," Amanda told Mable two days before the Larkland Christmas party.

She took an anxious look around the lobby of Larkland Technology Development. "I'll do a few more decorations on the day of the party but that's pretty much all there is left to do. The caterers are all lined up, I've arranged for the musicians...with no singing.

And I've had positive responses from almost everyone we asked.''

''You've done a great job,'' Mable murmured. ''This is going to be one heck of a Christmas party.''

''It better be,'' said Amanda. ''Everyone Josh wants to impress is coming.'' She leaned back in her chair near Mable's desk. ''I'm a little surprised at that. December twenty-third isn't a great time to be having a Christmas party.''

''Everyone is coming because of Josh,'' Mable explained. ''No matter what he does, people like him. I even like him, and that's not easy considering how difficult he is to work for.'' She paused. ''Of course, he's been a lot easier to work for since you've been around.''

Amanda blushed at the compliment. ''I don't think I...''

''Yes, you did. You dragged him out of his office and into the real world. That's been good for him. And you put him back in touch with his family again. That's been good for him, too—and for them. But I'm not so sure it's been good for you.''

Amanda felt a twinge of unease. ''What do you mean?''

Mable's blue eyes were warm and wise. ''You've fallen for him, haven't you?''

Amanda opened her mouth to deny it, then closed it and nodded.

''I thought so.'' Mable sighed heavily. ''He is fond of you, too, Amanda. I know he is. And he needs you—right now anyway.'' Her eyebrows came down. ''But I'm not too sure what's going to happen when Christmas is over.''

Amanda swallowed a couple of times. ''What do you mean?''

Mable winced. ''I don't want to burst your bubble, and I don't want to be an interfering old woman, either. But I've known Josh for a long time. True, I've never seen him act like this before, but it is Christmas. Josh gets a little strange around Christmas.'' She smiled slightly. ''Of course, it's hard to tell because he's a little strange most of the time.''

''Mable...''

Mable stretched forward and put her hand over Amanda's. ''What I'm trying to tell you is that this Josh—the one who is interested in you and spends time with you and wants to be with you—well, this isn't the Josh I'm used to. The one I'm used to spends most of his time at work, and doesn't think about anything but that.''

Amanda had a brief flash of Susan's beautiful face as she'd told Amanda much the same thing. *He just forgot about me,* she'd said.

Mable's blue eyes were crystal clear across the table. ''I just thought you should be prepared...in case that happens. It's not as if Josh is a bad person. He doesn't mean to hurt anyone, and he'd never do it on purpose. He just wouldn't know that he's doing it.''

''I know,'' Amanda said. She gave Mable a swift smile. ''You don't have to worry. I'm a Christmas elf, remember? Us elves can take care of ourselves.''

''I hope so,'' said Mable. ''Oh, and if it makes your job any easier, I should tell you that I've got my heart set on a bottle of brandy for Christmas.''

AMANDA ARRIVED at Josh's place that evening feeling tired and depressed. They'd planned on spending the evening at home, but when she walked in, Josh still had his coat on. He kissed her when she came in, and Amanda clung to him extra hard. He released her and used a finger to raise her chin. "What's wrong?" he asked. "You look worn out."

Amanda was touched that he'd noticed and then annoyed with herself for being touched. "I'm just tired," she said. "It's all this rushing around. Thinking up Christmas presents. Buying Christmas presents. Organizing parties. Going to parties. And you should see my apartment. I can't even move in there." She rested her head against his chest. "Sometimes Christmas gets to me."

"Me, too," he said. "Cheer up. Soon it will be all over and things can get back to normal."

"Now there's a cheerful thought," Amanda muttered. She eyed his clothes. "I thought we were staying here tonight."

"We can't," said Josh. "There's this...business thing we should go to."

The last thing Amanda wanted to do was go anywhere. "Do we have to?" she asked.

"We really should." He patted her shoulder. "Come on. It's the last Christmas thing you'll have to come to."

Was that supposed to make her feel better? "Terrific," Amanda muttered. "The North Pole looks pretty good right now."

"We're not going to the North Pole. Hurry up. Get dressed. Let's get out of here."

His aura of suppressed excitement made Amanda want to either smack him or throw herself at his feet and beg him to assure her that Mable was wrong.

She was still mulling over Mable's warning when

Josh stopped the car. Amanda had been so lost in thought that she hadn't noticed where they were. Now she realized they were stopping in front of an office building. She glanced over at him. "Is this the right place?"

"Uh-huh." Josh grinned at her, his eyes sparkling with excitement. "Come on."

Amanda hesitated. The building looked pretty much deserted. "But..."

He ignored her objections and guided her into the elevator, and pressed the button for the second floor. "Are you sure you know where we're going?" Amanda asked as the elevator rose.

"Absolutely positive," said Josh.

The elevator opened onto a hallway. Josh used a hand on her back to guide her down it, and stopped in front of a glass door. Amanda looked up at him, then at the writing on the glass door in front of her. A&B Executive Services, it said in big block letters.

Amanda looked back at Josh. "What?"

"It's your Christmas present," Josh explained. "I would have wrapped it but it's a little hard to wrap an office."

"An office," Amanda echoed. She looked back up at him. "You got me an office?"

"Uh-huh." He grinned down at her. "I even had a voice-recognition door lock installed. It's coded for Brandy's voice and yours, too." He gestured at the door. "Go ahead. Open it."

"I can't believe this," Amanda said, thoroughly astonished and thoroughly delighted. She looked from him back to the door. "Open," she whispered. The door swung open.

"It's not huge or anything," said Josh as he led

her through the reception area. ''But it's a lot bigger than your apartment.''

It wasn't huge, but it was exactly the right size. There was a small foyer at the front, a storage area at the back, a large square work area, and two interior offices. It was all completely furnished, and the cupboard in the back was filled with stationery supplies. ''These are from my family,'' Josh explained as he showed them to her. He held up a hand. ''I know you said you didn't want them to give you anything but it was impossible to talk them out of it. I finally gave up and told them to give you office supplies, so they did.'' His forehead furrowed. ''Except for Aunt Judith. She gave you a year's supply of toilet paper.''

''That was very kind of them,'' Amanda said, her voice choked with emotion.

''Hey, you haven't seen the best part.'' Josh led her over to one of the interior offices and gestured at the wooden door. There, on the door, was her name—Amanda Kringleton—carved in big block letters.

''It's what you said you wanted,'' Josh reminded her. ''An office with your name on the door. Of course, if you ever leave this place you'll have to take it with you.''

''Oh, Josh,'' Amanda said inadequately, so touched she could hardly speak. ''You...you did all this in just over a week?''

''I told you. I'm a fast worker when I make up my mind.''

''You sure are,'' Amanda breathed. She turned and threw herself against him. ''Thank you so much. I just...I can't...I...''

Josh chuckled and backed against the wall, taking her with him. ''I guess you like it, huh?''

''Like it?'' She took his face in her hands and kissed him hard. ''I love it.'' She pushed herself against him, running her hands down him, feeling him harden in response.

''Good.'' He raised his head. ''But is it...personal?''

''It certainly is,'' Amanda told him.

THE NEXT DAY she took Brandy over to show them their new quarters. ''It's rent-free for six months,'' she explained to Brandy, passing on the information that Josh had told her. ''If business keeps on the way it is, we shouldn't have any problem affording the rent after that.''

''It's...amazing,'' Brandy said, as she wandered around, touching the desks and staring at the stationery. ''I hope you got him something really good for Christmas.''

''I did.'' Amanda smiled in satisfaction. ''I got him a picture of his whole family. It's not exactly a surprise, since I had to get them all together to do it.'' She rolled her eyes. ''That was a real adventure. Alaina phoned me four times to find out what everyone else was wearing. Francine insisted on showing up in pink. Judith wanted to wear red, so she said she wouldn't stand anywhere near her. Marilla wanted to bring all her cats. Luckily, Josh was cooperative.'' Her smile faded as she said his name.

''We sure were wrong about him,'' Brandy said. ''Just like I was wrong about Harvy.''

''I'm not so sure,'' Amanda said slowly.

Brandy peered at her. ''Oh, no. You're not still worrying about that Christmas elf stuff, are you?''

Amanda sat down in her office chair. ''As a matter of fact, I am.''

''Well, don't. I'm sure Josh feels something for you. You're always together. He gave you an office...''

''Oh, he does feel something for me,'' Amanda agreed. ''At least, he does right now. But I'm not so sure that will last. He keeps talking about how he can hardly wait until this is finished. I swear if he calls me his Christmas elf one more time, or says, 'I'll be glad when this is over so things can get back to normal,' I'm going to smack him.''

''Why? People often...''

''I wasn't part of his normal,'' Amanda reminded her. ''I was hired to do a job. Yes, we're attracted to each other, and yes, we're having a great time now. But after Christmas, he isn't going to need me anymore. And then what will happen?''

''Amanda...''

''I don't want to be dumped again,'' said Amanda. ''It was bad enough when Dwight and Kyle decided they didn't need me anymore. I don't know that I want to hang around and watch Josh decide that he doesn't need me, either.''

''You don't know that's going to happen,'' Brandy said, but she had an uncertain look on her face.

''I know. And maybe I am being silly. But I want to be prepared.''

AMANDA SPENT the next two days rushing around, preparing for Josh's office party, helping Brandy with two other parties, moving into her new office, finishing the last of the shopping, and assuring herself that everything was wonderful between herself and Josh.

However, every time Josh jokingly called her his elf, she cringed.

And at his office party, she finally made up her mind.

It wasn't that things didn't go well. As a matter of fact, it was probably one of the best parties Amanda had ever organized. Even some of his family came, mingling with the business acquaintances, and oohing and aahing at the technology. Charmaine came with Wendell. "It's so connected to the universe," she exclaimed. She clung to Wendell's arm and looked up at him. "In a reality-based way of course."

"It's all so amazingly modern," Mimi said, while Judith admired the bathrooms and his mother admired everything.

"Your father would be so proud," she told him with tears in her eyes.

Even Josh seemed to be having a good time. He walked around, confidently explaining the technology to everyone. And he introduced Amanda to everybody. "This is the person responsible for all this," he'd say. "Amanda Kringleton. My very own Christmas elf."

When it was over, Josh was ecstatic. "We did it," he said to Amanda as they returned to his condo. "Hank says he's got people almost forcing their money on him." He led her over to the couch and pulled her down beside him. "This has worked out perfectly," he enthused as he stared at the Christmas tree. "I've got the investors lined up. We've got terrific personal presents for everyone." He chuckled. "You know, I haven't been this excited about Christmas since I was a kid. I can hardly wait for everyone to open their presents. I just hope they like them."

"They'll love them," Amanda said. "And the best part is, that you came up with most of them yourself."

Josh looked pleased. "I guess I did, didn't I?" He squeezed her shoulder. "But I couldn't have done it without my Christmas elf."

Amanda studied his features. "That is how you see me, isn't it? As your Christmas elf?"

"Of course," he said, obviously not getting the question. "My own personal Christmas elf."

Right, thought Amanda. She pushed herself to her feet, knowing the moment had arrived. "And speaking of elves, it's time for this one to go."

"Go?" Josh looked confused. "Where are you going?"

"The North Pole," Amanda reminded him. "That was our deal, remember? After Christmas, I'd go back to the North Pole."

Josh blinked twice. "Yes, but..."

"It's past midnight, Josh. It's Christmas Eve. On Christmas Eve, I'm supposed to go back to the North Pole."

"I know but..." He shoved a hand through his hair. "I didn't mean...that is, I didn't actually expect you to..."

"What did you expect, then?" Amanda asked. "I've done everything I was supposed to do," said Amanda. "We bought the gifts. They're all wrapped, and the gift tags are written. We had the office party. I played the part of your significant other." She put a hand on her stomach to stop the churning. "That's all I was hired to do, isn't it?"

Josh stared at her. "Yes, it is, but..."

"So you don't need a Christmas elf anymore?"

His gaze met hers. Then he lowered his eyelids. "I guess you're right," he said slowly.

Amanda's stomach sank with disappointment. She hadn't expected him to react any differently, but part of her had been hoping...

She drew in a long, deep breath. "Well, then," she said. "Thanks so much for everything. The office is fabulous. And you've done a lot for my business...not to mention my shopping skills. And I really enjoyed meeting your family."

"Yeah," Josh said. "So did I." He had a stunned look on his face, like someone who had just been run over by a truck and wasn't quite sure what was going on.

That was exactly the way Amanda felt. She kissed him on the cheek, picked up her coat, and walked out the door.

"I JUST DON'T GET IT," Brandy said.

She handed Amanda a cup of tea, sat down on a kitchen chair, and stared at her as if she'd lost her mind. "You broke up with him just because it was Christmas Eve?"

"We didn't exactly break up," said Amanda. "It just ended, that's all." She took a sip from the cup. "It was just a job and the job ended Christmas Eve."

"It wasn't just a job! You were practically living with the guy."

"I know."

"And it doesn't sound as if he wanted to break up."

Amanda recalled the stunned look on Josh's face when she'd walked out. "I don't think he did."

''So he didn't want to. You didn't want to.'' Brandy raised an eyebrow. ''So why did you?''

''I had to,'' Amanda said. ''It was going to end anyway.'' She drew in a breath. ''And do you know how it would end, Brandy? He'd just stop calling. He'd get all involved in his work—he'd forget to call me—then he'd walk into his condo some evening and look surprised to see me there. He wouldn't mean to hurt me, but he would.''

''This isn't hurting you? It looks awfully painful to me.''

''It's better than the alternative.'' Amanda wiped back a fresh rush of tears. ''I couldn't stand to hang around and watch him slowly discover that he doesn't need me.''

''You don't know it would happen.''

''Yes, I do.'' Amanda took another sip. ''And so do you. You're the one who said people don't change.''

''I might have been wrong,'' Brandy said. ''I was wrong about Harvy.''

''You weren't wrong about Josh,'' Amanda said. She took another sip of tea, but it didn't warm her. She felt cold inside, so cold she could have been at the North Pole.

11

"SATURDAY?" Josh said into the phone. "I don't know about Saturday, Mom, I'll have to..." An image of a small blond woman flashed through his mind. No, he didn't have to check with her anymore. "Yeah, okay," he said. "Saturday sounds fine."

"What about Amanda?" Edwina asked. "Do you think she'll..."

"No," said Josh. "Amanda will *not* be there."

There was dead silence from the other end of the phone. When Edwina finally did speak, her voice was filled with questions and concern. "We certainly haven't seen much of Amanda since before Christmas. It's the fifth of January. Surely she isn't still visiting her family?"

"I...wouldn't think so," Josh mumbled.

Edwina cleared her throat. "You two haven't... broken up, have you?"

"Not exactly," Josh muttered. They hadn't broken up. There wasn't anything to break up. It was a job that ended, that's all. "I'm just...not seeing her anymore."

"Why?" Edwina asked. Her tone sharpened. "You weren't cheating on her, were you?"

"Good God, no," said Josh. He couldn't imagine being with another woman.

"Then what..."

"I can't talk about this anymore," Josh interrupted. "I have to get back to work."

He hung up the phone and glowered at it. What was the matter with his family? They'd wanted him to have a relationship, and he'd had one. Okay, it hadn't really been a relationship, but they didn't know that. Why couldn't they just be happy he'd had one and forget about it? Then maybe he could forget about it!

That's what he wanted to happen. That's what he'd expected to happen. He'd forgotten about every other relationship in his life, including, at times, his family. But he couldn't seem to forget about his Christmas elf.

It had been two weeks since he had seen Amanda, and they'd been the worst two weeks of his life. When he'd woken up that first day without her there, his first instinct had been to phone her. But he'd been unable to think of a thing to say. She'd been right. The job had ended. He didn't have any more personal presents to get, or any more parties to plan. He didn't need a Christmas elf anymore.

He'd spent Christmas day walking around in a fog, watching his relatives open their presents, and listening to their praise and thanks. Naturally, they all asked after Amanda. "She's out of town," he'd told them. He didn't have the heart to ruin their Christmas by telling them the I'm-not-seeing-her-anymore story.

He'd thought after Christmas Amanda would slip out of his mind. That hadn't happened. He'd immersed himself in work. That hadn't helped, either. Nothing seemed to help. It was ridiculous. He seemed to have spent a good portion of his life forgetting about his relatives, and yet he couldn't forget about Amanda.

He picked up the photograph sitting on his desk. It was Amanda's Christmas present to him—a picture of his family. He ran a finger along it, pausing at his own face. The only person missing from it was Amanda.

Josh abruptly set down the picture, annoyed with everything and everyone in the world, and let out a bellow. "Mable!"

After a few minutes Mable stalked into the room. "What—"

"Do you have those technical specs I asked you to get?" Josh demanded before Mable could say a word.

"No, of course I don't. You just asked me for them ten minutes ago."

Josh glared at her. "I need them right now!"

"You need something right now, but it isn't technical manuals," Mable flung. "And if you bellow at me one more time I'm going to smack you over the head with my bottle of brandy." She came a few steps closer. "What's the matter with you, anyway? You've been in a lousy mood since Christmas. What happened? I thought you said your family liked their presents."

"They did like them." Josh smiled briefly at the memory of their enthusiastic responses. "They thought they were very thoughtful and very personal." His smile faded. They should have liked them. They'd been hand-picked by a Christmas elf.

"Then what's bothering you?" Mable demanded.

"Nothing is bothering me," Josh snapped, although to be perfectly honest everything bothered him. "It's cold outside. There's too much snow. And...and I just don't like January."

"Really?" Mable raised an eyebrow. "What do you want me to do about it? Get you a ticket to February?"

"No!" Josh snarled. He didn't think he'd like February much more than he liked January.

"Okay. Which month do you like?"

How about December? Josh thought. I liked December. "I don't know but I know it isn't this one."

"Perhaps it was December," Mable suggested gently.

Josh shoved a hand through his hair. "December wasn't bad."

"Oh, come on, Josh," Mable exclaimed. "You were happier in December than you've been in years. You only started getting miserable when Christmas came...and you broke up with Amanda."

"We did *not* break up," Josh snapped. "It was a job, that's all. It ended the way it was supposed to end—on Christmas Eve."

"Is that all Amanda was to you...an...employee?"

"Of course not," said Josh. "Amanda was more than that. She was...special."

"I think she thought you were special, too," Mable said. "As a matter of fact, for reasons that right now I'm hard-pressed to understand, I'd say that Amanda is in love with you."

"Really?" Josh felt a surge of elation that quickly died. "If she felt that way, why did she leave?"

"Because she didn't think you felt the same way."

"Of course I feel the same way," said Josh without thinking about it.

"Well, did you ever tell Amanda that?"

"No, of course not," said Josh. "How could I? I didn't know how I felt!"

"Well," said Mable, "now you do. What are you going to do about it?"

Then he picked up the phone. "The first thing I'm going to do is call my mother. I think she deserves to know the whole story." He grinned, suddenly filled with excited anticipation. "And then I'm going to get Amanda a very personal, thoughtful present." He took a deep breath. "I just hope she likes it."

"BUSINESS IS BOOMING," Brandy reported. "We won't have any problem paying the rent on this place for the rest of our lives—and paying ourselves a decent salary, as well."

"That's nice," Amanda said glumly. She wasn't sure she liked this office anymore. Every time she looked at it, it reminded her of Josh. Everything reminded her of Josh, from the snow on the windowpane to Brandy's face. She gave her head a shake. She'd cried all over her parents, and she'd cried all over Brandy, and it was time she got over this.

Brandy released a huge sigh. "Why don't you go home, Amanda?"

Because it's just as bad there, Amanda thought. As a matter of fact, it was worse. The place seemed empty without the clutter from the office, and Josh's relatives kept phoning and leaving messages on her machine. Amanda hadn't returned any of their calls.

The only person who hadn't phoned was Josh. Amanda hadn't really expected him to, but she couldn't help but hope that maybe he would.

She'd just arrived home and was in the process of making herself a cup of tea when someone rang her doorbell. When she opened it, she found Josh standing on the other side. His coat was open, showing his pink shirt, and his lack of a tie, his hair was mussed from the wind and probably his fingers, and just seeing him almost had her heart jumping out of her chest. For a moment neither of them said anything. Amanda couldn't think of a single thing to say and Josh just stared at her much the same way he had when they'd first met. Then he cleared his throat and gave her a small smile. "I'm staring, aren't I?" he asked.

"S-sort of," Amanda stammered. She peered over his shoulder, suddenly realizing that he appeared to have his entire family with him. "What..."

"I came to give you a Christmas present." He smiled faintly. "I know it's a little late, but I'm really hoping you'll like it."

"Oh." What? "You brought your family here, too so you could give me a Christmas present?"

"I had to," Josh explained. "They all helped me pick it out." He held up a hand. "I didn't intend for it to be a group activity, but...well, I told Mom the whole story and...she called Shelby and Shelby called Louise and Charmaine and..." He shrugged. "The next thing I knew, we were all there."

"Oh," Amanda said faintly. She had wanted him to spend more time with his family. She wasn't positive this was what she'd had in mind.

She opened the door wider. "Won't you...come in?"

"No, they won't," said Josh. He entered her apartment, closed the door and rested his back against it. "I will come in. They are going to wait in the coffee shop across the street. There are some things a man does without an audience and this happens to be one of them. We'll call them later.'' He hesitated with an uncertain look on his face. ''At least, we might, depending on how this goes.''

Amanda waited for a moment in a vain attempt to lower her heart rate.

Josh pushed his hands into his pockets. ''I should tell you that my family knows all about you.''

''All about me?'' Amanda said faintly.

''Yes. I told them the entire story.''

''You did?''

''Uh-huh.'' He winced. ''They weren't very happy about it. My mother said I was reprehensible. Shelby told me I was a jerk. Marilla said it was a good thing I didn't have a cat because I'm too dense to take care of it. And Charmaine told me that I was the most cosmically unaware person she'd ever met.'' He sighed and bent his head. ''And that was just the beginning.''

''Oh, dear.'' Why had he done that? And why was he telling her?

Josh raised his head and smiled faintly. ''I think I might have deserved it. After all, hiring someone else to find out personal things about your family probably is something only a real jerk would do. And blackmailing someone into pretending we were involved is even worse.''

''Actually it was extortion,'' Amanda corrected. ''And it seems to me I used the same tactics on you.'' She gave the door an apprehensive look. ''Is that why your family was here? So they can tell me off, as well?'' She wouldn't blame them if they did, but she didn't think she was up to hearing it.

''Of course not!'' Josh reassured her. ''I told them it was all my fault—which it was. I did sort of force you into doing it—although you didn't have to. I was going to offer to help out anyway."

"That's...uh...true," Amanda stuttered. "But does your family understand..."

"Don't worry. They're not mad at you or anything." His eyes gleamed at her. "They're not even that mad at me anymore. I pointed out that I was just trying to make them happy and give them what they wanted. That seemed to help."

Amanda wasn't surprised to hear that. Josh could soften up anyone with all that charm.

He took a deep breath, bent his head to study his hands and then looked back up at her. "Is that why you left me? Because you think I'm a jerk, too?"

Lord, she was crazy about him. "I didn't exactly leave you, Josh. The job just ended, that's all. I was your Christmas elf, and you said you wouldn't need an elf after Christmas."

"Actually you said that," said Josh. "And I thought you were right. You were right about everything else..." He frowned. "Well, practically everything else. I still don't think my mother would have liked a pasta maker."

"Maybe not, but..."

"You weren't right about this," said Josh. "I do need you. You would not believe how miserable I've been without you. I was even miserable during Christmas—even though everyone really liked their presents."

"Did they?"

"Uh-huh. They thought they were very thoughtful and very personal. Of course, they should have been. I had an elf to help me out."

There it was…that Christmas elf thing again. ‘‘Josh, I…’’

‘‘I’ve spent a lot of time thinking about this,’’ said Josh. ‘‘And I’ve finally realized that I don’t just need a Christmas elf for Christmas. I need one all year through…for ever and ever.’’ He reached into his coat pocket, pulled out a box wrapped in cheerfully red Christmas wrapping and handed it to her. ‘‘If I tell you that I want you and I need you and I love you, and that I’ll try very hard to get over being a jerk, do you think you might consider taking the job?’’

Amanda was too stunned to take in what he was saying. She stared at him and then at the present. It was small and square and just the right size and… She looked questioningly up at him. ‘‘I think you should open that before you make up your mind,’’ he said gently.

Was this actually happening? You shouldn’t jump to conclusions with Josh Larkland, Amanda told herself a little hysterically. He could be giving *her* a pasta maker, and not offering her what she thought he might be offering, after all.

She removed the paper, opened the box and stared at the sparkling diamond. ‘‘Oh, Josh,’’ she breathed. ‘‘It’s…uh…I don’t know what to say, I…I just…’’

‘‘Well, for God’s sake, say something,’’ Josh interrupted. ‘‘I’m going out of my mind here. Say ‘yes,’ ‘no,’ or ‘Get out of here, you jerk’ but don’t just stand there because I can’t…’’

‘‘Yes,’’ Amanda said quickly. She smiled radiantly up at him. ‘‘Although I believe the proper response is ‘Yes, thank you, I’d be delighted to…’’’

‘‘Terrific,’’ said Josh. ‘‘I guess now we’re officially engaged. And this time it’s for real.’’ He pulled her into his arms and up against him. ''I'm glad that's settled. I thought I'd have to do a lot more groveling.'' He brushed his mouth against hers, then deepened the kiss. Amanda responded passionately, holding his head down to hers, reveling in the familiar feeling of his body, his lips, everything about him. ''Oh, Josh, I love you so much,'' she whispered.

''I love you, too, Amanda,'' he mumbled. She started unbuttoning his shirt, then gave up on it, took his hand and started leading him down the hall. ''Come on,'' she said. ''I want to show you how us elves celebrate getting engaged.''

They were halfway down the hall, still clutching each other, when Josh stopped. ''What about my family?'' he said. ''They'll be waiting for us. Do you think we should...''

''Absolutely not,'' said Amanda.

There was a time for family. This wasn't one of them.

SANTA AND SON

Leandra Logan

For Marilu LaVoie

We can still be dangerous when we want to be!

★ ★ ★

Leandra Logan loves the holiday season, shopping for family and friends. Never one to pass up the chance to browse through a toy store, she's seen her share of Santas on duty, watched them in action from afar. Her husband has yet to endorse the idea of her posing on St. Nick's lap for a photo, but hope springs eternal for next year!

1

SHE WANTED SANTA and she wanted him bad.

Or so Ron Coleman suspected from the moment the shapely blonde entered Grace Brothers Toys late that wintry Monday afternoon. He had a bird's eye view of the store from the grand North Pole display located at the rear of the center aisle, and had noticed her the minute she'd burst through the sliding-door entrance on a tidal wave of bundled-up shoppers. While others rushed the customer-service area to grab yellow shopping carts and baskets, she broke free of the pack, and moved quickly and with determination toward the center aisle.

The bachelor in him enjoyed watching her. A pale blue parka with a fur-trimmed hood hugged her hourglass torso, and navy stretch pants set her slender legs to advantage. She would've been a welcome elfin addition to Gracie's—as the store was known locally—holiday kingdom. He envisioned her in one of the store's skimpy green-velvet skirts trimmed with white fur, a jaunty tasseled hat in place of her tam, a jolly grin supplanting her frown.

His journalist side, however, seasoned by years of traveling the globe as if it were a routine spin around the park, was concerned about that frown, and her lack of interest in the colorful Christmas gimmickry contrived to catch the eye and urge open the pocketbook. The store's lush brochure featuring Emmett Windom, Minnesota's beloved thespian as this year's Santa Claus, was the most ominous sign of all. By the way the glossy paper was clenched in her gloved hand, Ron was certain her thumb was pressed directly into his grandfather's jugular.

What had his Grandpa Emmett done wrong? Ron wondered. He'd been the store's Santa for two weeks and everything had run as smoothly until now. Ron knew so for a fact. He'd arrived in the Twin Cities shortly after Thanksgiving, and had moved into Emmett's St. Paul high-rise for the holidays to keep an eye on the free-spirited eighty-year-old so his folks could take a worry-free vacation in Arizona. He and his grandfather had bonded like a couple of rowdy boys despite the fifty years between them, and had been having a wonderful time hitting all the best restaurants and theaters during Emmett's off-duty hours.

What bad luck that Ron now happened to be rummaging through the lavish display for Emmett's precious gold pocket watch long after Santa and his entourage of elves were gone for the day. Had the Pole been empty, the Closed sign hanging from the gingerbread-shaped entrance might have been enough to discourage her.

As he dug around the white velvet cushion on the seat of Santa's giant chair, he managed to keep sight of her progress out of the corner of his eye. She was closing in fast. And spoke just as he spotted the timepiece wedged deep behind the cushion.

''Excuse me. Sir?''

The feminine voice was crisp and powerful enough to rise easily above the hum of the crowd and the instrumental version of ''Jingle Bells'' on the public-address system. Ron straightened and dropped the watch in the pocket of his tweed jacket. He slowly turned to confront her, hoping for a facial flaw—a wart on her chin, perhaps—to detract from her appeal, make this brush-off easy.

As luck would have it, she was even more stunning up close, with cheekbones set startlingly high in a heart-shaped face of the creamiest color and golden hair spilling over her shoulders and the fur ridge of her hood like melted butter. He was intrigued by the anger behind eyes a shade darker than her jacket, and couldn't help but imagine the explosion, when she did let loose.

Ordinarily he adored such fireworks, lit many a feminine fuse himself to start the sizzle. But this was Emmett's turf, not his! His folks were counting on him to keep the peace, make sure the old guy was safe and sound.

She seemed a little disconcerted by his appraisal. But her words were spiked with annoyance just the same. "Can you tell me who is in charge of Santa Claus?"

"Mrs. Claus?" he quipped.

Her smooth brown brows inched up her soft forehead with traces of suspicion. "You do work here, don't you?"

He glanced down at his sport coat and woolen trousers. He was dressed for the part and could pretend to be a store manager for the cause. With any luck he might even be able to keep this situation from Grace Brothers' true and tyran-nical manager, Stanley Bickel. "Santa is in my care," he replied carefully, pleased with his clever tap dance around the truth. "My name is Ron Coleman. And yours is..."

"Jeanne Trent," she said hastily, as though her identity was inconsequential.

"Snowing outside, Ms. Trent?"

"Not yet. I—"

"It's in the forecast I think. You hear anything on the way over?"

Ron's questions were outright manipulation, attempts at distraction. But it was obvious that this beauty couldn't be steered off course. Her dark blue eyes glittered with an unwavering intensity.

"Look, I'm not here to discuss the weather. I have a complaint about your Santa." Her fingers curled into fists, crushing Emmett's brochure with a crackle that made Ron wince. "He's...he's ruined me! And he's going to pay!"

"Shhhh!" Ron's panic rose with her voice. A few shoppers near a shelf of dump trucks turned to survey them. He scrambled down the throne's three steps, past the gumdrop lamp posts, beneath the hanging icicles, and joined her under the gingerbread entrance.

"I will not shush!" she cried, her cheeks aflame.

"Look, Emmett hasn't ruined a woman in ages."

"How can you possibly know that for sure?"

He didn't, of course. The bluff had been automatic. All he knew was that perhaps Emmett wasn't suited for this touchy public-relations job. Playing Santa was just another gig to him. An important one, yes, but a perilous stretch for the salty stage actor who'd never warmed to children outside of his daughter and grandson.

It seemed to Ron that he'd turned around and Emmett had grown old on him. Emmett still behaved like a rogue and his giant ego hadn't diminished any, but this visit Ron saw a frailty and vulnerability in him that hadn't been there before. All in all, how dangerous could one old man be? It took all Ron's courage to pose the all-important question. He cleared his throat, and forced the words to the surface. "Uh, exactly what did he do to you?"

She'd tipped her gaze up to his. "The unthinkable," she said succinctly. "The unforgivable."

Why, the old coot, he thought in stunned surprise. He didn't know whether to ground Grandpa or pat him on the back. How did he do it? Jeanne Trent had to be in her midtwenties! By all rights Jeanne Trent was more *his* style!

"Are you going to take action or not?" she sputtered.

"Would you mind lowering your voice?" Ron scanned the area for Stanley Bickel. The manager's radar for trouble zoomed in on more shoplifters and merchandise abusers in any given day than his own professional security people did.

"So much for the customer always being right," she fumed, tapping the toe of her black boot like a small jackhammer.

"Well, I'm sure you are right," he said placatingly. "About something. About everything!" He sounded patronizing and ridiculous.

"Oh, you're a typical store employee, all right," she huffed. "Full of empty charm."

Empty charm, eh? Despite the fact that he had no connection to merchandising, her words stung. Emmett wasn't the only one in the family with a huge ego, the only one who could cause some pillage and ruin! He gave her his most captivating smile—The Look. The big gun, the one he pulled out after the most fulfilling kind of lovemaking, the one that had gotten him the most in-depth interviews of his journalism career.

"Now do you really think you're being fair, Jeanne Trent?" he scolded silkily.

"Fair? Me?" Jeanne's voice had risen to a squeak. Where was this conversation headed? On a merry chase going nowhere, common sense told her. He was toying with her, using her complaint as an excuse to flirt—to distract her from her mission.

And distract her he had. She hesitated a moment and studied his gorgeous brown eyes and generous, wolfish mouth. She was a photographer and he certainly was photogenic.

She was also a woman, and it was at that moment that she realized a girl could get in a lot of trouble with a man like Ron Coleman. Knee-knocking, heart-skipping, mattress-dipping trouble.

He was getting places, Ron realized with satisfaction. She wasn't smitten, but she was...interested. If only there was more time to explore this captivating elf. But Bickel was an ever-present threat, as was Emmett himself, currently changing his clothes in the employees' lounge. "I still have no idea what the matter is," he said. "Can't help you till I do."

How sneaky to lay the blame for their verbal detour on

her! If the man wasn't a direct descendent of the Grace brothers, he ought to be adopted posthaste. He was a natural who could sell anything—especially himself. She cleared her throat. "My son had a talk with Santa yesterday, and you know what Santa did?"

Ron's eyes grew in confusion. "Hit on you?"

"He promised him everything on his wish list," she lamented as though not hearing him. "Now does that seem right to you?"

"Well—"

"Of course not! Far more tact was in order. I thought these guys went through some kind of training—in evasive tactics, subterfuge, surface platitudes." She paused then. "You mean to say you thought Santa tried to pick me up?"

Ron rubbed his lips, struggling for something clever. "Uh—"

"Why, I wasn't even along," she surged on. "My mother brought Toby." She glared down at the brochure featuring the very old man. "The idea of him hitting on me. The idea that you'd suspect it!"

"Guess I overreacted," Ron admitted resignedly. "A lot of men would be tempted to try to pick you up. I mean, with no wedding ring on your finger..."

Splashes of red appeared on her cheeks as she shook Emmett's brochure. "This guy's old enough to be your grandfather. How could you seriously think that he'd come on to me?"

Because Emmett *was* his grandfather, Ron thought, amused by the irony, and a one-of-a-kind actor character who considered any female old enough to order a martini fair game.

"Furthermore," she continued in a huff, "it's nobody's business why I'm not wearing a wedding ring. I didn't come here to discuss my life with you or anybody else."

Ron groaned inwardly. When had he lost control of this

conversation? Why had he deliberately strung her along when he should've gotten rid of her right off?

Because she was just too interesting. Too pretty and fiesty and testy. Too much!

"Look, I think the Better Business Bureau would be interested to learn of a toy store that makes such rash guarantees to encourage sales. It's—it's nothing short of blackmail!"

"Huh?" He couldn't resist touching her arm then. Just a little squeeze on her downy jacket sleeve. "You're jumping to all kinds of inaccurate conclusions. Why, Grace Brothers Toys is not just any store, its known around the world for its unique personality."

"So was John Dillinger," she retorted, "but I wouldn't have trusted him with my son's Christmas happiness."

A frown wedged Ron's brows together. "I happen to know our Santa very well and can absolutely guarantee that he operates with the best intentions."

She waved her glove dismissively, deftly loosening his gentle grip. "So you're willing to admit he may have accidentially slipped up?"

"Yes, of course."

"So what are you going to do about it?"

Damned if he knew. Ron glanced around again to see Stanley Bickel marching up the game aisle, a cross between a watchful sentry and a smug ruler as he inspected his castle. "I'm more than willing to make good here. Meet any promises." His impassioned words bounced back at his face with the sting of a heavy, wet snowball. What if the boy had asked for a four-wheel truck or a trip to Disneyland, or an addition to the house?

Her mouth curled mockingly. "You needn't look so frightened. He is only four years old."

"Oh." He grinned in relief.

"Besides, what I want is free."

Ron gave Bickel another glance. The manager was

closer, but had paused to check his reflection in one of the store's many mirrors. He was tugging at the suit coat buttoned over his tubby chest and had produced a comb to adjust his black, slicked-back hair.

He offered her a coaxing smile. "Free, you say?" As if anything in this world was!

"I'm a single parent, and therefore on a tight budget. There will never be a Christmas in my son's young life when he receives everything on his list. If your Santa would be so kind as to retract his promises, admit to making a mistake, I would consider the matter closed."

She was reasonable, lovely, and intelligent. Why did he have to meet her this way, caught up in a tangle of lies? "Your offer sounds more than fair to me." Ron slipped his hand into the lining pocket of his jacket and produced his ever-present leather notepad and pen set. "You can reach me here." He scribbled Emmett's number, and tore the sheet free with a quick snap. "If you don't mind, I'd like to settle this away from the store."

Jeanne put the paper in her small shoulder bag and presented him with one of her business cards. "Seems like a lot of trouble. Dressing up Santa for an extra showing. I could bring Toby back here to—"

"No, no, let's keep this between ourselves." After all, Emmett was bound to find dressing up easier than being strung up. If this leaked out to Bickel the old duffer would be through. "It would undoubtedly disrupt the customer flow," he said, striving for authenticity with some merchandising lingo. "And there is the photographer. We, ah, have an agreement with her about snapping each child who sits upon the jolly man's knee."

"Yes, about that photograph..."

He cringed as she launched into a spiel about how some better lighting, and different angles could improve the shots. Hope that she might perhaps be a forgettable know-it-all began to grow until he glanced at her card to find the slogan Pretty as a Picture printed on the top. She had every right to believe, as a manager, he'd be interested in her professional criticism. And dammit, it made her all the more intriguing.

But enough was enough. As much as he enjoyed her soft husky voice and the way her blue eyes danced, he had no more time to play store. Not only did he have to concern himself with Stanley Bickel, but Emmett as well. He was just emerging from the employee lounge several yards away, easing into his topcoat. A collision between all of them would be a disaster. Jeanne would unload, Bickel would explode, and poor Emmett would be forced to hit the road.

"Jeanne," he began with deliberate silkiness, "perhaps we could talk about all this later on. I have an important meeting to attend—some of my cashiers have been overloading the bags at the checkouts." The moment the excuse popped out, he realized how lame it was. All a real manager would have to do is walk over and tell the clerks not to be so stingy with the bags. Obviously, there was no time for a meeting during this mad rush!

"I see," she said succinctly between small even teeth. "This could really backfire if the press ever got hold of it."

Didn't he know it! He'd be the first in line to write an exposé if there was any reason to believe Gracie's Santa was dishonest! He couldn't help noting that Bickel was now closing in on them. "Look, I have your number."

"And I think I have yours," she returned icily. "Prove me wrong." With that parting gibe she turned on her heel and retreated down the wide center aisle.

"Ah, Ronald!" Emmett lifted his hand in greeting as he approached.

All traces of Santa had vanished. With his cashmere topcoat, his crest of carefully groomed salt-and-pepper hair,

Emmett now looked more like a visiting British aristocrat, his favorite image in public.

"Did you manage to find my timepiece, boy?" he asked with a dash of urgency.

Ron withdrew it from his pocket.

"Spendid, splendid." Emmett hooked the gold chain to his belt loop, seemingly unaware that Stanley Bickel had joined them.

"So, Emmett, how did things go today?" Bickel asked solicitously.

"Splendid, splendid." Emmett used this hearty refrain in the store in order to maintain a distant and positive image.

It was common knowledge among Gracie employees that Bickel was just looking for some excuse to dump this version of jolly old St. Nick. Bickel had been forced to take on Emmett by Wendell Grace himself, the eldest of the Grace brothers and a theater buff who considered Emmett's stage prowess second only to Sir Laurence Olivier's. Bickel fancied himself the real power behind Gracies, and he'd promised the Santa position to a cousin in advance. Apparently the cousin was waiting in the wings, until Bickel could justify the old man's dismissal.

How ironic that Bickel had let Jeanne Trent go without an introduction, Ron thought with grim satisfaction, when she was the answer to his prayers—Emmett's first and only critic on this gig.

"So, Ron," Emmett said, "who was the woman who cornered you under the gingerbread?"

"A friend," Ron replied evenly, picking up his brown leather jacket, draped over a plastic snowdrift.

"Somebody you know from the old days, eh?" Bickel ventured.

Ron shrugged into the thigh-length coat, and concentrated on the buttons to disguise his wry grin. "Your level of intuition never wavers, Stanley."

The prissy man beamed. ''Yes, I have a knack for such things. Tough to pull a fast one here in my kingdom.''

''I'm sure.'' With a curt nod, Ron took hold of Emmett's elbow. ''C'mon, Pop, I'm starved.''

''Won't be having chicken again tonight,'' Emmett cautioned him as they moved through the crowd. ''I want steak, burnt crisp with a juicy pink middle. To blazes with the cholesterol.''

''I have to admit that sounds good for a change,'' Ron admitted. ''We just won't tell Mom.''

They paused on the sidewalk outside the store for a moment and watched the rush-hour traffic on Snelling Avenue. Dusk had set in and it was snowing lightly. ''Let's head for the Countryview,'' Emmett suggested. ''It's close, on County Road B2.''

''Sure thing, Pop.''

Emmett turned the collar up on his coat and glared at his grandson. ''Stop calling me Pop! Here in the midwest it is a soft drink, not a person. And you know that, a Minnesota boy born and bred.''

Of course Ron knew. It wouldn't be fun otherwise. He extracted his keys from his jacket pocket, affecting an innocent smile. ''Okay, Grandfather, the car's over here to the right.''

Together they crossed the snow-packed blacktop. Even though the Santa display had closed, the lot was still jammed with vehicles.

''Remember, son, in the restaurant, it's Emmett. Ron and Emmett, a couple of fellows out for a bite. A couple of unattached males on the hunt.''

Ron inserted his key into the driver's door and released both locks on the rented two-door Plymouth. ''Isn't working enough distraction for you?''

Emmett winked at him over the snow-dusted hood. ''Why, it's a cover, boy, a sham, a way to meet the ladies.''

''Sure, Pop. Nothing comes second to your acting career and we both know it.''

''Hah! You used the setting for your own gain just now, didn't you? You may have fooled Bickel about that woman being an old friend, but I certainly didn't buy it. There was absolute terror in your eyes. I didn't think even an exciting stranger could scare the hell out of a seasoned gadabout like you!''

The two men eased into the car. Emmett rubbed his hands together gleefully. ''I dare you to tell me all the juicy details.''

Ron stared grimly out the windshield as he ignited the engine. ''I dare you to try and stop me.''

EMMETT BELIEVED it was his social standing that got them a fireside table at the Countryview Steakhouse. Ron didn't argue the issue, but figured his ten-dollar tip hadn't hurt. It was worth every penny to see the old man's chest puff with pride and Ron was enjoying the warmth of the flames. Though he traveled the globe for human interest stories, he spent a good deal of his time at his suburban Los Angeles home, where the climate was always tolerable.

Emmett watched him shiver slightly and take a gulp of his Scotch. ''Can't believe you're the same kid who used to toboggan in just a sweatshirt and jeans. Now you act like a trembling pup at the first dip to zero.''

''The blood thins after years away, Po—Emmett,'' he corrected. He nodded at the two middle-aged ladies at the next table who'd been eyeing his grandfather and had made little attempt to disguise their interest.

Ron felt like a fool for his mistakes with Jeanne Trent. To her, Emmett was just an old man but she didn't know his grandfather like he did. Emmett's good looks made him ageless and attractive in a most disarming way. Given the opportunity, Ron had no doubt that Emmett could have gotten her into some kind of delicious trouble.

Not that he wasn't a fitter man for the job, Ron told himself. Even now, he couldn't stop thinking about her, replaying their encounter for his own private pleasure. Unfortunately, it was high time he shared her complaint with Emmett. That should put an end to his fanciful dreaming.

Ron downed the last of his drink and signaled for one last round.

Emmett leaned over the linen-covered table. "I was thinking of inviting our charming companions over for a nightcap. What do you say?"

Ron's brown eyes blazed. "No."

Emmett settled back in his chair with a good-natured chuckle. "All right. Guess the three phone numbers I did get today are enough."

"We have to talk about the blonde—"

"There's something really sexy about that Santa costume, Ronny." Emmett interrupted with twinkling eyes. "The ladies must feel kind of naughty slipping old St. Nick a mash note. Maybe you should get a Santa job of your own. I mean as long as you're just sitting around all month."

"I'm not sitting around," his grandson argued hotly. "You know very well that I'm doing the guest holiday column for the Minneapolis *Clarion* while I'm here." He didn't have the heart to add that filling in for his folks as Emmett's guardian was proving to be a job in itself. It was more than driving him around and making sure he didn't slip in the shower. More than ever, Emmett needed an audience, an adoring audience. A lot of the time, Ron was it.

Emmett drained his Scotch as the waitress brought the fresh ones. "All you do is write in that damn diary of yours."

"It's a journal, Pop, and many a nugget of inspiration has jumped out at me from those pages. Besides, I wonder if you realize how coveted those Santa positions are, and how many men would bend over backwards for one—especially at Grace Brothers!''

''Never resorted to bending over backwards for anybody,'' Emmett said huffily. ''It's one reason why men like us choose to make a living in the arts. Makes it easier to slip by the corporate power-mongers cracking their whips over the pathetically prone.''

''Well, Stanley Bickel is a monger to look out for.''

''Don't I know it!'' Emmett shook his gleaming head. ''Poor clerks always dancing to his tune. I intend to have a long talk with Wendell and Arnold Grace. They should really take a deeper interest in store policy.''

''The Graces have so many business interests, Emmett,'' Ron pointed out. ''They have the pizza-parlor chain and the menswear stores.''

''So?''

''So, it appears they prefer to leave things in Bickel's hands. If you want to keep your job, you should stick with your, 'splendid, splendid' smoke screen. He doesn't seem clever enough to see through it.''

''You mean I shouldn't complain to the Graces?''

''At least hold off until the new year.''

Emmett's eyes hardened over the rim of his glass. ''You look deathly pale, like the time you drove your father's golf cart off the dock at Deer Lake.''

''Thanks for that reminder,'' his grandson retorted. ''But you're the one sinking like a rock today. Now about that blonde!''

Emmett reared back. ''No need to shout.''

Ron took a deep breath, then related Jeanne Trent's story. Emmett listened carefully, absorbing each word with a judge's fortitude.

''So you see, Grandfather, if you do value this job, you will have to try a little harder to work within the system,'' he said in closing. ''Agreeing to see the boy in costume seems like a fair compromise, doesn't it? Listen to his list again, rethink your response."

"Sheer poppycock. Impossible poppycock!"

"Why, Emmett, why?"

"Because I am a method actor," the old man returned coldly. "You've known that all your life. The cheesy model of the North Pole may be just so much child's play to you, but it is my home while I am there. Seated on that throne, dressed in red velvet, I *am* Santa Claus. The genuine article." He raised a long shaky finger, his voice gaining momentum. "Just as I was Hamlet at the Ordway, Othello at the Guthrie, Professor Higgins at the Old Log. The stage of the moment is my reality, the footlights my sunshine, the applause—or mash notes in this case—my manna. In short, Santa Claus does not do retractions. I stand by each and every performance."

Ron seethed. "But you promised this kid everything on his list!"

Emmett shook his head in helpless wonder. "Then I must have had the impression that he was to get everything. Nothing to worry about, son."

Ron pounded the table. "You know what I will have to do, don't you? I will have to make good your promises."

Emmett regarded him blandly. "Don't see why."

Ron was upset enough for both of them and couldn't disguise the fact. "Because Jeanne Trent can't afford to do so. If I don't deliver, she'll eventually get to Bickel and he will gladly fire you. You really should do as she asks."

"Santa does not renege!" A deep rumbling sound surged from Emmett's chest as he lunged to his feet. "Not even for a beautiful woman!" His rich baritone bounced off the paneled walls of the cozy pub-style grill. Heads turned toward him, the room stilled. He perused the tables with flashing eyes. "Nay, my good people. As it happens, the woman I discuss with this newsmonger reminds me of a few lines straight out of *Othello*." He took complete control of the room, his regal figure dramatically backlit by the roaring fireplace. His captive audience waited breathlessly, anxious to watch him deliver. And clutching the lapel of his suit coat, deliver he did.

"My story being done,
She gave me for my pains a world of sighs;
She swore, in faith 'twas strange, 'twas passing strange;
'Twas pitiful, 'twas wonderous pitiful."

The diners broke out in applause. Ron was sure he was breaking out in a rash. If he could have folded his six-foot frame underneath the small table, he would have done so.

"YOU SURE it's bedtime?" Toby Trent was asking at that very moment several miles away in his suburban Roseville bedroom.

Jeanne ruffled her son's thatch of thick, blond hair and leaned over his bed to kiss his soft cheek. "I am very, very sure."

"Tuck me real tight, so I'm like a mommy."

"Mummy, Toby." Jeanne made her way around his bed, securing the covers between the mattress and box spring. At one of the bottom corners her fingers touched upon some kind of paper. She pulled it free to find it was a business-size envelope. "What's this?"

"A letter to Santa."

"When did you write it?"

"Today."

"You mean while I was out?"

"Yeah." His eyes were shiny in the lamplight. "Sherry gave me the paper. Okay?"

She recognized it as her business stationery for Picture Perfect. Naturally the baby-sitter wouldn't know where the cheaper stock was. "It's fine, honey."

"Where'd you go, Mummy?" he asked in a teasing voice.

To tangle with a man so sexy he should be pushing love potions rather than roller skates. Even now, hours later, Jeanne couldn't completely focus on her original mission at Gracie's. Ron Coleman's runaround made her heart skip over and over again.

"Well, Mummy?"

"I'm Mommy," she protested in teasing dismay, sending him into a fit of giggles. She sat down on the mattress, bracing herself for another attempt to outfox this smaller male, the center of her life. "So, you ready to talk about your Christmas presents tonight?"

His lower lip jutted out above his sheet. "No."

"But you told Santa."

"Course I did."

"So I think you should tell me too."

"Nope. It's a big surprise. I told you over and over."

"I wish you'd try and understand that even Santa can't afford everything," she said gently.

"He said I could have everything. He said so."

Jeanne opened her mouth to protest, then closed it again. She was helpless here. She tried hard to be everything to the child, but she had to draw the line at Santa. He was one person she couldn't imitate, replace, or overrule.

"Santa wouldn't lie to a good boy, would he?" he asked hopefully.

"Not on purpose, Tobe."

"I want to mail my letter tomorrow. Need a stamp. You got a stamp?"

"I think you should draw a nice one."

"You got an address? I need an address."

"We'll do that together." She started a little when he took the letter back, and stuffed it under his pillow with a sly look.

"Did, ah, Sherry help you with your list?"

"Nope."

That was too bad. Sherry would have gladly ratted on him, to help the cause. She tried not to show the disappointment she felt. "So, what story would you like to hear tonight?"

"None." His lashes fell to his rounded cheeks. "I gonna dream all about Christmas."

Jeanne left the room feeling defeated. To discover what was on Toby's list would take time; to acquire all the items would take money. With bills and job commitments piling up, she had little of either. As always, she'd faced the holiday season with the best intentions, but for the first time in her life, she was beginning to identify with Scrooge!

2

"WHEN ARE YOU going to put that boy in school?"

Jeanne, seated at the kitchen table the following morning reading the newspaper, glanced up as her sister Angie entered the kitchen. All the Potters, including Jeanne herself, were aggressive and outspoken, and darn proud of it. But Angie Potter-Gilbert, the eldest of the Potter siblings, was all of these things in the extreme.

Just like their leader, their mentor, their mother: Catherine J. Potter.

Jeanne hid a wince behind her raised coffee cup. She especially hated it when Angie played the child-rearing expert. Big sister and her dentist husband, Brad, had no children as yet. Despite the fact that Angie had no practical experience to draw from, she never tired of offering Jeanne unsolicited advice concerning Toby.

Jeanne sighed. She and her younger brother Andrew had learned at a very young age how to deal with Angie: they allowed her to vent like a seasoned district attorney, then put forward a steady and firm defense.

"Toby is four, and too young for kindergarten," she said evenly. "He is enrolled in fall classes and until then, I feel more than capable of meeting his needs here at home."

"Do you know he greeted me at the door like a butler? 'Remove your shoes,'" Angie mimicked in a childlike squeak. "'Do you got a bappointment?'" She pounded the countertop. "Does he know how children are supposed to behave?"

Jeanne couldn't help laughing. ''He was only playing a game.''

''How can you tell?''

''For starters, I don't have any appointments scheduled until later on.''

''Oh, Jeanne!'' Angie lamented. ''Why should he even know that in the first place?''

''He's trying to be part of the business. The man of the house. And he really is trying to say 'appointment' properly, but he can't quite get his tongue around that big word.''

''He is a child who should be at play!'' Angie stripped off her ski jacket dripping with lift tickets and draped it over the empty chair, then pushed aside Toby's cereal bowl and juice cup.

Jeanne gave up on the paper. ''He doesn't open the door to strangers. Many of my clients have their pictures taken regularly and are good friends. And I always tell him who's expected. It's not like he hangs around the foyer just waiting to greet Jack the Ripper.'' There was no point in telling Angie that Toby loved to tease his Aunt Angie the most because she was so easy to bait. A boy didn't need nursery school to evolve into a well-balanced, insightful terror!

Angie poured herself a cup of coffee from the carafe on the counter. ''Yes, about the way you run your business,'' she forged on. ''You're still charging your clients hobby fees, aren't you, the way you did when David was alive and photography was only a hobby? The Drillmaster and I were discussing it last night and think you should reevaluate your position, strive to widen your profit margin.''

Angie and Brad ''Drillmaster'' Gilbert had a Dellwood mansion and country-club membership thanks to dental fees that gave them a very healthy profit margin. They gleefully admitted to a relationship full of nonstop discussion, which began during the day when Angie, who acted as Brad's hygienist, babbled incessantly over a steady stream of patients, then into the night while they snuggled in their massive king-size bed. Jeanne felt that if they shut up and rolled around on their plush carpet once in a while, they'd have a child of their own to smother in no time flat!

"I intend to raise my rates after the new year," Jeanne honestly reported. "There's something psychological about it. People more readily accept price hikes in January."

Angie approached the table to refill Jeanne's mug and remove the cavity-causing sugar bowl. "Sure, and all your customers will get their holiday photos at a steal."

"At a good rate, sure. But I'm still making a profit. I—" Jeanne broke off with a sigh as Angie sat down across from her, her nostrils flared like a wild filly, intent on a long gallop down a oft-traveled road. "Angie, I wish you wouldn't pick on me right now. I mean, I really, really wish you wouldn't."

Angie gazed directly into the forlorn face so much like her own, then wound down contritely. "You're right, kid, so right to stop me. You put up such a good front, I sometimes forget how fragile you are."

"I don't like that word, Angie. Fragile. It describes the first few months of widowhood. I'm about to clock in my first year of it. Because David died last January, the first Christmas without him comes on the tail end of all the other firsts. Can you understand that? It's like one last blast of pain, just waiting to grip me at the most sentimental time of year."

"Understand?" Angie crowed. "The whole family is acutely aware of the situation. Mom's baked three times her normal cookie quota. Dad's got the surface of the house plastered with light bulbs. And Andrew—" She stopped short, realizing Jeanne would know that their little brother hadn't gone out of his way at all. Andrew was a twenty-year-old college sophomore who boarded at school and always returned home at the last minute, just in time for all the fun, but none of the work. How Jeanne envied him!

And enjoyed his company. He was far too self-centered and fun-loving to butt into her affairs.

"Do me a favor and bully the folks into behaving like the boisterous, egotistical monsters we Potters have always been at Christmas," Jeanne pleaded, reaching across the table to squeeze her sister's hand.

"Don't know if even I can force cheer," she said doubtfully.

"Start with the Drillmaster," Jeanne suggested brightly.

"My husband's not an insane Potter," Angie objected. She took pride in the fact that she'd married a level-headed man with ties to the governor and other sober authority figures.

"Still, he's too solicitous," Jeanne insisted. "Denting my mashed potatoes at Thanksgiving was unnecessary. David looked out for me, but not even he did that."

Angie's voice rose defensively. "Brad just wanted to dent those spuds properly to dam the gravy. He can't stand not perfecting any kind of cavity within reach."

"Dam's a bad word," Toby peeped, peering in from the living-room doorway with huge shiny hazel eyes.

"Not the kind of dam that holds gravy," Angie hastily corrected. "Gravy dams are perfectly fine."

"Okay." With a grin, he vanished.

Angie's forehead puckered as she regarded her sister again. "I'll help you with the folks, if you enroll Toby in one organized activity this spring. The county sponsors all sorts of things—swimming, tumbling, painting. That kid should be needling his peers."

"Well..."

"Stop cringing. You're overprotective. Your son will walk out the door and return unscathed, over and over again." Her voice grew soft as Jeanne's eyes grew moist. "It's a reasonable assumption made by millions of parents each and every day."

"Hold that pose for a minute!" Jeanne ordered, then

studied her dumbfounded sister. "You remind me of somebody important. But who? Who?"

Angie did respect Jeanne's eye for imagery. She gave her tide of blond hair a pat, her eyes dancing anxiously. "Loni Anderson? You know I went to her old hairdresser last week for this trim."

Jeanne tipped her head pensively one way, then the other. "No, it's not the hair. It's something about the tone." Her eyes grew dramatically sinister. "Your whiny, demanding tone."

Angie clapped her hands to her cheeks. "Not her! Not Mother!"

Jeanne snapped her fingers. "How shrewd of you to figure it out. Catherine J. Potter uses that annoying voice when things aren't going her way."

"Stop! Stop! I beg you!" Angie became a Potter girl again, completely silly for a brief moment, giggling in a way the Drillmaster himself wouldn't even recognize.

"You stop making reasonable assumptions for me and I'll back off," Jeanne promised.

"Just listen to me on this one issue," Angie pleaded, struggling to recover. "If you want to survive the holidays, at least give the appearance of a budding social life, for both you and Toby. The scales will be out, ready to measure your progress. I have the feeling that if you're not happy, Mother is going to make you happy."

Jeanne lifted her chin in pride. "I'm taking small steps outward that don't have to be faked. I've been appreciating the opposite sex again. In subtle ways."

"Subtle? You mean squeezing mushy off-season cantaloupes at the grocery store with a silent, come-hither look?"

"No, I've graduated from the frozen-food section where I made real conversation. A scintillating debate over brands of chicken potpies and beef pita pockets."

"You never buy that stuff!"

"I know, but that didn't stop me from giving my opinion." Jeanne batted her eyes and puckered her lips.

Angie was openly impressed. "Way to go, flirty babe!"

"Yeah, the poor lamb listened with guileless faith, and bought what I told him to." She gave her head a hair rippling toss. "Oh, the dizzying feel of power."

Angie leaned forward eagerly. "Did he ask for your phone number? Have you seen him again?"

"Heck, no! It was just sort of an experiment. He was no one I'd care to catch under the mistletoe. He was a little pudgy and wore track shoes with rundown heels."

"Oh, sure, destroy the scene for me. I was envisioning 'The Young and the Restless' there for a minute."

"I wish." Jeanne braced her elbow on the tabletop and set her chin in her hand. "I do see what you mean though, about my holiday image. Everybody would relax if they thought I was involved."

"Even a commercial picture from a new wallet would ease the tension."

"What!" Jeanne sat up ramrod stiff, truly affronted for the first time.

"You know, something to flash and slip back into your purse before anybody realized it was a snap of Don Johnson in his salad days."

"I'm not that desperate," Jeanne said emphatically. "Don't you think as a professional photographer I can come up with a finer phony photo than that!"

"Gee, sis," Angie teased, "I apologize for underestimating your social skills."

As Jeanne searched for a scathing comeback, the doorbell rang. "Don't move," she said, bouncing out of her chair. "I'm not through with you yet!"

Toby collided with her in the hallway. "It's a real live stranger!" he reported. "So I just runned away!"

"Good boy." Jeanne ruffled his hair.

She returned to the kitchen moments later to find Angie

straightening the cereal boxes in her cupboard. Angie flinched, expecting the usual protest about her compulsive cleaning, but Jeanne barely looked at her. She smacked a red-and-green-striped envelope on the countertop. ''That was a messenger.''

''Good news, I hope.''

''Hah! He thinks he can buy me off with three hundred bucks!''

''Who he?''

''Him!'' Jeanne seethed. ''Can you imagine the nerve?''

''I can't even imagine *him,*'' Angie blurted out in wonder. ''Though I'd like to.'' Brimming with curiosity, Angie grabbed the envelope and peered inside. ''A gift certificate for Gracie's. Do you realize most people would kill for this?''

Jeanne jammed a hand on her hip, her mind full of questions. A good deed gone bad? A bad boy doing good? A bad boy paying off?

''What's this Post-it Note mean? 'All the best, Santa.'''

Jeanne snatched it away from her. ''Well, he was more like son of Santa, really—age-wise, I mean.''

''Who!''

''A guy named Ron Coleman.''

''The famous journalist?''

''No, the infamous toy-store superjock.''

''Guess there must be two,'' Angie mumbled. ''Never mind, go on.''

''Remember, after Sunday dinner how Mom was set to take Toby to Grace Brothers?''

''Yeah, I heard firsthand from her what happened,'' Angie admitted. ''So this is connected to that?''

''Of course. Didn't either one of you think I was going to handle it?''

Angie stroked her sister's flaxen hair. ''Simmer down. All Mom said was that you forbade her to go back to fix

St. Nick's hash. I understand full well that you couldn't turn her loose over there, with her temper."

"Exactly! We don't call her Cat for nothing." Jeanne explained the entire situation to her sister.

"It appears that you've done fine," Angie concluded. "So, it's over."

"But I didn't want this kind of payoff. I want Santa himself," Jeanne objected in a whisper, keeping her eye on the doorway for any sign of her inquisitive son. "I wanted him to backpedal on the promises."

"Ninety-nine percent of all Twin Citians would settle for the certificate," Angie declared with confidence.

Jeanne hated the way Angie made up statistics to suit her own viewpoint. "Maybe so, but I feel I've been giving in and making do ever since David died."

"What a dumb cause to start with."

Jeanne caught her sister's gaze and held it. Their blue eyes locked for a long moment. "Would you like to guarantee Toby everything he wants for Christmas, Ange?"

Angie's mouth sagged open. "I...guess it depends upon what he wants."

"He's keeping that a secret."

"Oh." The know-it-all sister was stumped. She took her ski jacket off the back of the chair, and shrugged into it.

Jeanne's voice was husky when she continued. "I figure we're at a crossroads. If he's disappointed this year, after losing David, he may grow up never believing in the spirit of Christmas again."

Angie gulped, thought hard, then said with a resurgence of confidence, "I see what you mean, but surely you can force an answer out of him."

"I've tried. And failed!"

Angie regarded her awe. "I can't believe it's you, sometimes."

Jeanne's pretty face went blank. "What do you mean?"

"The way you've stopped dreaming like a Potter, Sis.

The way you fully expect a shadow of disappointment to cross your path at every other turn. Since when is failure even part of our family's vocabulary?''

''It's tougher when you're spinning dreams all by yourself,'' Jeanne said patiently, but firmly. ''I schemed way too big once, and lost the whole jackpot.''

''There are other gambles out there, Jeanne. The biggest loss of all would be to stop trying.'' Angie zipped her jacket. ''It's about time I went to the office. Big root canal ahead.''

''Oh, sure, get along, you impetuous Potter!'' Jeanne tapped the edge of the envelope on her palm. ''I just can't believe this,'' she murmured. ''He seemed so anxious to please me.''

''Really?'' Angie gave her a quick hug, hope springing anew in her features. ''Is this Ron Coleman attractive?''

''Extremely so. Tall, muscular frame. Dark brown eyes, large mouth full of teeth you'd be proud to floss. So what's it to ya?''

''So I was just going to suggest you snap his picture for your wallet,'' Angie said sweetly, wiggling her fingers. '''Bye.''

''Don't tell Mom a darn thing about this, Ange. Not a darn thing!''

''A LADY ON THE LINE for you, Ron.'' A regal Emmett, bedecked in an emerald robe and black hard-soled slippers, held the phone out to his grandson later that same morning, his palm covering the mouthpiece. Ron, who had just finished showering and was wrapped in a towel, held out a wet hand for the receiver.

''Recognize the voicc, Pop?''

Emmett's lips thinned. ''No.''

''Big help,'' his grandson mouthed as he moved closer.

Emmett's gaze traveled over Ron's lean, damp body with

a measure of scorn. ''She is most assuredly a lady, however, and you are in no condition to speak to a lady.''

Ron nodded curtly, dropped the towel, then took the receiver. ''Hello,'' he said with a hint of laughter in his voice.

''This is Jeanne Trent.''

''Oh!'' Suddenly Ron felt uncomfortable with his nudity. He made a grab for the towel, but Emmett was a step ahead, already in the process of scooping it up. Ron, tethered by the phone cord, had no choice but to allow his grandfather his little game.

''Got your certificate,'' she went on, oblivious to everything but her own frustration.

''Hope it's enough. If not—''

''I thought you understood me yesterday. I want Santa himself.''

''But the money's better,'' Ron protested, pacing round like a bronzed warrior with an arrow piercing his hide. Adding insult to injury, Emmett was listening from a safe distance, more than happy to be the audience for a change.

''No, the money isn't better. You get Santa over to my house, ready to make a retraction, or I'll go above your head. There must be somebody in the Grace empire who can overrule you!''

Ron was horrified. This would crush the duffer for sure! ''No, wait!''

''I happen to know Santa's in the store from one to five every day of the week,'' she went on vigorously, pouncing on his distress like a cunning lioness. ''If I don't see him before tomorrow, I'll head straight for the North Pole!''

''But I can't. A retraction's—'' He broke off as a dial tone buzzed in his ear. He whirled on Emmett. ''It seems our late-night trip back to the store for that gift certificate backfired. She still wants you and only you.''

''A lady of discrimination and breeding,'' Emmett surmised.

Ron stomped up and snatched the towel off Emmett's arm. "I have to go out for a while."

"So close to curtain time?" Emmett glanced at the wall clock with a worried look.

"I'll be back in plenty of time to take you to the store." Ron turned slowly, a crafty smile on his face. "Better yet, why not ride along with me now?"

Emmett stroked his jaw. "Well, your sudden engagement does sound intriguing, but I have some things around here that need doing."

"You're just going to stand idly by and let me do your dirty work for you, aren't you?"

Emmett straightened indignantly and grasped the lapels of his robe. "How sharper than a serpent's tooth it is to have a thankless child."

Ron imitated his grandfather's stance, down to clutching an invisible lapel. "Thou shouldst be concerned with this pesky mother, after thy job, thy scrawny neck."

"I swear you could make it on the stage if you wanted to," Emmett marveled as he relaxed his pose. "Your dramatic flair skipped a generation, you know. Lord knows I love your mother, but Bernice is too mature for our extravagant ways."

"As Jeanne Trent seems to be. That kind always follows through."

"Yes, her sort make wonderful wives and daughters." Emmett lifted his sloped shoulders in resignation. "I suppose somebody has to run the shop for us lads."

Ron pressed a hand to his damp and hairy chest. "Please make the retraction, Grandfather. For me, as my Christmas gift."

The old man clutched his lapels harder, his gnarled knuckles whitening. "If I were to do so, I would be a liar to the nth degree. I have spoken what I know to be the truth to all the children and will not give in to a skittish mother who doesn't have enough faith, no matter how pretty she may be.'' He raised a brow and his voice. ''Ah, but that kind does things to a man. Despite the issues, the heart skips with delight.''

Ron's brown eyes grew larger. ''She's way too young for you.''

''Oh, yes, just by a margin.'' He smiled broadly. ''It's your ticker that's up for grabs this round.''

''Well, enjoy the show.'' Ron heaved a beleaguered sigh, and headed back for the bathroom to shave.

''MOMMY! It's a stranger again!''

Jeanne turned away from the tripod holding her best 35mm camera as Toby burst through the door of her in-house studio. ''A stranger you know?'' she asked, thinking of Santa.

''No way. It's a real stranger!''

''Excuse me a moment, Agnes.'' Jeanne nodded to her client, and went in pursuit of her son, already on the run again. To her chagrin, she found Ron on her doorstep.

''Oh,'' she greeted flatly. ''It's you.'' She turned to her son, panting at her side like a frisky, inquisitive puppy. ''Toby, go tell Agnes to take five.''

''Gotcha.'' With two thumbs up Toby scooted off.

Ron was primed to press his palm against the door if she tried to close it, but she fooled him by easing out onto the step beside him. He flinched beneath her cold scrutiny. ''You do awful things to a guy's ego, you know that?''

She surveyed him, and was aware of mixed emotions. He was so appealing, dressed in indigo jeans, a midlength leather jacket that fit to his broad shoulders and lean hips with tailored perfection. He had a stricken expression that he was attempting to realign into a bland mask of indifference. Was he worked up about Santa or her, or both? ''Well, you got here fast enough,'' she said, saying the only thing she could think of.

He bared his teeth in a cynical smile. ''Thank you very

much.'' Emmett's Como Avenue high rise was only ten minutes west of her Roseville home. For all he knew, she and the old man might even shop at the same strip mall on Lexington.

She folded her arms across her chest as the cold air seeped into her royal-blue sweat clothes. ''So where is he, Mr.—''

''Please, call me Ron.''

She eyed him warily. ''Where's the man in red, Ron?''

''You wear blue a lot, don't you?'' He ran an appreciative eye over her shivering form.

''Red, Ron, red! Where's Santa?''

He smiled faintly. ''It suits you.''

''What suits me?''

''Blue. Except around the lips. Aren't you freezing?''

Her mind raced to keep up with him. ''Yes, but I have a very nosy little boy with excellent hearing.''

''Well, the only gentlemanly thing to do is admit that the man in red isn't coming.''

''But why?'' Her voice rose shrilly.

''He flat out refuses,'' Ron reported, watching her dance from one sneaker to another on the cramped stoop.

''But you said you were in charge of him!''

''I said he was in my care,'' he corrected mildly. ''Please, let me in. We really have to talk.''

''Give me one reason why I shouldn't march right down to that palace of toys and have you fired. Give me one good reason!''

He lifted his hands in a helpless gesture. ''Because I don't work there?''

Her mouth sagged. ''Huh?''

''It's true. I'm sorry.''

She squealed in despair. ''After all I've been through, I won't even have the pleasure of making you squirm?''

''On the contrary.'' He reached over her and turned the doorknob. ''By all means, give it to me good.''

3

''HEY, DO I KNOW you?''

Ron was standing in the center of the Trent living room, removing his jacket when he heard the voice behind him. He swiveled round to find a small boy standing in the doorway, dressed in a green sweatshirt and blue jeans. ''No, you don't know me.'' Ron tried to keep up a merry front, but he didn't appreciate being parked in here, although Jeanne had seemed contrite as she explained that there was a client in her studio and she was in the midst of a photo shoot.

''Do you know me?'' the child asked intently, sidling closer.

''Nope.'' They studied each other for a long moment. Ron noted that the child greatly resembled his mother. He had her fair, Nordic features, and high, full cheeks.

''I'm Toby.''

Ron draped his jacket on an arm of the sofa and sat down on the center cushion. ''I'm Ron.''

''You Mommy's friend?''

Ron pressed his hands between his knees. ''I want to be.''

''Mommy's friends play with me.'' His eyes sparkled, full of hope and mischief.

''Well, I'm here for a talk—'' Ron started as Toby tossed a purple foam rubber ball into his lap. He promptly tossed it back to the boy. ''I really don't have time for catch.''

''Do so.'' Toby tossed the ball to Ron.

"I don't, Toby. Really."

Toby turned his back for a second, then spun around with a small vinyl glove on his left hand. When Ron tossed the ball back again, Toby made an unnecessary dive to grab it. "Line drive!" he shouted, reaching out as though he was making a tremendous save. He danced around on the tips of his tennis shoes. "Out on first. Crowd goes wild!"

Ron laughed. "Pretty good. So, you a Minnesota Twin in training?"

"Yup." With that the boy raced out of the living room.

With long-limbed restlessness, Ron rose from the mauve sateen sofa, and took a good look at his surroundings for the first time. He had no idea how long Jeanne had been on her own, but the room was done in feminine pastel tones. There wasn't a lot of furniture, but the stuff looked fairly new. He wondered if she'd recently moved in or had redecorated with a new beginning in mind. He was sure there was no male influence here, just as his Los Angeles bungalow reflected no feminine touches. Emmett's apartment reflected his love of the theater. The jumble of heavy pieces he'd collected throughout the course of his marriage to Olivia, Ron's easygoing grandmother made it resemble the set of a gothic stage play.

The glittering Christmas tree set in the corner against the eggshell-colored drapes crossed all boundaries, and would have been a welcome addition to any home. It was a tree in the real spirit of Christmas, Ron realized with a lift. He was often in Europe at this time of year and had nothing but a miniature tabletop tree that he dragged out if he needed it. A genuine, full-bodied pine was such a pleasant sight after all these years. He wandered closer, shutting his eyes, inhaling its pungent scent, recapturing the childlike wonder of the holidays for a brief moment.

Then—*whop!* Ron flinched as something hit him between the shoulder blades. He looked down to find the purple foam ball bouncing between his feet. "Toby..." He turned slowly and found the boy had set up a miniature baseball diamond with four washcloths.

"C'mon, pitcha-pitcha!" Toby was standing in the oversize doorway beside a washcloth turned to form a diamond, a gigantic yellow bat in his hands. By the way he was wiggling it over his head, it had to be hollow, feather-light plastic. A child-size navy-blue Twins cap was jammed over his thick thatch of blond hair, and he was squinting at Ron from beneath the bill.

Ron bent over, picked up the ball, and tossed it several inches into the air. Should he?

"You a pitcha or belly itcha?" Toby taunted in a squeaky sort of growl.

Disguising a grin behind pursed lips, Ron ran his hand over the surface of his tan chamois shirt, gave his imaginery hat a tug, and stared down the batter. He didn't know the first thing about appeasing children, but he did remember exactly how to play schoolyard baseball. With a huge windmill wallop, he sent the sphere of foam across the diamond.

And the boy hit it. With a *thunk* it sailed the length of the living room. Ron tried to catch it in midair, but was thwarted by an end table. In the meantime, Toby ran the bases with his arms in the air.

The game went on for a good fifteen minutes. Toby finally gave Ron a turn at bat, but not until he'd tagged the boy out three times.

Ron couldn't resist the urge to hit. Caught up in the moment, the excitement, the roar of the crowd that Toby talked about, he went for broke. One good smack sent the ball soaring high, directly for the tree. With an outstretched arm Ron leaped to try and intercept it in flight. Toby made a grab for his belt loop and together they tumbled onto the carpeting. They didn't graze the tree by much, but it shook the pine in its red metal stand, sending a shower of tinsel and ornaments from its branches.

"Boys!"

Cradling Toby in his lap, Ron looked up to find Jeanne standing in the doorway near home plate, shaking the plastic bat like a wild hitter. A middle-aged woman, in striking makeup, was hovering in the foyer beyond, more than a little interested. He felt like a kid again, exhilarated, and slightly ashamed. "I am so sorry," he apologized, scrambling to his feet, aware that Toby was using him as a shield. "So very, very sorry."

Jeanne set the bat against the wall and turned her attention back to her customer. As she held out the woman's coat, complimenting her on her cashmere scarf, Ron realized Jeanne's face was hot with embarrassment. She must think him a maniac and he couldn't blame her.

"C'mon, sport," he whispered to the child. "Let's get these ornaments back in place."

No sooner did he have one wooden soldier hanging from a branch than Jeanne was back, alone and livid. "Toby, I want you to take care of this by yourself. I have business with Mr. Coleman."

"He said his name is Ron."

"And I'm happy to help," Ron assured her.

"I'll bet." She gazed at him knowingly. Anything to escape their showdown. "But we have business, remember?"

"Gravy dam," the boy muttered.

"What?" Ron appeared perplexed.

"Just a little something my sister told him." Jeanne's mouth softened as she crossed the room to place her hand on Toby's shoulder. "Put these things back on the tree."

"All by myself?" he squealed with a stomp of his tennis shoe.

"Yes!" Jeanne pointed a finger at Ron. "As for you, mister, come with me."

Raking his hands through his thatch of chestnut-brown hair, Ron obeyed.

Jeanne ushered him into her studio and closed the door firmly behind them.

"That's a great kid you have," he ventured.

"Yes, I know." She picked a strand of tinsel from his hair. She found it difficult to believe him capable of stringing her along again over the very same boy. But he was doing just that.

He chuckled suddenly. "I remember having to blow off some steam at that age, especially before Christmas."

"Yes, I understand *Toby,*" she said, putting clear emphasis on her son's name. "But he knows better. Baseball is a basement game around here."

"He probably just saw an opportunity for play and didn't think much further. Kids can be impetuous. I always was."

And always would be, most likely. Jeanne watched him move, the ripple of muscle in his back and thighs. Now that he'd admitted that he wasn't a Gracie's employee, she could see that the job wouldn't suit him at all. This man needed action. Lots of sharp-edged action. Why, his tanned skin alone was a dead giveaway. So who was he? Where did he fit in?

Ron knew she was sizing him up, and found it kind of a turn-on. With his hands clasped behind his back, he roamed the room with equal curiosity. "How clever, transforming this master bedroom into a work area."

"Yes, it's the biggest room in the house, and the bathroom comes in very handy. It's the perfect little beauty shop for my clients. You see, I don't just take photographs, I provide the hairdo, the makeup. The works."

His interest was piqued. "A fantasy kind of photo?"

"Yes."

"That woman looked stunning. You really must know your stuff."

"I studied cosmetology before my marriage, and have dabbled in photography since my gig on the high-school newspaper. After Toby was born, it was a way to supplement the family income while staying home with him. A hobby with some profits.'' She paused, again feeling she was blabbing too much.

''Seems like more than a hobby now,'' he remarked, respect in his voice. He knew something about the business and this was a bona fide studio. She had a twelve-foot-wide backdrop along one wall as well as a host of props which included a door, Gothic pillars, a bookshelf and a mock fireplace. There were three quality cameras visible, a tripod, and a variety of electronic flash equipment.

''I suddenly found myself the head of the household,'' she explained. ''Got organized out of a sense of need more than anything else.''

There were many more questions he longed to ask. How had she ended up this way? What had led her to transform her bedroom into her place of business? What had happened to her husband? Was her bed, wherever it was, empty?

Jeanne watched his expression grow pensive, and cursed her big mouth. Why was she opening up to this stranger?

Because he was interested, that's why. And she was flattered by his interest. No matter what sort of stunt he and Santa were trying to pull, Ron Coleman was tall, dark and handsome, and far sexier than anyone she'd ever run into buying groceries. Despite her irritation, she wanted to know more about him as well. ''So, you're not part of the Grace's staff and their rebel Santa flat out refuses to see Toby?'' she prompted.

''Afraid so.'' He smiled tightly, hooking his thumbs in his belt loops. ''I may as well come clean here and now, Jeanne. I'm a journalist, not a salesman. And Emmett Windom is my eighty-year-old grandfather. I just happened to be at the North Pole when you showed up. I saw the chance to defuse a troublesome situation for Emmett and took it.''

''So you *are* the other Ron Coleman!''

''There are two?''

''No, I guess not,'' she conceded. ''But you are the famous one?''

''Yes.''

''So our conversation—your side of it—was a complete waste of time.'' She gasped as the encounter replayed in her mind. ''That was a mighty dirty trick, pretending to take my complaint seriously.''

''Oh, I did take it seriously,'' he hastily and sincerely assured her. ''Little else has been on my mind since. One conclusion I've reached is that we're in the same boat in many ways—''

''How can you say that!''

''We're both looking out for our own dream-chasing rascal, aren't we? When you think about it, my grandpa and your son have a lot of things in common—vulnerability, inflexibility, a tendency to throw tantrums!''

She absorbed the idea with a wry look. ''What does this have to do with the Santa issue?''

''Everything, really. Toby believes in him and Emmett believes he is him!''

''You're putting me on.''

''No.'' He shook his head emphatically. ''Emmett's a dapper old stage performer, a student of the method-acting school. He's convinced that he *is* Santa while in costume. So confident that he's done the job right in the first place, he can't comprehend the idea of a retraction.''

''Of all the Santas in the Cities to choose!'' She threw up her hands. ''So, in other words, you've simply come over here to give me the bad news in person.''

''Well, I hoped to intercept you before you did return to Grace Brothers,'' he admitted. ''Stanley Bickel, the manager of the store, is the real boss of Santa and is just looking for an excuse to fire Emmett. He has somebody else in mind for the job, you see.''

She sighed. ''Well, Emmett's certainly lucky to have such a protective grandson.''

Encouraged by these words, Ron hurried to add, "He's really a wonderful old guy, but at his age, his eccentricities are locked in tight. If you'd just try to understand."

"Can you blame me for trying to make things right for Toby? He's pretty wonderful, too."

"Look, I'm trying to make it up to you. Losing this job would be the end of Emmett. Not only does it pay handsomely, but he needs to maintain his image in the theater community. When he goes for coffee on Grand Avenue, he needs to have new stories to tell his cronies. If he didn't have purpose, he'd whither away like an autumn leaf."

"He looked mighty sturdy to me," she argued. "And my mother said he was quite a flirt."

"Oh, he loves the ladies still." Ron smiled fondly.

Like Santa, like grandson, she couldn't help thinking.

"My folks watch over him as a rule, and they really have their hands full. Emmett's memory and eyes are failing a bit, but he still has the lusty drive to make things happen."

She smiled a little. "So you're just pinch-hitting, so to speak?"

"While my parents are vacationing in Arizona. I have a home in Los Angeles. It's nothing special. I'm on the road a lot, gathering material for books and articles."

"But you're from here, originally?"

Ron knew Minnesotans, unlike transplanted Californians, always liked to hear about local roots. He couldn't help thinking how similar Jeanne was to the girls he used to date in school. Fresh, centered, generous. "Absolutely. I was raised on the south side of Minneapolis."

"Well, I think it's wonderful that a busy guy like you cares enough about his grandfather to come home and—"

"I do care. And you'd like him too, once you got to know him." He stepped closer to her, a dazzling smile of encouragement on his face. "Please reconsider, Jeanne, and accept the gift certificate for Grace Brothers in the spirit it was given."

"No, I won't!" She crossed the room to a small desk near the door and picked up the bright red-and-green envelope lying atop a heap of business papers. She whirled around to find he'd followed her. They collided with a thump.

Just as he'd planned, of course. He'd inherited enough of Emmett's acting ability to look suitably surprised, before sniffing her soft, fair head. "Mmm, lemon shampoo. My favorite."

Spicy masculine scent. A long-forgotten favorite of hers. She self-consciously realized that her nose was pressed into the softness of his chamois shirt. And she was enjoying it. Too much.

"Can't we be adult about this?" he asked huskily.

She tipped her face up to his, her brilliant blue eyes dancing suspiciously. "What do you mean?"

"Christmas is strictly for old folks and children, isn't it? The dreams, the tradition."

"And in what spirit was this gift certificate given?"

"The spirit of survival?" he replied with good humor.

"Oh, so this Christmas fuss is just an inconvenience to you?" she asked, assessing his position with dead accuracy.

"Well, yeah. It was super at Toby's age, of course. But at this stage of my life, I feel differently."

"Self-absorbed Reporter Plays Hero, Dragging Boy and his Santa Through the Holidays on a Rusty Sled." She fired out the words like a bold headline reporting a tragedy.

"That's about the size of it," he said with thinning patience. "I thought you'd agree, with all the stress you seem to be under."

She didn't answer immediately, and when she spoke, her voice was cold and distant. "Why, I almost believed you were…"

"Were what?" he demanded in bewilderment.

"A holiday junkie like me," she admitted disappointedly.

He inhaled in sharp surprise. He'd mucked this up even further it seemed. She was harried about her holiday obligations, but apparently enjoyed the condition. It seemed the harder he tried to please her, the closer the foot in his mouth came to nudging his tonsils. "Isn't it enough that I'm taking the blame on Emmett's behalf?" he asked. "That I want to pick up the tab?"

She regarded him with disgust. "So, life in your mind is one big tab?"

How quickly she could cut to the chase. "Hey, I didn't invent the policy, I just go with the flow. This seems so cut-and-dried to me."

"Have you ever been married? Have any children?"

"No."

"I didn't think so. Cut-and-dried," she sputtered. "You must get up close and personal on those news stories with nothing shorter than a ten-foot pen!"

The professional insult angered him, especially since he doubted she'd ever read any of his stuff. "I can understand a person's point of view, and report on it with insight."

She made a doubtful sound. "Nothing makes up for experience, something you seem to be lacking big-time."

That gibe, too, struck home. Gravy dam, it did. He wasn't accustomed to being unmasked or riled. Ron's eyes traveled round the room as he sought a comeback, something brilliant and unimpeachable. He gasped as he spied a large wall clock near the door. "That isn't really the time, is it?"

"Yes. Twelve-fifteen."

"I have to go. Emmett can't be late for work." He seized her by the arms so suddenly she gasped. "Please promise not to follow me."

She made an incredulous sound. "What!"

"Back to the store I mean, to play the tattletale. Give me some time, and I'll sort this out for Toby."

She shook her head as he dashed out of the studio. Sort

things out? There had been blind panic in his eyes when she'd challenged his skills and sentiment. Why, he couldn't hope to sort his way out of a gift-wrapped package!

"ONE NIGHT ON your own, Ron, and you're sitting in the dark with your diary." Emmett strode into the living room and stood in the glow from the streetlight outside the window.

"Hi, Pop." Ron shifted in the dilapidated chair of crushed rust velvet and oak that Emmett once gleaned from a *Hamlet* production. "I keep telling you, it's a journal, not a diary."

"Right. Tough guys don't do diaries. Even the toughest switch on a light, though." Emmett moved around the room, clicking lamps to life. His black topcoat, resting on his shoulders, trailed out behind him as he moved.

Ron stifled a yawn. "It was light when I sat down. Guess I dozed off."

"Appears you actually wrote something tonight," Emmett observed dryly. "That's a switch."

Ron flipped the book shut in a gesture of self-defense. "Venting my frustrations, I guess. So how was your evening?"

Emmett whisked off his coat and put it in the closet. "Dating women in the fifty- sixty-year range is such an inspiration," he rejoiced smugly. "They're still quite pretty and have the temperaments of angels. Tonight's granny picked me up right at the store, then wheeled us around town with dexterity and remarkable night vision."

"Going to see her again?"

"Indeed. She's picking me up at Grace Brothers after work tomorrow, then we're on to a choir concert at her church." He moved to a rocker opposite Ron that he'd acquired from a *Death of a Salesman* set. "So how is our pretty little mother managing?"

"Fuming. Still refuses to take that gift certificate."

The lines around Emmett's mouth deepened. "A matter of pride?"

"Yeah, I think the outright charity of it made her uncomfortable."

Emmett sighed. "That's too bad. Thanks for the effort, though. It was good of you to try, to care so much about the old man."

Ron was frustrated by resignation. "It isn't over by a long shot. I still have to resolve this somehow. Stop her from turning you in."

"She may have been tempted to report me," his grandfather said calmly, "but I think it was a bluff. As I said earlier, she's a lady of discrimination. I could tell by her voice. Beautiful diction, with an underlying charm."

"You do know voices, Pop, I grant you—"

"And now we know that she's not the type to grab an exorbitant payoff—even if it is one you could well afford. Another example of good character."

Ron set his journal on the end table, then leaned forward earnestly. "She's as down-to-earth as you can imagine. Runs a photography studio out of her home while taking care of her turbocharged boy. But you've got to understand. She is a protective mother first and foremost, who takes the role very seriously." Ron used the term deliberately. Emmett understood roles.

"I'd say the child is a lucky lad." Emmett pursed his lips in thought.

"She will put his holiday happiness way above your job security," Ron warned him.

"Well, in any case, I feel you gave it your best shot. Time to let Fate take it's course."

"I can't believe you're willing to run this risk!"

"I can handle myself, Ron, really." Emmett's old eyes hardened.

"Sure you can—"

"Are you?" His tone sharpened a fraction. "I expect

Bernice will always fuss over me because she's my only child, daddy's girl. And you see me through her eyes a lot of the time because she's often the bridge between us. How's Grandpa doing? How's Grandson doing? We ask her and she makes the judgment calls.''

Ron clasped his hands together. ''Guess that's true to a point.''

''I see myself in a realistic light always, despite what you and your mother think.'' When Ron's brows rose skeptically, he chuckled. ''I'm an aging performer who still likes to wring out a solid performance from the depths of my soul. True, I forget things and take ginger steps in the snow and the shower. But I can still handle Stanley Bickel!'' he bellowed with a shaking fist. ''Even if Jeanne Trent does her damnest, I have a defense. You know as well as anyone there has not been another single complaint.''

Ron swallowed hard. When he spoke, his voice was husky. ''I guess there's no reason to pursue the issue any further, then.''

''You sound disappointed.''

''Do I?''

Emmett's mouth curled mockingly. ''Yes, as though my dilemma was just so much fun and now it's over.''

Ron flushed. ''Begging beautiful women for mercy isn't my idea of fun. You know how tough it is to beg?'' he demanded plaintively.

The rail-thin man shivered beneath his dress clothes, as though repelled by the idea. ''Can't say I do. Never been a beggar myself.''

''Bickering too,'' Ron complained. ''Bickering and begging. All for you!''

Emmett rose stiffly and stretched his arms above his head. ''Always have enjoyed a good bicker with a hot-blooded woman. More than a few ended up begging in the end,'' he quipped, highly amused.

Ron smiled thinly. Emmett's love life sounded more fruitful and fertile with every passing year. It was amazing how the man could manipulate his own memories for entertainment purposes. "Just trying to help you, Pop. Seems only right you should cooperate."

"Really?" Emmett stood over him, his spine erect and his chin high, the imposing father figure suddenly. "I feel I must be honest for your own good, Ronny. We've always had a special bond, two headstrong fellows bent on avoiding the mundane at all costs. As much as I enjoy your visits, the camaraderie renewed..." He hesitated, weighing his words. "I can't help but feel you might be using me as some sort of excuse this time around."

"What!" Ron's strong jaw slackened.

"I'm not challenging your goodwill, but you are behaving strangely."

"How?"

"You're characteristically full of yourself when you come, hearty and sure, talking a mile a minute about life and your footloose cronies."

"Good lord, that's a description of you!"

Emmett's chest puffed like a rooster's. "Yes, and a flattering one. Furthermore, you're usually pounding away on that laptop contraption of yours about some adventure you've had or stolen from somebody else. This time, aside from tonight, you seem at a loss for words, and obsessively focused on me, as though I'm some kind of geriatric pet project." The idea obviously left a bad taste in his mouth.

"I'll back off a little," Ron grumbled, studying his laced fingers.

"That isn't enough! I'm telling you to dig, Ronny. Examine your motives. Perhaps you feel at a crossroads, son," he suggested. "You're thirty now, without a family, a clear direction, a significant other to run hot water for your feet."

Ron's mouth twitched then. Foot-soaking was a pleasure more suited to Emmett's advanced age. Ron had no trouble suppressing his glee, however. The picture Emmett had painted of him was all too accurate. How shrewd of the old man to put all the pieces together. Ron knew he was looking for purpose in his overbearing care of Emmett. He'd come back to hometown comfort hoping to recharge his creative batteries.

But he'd die before admitting it outright.

Emmett reached out to ruffle Ron's brown head the way he used to years ago. "Jeanne Trent is quite pretty and seems worth knowing. Is it possible that saving my job is only part of your motive for pursuing her? Could it be that you enjoyed meeting the lady yourself and hoped to milk it a little longer, using my plight as a front?"

"Even if I did try and pull that sort of stunt, she ended up hurling insults at me with your kind of skill. That's hard to take from a female a guy barely knows."

Emmett smiled blandly. "A little bickering and begging with the right lady may be just what you need."

Ron's self-control slipped. "She was brutal." He went on to repeat Jeanne's crack about the ten-foot pen. "I'm not an impostor, Pop. I've delivered the goods. Seen life and reported it!"

"Oh, I know, son. You've had tremendous success. Did you try to tell her?"

"Didn't have the time. Had to come back for you."

"You're just bound and determined to blame all your troubles on me, aren't you?" Ron couldn't bear the unmistakable hurt in Emmett's faded eyes.

"You're trouble for sure, Pop," he said gently. "But I definitely botched things up myself. I came across as a crass wise guy about Christmas, with the gift-certificate push and some other blundering remarks."

Emmett nodded his silver head in understanding. "A holiday that presumably means something to her."

"Oh, yes. Huge tree, lavish decorations throughout the

house. The sort of thing Mom and Dad delivered throughout my childhood.''

Ron's interest in Jeanne was disguised by the flimsiest of veils now. So was Emmett's disgust. ''Then the visual signs were there, Ron. Why did you make yourself look like a globe-trotting grinch right out of the bull pen?''

Ron had given that question a great deal of thought. ''Maybe I was hoping she'd try and convince me I was wrong,'' he suggested.

''She was to do all that? Hardly knowing you? With concerns of her own?''

''She could have,'' Ron argued. Despite her spunky stand, her qualities had shone through like the brightest ornament imaginable. He'd found her sassy, sexy, exciting. Why couldn't she have reciprocated?

Ron sat in sulky silence. Gravy dam, leave it to Emmett the tireless interrogator to dredge it all up.

''The Trent house sounds like a mighty nice place to be at Christmas,'' Emmett murmured, shuffling toward the hallway. ''No, I'm not going to worry for one minute about her son's interests. That woman, she knows exactly how to make wishes come true.'' Lifting a hand, he disappeared.

Ron had come to a similar conclusion. Jeanne's warm Christmas cottage was storybook inviting. Visions of her soft smile and feminine curves danced in his head like sugarplums, making him yearn for a place at her place.

But it was ridiculous to dream this way. A five-year-old fruitcake, run over by a mail truck, would be more welcome at her door!

4

"GRACE BROTHERS does not return cash on this kind of transaction, sir."

Ron stared at the prim female clerk behind the store's customer service counter Wednesday afternoon, tapping his three-hundred-dollar certificate on the glass surface between them. The red-and-green striped envelope was looking a little dog-eared and so was he. The idea of getting his money back with a dash of charisma had seemed like a cinch in theory, just as buying off Jeanne had. At first…

He was amazed as well as horrified by his circumstances. This retreat back into his wintry hometown had his nerves frayed to the limit. His visions of sitting by cozy fires with good books and wines were gone, along with the ice skates he'd imagined strapped to his feet as he'd skimmed across one of Minnesota's ten thousand lakes.

There seemed little doubt left. Not only was he flat out of inspiration, but it seemed he'd lost all appeal to the opposite sex.

But in his own defense, this clerk was more up Emmett's alley, right down to the name tag bearing the name Lenora. Emmett liked names that rolled grandly off the tongue. She wore a simple lilac dress most likely all the rage back in the fifties, and had a cap of steel-gray hair slightly longer than his own. He cast Emmett a beseeching look over his shoulder. Where was the old actor's magic when it could be truly useful?

Emmett's hand pressed against the leather sleeve of

Ron's jacket, signaling caution. "Couldn't you make an exception in Ron's case?"

Lenora's pale blue eyes hardened. "Listen, Hamlet," she snapped flatly, "I've manned this counter for thirty years, since the day Wendell and Arnold Grace themselves cut the ribbon to the front doors. Gift certificates are nonrefundable."

"I've been a friend of the Grace boys myself for even longer, you fussbudget," Emmett said loftily, his nostrils flared like a wild stallion's.

Lenora stepped back dramatically. "Deary me, you've bothered to make male chums along the way? When would you have had the time, you—you Santa Claus Casanova!"

Ron rolled his eyes. The name-calling suggested the worst: Lenora was a woman scorned, and intent on punishing Emmett for it. As Ron looked around the huge bustling store, he realized she would have a clear view of Santa's throne from here, and be able to watch Emmett's flirty antics. Unexpectedly, his grandfather's backup was sinking any chance of getting around the policy so boldy printed on a sign against the wall, right beneath a pledge of friendly service.

Mistaking Ron's thoughtful pause for his cue, Emmett suddenly shoved him aside, and leaned over the countertop until his head was close to Lenora's angry face.

"The name is Emmett," he hissed. "When I am dressed in street clothes I expect to be addressed as such. Or Mr. Windom, if you prefer."

"I prefer that you remove yourself from my sight," she returned huffily.

"That I can do!" With a flourish he removed the coat draped across his shoulders, and tossed it over his arm. "Just to clear up any misunderstandings or hard feelings," he said on a gentler note, "I feel it only fair to confess that I date only younger women."

Lenora's long bony fingers flew up in the air in mocking

surprise. "Good heavens, Methuselah, we're *all* younger than you!"

With a single sniff worthy of a thousand retorts, Emmett marched down the center aisle toward the employees' lounge.

Ron affected an amused chuckle as he turned back to Lenora. "You just gotta love the eccentric old guy, don't you?"

"I don't gotta," she fumed. "Just as I don't gotta give you a refund."

"Look," he said quietly, "a goodwill gesture fell through for me. Having no children of my own, or nieces or nephews, I've no use for the kind of merchandise you handle."

"I must say, you do seem like a fine young man," she admitted with gruff sincerity, "putting up with him and all. But I can't see my way clear to bending the rules this time."

Ron sighed heavily. "Emmett's the decider, isn't he? You just can't bring yourself to give him the satisfaction." Her stoic silence confirmed it. "How about we keep it a secret, just between the two of us."

Resting her elbow on the counter, she crooked her finger at him. He leaned over, boyish hope in his features. "All I can give you is some advice. Next time, drop the old buzzard. He doesn't do a thing for your image."

Ron closed his eyes with a solemn nod. "So what do you suggest I do about this certificate?"

"Shop till you drop." With an abrupt motion she pushed herself away from the counter to answer a ringing telephone.

Ron tried. Braving the crowded aisles, he surveyed row upon row of every conceivable kind of toy. Dolls that wet, dinosaurs that roared, planes that flew, cars that honked. He craned his neck every which way in the gigantic building, even upward, to the stuffed animals hanging from the ceiling.

He eventually bumped into Emmett in full costume as the old man made his way to the North Pole on the heels of two perky elves and the store photographer, a plump redhead in her early twenties. Ron suspected that the redhead had little interest in the art of photography by the careless way she handled the equipment. Naturally he couldn't help but think of Jeanne and her passion for the same kind of work. Her passions in general. He hadn't been so captivated by a woman in a very long time.

"Any luck with our store bully, Ron?" Emmett asked, breaking into his musings.

Realizing adoring eyes were already on Santa Claus, Ron kept a frozen smile. "No," he said between his teeth. "Told me to shop till I drop. Unfair, when all she really wants is for you to drop dead. Didn't you have any idea she was harboring a secret crush?"

Emmett was aghast. "Certainly not!"

Ron's eyes widened skeptically. "Her infatuation would be obvious to anyone. Admit to me that she was harboring a grudge. That playing sentinel behind me wasn't a good idea."

"How preposterous."

"That exercise in egotism cost me three hundred smackers!"

"Well, just call me the ghost of your Christmas Future," his grandfather retorted with a measure of pride. "We're so much alike...it's as if you're a walking tribute to me."

Ron studied him grimly. "Then maybe we're both in big trouble."

"Huh?" Emmett was about to ask what Ron meant by that cryptic remark when he noted parents and toddlers closing ranks on the Pole. "Ho-ho-ho, son!" he bellowed with a jolly belly laugh. "What would you like for Christmas?"

Ron patted the shoulder of Santa's red jacket. ''Let you know, old-timer,'' he said in a loud, jovial voice.

''Better to give than receive,'' Santa proclaimed. He got the expected round of applause.

Ron's eyes gleamed mischievously. ''Yeah, I would like to see you get it. Which gives me an idea. Think I'll shop for you here. Right here and now.''

Emmett's eyes grew wide in panic. ''I want a new VCR, you know that, Ronny.''

''That's boring,'' Ron whispered tauntingly. ''You hate boring.''

Emmett's lips curled over his beard as he mounted the white glittery steps to his carved mahogany chair.

Ron began to scour the store with determination. Surely there was something in the place that Emmett could use in his apartment, something that would antagonize him. Perhaps a small pool in which to soak his feet. He found a wading-sized one and paraded it past the Pole. When he caught Emmett's attention, he gestured to the pool, and his shoes.

''No-ho-ho!'' Emmett proclaimed heartily, before turning back to mug for the camera and the fidgety little girl on his knee.

Ron went through the ritual several times. He passed by the Pole with a giant wall clock framed with a bright yellow sunburst, then a shoe rack in the shape of a monkey, and finally a Mickey Mouse telephone. Emmett declined them all from his kingly perch with a shower of no-hos.

Ron strolled through the game aisle, wondering if there was some little gadget he could take on his plane trips. With hands shoved in the pockets of his leather jacket he stared at the stacks of boxes on the shelves. Children of preschool age were swarming around him like the residents of a huge ant farm, their small hands tearing treasures off the shelves for inspection. It had to be a toddler trait to settle on the floor with a bottom bouncing plop, because that's what so many of them did—as Toby had while the two of them scooped up the ornaments that had toppled from Jeanne's perfect tree.

A boy about Toby's size was seated at his left, playing with some kind of pinball game. Ron stared down to watch the metal marbles rolling and rattling inside a clear plastic box housing a baseball diamond.

An inspiration suddenly hit him. "Is that fun?"

The child tipped his freckled face up. "Yup."

Man and boy turned as a faded-looking woman about Ron's age rushed through the crowd, with a cart holding two other children. She met Ron's eyes for a stricken moment, then dropped her lashes like a shield. No question, he'd lost his touch with women. Why, he couldn't even blame Emmett for this one's lack of interest.

"Just playin', Mommy," the boy whined as the woman tugged him to his feet.

"You aren't supposed to wander off!"

The boy sidled up close to her with a sigh. "Sorry."

The mother looked at Ron again with nervous little glances, as though he was some kind of weirdo.

"I was, ah, just wondering about the game he was playing," Ron assured her with a gentle smile. "Had the idea to buy it for another little boy I know."

"You don't have a child, do you?" She asked the question abruptly, then pinched her lips together.

Realization dawned on him as he scanned her plain, cosmetic-free face, her pale, limp hairdo. She wasn't afraid he was a creep at all. She feared that he might recognize her! "Elaine," he said softly.

"Yes," she admitted with a spurt of laughter. "It's me all right."

His smile grew, a blend of pleasure and sheepishness. He'd made a choice after high school. Life with Elaine at the University of Minnesota, or a solo trip to UCLA. Thirsty for adventure he had chosen the solo trip. Elaine hadn't taken it well at the time, and had hooked up with a football jock even before he'd set out for California. Tony. Tony Rosetti, if memory served him. "Been a while, hasn't it?" he finally said carefully, aware that her eyes were swimming with emotion.

She laughed again. "Twelve years, come this summer."

"Three children." They were all dark, like Tony. What would they look like if he had been their father?

"Actually, Tony and I have five children," she said with forced gaiety. "Two older boys are in school."

"All boys," he noted, grinning at the bunch.

"Yes. A girl would've been fun, of course," she said awkwardly.

"You always did enjoy dolling up," he recalled fondly. "That little girl would've been—" He paused in midsentence, as a shadow darkened her green eyes. "Would've been nice." He'd been about to remark that the child would've been dressed like a princess. But that was unlikely, judging by the worn jackets they were all wearing.

It was obvious that Elaine's primping days were long gone. She was no longer a self-absorbed teenager, but rather a busy housewife, presumably budgeting money and hours to her family's best advantage. How hard this must be for her, to run into him this way, unprepared. Elaine was still lovely, but by the way she was moving her bare lips together, as though smoothing a new coat of lipstick, she felt dowdy at the moment.

"I still think of you sometimes," he admitted softly. "Wonder if you're happy."

"Really?" she lilted, relaxing a little. "Well, I am. We have all the regular problems, you know, over finances and kid stuff. But Tony and the kids are my life. They give me an indescribable feeling of fulfillment."

"Mommy, Bobby's nose!" The boy who'd been fascinated by the pinball game was gesturing to the baby in the cart.

Elaine swiftly produced a tissue from her purse and dabbed the child's lip. ''To you this must seem so dull, with all your adventures, the women you must know.''

''Oh, I don't know,'' he murmured. And it was a true statement! He just didn't know. In spite of all his travels and accomplishments he was currently as confused as an adolescent.

''Read your books of course,'' she said. ''And enjoyed them. I could hear your voice so clearly. First-person-singular suits your writing.''

''Thanks. I appreciate the fact that you can still stand the sound of my voice.''

''Oh, Ron.'' She sighed in affectionate exasperation. ''No hard feelings anymore, really.''

''I'm glad. And if it means anything to you, Laine, I'm beginning to wonder if I ever should've left town—and you—in the first place.''

She gasped in disbelief, flushing prettily in a way no makeup could match. ''Of course you should have! You'd never have been satisfied with settling down back then. You had to...discover things.''

She'd given their relationship a lot of thought, he realized. Presumably to work through his rejection. ''So, how is Tony?''

''Oh, fine, just fine,'' she assured him. ''He and a friend opened up a small service station in North Minneapolis, in our old neighborhood. Just a few pumps. They plan to focus mainly on repairs.''

''He always did dream of having his own shop,'' Ron recalled suddenly.

''Yes, and his dreams were put on hold for quite some time. It's a huge risk for us, but he deserves his chance. So, what are you doing in St. Paul anyway?'' she asked on a lighter note. ''So far from Los Angeles. Heck, it's even far from our old turf.''

"You remember my grandpa, don't you? He's settled here in St. Paul now."

"Emmett?" Her smile widened. "Why, I've often wondered if he's still on stage."

He tipped his head in the direction of the North Pole. "The most beloved role of all," he said cryptically, so as to not alert the children.

"Really? What a small world it is!"

"You really should go see him. He'd be delighted."

"All right. We'll stop. The kids will love it."

He touched the hand she'd curled around the cart handle. "It was so nice to see you again, Laine."

Elaine inhaled unsteadily. "Darn you for not behaving like everybody else! Showing up at the class reunions when a girl's at her best."

"You're the best anyplace, anytime. Take care now."

Ron turned to take a pinball game off the shelf and wended his way to the front of the store. Lenora was helping someone else as he stepped up to the service desk, so he patiently waited his turn.

"Knew you'd be back," she purred triumphantly, sliding her pen into the wedge of gray hair above her ear. "And if you want my opinion, I'd say the wading pool best suited the old boy."

"Good for soaking things," Ron agreed. "Feet, heads, egos."

Lenora laughed pleasantly. Ron wondered why Emmett hadn't noticed her qualities. She was bright, efficient and attractive. A tiger when riled. What more could Pop want?

"I'm afraid I'm going to have to disappoint you again," she clucked.

"How so, Lenora?"

"You wish to buy that item and get about two hundred and eighty dollars in currency, don't you?"

He might have, ten minutes ago. But life was slapping

sense into him at every turn. ''Not at all,'' he said, feigning hurt.

''Well, good, because here at Grace Brothers we just whack the purchase off the certificate. You'd still be running a tab.''

''I'm going to pay cash for this,'' he told her, enjoying her surprise.

''What's up your sleeve?''

''Patience, Lenora. First, I want you to look back at the North Pole for me.''

''Why?''

As if she didn't do it a hundred times a day on her own! ''Just because. Please?''

Lenora sized up the Pole over her reading glasses. ''All I see is a windbag in the red suit.''

''There's something more to see,'' he urged, slipping his hand into the lining pocket of his jacket for his wallet. ''A woman with three children. She's wearing a coral coat—''

''Oh, yes, at the end of the line. Somebody special?''

Hmm, nosy like Emmett, too.

''Oops, she's looking back at me.''

''Then look away,'' he whispered in distress. ''Play along, please.''

''I have a job to do here,'' she protested halfheartedly. ''If you'd get to the point.''

''Okay, okay.'' He produced the red-and-green envelope again. ''I would deeply appreciate it you'd award this to that lady.''

Her long fingers fluttered. ''How? For what?''

''Oh, I don't know, for having the brightest coat! Doesn't matter much. She's got five sons and isn't going to examine your motives too thoroughly.'' He made an exasperated sound. ''Don't you see? It would get spent and settle the matter.''

Her eyes searched his face, then she nodded. ''You're

trying to do something nice, I can see that. But we don't have policies for this kind of thing.''

''Thirty years at your post surely give you the freedom to rig policy,'' he argued. ''Especially at Christmas.''

''You're right,'' she relented, flattered. ''I can do it and I will.'' She snatched up the certificate. ''But you are leaving now, aren't you? It's only fair that I serve other customers some time today, too.''

''Consider me kin to the wind,'' he said airily.

She laughed then, a lyrical sound that turned employees' heads in wonder. ''Now blow before I change my mind.''

IT WAS ABOUT two-thirty that afternoon when Ron eased his burgundy rental car to a stop in front of the Trents' one-story brick house. Like most of the other homes on the street, hers was shaped like a shoe box. But it was adorned with extras that set it apart; white window boxes and shutters, a handrail on the concrete stoop, new-looking gutters edging the roof.

Jeanne dressed in her blue parka and jeans, was the most eye-catching adornment.

It had snowed heavily during the night and she was in the process of shoveling her sidewalk and stoop. She was nearly finished; only one step remained snow covered.

Though she didn't turn immediately, Ron knew she had heard the slamming of the car door and the click of his heels on the concrete path. She was holding her body alertly, like a sleek and beautiful cat. He envisioned her turning to discover the man she adored, dropping her shovel, running at full tilt, then bowling him over in the snow and smothering him with kisses.

He stumbled a little on a slippery patch, his pulse pounding as he imagined being that man. Oh, how he wanted to be here. How he yearned to be wanted by this woman. How he would manage to become part of her life he didn't know, but one obstacle had been hurdled. He'd found the guts to return.

Ron was so absorbed by these thoughts, he didn't notice exactly when she really turned to face him. She was now leaning on the handle of her shovel, regarding him with a wry expression.

"You're back."

"Yeah."

"I wasn't expecting you."

Naturally not. He was as surprised by this visit as she! He'd even fought the urge to return for a couple of hours after leaving Grace Brothers. Ultimately, in spite of the fact that he knew he wouldn't be welcome, he simply couldn't stay away.

It was seeing Elaine that had done it. It had been twelve years since he'd left Elaine for California and adventure, and in all that time he had never found another woman like her. Until now. After he'd left the store he'd come to the sudden, disturbing realization that Jeanne was more appealing to him than Elaine had ever been.

Jeanne, not having had the same revelation, was annoyed and suspicious. But awaiting his reply just the same. If he had to settle for curiosity at this juncture, he would.

"I said I'd sort things out for Toby," he ventured confidently.

Her slim brows rose speculatively. "Have you?"

"Uh, the plan is in progress." He held up the sack. "For now, I did come across something I think he might like—"

"Ten days before Christmas, Ron?" She gave a snort of derision. "What an amateur you are!"

He stalked up to the bottom of the stoop. "Hey, I know how the process works. I was a kid once myself."

Her mouth crooked in a smile. "Grown up since the tree-bouncing baseball game yesterday, have you?"

"That was an accident," he said defensively. "Actually, this toy is a gift to you in a way, something to slow Toby down.'' He dropped his car keys in his jacket pocket and fumbled with the bag. The slippery plastic was like liquid butter in his huge, chilled hands. ''Whoa!'' He nearly dropped the works into the snow.

Her spontaneous laughter filled the air as she rested her shovel against the house. ''Come inside, Mr. California, before you land on your butt.''

''The older I get, the quicker I freeze up in the arctic air,'' he said, trailing after her into the warm holly-trimmed foyer.

''Your ears are certainly red,'' she noted. ''You need a cap.''

He would rather she concentrated on his butt, but would have to take things in the order they came. Did she have any idea how appealing she was with that furry hood circling her heart-shaped face, her full lips parted with humor? She peeled off her outer clothes and invited him to do the same. He handed her the package, eased off his jacket, and hung it on a peg inside the closet door.

She peered inside the bag. ''Toby's napping right now.''

''Perfect time to take a look at that and see what you think,'' he suggested.

She looked at him gratefully as she held the box lengthwise in her hands. ''This was a good idea. Might appease him until he can take his game outside.''

''Good. Then you'll keep it.''

''Yes, thanks.'' She drew a hesitant breath. ''Would you like a cup of coffee?''

''Very much.''

She set a plate of Christmas cookies out on the table as well and he wolfed them down. His stomach had been so tight over this visit that he hadn't stopped for lunch. Now that he was with her again he was ravenous.

Ron swallowed self-consciously, aware that she was studying him intently. ''You're staring,'' he said mildly. ''With eyes glazed over in shock.''

Jeanne's wind-flushed face grew a trifle rosier as she busily raised her steamy mug to her lips. She was staring because she was half-certain he was an apparition. Not since David had a dynamic man sat with her at this table. He was trying to play it cool, but she could see the vulnerability and interest in his expression.

"Sorry," she said laughing. "I really wasn't expecting you back."

She had the sudden, irresistible urge to make sure he was flesh and not some little diversion she'd created for herself. With as much grace as possible she reached out and grazed her forefinger along the cleft in his chin. "There! That takes care of the sugar." And her doubts. He was the real thing, all right. Her fingertip was on fire. And the heat was slowly spreading, giving her a sexy and desired feeling.

"I didn't handle myself very well yesterday, roughhousing with Toby," he admitted, shifting on the smooth chair as lightning coursed through his veins. He hadn't expected her to touch him without warning. That was one of his old tricks! He cleared his throat, struggling with his composure. "Guess I got carried away."

"Well, it suggested that you do like Christmas a little more than you were letting on," she said pleasantly. "Or did, once upon a time."

"Yeah, guess those feelings have faded some over the years." He looked around the cheery, cluttered kitchen with a smile. "Your house reminds me of my folks' place in North Minneapolis. And, well, Toby reminds me of myself at that age."

Her blue eyes twinkled. "Bet I would've liked you a lot back then."

But what about now? The question bounced around the confines of his hollow heart.

"I have to take part of the blame for our quarrels," she went on. "I've gone over things in my mind and see how you could've gotten the impression that I might settle for a payoff. I did talk of budgets, affording things. It's true as far as it goes...." She trailed off uncomfortably.

He raised a hand. "All that should matter is that I want to make up for Emmett's stunt."

"But your grandfather is the only person who can right this situation."

"I refuse to accept that," Ron argued. "Toby liked me, too."

She tucked her blond tresses behind her ears and nodded in slow affirmation. "I have to admit he hasn't stopped talking about you since yesterday."

"Surely together we can—" He stopped short. For just a second, before she lowered her lashes, he saw longing in her eyes. Was she envisioning the two of them together, on an intimate level, as he had outside? "Together we can bamboozle one little boy into believing Santa's come through," he finished brightly. "Can't we?"

"I really don't see how," she said, nibbling on a bell-shaped cookie. "It's complicated."

"Please tell me about it," he urged quietly. "I want to understand."

She shrugged her thin shoulders, and continued to hide her eyes beneath her lush lashes. "This is our first Christmas without my late husband David. Despite his young age, Toby does remember last year, the fun we all had."

Ron absorbed this new insight. No wonder he was such a little pistol! "He's having fun with the holiday, Jeanne. It's obvious."

"I know he is, so far. But if something goes wrong, this first Christmas after David's passing, he may forever feel sad at this time of year. It's certainly the last thing David would've wanted."

Her compassion and her distress overwhelmed him. "Children his age aren't that tough to satisfy, are they? He may not even remember every single thing he asked for."

''Ron, if Toby made some sort of request concerning his father, he's going to remember.''

''Oh, my Lord,'' he moaned. He rubbed his face in his hands.

''The last thing I'm looking for is sympathy,'' she hastily assured him. ''I've had a truckload. I'm in the process of rebuilding, looking ahead.''

The news excited him. She wasn't going to crumble and she was available. He struggled to keep his voice even and his manner patient as he waded further into personal territory. ''What happened to your husband? Do you mind talking about it?''

She smiled sadly. ''David died last January in a single-car crash. He was on his way home from work one evening and had stopped on Rice Street for Chinese takeout. The weather was bad. It was snowing, the roads were icy. Anyway, he took one of the curves on Wheelock Parkway a little too sharply and lost control. Hit a tree. Died instantly, they said.''

Her voice had become a monotone and the way she related incident sounded a bit like a recitation. He realized it was a shield against her emotions, a way to relate the tragedy from a safe distance. He'd seen it hundreds of times in his work.

''Bet this year's been rough.''

''Yes,'' she agreed breathlessly. ''But I couldn't fall apart, you see. For one thing, Potters—my family—just don't do that. We're too eccentric, too strong. And I constantly reminded myself that Toby deserved a mother running on all cylinders.'' She laced her fingers around her mug and smiled. ''Anyhow, the situation today is that we're at the tail end of enduring a year's worth of milestones without David. The Christmas holidays are the last. I feel if I can just fulfill Toby's most important wishes and convince my suffocating family that I'm fine… Well, that's what I want for Christmas this year!''

''It sure would help to know what he wants most,'' Ron sympathized. ''Funny, most kids can't stop talking about it, can they?''

''Toby is a bit of a tease,'' she replied. ''He likes to put me in tight corners.''

Ron stroked his jaw, hoping to conceal his twitching mouth. He and Toby had things in common, no question. ''If we could just wheedle that list out of him, find out what we're dealing with.''

Jeanne was overwhelmed with a fresh wave of warmth. *We.* He kept adding himself to the picture. And did it so naturally, with a deep, soothing baritone that no doubt had women opening up in all sorts of ways. ''These are the times when I miss David most,'' she blurted out. ''When I need a partner to outwit that child!''

''So how long were you married?'' he asked gently.

She gazed at him mutely, her temperature on the rise again. When was this confirmed bachelor going to flip back to his self-centered self again? She was more comfortable with that side of him. He was easier to battle, easier to dismiss. Maybe if she refused to answer any more personal questions, he would storm out. ''Seven years,'' she heard herself say in a wispy way no aggressive Potter would even recognize!

''High-school romance?''

''Yes. Puppy love that grew into something deep and adult.'' She studied her nails with a brief smile. ''We seemed to belong together right from the start.''

''A lot of Christmases clocked in, I imagine.''

''Wonderful ones.'' She propped her chin in her hand and studied him curiously. ''So tell me more about you.''

''Like what?''

''Like your Christmases, for instance.''

''Well, once upon a time they were full of tradition like yours,'' he replied. ''My youth was great in general, really.

I'm an only child who was probably spoiled a little. My parents are normal, the kind other kids like to talk to."

"So how did you ever escape Minneapolis in the first place?"

His chocolate-colored eyes twinkled teasingly. "Well, the folks made the mistake of encouraging me to think too big—or so they say now that I haven't married and reproduced. Seriously though, I grew restless during high school and longed for more. I headed for Los Angeles and beyond."

"Did you find more? Out there?"

"Oh, yes." He stared out the window facing the backyard, and spied a gigantic snowman. "Always a new rainbow to chase. Wrote all about it."

"Did you eventually find your pot of gold?"

He continued to stare at the snowman. "I guess the treasure is relative. Guess we know for sure when we stop digging for it."

"Or running from it." The words popped out of her mouth before she could stop them. "I meant that in a general way, really."

He slowly swiveled to face her. She was backpedaling to save his feelings. But it was no less than he deserved. The way he'd swooped in to play Emmett's diplomatic deputy with egotistical gusto, he must seem like a shallow, careless playboy. "I never stop discovering," he went on evenly. "People read my work and like it!"

She gave him an approving smile. "I'm sure they do. And you shouldn't be offended because I'd never heard of you."

No, he shouldn't. But how easy this would be if she respected him in advance, as so many other women had. If she'd read his previous work and gave him due credit for it.

But nothing was going to be easy with Jeanne Trent. He'd be forced to prove himself from scratch. At a time when he had nothing fresh left to say to his readers or anyone else.

"If it makes you feel any better," she said encouragingly, "my sister Angie has heard of you."

"Wouldn't mind meeting this sister," he said half-teasingly, hoping he didn't sound too eager. "And I know Emmett would like to meet you in spite of everything. He likes the sound of your voice already. Hey, maybe we should get the families together. Sound like fun?"

"Do you think Emmett might remember Toby if he saw him again?" she asked hopefully. "Remember any of his list?"

"No, I asked him and he said there are just too many faces every day."

"Oh."

"But we still could join forces for some holiday cheer. For drinks, or something."

"No," she said dully. "Without a real reason, I don't think it's worth exposing you to the brood at this time."

He stiffened defensively in the maple chair. "Would they disapprove of me?"

"On the contrary! They'd cuff us together, station us under the mistletoe until you cried for mercy."

The very idea brought a grin to his face. "I'm free for dinner."

She chuckled. "When?"

"The rest of my life."

His voice was liquid honey, and the message made her heart to skip a beat. "I'm battling the Potters' protective shield right now," she tried to explain. "Trying so hard to be independent. Despite the fact that Mom brought Toby into Gracie's, they know nothing of what's happened since. For the time being, I'd like to keep it that way. It'll cut down on their interference, and protect Emmett from being unmasked as the rogue Santa."

Ron released a sad sigh. ''Okay, if that's the way you want it.''

He was so interested. And she was flattered. But just the fact that she was flattered sent hazard signals flashing before her eyes. Real relationships weren't built on a foundation of flirtation and flattery. She was determined to search for something real and lasting again, like she'd had with David. This man traveled all the time, no doubt leaving many interested women by the wayside. She could only wonder how many times a year he affected the right kind of come-on to serve the moment.

Right now he seemed in need of a traditional Christmas, and she just happened to be serving up one.

He was probably the worst kind of choice for a begin-again romance. He'd make his mark and be gone.

If only his brown eyes weren't as tempting as rich, creamy chocolate syrup. If only his mouth hadn't been so hard and kissable under her fingertip.

A smart woman would send him on his way right here and now. If she stalled much longer, Toby would awaken and insist he stay.

She barely recognized her own voice as she offered him another cup of coffee.

5

"HEY, IT'S YOU again. Hi, Ronny!"

Toby burst into the kitchen a short time later, just as exuberant as Jeanne had predicted he'd be. She averted her gaze, hoping Ron wouldn't realize how relieved she was. Toby's presence would keep him here and buy her time to figure out what on earth to do with him.

"Hi, buddy." Ron cheerfully greeted the boy, who was dancing excitedly around the room.

Toby stopped in front of Ron. "Why'd you come back?"

"Well, for one thing, I brought you a present."

The pinball game was an instant hit. Toby plopped down on the floor, and set the game on his legs. "Pitcha! Pitcha!" he shouted, launching a marble-sized baseball into the hollow box. "Can I have a snack, Mommy? Before Fu-Fu comes?"

Ron watched Jeanne move to the cupboard for a plastic glass, then to the refrigerator for a jug of apple juice. "You attached after all?"

"Very funny," she snapped saucily, filling the glass. "Fu-Fu's a pet."

He chuckled. "Could've been a pet name for a frisky friend."

"I'm sure you realize I'm not the kind to give out gooey names like that to even the friskiest!"

Toby climbed onto a chair, and reached for his juice and a handful of cookies. "He is a dog, Ronny," he explained with authority. "A poodle dog."

''Does he come on his own?'' Ron asked.

''Fu-Fu brings Eddie,'' the child replied, stuffing a star-shaped spritz cookie in his small mouth.

''General Edward Chambers is the man with the appointment,'' Jeanne inserted. ''He's an old army man who has his portrait taken biannually with his pooch.''

''Sounds like you'll have your hands full,'' Ron remarked, eyeing the door leading to the hallway.

''But I'm sure Toby would love for you to stay on,'' Jeanne hastily added. ''For a late supper.''

He grimaced. She was using the boy as an excuse! She was no better at staking a claim than he was!

''Don't you get it?'' the child interrupted, never looking up. ''She wants you to sit with me. So I don't run willy nilly.''

Ron pretended to be shocked. ''Willy-nilly, eh?''

Toby flopped his blond head once. ''Yup.''

''Not sure we can be trusted together, Toby,'' Ron said, struggling to remain earnest. ''I mean, we got into trouble yesterday.''

Toby grinned toothily. ''Yeah, it was all your fault. I told Mommy on you.''

Ron chuckled then. ''Guess I've caused more than my share of mischief round here. Your mommy probably thinks I need a sitter.''

Jeanne was disgusted with herself. Why had she used Toby to bait Ron into hanging around? But Ron wasn't just any man. He'd shaken her up in a crazy, tantalizing way. ''Toby usually watches the studio's portable TV,'' she said with a dismissive wave, giving him a way out. ''It's no big deal, Ron, really. We manage.''

''It's a big deal to me,'' the boy objected. ''I want to play with Ronny.''

''Be glad to stay,'' he quickly told her.

''Good,'' Jeanne said with undisguised delight. ''We'll have some of my homemade chili afterwards. All I have to do is heat it up.'' She accidentally grazed him as she passed by. The jostling contact made them both pause for a heart-racing moment. ''I, uh, have to get things ready,'' she murmured. ''We won't impose too much, I promise.''

Famous last words. Ron hadn't been run so ragged since his last African safari. Not only did he and Toby end up in the studio helping Jeanne properly light the finicky clients, but the general insisted Ron hide beneath the table Fu-Fu was perched upon, and place his larger, stronger hand atop the dog, as though it was Edward's own!

The session dragged on with some background and clothing changes. Ron eventually offered to heat up the chili for a hungry Toby, and begrudgingly served it to order, minus the beans, with exactly three saltines ground into it. Then it was a trip to Toby's bedroom for a pajama roundup, a trip to the bathroom and finally, a bedtime story. Ron was delighted to discover he enjoyed himself every bit as much as the boy.

As Ron tucked Toby in, he couldn't resist quizzing him about his Christmas list.

Toby gasped, scandalized. ''It's a secret, 'tween me and Santa.''

''But I'm good at keeping secrets.''

His lip protruded. ''No, Ronny.''

''Please.''

''Go see Santa at Gracie's with your own grandma.''

Ron smiled tightly. Outfoxed by a four-year-old. But rather than risk pushing the child too far, he gave up, and circled the twin mattress to tuck all the edges in snugly.

''Get 'em tight, Ronny. I can fall out.''

''Know what you mean,'' Ron said dryly.

The boy's hazel eyes grew wide. ''You fall out too?''

Ron paused, with a far-off grin. Technically, he'd been kicked out on occasion by a tempestuous woman.

''Well, do ya?''

Ron cleared his throat. ''Tell you all about it when you're older.''

''Tomorrow?''

''We'll see.'' He moved to the desk where a clown-shaped lamp glowed. ''You keep this on all night?'' Before Ron could stop him the child had wiggled out of his cocoon, and was flying across the hardwood floor. With small nimble fingers he flicked off the clown's head, and clicked on the lamp's night-light base. As Toby turned, preparing to scamper away, Ron caught him by the shoulder. ''Hey, buddy, what's this?''

Toby stared at the envelope Ron had removed from the desk. ''My letter to Santa,'' he said soberly. ''Private first-class mail.''

''So it is.'' Ron tried to disguise his delight. What a break! Surely all the things Toby had told Santa at the store were written down here.

Toby leaned against him, yawning hugely. ''I drew that stamp for the postman.''

Ron's brown eyes shimmered in the dim light. SANTA, NORTH POLE, was written across the front in bold, crooked crayon letters. ''So it's ready to mail?''

''Yup.''

''Want me to mail it for you?''

Toby bobbed his head eagerly. ''Wouldya, please?''

Ron ruffled his hair. ''You got a deal! Now, back under the covers.''

''Tuck me more.''

''With pleasure,'' he said grandly.

Jeanne was just sitting down with a bowl of chili when Ron wandered into the kitchen minutes later. He had a crafty gleam in his eye that reminded her of Toby when he was up to something.

''Toby settled?''

''I think so.'' He chuckled. ''Are you ever sure?''

''No.''

Ron noticed her glass of milk on the counter and brought it to table, then slid into the seat beside her. "Fu-Fu and his master all taken care of?"

Jeanne took a long sip from the glass, giving herself a milk moustache. "Finally! Edward sends his thanks for the use of your hand."

"Hard to imagine that anybody will believe a hand that's younger and nearly twice the right size is really his."

"Perhaps not, but I used a soft-focus lens to buffer the clarity."

"You are a sneak."

Jeanne stirred the steamy chili set before her. "You're a bit of a sneak yourself, Ron. What were you and Toby up to?"

"A little of everything. I have a new and great admiration for parents. I haven't hustled this fast since profiling the rodeo circuit for *Time*."

"Yeah, right. You look like a sleek panther who's just bagged a big one."

He reached out then, and slipped his hand beneath her curtain of hair to make contact with the silken skin at the base of her neck. "And you're a kitten," he crooned. "Caught in the cream." She heard a deep delicious sound in his throat as he leaned across the table and pulled her closer, until he could capture her mouth in his own.

Hot, wet fire. Jeanne's body went limp with longing as his lips grazed hers. His tongue flicked at the ridge of milk beneath her nose. She'd almost forgotten how good a passionate kiss could taste. Almost. A burst of desire buried deep in her belly was rising to the surface and spreading through her with a molten heat.

It had happened with David this way, on their first date in his battered old Mustang. An instant powerful chemical connection. But Ron wasn't like David. He wasn't her type at all! So how could she be letting go this way?

When they finally broke apart and settled back in their chairs, both were a little shaky.

"I should be going," Ron said raggedly, raking a hand through his shag of brown hair.

She gazed at the stove clock to find it was nearly eleven. It had seemed like time had stopped during their kiss, but naturally it was an illusion. A long, fifteen-minute illusion. They'd made out! In fifteen minutes! He'd scraped his chair over beside hers and she'd climbed into his lap!

Ron followed her eyes to the clock and read her thoughts. She was surprised by the passage of time, whereas he'd been achingly aware of each and every second. He'd debated whether he dare palm the underside of her breast over her sweater, or slide his hand beneath it to stroke her back. He'd ultimately done neither, and had broken away when he could no longer control himself.

It had been the right choice, he was sure. This was probably her first intimate encounter since David had died. All in all, he was hopeful and satisfied. He was also fearful and confused. To his delight and dismay, he was falling hard for someone for the first time in ages. A woman he barely knew, had barely touched.

Maybe Christmas miracles could happen to anybody.

They stood up together. Jeanne smoothed her tide of golden hair. "So, you ready to fess up?"

"About what?"

He looked so panic-stricken, she had to laugh. "What you and Toby were up to."

"Tell you tomorrow," he promised.

"You can't mean it!"

"I do believe I have this whole Santa problem licked," he crowed. "If that makes it any easier for you to sleep tonight." Pivoting on his heel, he headed for the front door. She trailed him down the hallway, then moved ahead to block his way.

"I want to know. Right now."

"It's something you should've thought of," he teased, tapping her nose as he reached into the closet for his jacket.

"C'mon, Ron," she coaxed with a hint of irritation. Maybe she was overprotective of Toby, an issue all the Potters agreed upon, but she couldn't abide being left out.

He stepped outside. "Hey, you didn't turn on your Christmas lights."

"It's too late now."

"Oh, please, do it for me."

The words were so natural on his tongue, as though he'd used them over and over again. In bed, out of bed, maybe even under the bed. After a year of just making the bed, she felt a rush of fear and inadequacy. She did her best to conceal it all behind a frown. "Don't know if you deserve the lights when you're being such a difficult fiend."

He descended the stairs, moved halfway down the sidewalk, then waited there with hands clasped. Sighing in resignation, she moved her hand over the switchplate beside the door. The exterior of the house sprang to colorful life. He gave her an enthusiastic thumbs-up, then continued on out to the street.

"Hey, I'm not through with you yet, mister!"

Lord, he hoped not. "You're an incorrigible flirt, Jeanne Trent. 'Night." With a wave, he eased behind the wheel of his rental car.

Jeanne watched his taillights wink into the dark distance, then flicked her lights off in a huff. Outsmarting Toby couldn't have been that easy for him. It simply couldn't have been. He was the incorrigible one, a know-it-all bachelor who needed a good swift kick in the pants. Why, the idea that Toby had told Ron a secret he wouldn't share with her was intolerable, if not impossible! With her chin held high, she marched off toward her son's room for some answers.

"WAITING UP for me, Pop?" Ron entered the apartment thirty minutes later to find Emmett pouring himself a brandy at the portable bar beside his large floor-to-ceiling bookcase.

"No, just took a taxi home from Victoria's." He immediately reached for a second glass, and filled it as well. "We went there after the choir concert, and I didn't want her to brave the roads again."

"Good thinking." Ron eased out of his jacket, accepted the snifter Emmett offered him, then settled into an easy chair.

"Nice seeing Elaine again?"

"Sure was." Ron took a long sip of the strong amber liquor. "Five kids by Tony Rosetti. Wow."

"Could've been you, married and content."

"Tony's not my type."

"Don't be flippant at this hour."

"Okay," Ron relented, laughing. "The same thought passed through my mind. What would've happened if I'd settled here and married Elaine? But I've concluded that I wouldn't have been satisfied, Pop. She said even Tony had been waiting for the chance to fulfill his first dream, and I would've been too. Easier for him to open a garage than it would've been for me to hop a plane for stories."

Emmett's chest heaved beneath his black-velvet dinner jacket. "Ah, then she's but a Ghost of Christmas Past."

Ron affected a shudder. "First you say you're Christmas Future, and now Elaine's Christmas Past. What's my present fate, I wonder."

Emmett's regal face beamed. "If you've begun to wonder, my point is made."

"You should be more concerned with your own affairs," Ron retorted, lifting his lean hip to extract his wallet from a back pocket. He opened the worn leather billfold and extracted an envelope. "I'm still working the damage-control shift for you."

"Thought this was settled, son. No retraction. You had no reason to pursue this matter on my behalf."

Ron was in no hurry to admit he simply couldn't stay away from Jeanne Trent, that he'd opted for some bickering and begging after all. Emmett would crow so loud, he'd wake the entire high-rise. "Well, call it inherent pride, but I couldn't believe there wasn't some simple answer to the Trent family's problem."

"And you claim to have discovered it?" the old man asked loftily.

Ron's mouth crooked triumphantly. "Got hold of Toby Trent's letter to Santa. And presumably the list he whispered in your ear."

"What do you intend to do with it?"

"Steam it open for a look, see if I can't make it right."

"Is it all really worth it, when I can assure you things will work out?"

Ron resisted the urge to suggest that perhaps Emmett should be telling fortunes instead of playing Santa. He turned the envelope over in his hands. "You'd think that Jeanne would've done this herself. But I figure maybe she didn't know about it. In any case, the kid insisted I mail it."

"Sounds like a lucky break."

"Skill and luck." Ron drained his glass with a satisfied sigh. "I feel I'm really getting the hang of this family stuff."

"Really?" Emmett's query was accompanied by an unbecoming snort, but Ron didn't seem to notice.

"Oh, it goes way beyond finding the letter. I took to Toby's routine in a snap—play, dinner, bed." He waved the envelope. "Pull this off, and I'll really be in with Jeanne."

"I'll put the kettle on for a little steam," Emmett announced, heading for the kitchen.

"Why, when you obviously think it's a waste of time?"

The old man paused at the doorway, lifting his snifter in toast. "I don't know how you're going to get skunked, but I can't wait to find out."

JEANNE WAS half expecting the telephone to ring that night. And it did. About one o'clock.

"Why didn't you tell me!"

She sat up a little straighter in bed, and set aside her book. "Now, Ron, you know you didn't give me the chance."

"So you figured it out."

"Yes, a look around Toby's room and I realized."

"I must've come off as an arrogant jackass."

Jeanne tipped her head back against her bank of pillows with a smile. "In a fun, naive way."

"So Toby can't write yet, eh?"

"No, I helped him address the envelope, that's all. He didn't want to show me the inside, and I knew it wouldn't help the cause anyway."

"In case you're wondering, it's bunch of blue squiggles—six in all—with a row of red candy canes at the bottom, along with a big T for Toby."

"You translate those squiggles and the CIA will recruit you for sure."

"Maybe the candy canes mean something," he suggested in desperation.

"Oh, they do—they're kisses. The Potters give candy-cane kisses out at this time of year, and Toby picked it up."

Ron made a soft groaning sound that curled her toes beneath the covers. "You're making those Potters sound mighty inviting. Especially the blond, elfin one with a mean sense of humor."

Her soft laughter rang a little off-key.

"You aren't angry that I took the letter, are you?"

''No. But be sure to mail it, won't you, just as Toby intended?''

''Really, without a stamp?''

''Post offices around the country handle hundreds of them, believe me. And it's only fair to follow through.''

''If that's what you want, sure.''

''Thanks so much for trying so hard with him, Ron,'' she said sincerely. ''It was very, very nice of you.''

''But I haven't succeeded yet.''

''I'll think of something.'' Her tone was formal and distant.

''But I'm committed to helping, Jeanne.''

''Surely you've come to realize that I won't be turning Emmett in to Grace Brothers—''

''Well, I did figure—''

''That was more my temper talking than anything. And I'm over it. If there haven't been any other complaints to the manager, I don't want to be the villain who pulls the plug on him.''

''Amazingly, as I told you, there hasn't been another one. Aside from the lady at the customer-service counter,'' he joked. ''But I think Lenora's problems with Emmett stem from his off-duty habits.''

''Well, anyway, as far as I'm concerned, you and Santa are off the hook. If I could survive this past year with my sanity intact, I can certainly round it off with an answer to this last crisis. Good—''

''Hey, wait! You can't be dumping me! Can you?''

She gasped. This didn't sound like the cocky guy who'd strutted down her walk two hours ago, the guy she'd prepared herself to brush off. This anxious suitor was a lot tougher to deal with. She released a nervous breath. ''Oh, Ron. I just don't want to impose.''

She was the worst liar he'd ever met! ''I thought we were really on to something, Jeanne.''

"Is that possible? I mean, we're so different, you and I."

"I'm a man, you're a woman. It's the age-old difference. The most intriguing difference." The sharp intake of breath on the line gave him the same satisfaction. "I should make you kiss me hard and long every time I find out an item on Toby's Christmas list. Presumably we're dealing with six items—"

"As if you can!"

"Kiss you hard and long? You know I can."

How like him to say something like that, to force those intimate memories to the forefront of her mind. As if she needed inducement. She could think of nothing else.

"One thing on the list is something called a Mighty Mite Gas Pump," he announced with pride.

"Are you improvising?" she wondered suspiciously.

"That's a fancy word for lying. But no, Toby let it slip that he'd be getting one soon to gas up his bike and sled." A silence fell over the line. "So it seems like somebody owes somebody a smooch already."

"You were paid in advance."

"And next time?"

"Don't you get the hint?"

Her tone was husky with desperation, but he wasn't going to let her off the hook because of it. He was even more desperate. "Don't try to tell me you're not ready, Jeanne. That kind of bluff would be beneath you."

"No, you're right," she said after a long pause. "I do want to get back in the game. It's you, Ron. The fact that we don't seem particularly compatible. I'm sorry."

"But we hardly know each other!"

"True—"

"So what are you afraid of?"

"Falling for the wrong man, I suppose," she replied honestly.

"How can you know that!"

‘‘I have to think of Toby, too. How disappointed he’d be if it flopped.’’

‘‘Toby, Toby,’’ he scoffed in disgust. ‘‘First you use him to keep me close, now you’re using him to dump me!’’

‘‘And you didn’t use him yourself, trying to get to me by solving his problems?’’

‘‘Maybe, but I like him very much. Very much.’’

‘‘Don’t you think you could hurt him, Ron, if you hung around for the holidays, then became bored and disappeared?’’

‘‘I wasn’t thinking that far ahead.’’ There was surprise in his tone.

‘‘I think way ahead, Ron. I feel I must!’’

‘‘Really, Jeanne? Did that policy work for you the first time around?’’ The angry words poured out and he didn’t stop to monitor them. ‘‘Do you think your late husband wouldn’t give anything to go back and be crazy and impetuous and daring with you? That he wouldn’t want you to do the same now if you had a second chance at a relationship?’’

‘‘If you were here I’d slap your face so hard your inflated ego would burst like a balloon,’’ she seethed.

‘‘You just don’t get it, Jeanne,’’ he attempted to explain. ‘‘I haven’t taken enough risks myself—’’

‘‘A man who’s been in most of the world’s danger spots?’’

‘‘I mean on an intimate level,’’ he confessed. ‘‘I’ve waited way too long to jump into a real kind of relationship. If we could just take the leap together.’’

‘‘How many times have you used that line?’’ she snapped.

‘‘Huh?’’ How could she possibly mistake him for a silver-tongued Romeo, when all he could manage was that single-syllable retort?

‘‘Can’t you see I’m struggling? Can’t you see I’m having problems coping?’’ Her voice broke a little. ‘‘Even a hustler like you should have the goodwill to back off and pursue other prey. When asked to do so politely.''

Politely? He overlooked that inaccuracy. ''But we were fine tonight,'' he said instead. ''What happened?''

''I didn't mean for this kind of fight to erupt, really,'' she admitted in a milder tone. ''I've done some thinking since you left and it's clear to me we're all wrong for each other.''

''For somebody who'd never heard of me, you sure have drawn some hasty conclusions.''

''This wouldn't have gotten so ugly if you'd have just accepted my decision. Goodbye.''

The dial tone buzzed in his ear with the ferocity of an angry bee. Ron returned the slimline phone to his nightstand with a frustrated growl. On one hand she'd accused him of being too crass, and on the other she'd been begging him for the understanding of a sensitive male. How could he be both?

He'd never met anyone quite like her. An overprotected mother with the passions of Venus. An overly organized spitfire with the kiss of an angel.

She certainly had a nerve being all those things at once. He punched his pillow and twisted and turned beneath the covers. It would serve her right if he didn't give up, if he forced her to reject him for a saner reason, like disliking his taste in clothes or his snoring. Yes, it would make him feel a whole lot better if she dumped him because he snored too damn loud. All night long. After wild, passionate lovemaking.

Yessiree, being rejected for a good tangible reason like that would make him feel a whole lot better.

6

"SHOULD RUN LIKE a top with these new spark plugs, Jeanne."

Martin Potter's jovial voice echoed through his old high-ceilinged garage, as he closed the hood of his daughter's green Buick the following Sunday. A giant, robust man in his midfifties, with a ruddy complexion and a thick head of straw-colored hair, he was an ideal patriarch in the eyes of his family. Especially to the middle child, Jeanne, presently shivering near the space heater on the workbench. As she stepped forward to hand him a rag to wipe his blackened hands, her pretty face was aglow with hero worship.

"Thanks, Daddy." She had to stand on tiptoe beside the towering, large-boned man to kiss his smudged cheek. "You're my knight in greasy coveralls."

"And you're my princess in denim and flannel," he returned gruffly. "What are you doing skipping around without a coat?"

"Just dashed out to tell you Mom's waiting dinner. Just the kind of Sunday meal you like best. Roast beef and all the trimmings."

Martin lifted a bushy brow. "So the Christmas cards are taken care of?"

"Yes, Toby took your place licking the stamps."

Martin inhaled deeply, unzipped his moss-colored jumpsuit, and peeled it off like a banana skin. "Suddenly I'm starving!"

He shut off the heater and the lights, then angled an arm

around Jeanne's shoulders and guided her outside into the snowy twilight and down the narrow backyard path that led to the family's rambling old gray two-story. Jeanne couldn't help noting that, just as Angie had said, the house was plastered with small colored bulbs. Ten times the number on her own place, by conservative estimate. This was supposed to help her and Toby feel more festive?

"The house looks like a movie marquee," she remarked.

Her father pressed a kiss on her flaxen head. "Do you know they make self-adhesive stamps now, baby? You peel 'em off, then stick 'em on. Easy."

"Mom's old-fashioned about her stamps. Said they didn't have self-adhesive angel ones. About these lights—"

"Ah, the hardware store was having a sale, darn near giving them away." He avoided her gaze as he clomped along the slippery walk.

"Sure, Dad."

"Always been a sucker for a sale."

A sucker for his kids was more like it, she silently corrected. Her parents, social workers for the county, had never had extra income to lavish on their children. But she and Angie and Andrew had been loved equally throughout the years and it was the most important kind of wealth Jeanne could imagine. Since her husband's death, however, they'd begun to focus on her and she'd grown to absolutely hate the smothering. How she longed for the old Potter system of democracy.

The old house boasted a small service porch on the back, perfect for storing seasonal clothing and equipment. Martin stopped in the long, narrow room to tug off his boots, leaning against their boxy old freezer for leverage. He expressed surprise to discover Jeanne had lingered alongside him. "Go along into the kitchen, honey," he said. "It isn't more than fifty-five degrees in here."

"Wanted to speak to you, first, Dad. About my life right now."

The crack in her voice set his teeth on edge. He straightened up in his stocking feet, and met her gaze squarely. "If you want to move back in here with Toby, we'd be happy to oblige."

"Oh, Daddy." Her tone insinuated he'd offered her a trip to the moon on the tail of a kite.

"Do anything for you," he blurted out with Potter directness. "Just name it."

"You're doing too much," she said softly. "I appreciate the extra efforts this year. All year long you and Mom have hovered close, paving the way for me. But now, this finale of a million lights and spritz cookies." She rubbed her chilled hands together, undaunted by the fact that he hardly seemed to be listening. "It wasn't necessary. It really, really wasn't."

The big man straightened up, a force to be reckoned with in his rumpled twills and stocking feet. "Can't argue the point."

"You can't?" It wasn't like her father to give in without an argument.

"Nope. Potters aren't known for their subtlety, but we're sharp on the facts, right?"

"Right." She beamed in relief.

"It was a silly waste," he scoffed. "We know that now."

"Now?" she repeated confusedly. "How now?"

He opened the door leading to the kitchen, motioning her ahead. "Now that you got yourself a boyfriend, of course. C'mon, step lively. You'll turn into an icicle standing there with your mouth hanging open."

"I DIDN'T TELL anybody anything and I resent your accusation!" Angie stood erect, hugging their mother's precious china plates at her chest as she glared at her little sister across the dining room table a short time later.

Jeanne shifted from one foot to the other. She'd waited

for the chance to speak to Angie alone, then she'd barrelled in here in a fit of white-hot anger to accuse her of nothing less than a felony between sisters—the breaking of a confidence—and was being quickly and efficiently defused. Angie was quite the opposite of the humble blabbermouth caught in the act. "You, ah, didn't?" she spluttered, reaching down to pick up the stack of paper napkins on the crocheted tablecloth.

Angie began to round the rectangular table, slapping down the dishes as if they, too, were paper. "No. Quite frankly, I didn't think anything would come of it."

"Thanks a lot!"

Angie paused impatiently. "Let's face it, sis, at twenty-six, with a son to raise, you'd have to do more than flutter a lash at a celebrity bachelor like Ron Coleman!"

Jeanne's face flamed. "As it happens, he appeared interested enough."

"Oh?"

"Yes," she affirmed with a measure of pride. "And as it happens, I think I'm still a fairly good catch."

Angie chuckled. "Good to hear that you know it. Decide you want to be caught and you'll be on your way."

That was the heart of the matter all right, the process of making the right decision. She intended to approach the dating game with the same kind of care and sense she'd been using to expand her business.

A man like David seemed in order, someone rooted in his hometown, a nut about traditions, an orderly businessman who paid bills well in advance and planned vacations with a set and secure itinerary.

All the things Ron Coleman wasn't.

Ah, but when he'd kissed her, she'd forgotten all about her mental list of qualifications. Forgotten everything, except how she felt. He had the power to coax a woman into blissful submission. But she wasn't foolish enough to believe it was accidental; Ron was a man of experience—another trait foreign to her.

"Hello?" Angie tapped on her head. "Anybody home?"

Jeanne laughed. "I don't blame you for wondering lately. Sorry I accused you. Toby has to be the stool pigeon."

"Naturally. The folks have been pumping him like a well all year long about your activities and emotional state."

"He comes cheap too, doesn't he? A few gumdrops, a can of soda pop, a nose nuzzle from Grandma Cat."

"Since you can trust me—as always," Angie said in a huffy whisper, "give me the scoop!"

Jeanne turned to make sure the swinging door leading to the kitchen was still, then made her way around the table, slipping napkins underneath the silverware. "I haven't seen him since Wednesday."

"That's only four days," her sister pointed out encouragingly.

"It's over, Ange," she whispered adamantly. "Whatever there was, is over."

Suddenly the old oak door behind them creaked. Jeanne tensed as her parents, Angie's husband Brad and Toby filed in, chorusing that it was dinnertime. Martin led with a platter of beef, Catherine followed with vegetables, Brad and Toby trailed after with milk and rolls respectively.

Catherine set her platter on the table and turned to tweak her daughter's cheeks. "There's my crafty girl! Finding a boyfriend all on her own."

Jeanne stared at the slender, misty-eyed woman, still so attractive at twice Jeanne's age. She hadn't seen such raw emotion on Catherine's face since the night of David's accident. "But, Mom, I— He isn't a boyfriend. Not a boyfriend."

Catherine made a clucking sound with her tongue. "Should've told your mother right away."

"Thanks to Toby, we know all about it," Martin chuckled, ruffling the boy's hair affectionately.

"I told ya Ronny's *my* friend!" Toby exclaimed, and pouted when a knowing ripple of laughter filled the air.

"You know, guys, Toby has a point," Jeanne attempted to explain.

Catherine suddenly squeezed her younger daughter fiercely. "We've been so worried. But no more of that nonsense." She released her again. "It's over and you're all right."

Jeanne gasped indignantly. "I have been all right all along. Being a single parent isn't impossible. Millions of women manage it for years."

Her parents exchanged a doubtful look.

"Of course I want to get married again. Someday. To a man as wonderful as David."

"And it's smart to know what you're looking for in advance," Angie said in support of her sister. "No sense wasting time on a fling. Right, Brad?"

The Drillmaster shrugged. "A fling sounds kind of fun."

Jeanne seethed. Couldn't he pick up a simple cue?

"Well it does—*yowee!*" he added, wincing as his wife's heel landed on his suede shoe.

Martin nodded, beaming with his stamp-of-approval smile. "Doesn't hurt to sample all the treats in the window before you buy."

"Daddy!" Jeanne was mortified.

"It doesn't matter whether this Ron is the one," Catherine added sweetly. "We're just thrilled that our wounded duckling's ready to fly again. Finally, we can sleep through the night again. Have a merry Christmas after all!"

A merry Christmas after all? Jeanne's heart dropped clear to her feet in one painful bounce. Their yuletide cheer was in the hands of Ron Coleman? A virtual stranger? A man she'd insulted beyond repair?

They gathered around the table for the meal. Jeanne

found it hard to swallow even the soft vegetables. The depth of her parents concern over her solitary life-style really rocked her. Sleep was still lost over it? She surveyed their bright faces, wondering how she'd ever straighten this out.

"So how did you meet a famous man like Ron Coleman?" Catherine asked, leaning over Toby's chair to slice his meat.

"He just rang the doorbell," Toby chirped.

"I met him at Gracie's," Jeanne replied over their amused chuckles.

"Buying me toys?" Toby asked.

"Let's say I was there on your behalf."

"What an odd place to run into a bachelor," Catherine mused. "I imagine the whole thing was a romantic whirlwind. But a man who writes such witty books and articles about exotic places is bound to be adventurous."

"Like a Potter!" they all chorused.

Except for Jeanne, of course. "Surprised you know of him, Mom. You read mysteries mostly."

"Everybody reads Coleman," Martin inserted, jabbing a large potato. "Any sour cream, Cat?"

"No. Use the margarine." Catherine shifted her attention back to her younger daughter, her eyes sparkling. "Why, he wrote a whole book about the way deep-sea fishermen live in the Florida Keys."

Jeanne made a doubtful sound. "Fishermen? You?"

"It's the way he does it, dear," Catherine explained good-humoredly. "Always gets to the heart of the human condition."

"That was the book right before his report about exploring in the Himalayas," Martin recalled with a chuckle. "You know, Jeanne, those mountains along the border between India and Tibet."

His daughter smiled thinly. "Never been there, but the location rings a bell."

Martin was seemingly unaware of her sarcasm. ''He backpacked his way through that range. Ran into some way-out Tibetan sect who took an instant liking to him. Wasn't sure if they wanted to string him up or crown him king!''

The Potters' voices swelled once again, this time in laughter. Jeanne shook her head dazedly. She knew the signs. Ron had been unanimously inducted into the Potter clan—sight unseen!

''He seems nice enough,'' she ventured carefully, ''but he isn't in town for long. Pass the salt, please.''

''Where does he live?''

''Uh, Los Angeles.''

''With whom is he staying?''

''His grandfather, I believe.''

''Where might that be?''

''Como Avenue. Senior high-rise near the lake.'' For someone who claimed not to be interested, she knew she had too many hard facts on the tip of her tongue.

''And boy, oh, boy, can he play baseball!'' Toby announced gleefully.

Jeanne and Angie offered to bring in the dessert and coffee a short time later. Jeanne had baked the tall chocolate cake standing on the counter in the kitchen, so she sliced it while Angie got plates from the cupboard.

''Don't feel bad, Jeanne,'' she said, setting the dessert dishes on the counter at her sister's elbow. ''Playing along was the most merciful route.''

''They are pathetically happy, aren't they?''

''Yeah.''

''I just didn't know how they felt.'' She sawed the cake like a lumberjack attacking a mighty oak. ''What a dirty trick to spring on me at Christmas.''

Angie skimmed her finger through some fudge frosting edging the plate. ''Timing isn't their fault, or your fault for that matter. Things just happen. It's fate.''

"It's Ron Coleman's fault, pure and simple! And his loony grandfather's."

"Well, you gotta admit, this encounter with him sure beat the heck out of cooing over a half-baked frozen-food fanatic in the supermarket!"

Jeanne turned, a slow and dangerous smile forming on her lips. "Don't you start taking this seriously, too. I need somebody to shed doubt on Ron's potential."

"And if I refuse?"

"I'll tell Brad you failed your dental-hygenist exams the first try."

Angie clapped her hands to her pretty face, mortified. "You wouldn't! You know how picky he is about his work. Why, if he found out, he might never totally trust me again."

"Then play the role that best suits you, the devil's advocate."

As hard as Jeanne tried to steer the after-dinner conversation in other directions, it kept drifting back to Ron.

"Do you have any pictures of him?" Catherine asked. "You always take pictures. Always."

Toby giggled as he licked frosting off his fork. "We got one. Remember, Mommy?"

The child was right. "One did just come from the developers." Jeanne rose, and went to the front hall where she'd left her tote bag. When she returned, she was waving an envelope. She handed it to her father and he edged it open with his large thumb. Everyone popped up and crowded around them.

"Why, this is a picture of the general and his poodle," Martin complained.

Jeanne, standing on his right, leaned over and gestured to the dog. "See that hand on Fu-Fu? That," she told them triumphantly, "is Ron's hand."

Murmurs of interest filled the air.

"What a strong, handsome hand!" Catherine enthused.

Martin studied it. ''Doesn't look like he gets a prissy manicure.'' He glanced at Jeanne for verification.

''No, his cuticles were a bit of a mess.'' She tapped the photo. ''I think the forefinger nail may have even been bitten off.''

''An animal!'' Angie squealed, forgetting herself. ''Wild, virile—no office hours to keep.''

For the first time Brad looked a little unsure. ''Maybe Jeanne'd better be careful with this guy. Give some thought to her choice.''

Jeanne smiled. ''I am so sorry my sister stepped on your foot, Brad. It was a mean thing to do.'' She turned to Angie. ''You can't trust some people, that's all there's to it.''

7

RON WAS ACCUSTOMED to being sized up at public appearances. Talk shows, college lecture halls, book signings at stores large and small, he'd done them all. He figured that by and large, over the course of time, he'd seen it all.

But this last Thursday before Christmas, settled into Emmett's favorite Grand Avenue bookstore for his only autographing of the season, he seemed to have picked up a new kind of fan club. Or should he say hand club?

His right hand in particular, seemed to interest a bundled-up trio. As he sat at a small square table adjacent to the cash register, putting his signature to books and various clippings bearing his name, he was constantly aware of these people, a middle-aged couple and a woman in her late twenties, who watched his every stroke of the pen. The bookstore, as old as Grand Avenue itself, wasn't very large so customers were in the way if they lingered.

But this small group had the guts to linger unabashedly. Stubbornly planted several feet away from his line of well-wishers beside a display of romance novels, they watched him in wide-eyed wonder.

He tried to put them out of his mind by concentrating on his fans and his grandfather, who was standing beside him to soak up the limelight. Ron was here as a special favor to the old man. The surrounding Grand Avenue shops and cafés were thick with his friends, and he'd promised to deliver his prized grandson to boost revenues and spirits.

Emmett was in his glory at the moment. He'd delivered

the hometown hero and intended to reap the rewards with a grand showing. While Ron was dressed in casual khaki, the proud grandpapa was decked out in a tuxedo. While Ron spoke in personal murmurs to his readers, Emmett bellowed platitudes that bounced off the varnished pine walls.

As usual, nothing got by the old fellow, however. As a woman dug through her shopping bag for a clipping she wanted signed, Emmett placed a hand on Ron's solid shoulder and whispered in his ear, "Do you know them, son?"

Ron looked up at him, keeping his expression nonchalant. "Figured they were part of your crowd."

"All bundled up, it's sometimes hard to tell."

"Just hope they're not distant relatives I'm supposed to remember, or old neighbors of my folks."

"Highly unlikely," Emmett assured him. "Though the older lady looks a bit familiar. If only I could place her...."

"She's wearing a wedding band, so I'm sure she didn't make a big impression," Ron retorted under his breath before returning his attention to his task.

The line eventually thinned out, something the trio had apparently been waiting for. They approached the table now. Ron immediately noticed that the younger woman was carrying today's paper under her arm. The store's advertisement announcing his appearance was in plain sight.

"He looks better up close and in the flesh," the older woman proclaimed, eyeing his hand.

Ron swallowed hard. "Excuse me?"

"Can't you guess who I am?" the woman asked. "Who we are?"

Ron's jaw worked as he searched his brain.

"Now, dear," the man chided the lady. "You should pull down your scarf and show your face."

The woman laughed, and playfully complied. That did it for Ron. The combination of the dancing blue eyes, the heart-shaped face, and the blond hair was all too familiar.

She was related to Jeanne. All of them were, as a matter of fact. Presumably they were her mother, father and sister.

"The Potters, of course!" he said smoothly. The crazy Potters. Isn't that what Jeanne herself had called them?

"I'm Catherine," the older woman continued. "This is my husband Martin and my elder daughter, Angie."

"Pleased to meet you," Ron said, standing to shake hands with all of them. "I'm assuming you saw the photo of my hand on the poodle."

Catherine gestured to Angie's newspaper. "That's all we had to go on until we saw this appearance advertised in the newspaper. Figured it was about time we saw the rest of you!"

Ron watched them in wonder. They actually made sense. They made staring at his hand for thirty minutes sound reasonable!

"Enjoy reading about your adventures," Martin told him, interest and respect in his features.

"I am the grandfather," Emmett proclaimed heartily, not about to be forgotten for a millisecond.

Introductions were exchanged all around, and Catherine took over the conversation from there. Her eyes sparkled like gems as she surveyed Ron. "It's so nice to finally have more than a hand to go by. The rest of you measures up quite nicely."

Ron shook his head slowly. "I can't get over how much you Potter women look alike." But Catherine was different somehow, not just because of her age. Suddenly he knew. Catherine was happy to see him, genuinely delighted. He could envision just such an expression on Jeanne's sober face, and it made his heart ache. Why couldn't she let go and accept the attraction between them? The rest of the Potters were giving in. He couldn't begin to imagine what they thought or what they wanted, but they were downright delightful about it in any case!

"We felt, under the circumstances," Martin ventured, "that we should get to know each other better."

"Circumstances?" Ron's heavy, dark brows lifted a fraction as he scrambled for equilibrium.

The sister, Angie, who'd been nervously fingering her pale hair till now, interrupted with a hoot. "Now, Ron, you don't have to play dumb for Jeanne's sake."

Dumb? Why, this sister was every bit as irritating as the other, right down to her glum, wary expression. "Meaning?" he queried with a dangerous smile.

"Why, that Jeanne wanted to keep your relationship a secret until you knew each other better!" Angie supplied in a rush. "The jig is up. Toby told the folks everything."

"Oh, I see." He smiled broadly. But his pleasure was short-lived as Emmett cleared his throat. Ron had his own crazy kin to worry about. Mixing them all together might be a sin Jeanne could never forgive.

"So these are the parents of the Jeanne who—"

"Yes, that's right," Ron cut in curtly. "The Jeanne I've been spending time with." He looked from the Potters to Pop. "You really don't know much about our relationship either, Emmett," he said with a cautionary gleam in his eye. "But now that's the cat's out of the bag, I suppose I'll have to fill you in. Later."

"As you say, I suppose." Emmett reared back a fraction, enjoying this new and unexpected game.

"We must have lunch together," Martin announced. "How about right now? My treat."

"You don't have to do that," Ron said politely, though he was curious about this family and, hungry for any information about Jeanne.

"We insist," Martin said.

"Splendid, splendid," Emmett intoned, always one for socializing. "The Café Bon next door serves wonderful salads and sandwiches."

"It's settled then," Catherine said happily, readjusting

her scarf. She studied Emmett's face thoughtfully for a moment. "You know there's something about you. I feel we may have met, but I can't imagine where."

Emmett nodded his silver head, giving the matter grave consideration. "I feel it, too...."

"I have some loose ends to take care of here," Ron announced, putting a detaining hold on Emmett's elbow. "Shall we meet over there in ten minutes?" The Potters chorused their affirmation, and filed out of the store with cheery waves.

"Why couldn't I go along with them?" Emmett demanded gruffly, wrenching away from Ron. "The younger one had no man's arm."

"Look, if you don't back off, you could lose that arm of yours. Maybe even your neck."

Emmett's nostrils flared. "Whatever do you mean?"

Ron sighed. "Now that I have all the facts, I can say with certainty that you *have* run into Catherine before."

"Ah, yes, I thought so," Emmett said dreamily. "Following through the first faint glimmers of recognition is such fun. A bonus of mystery to enjoy as one gets older. Where did we meet? In summer stock during the sixties? What did we say to each other? Something sweeter than the most polished script?"

"You were in Grace Brothers a week from last Sunday, telling lies to her grandson," Ron supplied flatly.

"Oh. So she brought the Trent boy in." Emmett sighed wistfully.

"Does it ring any bells, Pop? Any chance you remembering anything the boy wanted?"

"I told you there were too many children to remember anyone in particular," his grandfather said. His features softened as he went on. "This Catherine would've been quite a dish in the sixties, I imagine. I would've liked to have known her then, surely."

Ron rolled his eyes. Emmett was happily married to

Grandma Olivia back then, and never would have given this woman or any other a second glance! How could a man so lost in fantasy insist his decisions as Santa were beyond reproach?

"I'm going to ask you one last time, Pop. Will you please reconsider your stand with Toby? Speak to him again?"

"I wish I could be confident that you are sincere when you promise never to broach the subject again," Emmett returned silkily.

"You can!"

"Good, then I can be assured this will be the last time you ask me to compromise my principles and speak to this boy!"

Ron glared at him. "Okay, Pop, okay. But don't miss my point about the lovely Catherine. She's as livid as Jeanne about your stunt. Apparently it took all the Potters and an in-law to keep her from a return visit to the North Pole." Ron shook a finger in his face. "Jeanne somehow convinced Catherine that she would and could take care of the matter—take care of you!"

"How preposterous!"

"For your own protection, Pop, you mustn't let any of them know you're the offending Santa Claus."

"Oh, I think I'm beginning to see," his grandfather said stiffly. "You're uninviting me to lunch."

"As a start, yes!" Ron all but thundered.

Emmett's lined face drooped in disappointment. "But they seem such fun."

"Even if you were to be careful in conversation, Catherine might recognize you at any moment. As it is, we're damn lucky she never got hold of one of your store brochures."

"But you are going to lunch," Emmett pressed. "Jeanne Trent wants nothing to do with you, and still you go to lunch."

"C'mon, Pop. Stay out of this, please."

"I just wonder what you're trying to do."

"I'm not sure myself," Ron hedged, rubbing the back of his neck. "I just can't let go of Jeanne, not yet. Guess I hope that this is a lucky break for me. A chance to approach her from another angle."

"Now was that so hard to admit?" Emmett said in a gentler voice.

Ron stared at his feet. "Yes. I'm not accustomed to being turned down."

"I know. But it happens when we least expect it. When we want things the most. You do really want her, don't you? I mean, you're not pursuing this girl just for the sake of winning?" Emmett asked.

"I wouldn't!"

"It's your nature to chase things the hardest that are just out of reach. Why, you've made a career out of it."

Ron couldn't argue the point. But Jeanne was doing things to his heart and soul that he couldn't begin to explain to his grandfather.

JEANNE WAS IN the midst of scrubbing her kitchen floor when the telephone rang. She slipped on the wet linoleum as she lunged for the wall phone. "Hello."

"Drop everything and get over to the Café Bon."

"Nice to hear your voice, Angie."

"There's no time to waste, Jeanne," her sister hissed.

"Why, they giving something away?"

"You!"

Jeanne frowned, leaning against the handle of her sponge mop. "Have you been drinking?"

"Not yet!" Angie's voice dropped even lower. "I'm on Grand Avenue with Mom and Dad. Grand Avenue, Jeanne."

"I don't mind being left out. It'll give them time to buy me a super Christmas gift."

"This is one gift you don't seem to want!" Angie paused, then her voice rose. "Coming, Mom!"

"Angie—"

"Didn't you see this morning's paper, sis?"

Jeanne chuckled dryly, surveying her damp floor and sink full of scrubbed pots. "Haven't had the time."

"Make the time for the Entertainment section. Page six."

"Why?"

"Not supposed to be telling you at all. Just hurry. Hurry!"

The dial tone buzzed in Jeanne's ear as she stared at the newspaper, still rolled and bound, lying on the table.

"SORRY GRANDFATHER COULDN'T join us," Ron apologized a short while later as he slipped into one of the empty seats at the Potter table. "But he has another appointment he couldn't break."

Their table by the window offered them a clear view of Grand Avenue and Emmett climbing into a taxi with a jaunty wave.

Angie met his eyes then and Ron knew that she was aware of what Emmett did every afternoon.

"Then it seems we didn't need such a large table," Martin declared, looking round the bustling café for the waiter. "Maybe they'd like to switch us to make better use of this space."

"Oh, no," Angie protested. "This view of the avenue, with its decorations, is too pretty to pass up. So easy to be spotted—I mean to spot things from here."

"So what did Brad have to say?" Catherine asked.

Angie regarded her blankly. "When?"

"You just called him, didn't you?"

"I won't be needed at the office until two," Angie said evasively.

"But you knew that already."

"Hmm, so I did."

Catherine gave up on her eldest child, and smiled at Ron over her water glass. ''Our cornering you this way may seem strange, I suppose.''

''I don't mind,'' he assured her.

''Good. It's just that, well, Jeanne tires of our interference so we've been trying to accommodate her by doing it behind her back when possible.''

His mouth curved politely. ''How thoughtful.''

''She's delicate right now,'' Martin explained, his large face pinched in concern. ''I'm sure you understand.''

''I know about David, of course.''

''Tragic, tragic,'' Martin rumbled. ''But it is high time Jeanne got back in circulation. If we seemed a little overexcited about your hand, well, it's because it's the first hand our baby's shown an interest in.''

''Nobody could bear to see Jeanne hurt any more,'' Angie put in. ''We just want her and Toby to get through this Christmas with some new and valuable memories to look back on.''

''It isn't easy,'' Catherine said huffily. ''She doesn't want our help. And she needs it, with all the problems that keep cropping up to threaten our holiday.''

Martin patted his wife's hand. ''Now, dear, I told you to forget all about that Santa incident at Gracie's.''

Angie took fiendish pleasure in relating the tale to the hapless Ron.

Catherine opened her napkin and slipped it over her lap. ''I had only the best intentions when I took Toby there. Who'd ever guess the Santa would go haywire and promise the boy everything he desired?''

''A careless thing to do,'' Ron said, looking directly at Angie, hoping for mercy. ''But I'm sure it will all work out. I've been quizzing Toby myself and have already gotten him to admit he wants a Mighty Mite Gas Pump.''

The elder Potters expressed their approval. Only Angie's

sour expression did not change. Couldn't she see that he was trying to make up for Emmett's blooper?

"And I intend to question Toby until I find out what all six squiggles on his list stand for," he promised.

The Potters expressed delight over the squiggle revelation. So there were six in all. With the gas pump revealed, that left five more mysteries. Even Angie seemed impressed with his investigation.

"So nice of you to care so much," Catherine said sincerely.

"Glad to do it," Ron assured her. He was beginning to feel more relaxed. "But don't underestimate Jeanne's capabilities. She runs that house and business of hers with amazing skill. There's not a problem she'd shy away from, I'm sure."

Angie nodded, and her eyes slanted to the empty chair. "You can count on it, Ron."

Ron's heart stopped at Angie's cryptic remark. The call Angie had seemed so uncomfortable about wasn't made to her husband, but to her fiesty, temperamental sister. Jeanne was on her way over to take the romantic reins away from her family.

The very idea sent a delicious tingle down his spine. She was going to answer the challenge, after all. Naturally she'd be working against him, trying to prove they were mismatched. But what better way to create some sparks, than with some up-close friction?

THEY WERE EATING their sandwiches when Jeanne burst through the glass door on a gust of chilly air. Ron had never seen her eyes so huge. But it had to be a shock, seeing him cozily ensconced in her family unit.

"Jeanne!" Her parents chorused her name in surprise.

"Hello. Everyone." She sank into the chair originally reserved for Emmett. Ron was captivated by the way her hair lay on her rosy-colored sweater in a soft blond puff, and the way the Angora knit picked up the pink in her cheeks. How refreshing it was to savor the simple things he used to enjoy: a sandwich, laughter over family matters, a pretty girl just in from the cold. It was a much-needed change from being on the run all the time, viewing people and places from a safe, objective distance.

"Angela," Catherine said snappily. "Why didn't you tell us your sister was coming?"

"It's a surprise?" Angie said feebly.

"You don't mind, do you, Mom?" Jeanne challenged.

"Naturally you're welcome," Martin intervened evenly. "Had we known, we could've ordered for you, that's all." He hailed the waitress, who efficiently took Jeanne's order of the broccoli-soup and chicken-sandwich special.

"So you were signing autographs next door, Ron?" Jeanne remarked as she allowed him to ease her jacket off her shoulders and drape it over her chair.

"Yes, this appearance was for Emmett in particular. All his theater cronies hang out around here."

Catherine fluttered her lashes like a teenager. "Isn't that Emmett a dapper man, Jeanne?"

"Quite the character," Jeanne murmured, moving her table setting closer.

"Has Toby met him yet?" her mother pressed. "Oh, how they're bound to get on."

Jeanne opened her mouth to respond, but Ron beat her to it. "Everything's so new still," he pointed out. "We thought it might not be wise to blend the families until we're on more solid ground ourselves." Ron's hopes rose as he glanced at Jeanne's delicate profile. She'd actually brightened a little over the dodge.

"How ridiculous," Martin rumbled. "We expect you and yours for some Christmas cheer. Why, being a bachelor with no home here yourself, we'd simply assumed we'd be joining forces."

"We'll see, Dad," Jeanne said with finality in her tone.

"So where is Toby?" Ron asked, to change the conversation to a safer subject.

"I left him with the next-door neighbor," she said, upturning her cup for the waitress hovering with the coffee pot. "Pass the sugar, Dad?" Knowing the Potters were all watching her sugar intake, she poured two sacks, rather than the usual one into her cup. They wouldn't gain control of everything!

"Toby's playing with that Jason boy?" Catherine beamed with pleasure as she moved the sweetener back out of reach. "How nice."

Jeanne's forehead puckered in doubt, as she stirred her steaming brew. "He is a year older. And in school... He takes advantage of Toby sometimes."

"Toby-boy's sharp like his grandpa," Martin protested. "David was more of a gentle sort, but that Toby can mix it up with the best of 'em."

"And Jason's mother seems very responsible," Catherine added. "I've spoken to her several times over the fence and was very impressed."

"And they won't even be going anyplace by car," Angie blurted out. She clamped her mouth shut again and cringed when it became clear by the disapproving gasps that she'd gone too far.

Jeanne spoke next, in a tone frosty enough to rival the December weather. "I don't care to have all my fears, all my business exposed this way! In—in—front of strangers."

Ron didn't like being called a stranger but he could understand how she felt. He believed she was doing just fine as a single parent, but her family didn't seem to think so. Sure, it was obvious that she was shielding Toby a little too much. But she'd get over it, Ron was certain. Couldn't these Potter people see that their interference was Jeanne's biggest cause for anxiety?

Jeanne simmered beside him, sorely tempted to leap up and announce that charming Emmett was the Santa they so badly wanted to string up, that she and Ron were no couple at all.

That was when Ron played a monstrous trick on her. He reached over, covertly, casually, and grasped her hand under the table. Seconds passed, minutes passed while he held her trembling fingers with a strong and steady pressure. Astonishingly, he'd done the right thing. His touch translated into a quiet, comforting show of support.

There was no denying it, they'd formed a union. Against their mad, web-spinning families. All of a sudden Jeanne found herself part of a couple after all.

But she was not going to admit it. When Ron excused himself to use the rest room in the rear of the café some twenty minutes later, Jeanne followed and was waiting for him by the very pay telephone Angie had used to summon her. She stepped up to block his path in the dim hallway. Ron grinned crookedly and did nothing to avoid the subsequent collision. The angora of her sweater tickled his wrist with a teasing tingle, the tips of her breasts flattened on his chest. How he wanted to put his hands all over her sweater, to envelope himself in her curvy softness.

"How could you let this happen, Ron?"

He eyed her lazily. "Which part?"

"The 'let's have lunch' part! The part that started it all!"

"Oh, no, that's where you're wrong. This deal got brewing the minute the Potters walked into the bookstore for a look at my hand." He snapped his fingers suddenly. "No, that's wrong, too."

"Wrong?" she repeated mutely.

"Right. Wrong."

"Never mind!" She tried to whirl away from him, but he made made a deft grab for her arm.

"Okay, okay. This all started because you showed off that snapshot of Fu-Fu. What a conversation piece, Jeanne. You had to have some motive when you did that." Had she hoped to spur her family into action, to force her to spend time with him against her better judgment? She was obviously getting way too much help from them, but it would be reasonable to suppose that she relied on it to some degree. Families were a blessing and a curse all at once.

''I'm not a snitch as a rule,'' she said, ''but it was Toby who put them on to you. They couldn't believe I hadn't taken any shots of you—''

''Why?''

''Because it's my thing. I take pictures of everyone. Especially in natural poses.''

''No wonder you haven't taken my picture. We haven't been in any natural poses yet.''

He looked innocent enough, but she couldn't be sure if the innuendo was deliberate. With David, she'd always been sure. She was accustomed to being sure. Why did Ron have to keep pursuing her when he knew he was all wrong in every way!

''I admit I was caught up in the moment, and trapped into trying to please my parents. They wanted to see a photo of you and I happened to have the hand in my purse.'' He was grinning now, with smug pleasure—as though immensely enjoying her discomfort! ''Toby had already told them about your visits,'' she continued defensively, ''and I sort of got caught up in their joyous relief.'' She threw her hands in the air. ''Not only do I have Toby's Christmas to worry about, but the Potters' happiness too. Apparently it rests on whether I have a boyfriend.''

''I'm sure they'll get over this obsessive need to meddle in your life,'' he said consolingly. ''And if it makes you feel any better, I agree that they're overdoing it. Everyone mends at different speeds, handles setbacks in different ways. You're doing just fine, Jeanne. And I told them so.''

There was that soothing liquid-honey tone of his again, such a nice complement to his comforting handclasp. She suspected it was just a smooth technique, but it still washed over her agitation with amazing effectiveness.

‘‘It’s grown worse, when it should be better,’’ she confided. ‘‘Whenever I come up for air, they push me under again!’’

His brown eyes crinkled with humor. ‘‘Just because it’s Christmas.’’

Catherine flew in from the dining area just then, and announced breathlessly, ‘‘I just had a brainstorm.’’

Jeanne smiled tightly. ‘‘Take two aspirin and call me in the morning.’’

Catherine chuckled at her daughter, and absently patted Ron’s solid forearm. ‘‘I was thinking, dear, why don’t I just go around to your house this afternoon and baby-sit Toby. That way you and Ron can spend some time alone, perhaps do some Christmas shopping. That is, if Ron is available.’’ She turned to him then, with a sunny smile.

Ron smiled right back, again wishing he could transfer Catherine’s enthusiasm for him to Jeanne. At this moment, Jeanne’s expression was strained with thought. She was most likely looking for a way to escape.

‘‘Mother, how do you know I don’t have any appointments?’’

‘‘Because I took a look at your appointment book yesterday,’’ Catherine fired back matter-of-factly. ‘‘So how about it?’’

Jeanne wrestled with her annoyance. ‘‘Oh, Mom, I don’t know. I have my car. Ron must have his.’’

His lips twitched. Jeanne was a capable photographer, but an alibi-spinner she wasn’t. She’d have to come up with a better excuse than that!

‘‘I’ll drive your car back. No problem.’’ Catherine looked from her daughter to Ron, waiting for whoops of glee. ‘‘Give you a chance to get that gas pump Toby wants.’’

Jeanne took a breath. ‘‘You know about that?’’

‘‘Yes, Ron explained how he’s trying to wangle Toby’s

list out of him. Dad and I think he's so clever. Why, we'll have a countdown. Five squiggles to go.''

Ron wondered if Jeanne would dare defy her mother. But it was so clear that Catherine was a well-meaning basket case of hope and concern that he doubted it. He wouldn't have dared make the comparison openly, but both women were the same sort of mother, protective, prying and gushing with warmth.

''So, Ron, would you like to make Mom the happiest woman in the world?'' Jeanne asked sweetly, sending him a look that begged him to decline.

As if he wanted to take the rap for this imaginary romance going sour. Or miss the opportunity to try to make it the real thing. ''Sounds like a great idea to me. We'll shop for Toby, and maybe my parents if you're willing.''

With a wave and whirl, Catherine rushed back to the dining room.

Jeanne stomped her boot. ''You could've said no.''

Ron's handsome face crumpled. ''That attitude hurts.''

She nodded vehemently. ''Good. A little pain will give depth to your performance.''

''Then I have the part of the boyfriend?''

She frowned, but there was amusement in her eyes. ''For now. But don't let it go to your head. You're the only one who auditioned.''

Probably the only one who had guts enough to do so, he thought. Just the same, he truly wanted the part. Ah, Emmett would be so proud when he heard the details of his gig. A starring role in Potter Productions, Unlimited. Live theater at its most challenging. And the payment... Candy-cane kisses were what he had in mind, from his very tempting leading lady.

8

''DESPITE YOUR FAMILY'S obvious problem with snooping, I like them.'' Ron made the remark as they wandered through Rosedale Mall some forty minutes later. Jeanne hadn't wanted to go to Grace Brothers for the gas pump and he couldn't blame her. Not with Emmett appearing there live and uncensored, doling out dreams to a bunch of wide-eyed innocents like her son.

''I know you're busting with pride because the folks like you,'' she returned with a saucy lift of her chin. ''But don't you think feelings mean a whole lot more when they have substance?''

''What are you driving at?''

''Only that my parents don't really know you, apart from your public image. They have—''

''Haven't gotten close enough to know I'm a self-centered bachelor who doesn't fit in?''

''Mmm, you are in the right business, aren't you? So quick with just the right words.''

She wasn't supposed to agree! Anger swelled inside him as they moved along with the flow of shoppers. Never had he tried so hard to please a woman, never had he felt so frustrated. He could hardly believe it.

It was then he thought to look down at her. Why, she was teasing him! The merry twinkle in her vivid blue eyes made her all the more striking. All the more desirable.

''What I was going to say,'' she began again, ''is that,

well, my family has no reason to try and palm me off the way they are—''

''You mean you're not a desperate hunter?'' It was his turn to tease, and he enjoyed her gasp.

''Haven't you heard a word I've been saying since the moment we met?''

''Of course I have.'' He curved an arm around her back. ''I get the picture, really. Still, I'm glad your family came to check me out. It was my pleasure to meet them. They're genuine and kind and a lot of fun.''

She opened her mouth to say more, but he gave her shoulders a squeeze. ''Let's just enjoy the moment, Jeanne, and keep our sense of humor. Okay?''

The truth was Ron didn't want any more serious talk. He was afraid she was working her way back to the big brush-off. If he could throw diversions in her path, anything to keep her confused and interested, he was going to do it. Despite her teasing remarks, she really didn't know him well at all. At least not well enough to unceremoniously dump him!

They combed the vast mall in search of the gas pump, and came up empty at toy stores and department stores alike. They did, however find some gifts for Ron's parents, a silk scarf and perfume from Dayton's for his mother and some casual wear from Mervyn's for his father. He'd still wanted a gift his folks could share and show off so Jeanne had steered him to an art gallery, where they'd come upon a limited-edition print by a local artist of Loring Park.

Ron arranged for the print to be framed and delivered to Emmett's. As he dug for his credit card, he noticed that Jeanne, who'd been wandering through the shop, had paused to admire a print of the Como Park Conservatory, a St. Paul landmark boasting a huge variety of plant life in a controlled setting.

He sighed wistfully from his view at the counter. If only she'd smile at him the way she was smiling at that picture.

He hastily arranged for the Conservatory print to be delivered to her house, and tipped generously to make certain it would arrive on Christmas Eve. Hopefully, by then, she wouldn't perceive it as some kind of bribe to get her between the sheets. Hopefully, by then, she'd be wearing that smile morning, noon and night!

It was about two-thirty when they left the mall in search of other toy stores. They tried several, but no Mighty Mite Gas Pump could be found. Apparently it was one of the hotter items of the season.

Ron started the car in the parking lot of the last of the bunch, and turned to Jeanne who was rubbing her arms against the winter chill. "I'm so sorry, but—"

"I know! And I know what you're going to say."

"I can't help it!" he squawked.

She waved her gloved hand at the windshield. "Just do it. Get going."

"All right. Next stop, Grace Brothers Toys."

It was close to four o'clock when they entered Gracie's sliding doors with the ever-present customer flow. Ron took hold of her arm, as a burly woman in an artificial fur coat attempted to barge between them.

Jeanne looked harassed. "To think I'd hoped to get Toby's toys on sale. Now, at this late date, it seems I'll be lucky to get them at all, at any price."

"Should've kept that gift certificate," he chided.

She shook her head, still uncomfortable with the idea of such indebtedness. "Emmett's only half-responsible for my fix. He did promise Toby everything. But that darn Toby is to blame as well! Imagine, being coy at that age. If only he'd told me what all those squiggles meant."

"I'll get that list out of him yet," he promised.

"Have to admit I'm warming to that idea." There was a catch in her voice. In this busy store, she felt all the pressures of Christmas, all the pressures of widowhood. She stared at Ron with the huge blues eyes of a lost little girl.

The look pierced his heart clean through. Never had he cared so for a woman. The truth of it washed over him like a tidal wave, making him tremble with fear and desire. At that moment he'd have bought out half the store, done anything possible to put the confident shine back in her eyes.

But storming her with grandstand plays hadn't proven successful, he reminded himself. The only way to win her was with gentle nudges of support. Work his way inside her until she woke up one morning to find him completely indispensable. Suddenly an idea occurred to him. "Go look for the pump," he directed above the merry jingle coming over the public-address system. "Meet me back up here, at the service desk."

"Why?"

"Because I have an idea."

Jeanne mouthed something that might have been "You're crazy," and melded into the crowd.

Crazy like a fox. She'd see.

The line at the service desk wasn't especially long at the moment. Lenora was on duty of course, taking care of customers with brisk efficiency. Despite the static between her and Emmett, he simply couldn't stop imagining them as a couple: The blustery big mouth and the clear head of reason, both with vinegar-dipped tongues. Lenora would be good for Emmett, and there was no question that she already had a thing for him. If only he could make them both see it!

"Next, please."

Ron stepped up to the counter.

"Well, where've you been all day?" Her tone was snappy, and edged with amusement.

"I do have a life outside of Gracie's," he told her airily.

"Yeah, right. What's on the wish list now?"

He made a clucking sound. "You're so sure I want something."

She nodded knowingly. ''Decades in customer service have made me a shrewd judge of character.''

''Don't think you have Emmett figured out yet,'' he challenged. ''Or do you?''

Her long, thin face flushed prettily. ''I'm busy. Extremely, thoroughly and totally engaged.''

''Now there's the kind of line Emmett would appreciate.'' Ron rubbed his belly. ''Just speak more from your diaphram, he'd say. Project with force.''

She pursed her lips, as though savoring a sweet taste. ''If I accused you of shoplifting, you'd be in a spot for a few delicious minutes.''

''Okay, Lenora, you're too good for me.'' He leaned over the counter, bringing his face close to hers. ''I'm here to inquire about Emmett's employee discount.''

''What!''

His face split with pleasure. ''Now, you see, Lenora? See what you can accomplish when you pull that voice out of the depths? Why, you'd be a most convincing Juliet to any man's Romeo.''

She planted her hands on the counter, her face resembling an irate mother's. ''You're playing Santa again? With this other girl?''

''Sort of.''

''How many you got on the string?''

''This one has me on the string,'' he confessed softly. ''I swear, she's the one who counts the most.''

Her forehead puckered. ''Methuselah know you're pulling this?''

Methuselah, he mused with silent chuckle. How could Emmett disregard this woman's apt wit, her straight-faced delivery? ''He doesn't know yet, but he won't mind.'' His voice grew furtive. ''Can I trust you with details?''

''No.''

''Okay, okay,'' he said good-naturedly. ''But you wouldn't want that pretty young widow's son to go without a fine Christmas, would you?'' Ron could all but see the gears in her head turning. That ''a pretty young widow'' stuff would surely soften this store veteran, set in her ways.

''But the discount is for the direct benefit of the employee in question,'' Lenora finally asserted.

''Trust me, Lenora, any purchases that widow would make would benefit Meth—Emmett. He owes this woman for those details that you didn't want to hear about.'' Her face filled with rage. ''No, no, nothing amorous,'' he hastily added. ''This one's my girl. Honestly. Mine, mine, all mine!'' Oh, how he loved saying it. Even if he did take a quick and furtive look around to make sure she wasn't close enough to contradict him.

She was visible, struggling with a large box near a teddy-bear display, but certainly not within hearing range.

''Hmm, she was gosh-darn lucky to get that Mighty Mite,'' Lenora noted.

He didn't dare step out of line to help Jeanne with the bulky box. She gave him a drop-dead glare as they locked gazes, but all he could do was beckon her over.

Suddenly Lenora put a Closed sign out at her station and called for counter assistance. Ron breathed a sigh of relief as a clerk came to handle the line. Lenora was freeing herself to help them out. She held out her arms over the counter, startling the weary-looking Jeanne. ''Give the box to me, dear.''

''Why?'' Jeanne asked testily.

Ron took the box and set it on the counter. ''Because,'' he whispered in Jeanne's ear, ''I've wangled you Santa's employee discount.''

Jeanne's eyes grew as they rested on Lenora for verification.

Lenora measured her as though looking for some verification herself. ''So young to be a widow.''

''Yes,'' Jeanne said bemusedly. ''Have the Potters been in to see you about my personal life, too?''

The older woman looked surprised. ''What is a Potter?''

''A wild species that could clear this crowd within seconds.''

Lenora laughed. ''I'd like to meet these Potters one day.'' Handling the box with strength and dexterity, she set it on the floor and put a large band of green Gracie's tape across the top to verify payment. She then produced a receipt book from beneath the counter. Curling her fingers around her pen she began to fill it out.

''Just accept that Emmett owes you this much,'' Ron suggested, giving Jeanne's shoulder a pat.

''All right, but I'm paying cash,'' she said as Ron's hand moved to the back pocket holding his wallet.

''That would work best, with the foggy connection to the employee,'' Lenora said, pleased. ''All I will need is Emmett's signature.'' She came round the counter, receipt book in hand. ''Shall we pay a visit to the North Pole?''

Ron's face lit up like a boy's. ''To Santa? Let's go!''

Lenora led the way, blazing a trail down the center aisle. Ron and Jeanne followed a few steps behind. There was a line at the Pole's gingerbread entrance, but that didn't stop Lenora. While her followers paused near the plump photographer, the service clerk kept on moving, her slender form gently jostling people on her way to the throne. Cries of dismay rose. Parents had no quarrel with Lenora's moves, as she was so obviously there for business reasons, but the children viewed her as a low-down line crasher.

''Do something, Ron,'' Jeanne whispered.

Ron smirked. ''Oh, no, those two old-timers are on their own.''

Lenora stood at the bottom of Santa's small glittery staircase and the moment a pair of preschool girls bounced off his lap, she handed the pen and receipt book to Emmett. He studied it in confusion.

Suddenly Ron realized that method actor Emmett was in character up there in the big chair and couldn't understand this intrusion. Ron hadn't thought of this glitch. Lenora, her patience about to snap, moved up the first step, making signing motions in the air.

"Get out of there!"

"Take your turn!"

"Line crasher!" All these chants filled the air. Still Emmett sat, blankly staring.

"You silly old coot!" Lenora hissed, as she set a low-heeled pump on the second step. "Sign, sign, sign!"

Suddenly the next second, a chunky boy of about six bounded up behind her and gave Lenora a mighty shove that sent her reeling forward.

"Take your dang turn, lady!" he shouted. "Just hurry up!"

Lenora lost her balance, and her arms flailed in an effort to catch the candy-stripe handrail. It was no use, however. She was a sleek missile, destined for Santa's red-velvet lap. Cries and laughter filled the air as she plopped down on Emmett's thighs, her limbs akimbo.

The old couple looked like animals trapped in headlights on a dark, deserted road.

"That's cute," Jeanne murmured. Ron turned and was surprised to find her standing behind the tripod with a firm grip on the Polaroid camera. To Jeanne, it had been the most natural move on earth. The redheaded photographer had stepped away to help the elves calm the crowd, and Jeanne, anticipating trouble from the angry little boy, had primed herself for the ultimate shot.

The redhead returned, uncertain and harassed. "He'll kill you, Ron."

"No, he won't," he argued with a wink. "Especially when he sees how good he and Lenora are together."

Jeanne expertly took the finished photo from the camera. She showed it to the redhead. "If you just concentrate more, get ready for that smile you know is coming, you get a much more spontaneous shot."

The redhead nodded. ''Thanks for the tip. And please keep the picture, my treat.''

''IT CERTAINLY WAS NICE of Lenora to sign off on the receipt with her own employee-discount number,'' Jeanne remarked as they strolled up her walk sometime later. Dusk was closing in and the residential street was alive with colorful lights, including the Trent house.

Ron was moving slowly, reluctant to let their date end. ''I'm sure she wishes she'd thought of it in the first place.''

''Does this mean my discount days are over? I mean, Emmett looked furious. He even refused your ride home.''

''Don't you worry. Once I get Emmett's feet soaking tonight, I'm going to strike some kind of deal with him for the unlimited use of his number.''

Jeanne skipped up the snow-dusted steps, and turned to face him with shining eyes. He'd crowded in close but she didn't seem to mind. ''I doubt we'll ever be allowed back in that place, though. The manager, Bickel, was beside himself.''

Ron lifted his broad shoulders beneath his leather jacket. ''Thank goodness Lenora managed to calm him down. She certainly went to bat for Emmett. And then when he scooped her up in his arms near the candy machine for that grand kiss… Wow.''

''Wow is right. I simply assumed they were already a hot item,'' Jeanne admitted. ''Don't see that kind of chemical explosion very often.''

''Don't you?'' His voice was a husky croon as he cupped his hand under her chin.

Jeanne trembled as he tipped her face to his. He smiled gently, feeling the vibration. ''You're quivering in your boots.''

''Guess the whole scene just got to me,'' she offered weakly. ''I do believe this kind of thing could become addictive.''

He smiled wolfishly. How could he help it, huddled so close to the sexiest woman ever to wear a hood! "Care to tell me what you mean? Exactly?"

"Why, the employee discount, of course! That glorious twenty-percent reduction lopped right off the top."

He chuckled dryly over her feigned innocence. "Torturing me must be at the top of your wish list this year."

She made an airy gesture with her gloved hand. "Someplace near the top."

"What would you have done if we hadn't met?" He posed the question teasingly, but was really quite serious about the answer. He would undoubtedly be dwelling on Christmases both present and future well into the night and didn't want to be the only one losing sleep.

She didn't reply, however. But by the distress and delight on her delicate features, he figured the odds were good that she would indeed think about his question.

"All teasing aside, Ron," she eventually said, "I do want to thank you for the adventure today. What I thought was going to be a grim mission turned out to be delightful. And so successful."

"I think you'd rest easier if you looked upon Toby's mystery list as some kind of scavenger hunt. I know I do. I haven't had this much fun at Christmas in years. And for that, I want to thank you."

And words weren't going to be enough for him, she realized, her pulse jumping to life. The glitter in his brown eyes flashed the message that he wanted to kiss her.

Jeanne could feel the knob of the storm door pressing into her spine as she leaned back. She could easily slip inside the house, but then her eyes dropped to his mouth. It was curving seductively, reminding her of their last long, searing kiss. She could still get away, she knew. Until she licked her lips. At that point it was too late. His mouth was on hers in a flash, with a hard, steady pressure.

It was as good as the last time. Jeanne could feel her

knees giving way. But Ron was right there to catch her, to snare her in his arms and tug her as close as their jackets would allow.

"You owed me that," he murmured into her hair.

"How so?"

"It's all part of the scavenger hunt." He stroked her cheek with his gloved finger. "One gift revealed, one candy-cane kiss delivered."

"What!"

"Remember for every item I discover on Toby's list, I get a Potter candy-cane kiss."

She rocked back on her heels, and sized him up in the twinkling light. "Seems there are a lot of rules to this game of yours."

"You make finding kissing excuses tough on a guy," he complained. "Do you realize there isn't a single sprig of mistletoe in your entire house?"

"Yes, sure, I know." He'd actually looked for the stuff. For the excuse. She was flustered and flattered and confused. And she wanted to get away from him, to think. She anxiously tried to wiggle away from the doorknob, but he leaned closer and slid his arm over her head, bracing himself with his palm on the door. "What do you think you're doing now, you—"

"I'm making a good show for your mother," he calmly interrupted. "She and your son have their noses pressed to the window on your right."

A moan escaped from her as she resisted the urge to turn for a peek. "Oh, no! The Potter push again."

"Must say I'm taking a shine to that push."

A flicker of the old fire flashed in her eyes. "Depends how a Potter uses it, Ron."

"So show me how it's done right." Grasping her slender face firmly in his free hand, he kissed her again, deeply, passionately, desperately.

Her long, pale lashes fluttered in surrender. The only heat

in the whole ice-cold universe suddenly seemed centered in their hot, wet kiss. The fact that it was a show for her mother should've taken the edge off it. But it didn't. She couldn't think beyond Ron and the dormant longings he was awakening inside her. The way his masculine scent made her think of uncomplicated sex.

He released her then, and she sagged against the door frame. Deprived of his heat she was lost. Chilly and lonely, too.

Just as she was working up the energy to flounce into the house, Catherine popped out, like a champagne cork from an extra-lively vintage. She was attempting to look exasperated, but the glee in her faintly lined face was unmistakable.

"Don't forget I have a husband to feed tonight," she greeted them, shivering inside her bulky cable-knit sweater.

"Ron was just leaving."

"He doesn't have to!"

Jeanne was mortified. "Mother! I think I can handle this goodbye without you."

Catherine's face remained cheery. "So did you find the toy?"

"We did," Ron told her with a measure of pride. "Even got a dis—"

"A discount from a woman at the service desk," Jeanne cut in, wanting to make certain that Ron didn't slip and mention that Emmett, the offending Santa, was on hand at the store.

Ron took the hint. "She's a dear old thing, a friend of my grandfather's."

"How that man gets around," Catherine marveled. It was obvious she found the trait a charming one.

"He's smooth," Ron said, not quite up to matching her enthusiasm.

"Did Toby have a good time next door?" Jeanne asked.

Catherine rubbed her bare hands together. "He certainly

did. As a matter of fact, he brought Jason along and they played in Toby's room for the longest time. And you'll never guess what happened."

"Mother, don't make me guess," Jeanne chided. "Not about Toby."

"But it's good news, dear. You see, I was passing by the bedroom and heard the boys talking. When I realized they were discussing Santa I paused to listen."

"Oh, Mother!"

"Well, we need that list, don't we?"

"I hope you didn't stand there thirty minutes, prying into their business."

"Barely twenty," Catherine assured her.

Jeanne inhaled sharply, then noticed Ron's twinkling eyes. There was humor in the situation, she realized. And it wouldn't hurt her blood pressure to remember that.

"Did you find out anything?" Ron asked the older woman, who was clearly about to burst with excitement.

Catherine made an X in the air. "We can cross off squiggle number two. Toby is expecting a remote-control car!"

"A what?" Jeanne all but shrieked.

"They make them for preschoolers," Catherine said soothingly.

"But they run those things in the street!"

"Not necessarily," Ron said gently. "You can take him to a park, or parking lot."

Catherine squeezed his arm. "I was going to pick one up someplace, but if you have a discount at Gracie's..."

"I'll be glad to take care of it," Ron offered. "The pump is still in my trunk.... Hey, why don't I keep Toby's stuff at Emmett's place, until we can get it all collected."

"Use your place as Santa Central, you mean?" Jeanne asked.

"Sure, why not?" Ron pretended to mull it over, as though the idea was brand-new and spontaneous rather than hours old and contrived. He hadn't brought it up earlier because he'd expected to be turned down flat. But that wouldn't happen now. Catherine wouldn't let it.

As expected she nodded vigorously. "Considering that Ron's committed—"

"Mother, really! Committed?"

Catherine looked a bit sheepish. "Can you deny it? Not only is he on the trail of the list, but he's going to make the buys through Gracie's."

"But—"

Catherine forged on. "And I must warn you that Jason is already searching his own house for gifts. It may be impossible to stop Toby from following suit."

"Well, if he proves to be a snoop, we certainly can't blame a neighbor for it, can we?" Jeanne retorted. "Not with his heritage."

Catherine folded her arms indignantly. "I hope you're not implying anything."

"I'll even wrap them," Ron broke in to promise. "Tie them up in neat ribbons."

Catherine beamed again. "Ah, so sweet."

"Ah, the ties that bind." Jeanne added, with less exuberance. She'd always been in charge of Toby's things. She certainly hadn't intended to entrust Toby's Christmas presents to Ron. In a way, it seemed riskier even than lovemaking.

Now where had that idea come from? she wondered. Why, he wasn't even kissing her.

The door creaked open and Toby popped out of the house in jeans and a sweatshirt. "Hey, I wanna have some fun too." He tipped his face up to survey the adults. "What's goin' on?"

Ron ruffled his blond hair. "Nothing at all."

Toby squeezed his fingers. "C'mon inside, Ronny. Let's play."

"I can't tonight. I have some writing to do."

Catherine clucked in regret. ''I thought you were on vacation!''

''Well, I'm doing an article for the Minneapolis *Clarion*. Hometown boy angle,'' he explained. He gave Jeanne's nose a playful tap. ''But don't worry, our special deadline is my first priority. 'Night everyone.''

Jeanne herded her family inside, determined that they not all stand on the stoop, waving farewell like a bunch of dopes. Catherine left soon after, blissfully convinced that Jeanne was on the road to an exciting romance.

Jeanne attempted to push all such thoughts out of her mind as she went about the business of making a hamburger hot dish. She found herself twitching her nose like a bunny's, however, over and over again in an effort to shake off the tingle his tap had left behind. In spite of her best efforts, she couldn't stop wondering just what it would be like to be really touched by him. All over...

She reached for her frying pan, then slammed the cupboard door. How dare he do this to her! Tempt her when she'd made it all so clear— She stopped herself abruptly. Clear as mud. That's what her message was like. She melted into his kisses, kissed him right back. And when he pressed her body to his, did she stiffen or wrench free? Oh, no, she turned into a soft pliable Raggedy Ann doll.

But it was all his fault just the same. If he weren't so sexy, so handsome, so strong all the time, she wouldn't be so attracted to him.

It simply wasn't fair. He was all wrong for her and had no business trying to convince her otherwise. How dare he act so irresistible when he was so obviously unsuitable?

9

RON WAS BUSY pounding the keys of his laptop when Emmett arrived home about ten. He couldn't see the front door from the dinette table, but he was quickly alerted to the fact that his grandfather wasn't alone. He listened intently for a moment, then relaxed again. It was Lenora's soprano blending with Emmett's rich bass. Soon they appeared in the room, minus their coats.

"Oh. Ron. You're here."

Emmett's greeting was flat, but Ron wouldn't give him the satisfaction of noticing. Instead he feigned raw terror. "Grandfather, Lenora. Together! If you two have joined forces, what chance do the rest of us have?"

Lenora shook a finger at him. "As if this isn't what you wanted in the first place!"

Ron grinned. "Okay, I confess. But you can't blame a guy for wanting to ensure his Gracie's discount."

"We'll help with the widow's boy, won't we, Santa?" Lenora lifted her chin as she regarded the grumpy Emmett.

"A grandson should use his own kin's discount! Not a lady's! Even if the lady is splendid in every way," he added silkily.

Ron rolled his eyes. Emmett's Romeo, as usual, was way over the top. "But you forced me to turn to another, Pop."

"That wasn't your Pop. It was Santa Claus, busy with his job."

"Well, I'll give you another chance tomorrow. We need a remote-control car. Suitable for preschoolers."

"If he doesn't make the purchase, I'll come through again," Lenora promised.

"I'll do it. Out of costume, before curtain time, as it should be." Emmett took special interest in the fact that Ron was typing. "Working on that article for the *Clarion*?" He turned proudly to Lenora. "Ron's snagged a job, doing an article for the paper across the river."

Ron rolled his eyes. "I never feel unemployed, you know that. All in all, I work more hours a year than most."

"Just like to tell people you're working, is all."

In truth, Ron hadn't even started the article until tonight, he'd been so wrapped up in writing about his experiences with the Trents. Writing about Jeanne and her family had helped him clear his head and put the situation in perspective. The people in his trade always said it was the cheapest form of therapy. And Ron agreed.

Emmett stalked to the table, clutching a stack of mail. Ron saved his work and cleared the screen. The old man was too wound up in himself to notice the bid for privacy.

"I stopped by the box downstairs. Something for you."

Ron held out his hand, but Emmett slapped the square green envelope on the table instead.

"There! How do you like having the unexpected thrown at you?"

"Not fair, Pop," Ron replied calmly. "I throw a whole girl at you, and all I get is this crummy card." He studied the return address. "Hmm, from the old neighborhood." Emmett handed him a letter opener, then came around to spy over his shoulder. "It's a party invitation. Sleigh ride up at the apple orchard, just like back in school."

"That Elaine was always a nice child." Emmett turned to Lenora. "She's the one you presented the gift certificate to last week."

Lenora smiled. "Seemed very nice."

"Yes, Ron could be settled with her, you know, but he dumped her after graduation." Emmett set his hand on

Ron's collarbone. "Wonder what she wants with you now? To show you she's done all right, maybe?"

"Most likely," Ron conceded, remembering how uncomfortable she'd been, caught looking anything but glamorous.

"Well, from a feminine perspective, I feel you owe her the chance to show off a little," Lenora observed. "It's no fun to be dumped at any age."

Ron objected. "I didn't mean to hurt her. Don't know if I even did."

"It'd be a proper closure to Christmas past," Emmett recommended.

Ron twisted in his chair, his temper rising. "I'll decide if I'm going."

"Take that widow along," Lenora suggested with brisk practicality. "Then everybody can impress everybody and part friends."

Or more than friends, perhaps. How nice it would be to get Jeanne away from the pressures of Christmas and her family. Maybe it would advance their relationship beyond Santa and scribbles. Ron nodded, smiling at Lenora. "I really like this one, Pop. Don't you let her slip away!"

Lenora scoffed. "I'm no passing fancy to any man, no matter how dynamic he may be!"

Emmett shook a fist. "Don't start with that Casanova stuff again."

"You promised me sherry, old-timer. Don't offer me any of those sickening wine coolers!"

"Wouldn't have the things under my roof!" the elegant actor thundered.

Lenora glanced at her watch. "It's a work night, you know. If you don't get moving, you won't have me under your roof, either. Or in your lap again."

Emmett frowned as he rummaged through his liquor cabinet like a common thief in the night. "Where is the blasted sherry, Ron?"

"In the kitchen. We used it in that cherry dessert thing, remember?" Taking up his notes and computer, Ron quickly headed for his bedroom.

"A SLEIGH RIDE this Friday night? Two days away?" Jeanne moved around her studio the following morning, her cordless telephone tucked under her chin. "Of course I sound breathless, Ron. I have a boy shoveling in cereal and a church choir coming for a portrait!"

"Can you keep Toby occupied without me?"

Jeanne smiled faintly at his interest. He really did seem to like being in the thick of their ordinary life. Crazy, but sweet. "We'll manage." She took some film out of a wall cupboard, set it on a table near her tripod, and examined the box to make sure it was the right speed. "Just have to keep him in view. So why is this date so last-minute?"

"You're not an afterthought, if that's what you think."

She fell silent. That was what she'd figured. How many afterthought invitations had she received this past year? Oh, yes, let's invite the poor widow. Or let's not. How many times had she been overlooked? Oh, how anxious she was to get to the end of this awkward year of firsts!

He swiftly went on. "I just got the invitation yesterday. A bunch of my old school pals get together every year for a sleigh ride. We've been doing it since the tenth grade."

"Oh, I see." She felt better, and it showed in her tone.

"I'm rarely in town, but I happened to run into my old girlfriend—happily married with five children, by the way—and she must've thought of me for that reason."

"How'd she look? The old girlfriend, I mean?"

"Happy. Can I please come over!"

"Wish you wouldn't."

"But why, Jeanne?"

"Just a minute." Jeanne hurried to the studio door and closed it firmly. "Listen, I have another mission for you. If you're interested."

"Oh?"

"Don't make that sound."

"What sound?"

"That purry growl."

"Didn't know I was."

"Liar." Her own voice was a growl now but more threatening.

His chuckle rippled over the wire. "Okay, tell me what you want."

"I've uncovered another of the scribbles," she confided happily.

"Good for you! What is it?"

"A basketball."

"That's an easy one. I'll get on it today, along with the remote-control car."

She took a hesitant breath. "You don't mind, do you?"

"Give me my candy-cane kisses in return and we'll be square."

Her laugh was merry and spontaneous.

"You know, Jeanne," he said with sudden inspiration, "I bet we can guess the next scribble as well."

"How so?"

"Well, don't you think Toby would expect a hoop with that basketball?"

"You know, he would," she agreed. "He's wanted one since last summer."

"Great. I'll add it to the shopping list."

She sank into the chair at her cluttered desk, a deep sound of relief rising from her throat. "I know I seem a wreck about all this, Ron, but every scribble we decode, well..."

"I understand, honey," he said gently. "It decreases the odds that Toby made a wish that had something to do with his father."

She blinked her moist eyes. "Yes, exactly."

"We're almost there. Four wishes down, two to go."

‘‘You’ve been wonderful about everything,’’ she said with a sniff.

‘‘Wonderful enough to get a real date out of you?’’

She made a doubtful sound. ‘‘Meeting your old girlfriend?’’

‘‘And my other long-lost friends.’’

‘‘I’m surprised you don’t want to dazzle the old crowd with some knockout. A foreign correspondent, a Miss America.’’

‘‘It’s probably what they would expect—’’

‘‘See!’’

‘‘And maybe a few years ago I might have done it, just to show the guys.’’ He sighed heavily, then spoke as though dredging up his words from the depths of his being. ‘‘But I’ve come full circle, Jeanne. I started out with an angel of a girl and I’m back on track again. With you.’’

Damn him for saying the right thing! Jeanne tipped back in the springy chair, and rubbed her temples, then the lips he’d kissed so long and so well. She had, of course, imagined dating him for real. It fit right in with making out in her kitchen and dining with her family. Why, most people would have started right off with a date or two before all the rest.

But to start off with his old crowd? That would be a tough, bonded audience full of preconceived notions and expectations. No way would they mistake her for some sophisticated global player. Oh, how she’d love to pass on this one. But he wouldn’t want to go alone. If she said no, she’d run the risk of losing him to another date. The idea of losing him to someone else sent a painful jab clear though her. Despite all her precautions, she was growing more and more attached.

‘‘Jeanne?’’

‘‘I’m thinking,’’ she claimed nervously.

‘‘I know you must have reservations,’’ he pressed on. ‘‘I expected it.’’

"Oh, really?" she challenged in a sharper tone.

"You'll perhaps be the only stranger," he went on evenly. "Won't know the inside stuff. And then there'll be the curiosity to face, the questions about your life."

His insight gave her the strength to play devil's advocate to her own fears. "I'm sure everyone would be most friendly."

"I can guarantee that much."

"And there won't be questions I haven't answered before."

"So true."

"And we won't have to tell any lies together, for the first time."

His rich laughter filled the wire. "Now who's selling whom?"

"Okay, Ron," she decided abruptly. "It's a date."

There was joy and surprise in his tone. "Great. Don't know what tipped the scales—"

"That's easy," she cut in saucily. "I see my chance to be needed by you for a change." Without giving him the chance to respond, she slid her finger over the Disconnect button.

IN ALL HIS LIFE he'd never understand women. When Ron stabbed the Trent doorbell on Friday shortly after four, he should have been the happiest man alive, but instead he was angry.

More than ever, he was sure that Jeanne was the woman for him, but he couldn't help but wonder if he was getting through to her at all. Could she truly be blind to the fact that he needed her? This was much more than a game to him, a scavenger hunt over a Christmas list. Did she really think he'd go to all this trouble just for a little holiday fling?

He most certainly wouldn't. And she should know better by now!

Was he somehow at fault for her nagging misconceptions? He shifted from one boot to another and adjusted his new royal-blue ski jacket, self-recrimination oozing over his flaming temper like extinguishing foam. Maybe he hadn't made his stand clear enough in his effort not to push her. Maybe he was still coming off like one of his press releases: reckless, tough, larger than life.

She opened the door then, hopelessly pretty and fragile in a bulky, red-nylon ski suit. "Sorry to keep you waiting."

He stared at her mutely. At that moment, every setback they'd shared was melted to nothing by her wide and lovely smile. She looked nothing short of a dream date just then, nervous, breathless and ardent. At twenty-six she could easily pass for an impatient teenager.

What was he angry about? For the life of him he couldn't remember. He walked Jeanne toward the car feeling more than a little like an eager teenager, himself.

"Where are we headed?" Jeanne asked as she clicked her seat belt into place.

"East to Marlowe, a small town near the Wisconsin border." Ron made the reply as he backed the rental car down her narrow driveway with a little more speed than was wise. He couldn't help but notice she was staring at her neighbor's house, the white stucco one where Toby would be spending the evening with his pal Jason. He hoped she'd be able to leave family concerns behind, that they'd be able to forge a new path as a couple.

"Elaine's Uncle Chet has an apple orchard up there," he continued. "He runs sleighs through his property at this time of year to supplement his income."

Jeanne studied his profile. "So, Elaine must be the one? Your high-school flame?"

He gave her a surprised look as he slowed for a stop sign. "Yes, how did you know?"

"Your tone, that's all."

"It was all over long ago," he assured her.

She reached over and patted his thigh. "I'm sure it was,

Ron. All I mean is, because I married my school sweetheart myself, I know just how you must feel. I'm touched that you're still fond of her."

Ron shook his head in wonder. A woman who understood him. It seemed almost too good to be true.

LITTLE HAD CHANGED in Marlowe. Ron remembered the general location of the orchard and with the help of some road signs, and easily rediscovered the long private road leading to Chet's old, rambling farmhouse and barn.

There already were several cars parked in the small roped-off lot near the barn. Ron came to a stop there. Jeanne didn't get out in the open spaces much and popped out of the car with enthusiasm.

"It's right out of a Christmas card, Ron!"

He rounded the car and curved an arm around her red-suited shoulders. She hugged his waist, and together they marveled over the landscape. Dusk was setting in fast and the moon was illuminating the snow on the ground. Rows and rows of small trees lined the property, their branches heavy with tiny white lights.

There was activity near the barn, so they slowly strolled in that direction. Once they cleared the house they had a clearer view of what was going on. Two dark Morgans were harnessed to a large black antique sleigh. A group of joyous adults, six in number, were clustered nearby around a small bonfire.

Ron called out to them.

Hoots and hollers followed, and many expressions of shock over his appearance. Ron took all the teasing like a good sport and introduced Jeanne at every turn.

When all the hugs and handshakes had been exchanged Jeanne stood at his elbow, digging her toe into the mix of snow and dirt, feeling awkward. As was common with old friends, the men and women had divided, forming separate groups on either side of the fire.

Jeanne was unsure what to do. Her dating skills were dead. That was all there was to it. From the frozen-food section in the supermarket to the vast frozen tundra was too broad a jump to make so soon.

"Jeanne, is it?"

Jeanne turned to find Elaine squeezing her elbow. "Yes."

"Come join the girls," she invited in a merry whisper. "We want to hear all Ron's secrets, the ones his folks don't know or won't tell us."

"Hey, Laine!" Ron made the mock protest, but was relieved. Jeanne knew nothing particularly juicy about him to share and in his opinion she needed the female companionship.

Before Jeanne knew what was happening, she'd downed two hot-rum drinks and was telling everyone about the time she and her friends traveled to a fair not far from here in Wisconsin to get an interview and photos of the Beach Boys for their school newspaper. The story, which involved the police and local radio station, gradually caught the attention of the men, who in turn edged their way around the fire to listen.

"And that was the inspiration for Jeanne's chosen career," Ron proclaimed, tugging her close.

Hoots and laughter followed.

Elaine's Uncle Chet made his way down the lane from the house, announcing that it was time to climb aboard the sleigh. The men and women paired off, adjusting each other's mittens and caps.

Ron removed his glove for a moment to tap Jeanne's nose. "Having fun?"

Jeanne giggled, her face flushed by the chilly air and alcohol. "There's that purry growl again. And yes, I am. I'd forgotten how nice it is to let go and mingle this way. A lot of our old friends, David's and mine I mean, sort of drifted out of my life this year." She shrugged beneath her bulky clothing. "Guess they didn't know what to do with me."

Ron didn't even know them and still found himself angry.

She easily read his frown. "Can't blame them, really. I wasn't ready to date, and was the odd person out at a dinner party."

Ron found this strict social code surprising, but he responded lightly. "All those women were probably afraid you'd attract their husbands."

She laughed and rapped his chest with her mitten. "You obviously mingle in a whole different way."

"We'll just have to experiment and see."

"Hey, c'mon, Ron!"

He turned toward the sleigh. Everyone was crowded together on the cushions. Chet gestured to a spot big enough for one. A perfect fit for the two of them. With a grand sweeping gesture he scooped Jeanne into his arms and climbed aboard.

The powerful horses trotted along the snowy paths between the rows of lit-up trees at a brisk tilt. The wind was pretty nippy, but Elaine's husband Tony started a round of Christmas carols to warm things up. Everyone joined in, frequently botching the words of the famous songs.

All the while Ron held Jeanne in his lap. Under other circumstances she might have been uncomfortable with the way he was nuzzling her neck and pressing his hands into her belly. But in this crowd of people who'd been married for eons the atmosphere was casual, and very affectionate. Did she dare begin to think about rebuilding that kind of relationship so soon? Had she been so fortunate as to find someone right all over again without a lengthy search? Only time would tell. All she knew for sure was that it felt so incredibly good to belong to someone again. To let go and have some fun.

A huge buffet dinner followed in the farmhouse kitchen.

Elaine's Uncle Chet and Aunt Doreen followed their guests round the main floor of the house offering food and pitchers of hot-rum drink. The hours slipped by in a glorious blur of singing, talking and smooching under the mistletoe.

Ron was sitting on the large rust-colored sofa with Jeanne when it occurred to him that he should hunt up Elaine. "Naturally, everybody chips in for this extravaganza," he murmured to Jeanne before rising on unsteady legs. Jeanne blinked dizzily as he cornered his old girlfriend near the dining room.

There was nothing to worry about, she told herself sternly. Elaine was a happily married woman. Still, Jeanne couldn't help but envy the easy body language between them, the way Ron pinched her chin. It was the same way he pinched *her* chin!

"Ah, Jeanne."

Jeanne slowly turned to find that Cathy, a tall brunette married to a plastic surgeon, was sitting down on the cushion beside her. Cathy was definitely the most monied of the bunch. Jeanne's plaid blouse and black slacks probably cost less than the woman's silver headband.

"You look like you're in a daze," Cathy observed with good humor.

"Not used to drinking so much," Jeanne admitted, tipping her glass mug in a toast. "And I've just been admiring the Christmas tree in the corner," she thought to add. It was on Ron and Elaine's left, a perfect cover for spying on them.

"Yeah, must be nice to have so many ornaments. Different kinds with memories attached." Cathy sighed wistfully. "Doug and I have gold bells all over the tree. He likes things orderly, you see."

"Some people do," Jeanne said absently. Ron was squeezing Elaine's shoulders now, digging his fingers into her inexpensive pink-and-white sweater. What were they saying to each other? She turned back to Cathy with searching eyes. How could Elaine look far more stunning in her discount-store sweater than Cathy did in her elegant, melon-colored cashmere pantsuit?

"Ron says you have a son," Cathy prompted.

"Yes, Toby." Jeanne's expression softened as she gave the woman her full attention. "He's four."

"I have a four-year-old girl," Cathy told her. "We really should get the children together."

"That would be nice."

"I don't live all that far from you. In North Oaks."

Jeanne smiled. Everyone in town knew of the elite community. "Sounds wonderful. We'll arrange something after the holidays." She stood up. So did Cathy.

Cathy reached into her small handbag. "Here's one of my cards. I'm a realtor by trade. You can reach me at home or at work."

"Sounds wonderful." Jeanne struggled to keep her features even, though the mission to disrupt Ron's rendezvous was eating at her like a fever. "Now, I believe I'll just go have a closer look at some of those fine old flames—I mean ornaments." She patted Cathy's arm. "Excuse me."

Jeanne was disappointed when she swiveled around, however. Ron was nowhere in sight. And neither was Elaine.

With as much indifference as she could muster, Jeanne paused by the tree to examine its treasures. She peered through the doorway into the dining room to find that most of the guests, including Tony, were in the middle of a boisterous round of poker. But Ron and Elaine were not in sight. It took all her self-control to stay in place for several seconds, admiring a hand-painted angel on a loop of gold lamé.

Was Elaine the one he still wanted? It was unlikely that he could have her ever again, Jeanne speculated. She and Tony seemed hopelessly in love. And Elaine's Uncle Chet had proudly shown her the framed photographs of the Rosetti children lining an upstairs hallway.

Of course, whether Ron would succeed at this game was beside the point. All that mattered to Jeanne were his intentions. With a contrived air of nonchalance, Jeanne sauntered through the dining-room area. She declined the round of invitations to blow on cards for good luck, sit on laps for better luck, or join the next hand to try her own luck with as much grace as she could manage, then whizzed through the opposite door leading into the kitchen.

The bright room was full of outdated olive-colored appliances and devoid of life, aside from Aunt Doreen. The stout, dark-haired woman had a blue gingham apron on over her holiday dress and was replenishing the food supply still spread out on the oval table. She met Jeanne on a return trip to the refrigerator. "Hungry, Jeanne?"

"Maybe a little," she fibbed, reaching for a soft, minty piece of taffy. She held it up before popping it into her mouth. "You pull this yourself?"

"No, there's a sweetshop in town. You should have Ron take you there tomorrow. Why, he and Elaine used to spend hours in there, back in the days when they had a soda fountain."

Jeanne nibbled at the candy. "I'm afraid we won't be around tomorrow."

"Aren't you staying the night? Everyone else is."

She paused. "Oh? First I heard of it."

Doreen clicked her tongue. "I wouldn't have been serving Ron all that rum if I'd known he intended to drive back."

"I'd better find out if we're staying. Have you seen Ron, Doreen?"

"He trotted through here with Elaine just a few minutes ago." She curled her fist. "Wait till I get my hands on that boy."

Jeanne curled a fist, too. Beautifully put.

Doreen filled a tray with drinks and cookies and headed for the dining room. Jeanne moved in the opposite direction, past the sink, toward the door into a hallway and the open staircase which led to the next level.

She started slowly down the dimly lit hallway. That was when she heard a squeal and a rumble coming from behind a closed door. A familiar, purry kind of rumble. It was a bedroom, too, the one where they'd stashed their things. Winding her arm up for the pitch, she lunged inside the room.

Unlike the hall, this room was well lit. And there stood Ron, holding Elaine in his arms. Kissing her for all he was worth.

10

''JEANNE!'' the pair chorused, breaking apart.

Jeanne couldn't believe what happened next. Elaine was actually reaching for her—as if she could smooth things over! She quickly stepped back, speechless and furious. ''Don't...let me bother you.''

She wasn't sure where she got the poise, but Jeanne managed a sure-footed retreat, and slammed the door shut within inches of Ron's nose. The hinges creaked open immediately and she heard Ron's footsteps behind her.

''Jeanne!'' he whispered. ''Wait!''

''Keep quiet, you mean!'' she whirled back to fling at him. She squinted in the dimness, frustrated that he didn't look terrified. Christmas music blared in the background, along with all the jolly human noises of those Jeanne suddenly perceived as blissfully naive. ''I'm nothing but a cover, a front for your shenanigans!''

''That's silly.''

Hissing a few well-chosen phrases she hadn't said or heard since her adolescence, she charged back into the kitchen and through a door she was certain led to the mudroom and the yard. Unfortunately, she found herself in a dark, stuffy, unfamiliar space.

Ron was chuckling as he joined her. ''Jelly, anyone? Jam maybe? How about some pickles?''

''Huh?'' She could feel his arm grazing her temple, and within seconds a bare bulb flicked on overhead. They were in a pantry about four feet square, surrounded by Doreen's canned goods. "Damn you, you beast!"

"Can I help it if you have no sense of direction?" He leaned against a shelf of peaches, a lazy smile on his lips. "Besides," he said more sternly, "this is no night to be running around outside. It must be close to zero by now."

Jeanne felt her eyes moisten and covered her face with her hands. "I think I hate you. I really think I do."

His eyes grew with the revelation. "Finally taking a stand, then?"

"What's that 'sposed to mean?"

He peeled her hands off her face with a growl. "I mean you've been avoiding all kinds of feeling for me. Until now. When you think the worst."

"Hah! And what about poor Tony and all the little Rosettis?" She extended her lower lip poutily.

"Don't change the subject. Let's talk about me and you."

She inhaled. "Okay. Let's talk about me, and how you decided I'm a replacement for Elaine—"

"Replacement?" he squawked in amazement.

"We do have a lot in common," she said bitingly. "Coloring, home-fire instincts."

"Oh, Jeanne." He exhaled and paused to choose the right words. "Look, I admit had I been ready way back when, Elaine would've been the one for me, but you're not a replacement. You're you. What I want now."

"But you just had to sample the old vintage, didn't you?"

"No," he denied hotly. "You're the one holding up the show here, walking on eggshells, reluctant to express yourself. I've tried so hard to get you to open up, and you lay this on me now of all times."

"Well, I don't hold my liquor very well," she explained defensively. "We Potters tend to express ourselves better while tipsy. But of course I've had feelings for you all along. Would I be here if I didn't?''

''You've made me feel like an intruder in your life from the start,'' he said angrily. ''Made me feel like a reckless bum who breaks every heart in sight, and has a hungry eye on yours. Do you have any idea how much it upset me to hear you say that I finally needed you for a change? How could you miss the fact that I've needed and wanted you all along?''

She swallowed hard, as she absorbed the admission. ''I guess I've been so wrapped up in my own situation, so frustrated by the trap set by my family, I haven't seen the clear picture.''

''Helping you is what I needed to do,'' he sought to explain. ''I needed to be needed, I guess you could say. It's been my pleasure to be there for you. I haven't had much experience in the giving department. I've been on my own so long with only myself to take care of.''

''That's right,'' she fired back with a poke to his chest. ''Your public image isn't a home-fires composite. Naturally I'd be cautious.''

''But you should be over that by now!''

''How can you say that, when I just caught you with Elaine?''

''Forget Elaine till later. Trust me, it was nothing.''

''Tony's the poor guy who will have to forget—''

''Hush!'' He clamped a hand over her mouth, his brown eyes blazing. ''Okay, here goes. When you returned the gift certificate to Gracie's, I went back to the store intending to return it. Lenora refused to give me a refund. I decided to shop for Emmett's gift there.''

She wrenched his fingers off her mouth. ''At Grace Brothers?''

''He's been behaving like a child, so it seemed fitting. Anyway, by providence I ran into Elaine there, for the first time in years. Jeanne, you should've seen her, with kids in tow, dressed in an ancient coat, disheveled as mothers sometimes are."

Jeanne blinked as her eyes moistened again. She had an idea of where he was headed.

"Anyhow, we talked, about Tony and his new garage. I realized money was tight—"

"And decided to give the certificate to her?"

"Indirectly. Lenora helped me."

Her features softened. "No wonder Lenora's so fond of you."

"Well, the rest is obvious. I paid Elaine for our part in this party and it reminded her that she wanted a showdown about that windfall in Gracie's. She dragged me into the bedroom—"

"Dragged? A first for you, I bet."

"Jeanne..." he muttered threateningly.

"Oops, old habit. Go on."

"She suspected the certificate deal was rigged from the start, and wanted to know if I was behind it. I confessed, and she was kissing me in thanks."

"Oh, Ron, I'm sorry."

"Tony knows all about it," he added dryly. "And to tell you the truth, I'm just as glad he decided not to kiss me, too. Now can we please forget about the Rosettis?"

"All right," she agreed quietly. "And if you're still interested, I do care for you."

"But why have you fought it so hard?"

"Because you weren't in the plan," she blurted out. "I had it in my head that I was going to get back in circulation after the holidays, and I thought I wanted a man like David." She shook her head dazedly. "I just didn't figure on falling in love at this time, especially with a man so different." She raised her palms in surrender. "But you've got me cornered every which way. Why, I was ready to duke it out with Elaine back there! Take it outside into the snow."

"Wow." He seized her in his arms then, and pulled her flush against him. "When you let go...wow!"

She sighed softly. "It's the Potter way. A little Christmas, a little rum and you've got yourself a basket case."

He pressed his lips to her hairline. "Oh, Jeanne, I absolutely adore you, honey. You drive me crazy, but I still can't resist the trip."

Her eyes grew large. "Is that the best smooch you can come up with?"

He rocked back on his heels. "'Fraid so. I kiss you anyplace else and I don't think we could walk out of here."

She instinctively smoothed her clothing. "That reminds me, Doreen wants to speak to you."

"Why?"

"Something about drinking and driving."

"Oh." He clearly understood.

"Seems everybody's accustomed to staying the night," she said scoldingly.

He nodded. "I didn't think you'd come at all if you knew about that tradition."

"I'm not sure we have a choice now. Both of us are unfit for the road."

"Can you manage, with Toby at Jason's?"

"Yes," she decided, glad that he thought to ask. "But I do think I'll give them a call and explain."

"Let's do it before it gets any later." Ever so gently, Ron eased open the pantry door a crack. He could see no one from his vantage point, so he hustled Jeanne out into the kitchen. Christmas tunes wafting in from the living room provided the background music for the expectant crowd hovering around the kitchen table, snacking with their fingers. Waiting for the closet show's dramatic climax.

Jeanne scanned them all with amazing aplomb. "There was no telephone in there, after all."

Chet, munching on a lemon bar, chuckled. "I swear,

somebody ends up in that cupboard each and every year! Virtually soundproof, too, darn it.''

Elaine sidled up to Jeanne with a captivating smile and shining green eyes. ''You really need the phone?''

Jeanne smiled apologetically. ''Yes. Not like me to take a wrong turn that way.''

Elaine nodded, understanding and accepting her apology. ''Calling the baby-sitter, I bet.''

''Yes.''

''Come along, there's a more private one in Uncle Chet's study.''

The crowd dispersed thereafter. Some headed for the dining room parlor game, others drifted to the bedroom for their overnight totes.

''So, uh, do you have room for us to stay, Doreen?'' Ron asked rather awkwardly.

'''Course we do,'' Doreen assured him with wink. ''Up in that attic you helped me clean out fifteen years ago.'' Her voice dropped a notch. ''Speak to Jeanne about the arrangements. If she prefers feminine company, I'll join her and you can bunk with Chet. A little cotton in your ears, and you won't notice the snoring half as much.''

Ron rolled his eyes. Jeanne wouldn't do that to him, would she?

''GUESS WE'RE LUCKY to have a room to ourselves,'' Jeanne commented, sizing up the twin sleigh beds in the third story attic. Her eyes came to rest on the left one, on which Ron was stretched out beneath a pale yellow comforter, pillows propped against the sloping headboard. Presumably he'd stripped down to his skivvies. His white T-shirt was still pulled tight across his chest.

Ron smiled, thinking how lost she looked in Doreen's spare flannel nightie. ''It's a full house all right. This space is the last choice because of the cold. I suppose it's tough to heat.''

''You weren't even going to tell me about Doreen's offer, were you?'' Jeanne said accusingly.

Ron stretched his strong arms with a groan. ''Aw, gee, Jeanne. I couldn't stand to sleep with Chet. He snores and mumbles.''

''Okay, okay.'' She shuffled closer. He flicked back his covers and moved to the far edge of the mattress.

''Come here, honey.''

She stared at his body for a long, startled moment. Long, lean limbs, so strong and dark on the taut white sheet. ''I don't know, Ron. If I'm ready, I mean...''

''We can at least hold each other, can't we? Keep warm?''

A soft sigh escaped her. David had been the only man she'd ever slept with. This kind of invitation was no doubt commonplace to Ron. And most single women her age probably wouldn't have a qualm. She finally cleared her throat. ''You know my own nightie is a lot like this one.''

As if he hadn't already guessed! She was a practical woman accustomed to dressing for her own convenience. Big deal. Couldn't she see that he liked her exactly as she was?

''You know what I'm driving at?'' she asked tentatively.

He couldn't resist giving the matter the consideration she expected. ''That you like being warm?''

''Well, yes, but—'' She broke off, spotting the teasing glint in his eye.

He patted the mattress. ''Me, too.''

''But I wasn't expecting anything like this!''

''I wasn't either,'' he admitted gently. ''Wasn't expecting to find myself caring so much for a woman that I'd be willing just to hold her through the night if that's all she wants.'' His handsome face grew dark with emotion. ''I need you so close, so badly, Jeanne, that I'm willing to do it any way you say.''

''Oh, Ron.'' With a surrendering moan she climbed in

beside him. He swiftly closed the covers over them as though to seal her in.

He cradled her against his chest and buried his face in her hair. It smelled of the outdoors, woodsmoke and dinner. "I know this is all a spinning cyclone in your mind. That it's been tough to leave Toby overnight with the neighbor, venture into a group of my old friends. And now, end up in bed with me."

She quivered along his length, her softness sheer torture against his hard, sinewy muscles. He swallowed hard, struggling to keep his voice steady. "I would never pressure you..."

He wouldn't force her. But pressure? It was a natural part of his character. As she nuzzled her cheek into his rib cage, her mouth crooked in a smile.

"But if you'd be interested..." He trailed off in a tempting rumble.

She tipped her head up then, and planted her mouth on his for a featherlight taste. Ron wanted to take hold of her and pull her down for a grinding kiss. But he resisted. It had to be her move. Her choice.

The decision was a good one. Jeanne seemed to enjoy setting the pace. She set her hands on his chest and kissed him more deeply and wantonly. Lustily. There wasn't a nuance he missed.

The way her breasts were crushing against his ribs.

The way her hands were grasping his hips.

The way her thigh was nudging his groin.

The way she was climbing on top of him...

With a groan he stretched out flat on the bed. Her mating moves were so slow and so subtle, he felt he had to be dreaming. And the forever kind of kiss went on and on throughout. Their slicked lips slid over each other's, whetting their appetites.

Ron's control was slipping. Confident that she was willing and ready, he ever-so-gently pulled her nightgown up over her head and tossed it aside. With a desire-roughened touch, he skimmed his hands over her silky back, massaged her hips, clenched her bottom. His erection was rigid behind the cotton barrier of his briefs. Over and over again, he pushed her groin into his with a pressure-packed undulation.

Jeanne inched up his T-shirt, tugged it off, and began nibbling at his nipples, She licked and nipped them to sensitive pebbles in the chilly room, and caressed his skin with bolder and bolder strokes. With a shiver, Ron pulled the covers over their shoulders. As he did so he could feel her fingers on the elastic of his briefs, inching them down. She caught them with her toes at midthigh, then pulled them clean off with sort of a flutter kick. Their naked bodies rubbing together made them shiver with anticipation.

Tipping his head up, Ron lost himself in the softness of her breasts. Her heart pounding wildly in her chest made him think of a new and unsure filly. But all she needed was encouragement, assurances that she was all he wanted in this world. A flame to reignite her fuse.

With an abruptness that jolted him to the core of his being, she suddenly arched and swallowed his shaft in her feminine opening.

The moist grazing friction made them both gasp and quake.

''You witch,'' he uttered hoarsely, blinking up into her eyes of blue fire.

The fuse was lit all right.

Clamping his hands to her hipbones, he raised and lowered her over him.

Jeanne grasped his arms for balance, entranced by his strength, the tantalizing, burning rub of their bodies. And the motions. Faster and faster their bodies moved together until their passions reached a pinnacle.

Jeanne's slender spine arched back, her hair tumbled in a golden shimmer and she cried out ever so softly in complete fulfillment. Ron climaxed soon after with a guttural, masculine, triumphant sound.

She collapsed on his heaving chest to share a deep carnal kiss as their breathing slowed. Finally she rested her head in the curve of his shoulder.

He reached up and rapped his knuckle on the curving headboard. ''Now, didn't I promise you a fun ride? And you, lucky lady, ended up with two!''

Jeanne laughed, bending the pillow into his face. ''Get too smart and you'll end up in the barn—in the other sleigh.''

He chuckled deep and low, and drew her under the quilt. ''Just try and get rid of me now. Give me some more of that body rub. I dare ya.''

So she did.

11

"GOOD MORNING, POP." Ron glanced up from his laptop computer as Emmett appeared in the kitchen doorway, still dressed in his silk pajamas. "Getting off to a slow start, eh?"

Emmett yawned hugely. "Well, it is a Saturday. What time is it?"

"Nearly ten." Ron motioned with his disheveled brown head toward the side counter. "There's some fresh coffee there."

Emmett helped himself to a mug. "Aren't *we* chipper," he observed in dry surprise. "And ambitious. Out all night and straight on to work."

"Got a fair amount of sleep. Enough to last me." Ron paused pensively, wondering if in truth he could ever get enough sack time with Jeanne. The ritual of intense, impetuous sex followed by a deep, sound sleep was one he could easily grow accustomed to. "Anyway, I have to stick with this article for Burt Waters over at the *Clarion*. Tomorrow's my deadline."

"So you decided on a title?"

"Recapturing the Spirit of Home." Ron noted Emmett's approving noises, then went back to typing. "Yesterday's reunion gave me the insight I needed to finish. So glad I went."

"Did you stay up at the orchard with Elaine's relatives?"

"Everybody did, just like the old days."

"Jeanne have a good time?"

Ron struggled to keep his expression indifferent. "Oh, I think so."

Emmett rummaged through his bread box, and pulled out a loaf of whole-wheat. "Yes, I scored myself last night."

Ron's fingers flew up from the keys. "Better watch your terms, Pop. Might land you in trouble."

Emmett regarded him crossly. "Your ears suddenly delicate? Frostbitten, maybe?"

"I mean you wouldn't want to slip in front of Jeanne or Lenora. They're irreplaceable."

"Yes, right. But we lads are alone, aren't we?"

"Yes, it does seem to be our condition too often." Ron made a show of returning to the keyboard. Hopefully, Emmett would drop the issue.

Emmett moved closer, though, his pale eyes bright with curiosity. "So you going to marry this Jeanne?"

Ron met his gaze smugly. "You marryin' Lenora?"

Emmett arched like a mighty eagle. Ron prepared himself for a lengthy lecture.

"Asked you first," the old man said childishly.

Ron roared with laughter. "I expect an applause-getting soliloquy and get, 'asked you first?'"

"Well, I did. And I expect an answer."

"To be honest, I just don't know yet." Ron steepled his fingers and used them to prop his chin. "But it's very possible."

Pleased with himself and the news, Emmett wandered over to the counter and set two pieces of bread in the toaster. "Well, I have to admit you were right about Lenora's being quite a dish. But in my case, I'm not so sure about a legal knot. It's so important, picking a mate for life!"

Ron made a thoughtful sound. "Tough decision. She is about twenty years younger than you are. Probably has a bit more zip, and a more active life-style. And she's liable to work full-time for another few years, until she's sixty-five.''

''Are you insinuating that she might not be ready and willing to accept my proposal, if I choose to make one? Why—'' Emmett paused in midstorm. ''Oh, yes, see what you mean. She might not see me as the catch of the year.''

''Then again, she might,'' Ron returned kindly. ''I just think you should give her the option.''

''Agh, sometimes I forget I'm eighty.''

''So do I,'' Ron agreed. ''One day you seem five, the next fifty, then seventy. You're all over the map.''

''Still, you're right. A little humility with a hot babe like Lenora might help the cause.'' He brought his toast to the table and sat beside his grandson. ''Speaking of things hot, son, I'd like that photo Jeanne took of Lenora on my knee.''

Ron chuckled in reminiscence. ''Jeanne is having some copies made for you.''

Emmett brightened. ''Good. Saves me the trouble.''

''Oh, by the way, thanks for picking up Toby's toys.''

Emmett sniffed. ''Nothing to it. That reminds me, though. The mother called.''

Ron's jaw tightened. ''Catherine?''

''Yes. She certainly is bubbly, isn't she?''

''But she's trouble for us right now, Pop. If she comes to realize that you're the no-good Santa who spoke to Toby, we'll both be done for.''

''Find her quite irresistible just the same,'' Emmett went on grandly.

''So, what did she want?''

''Wanted to know if she could come over and wrap Toby's presents. Gave me a delightful line of patter about how all the gifts should be done up in the same paper, with a neatness worthy of Mrs. Claus. If you ask me, I think she's angling to get to know us better.''

''Hope you said no.''

''Naturally. And most regrettably. I covered by saying

that she might as well hold off until you've unearthed the last items."

"Perfect answer, Pop."

"So, how many more scribbles are left?"

"Well, presuming that I'm right about the hoop, two."

"Better hurry up."

"I'm trying to, Pop. Christmas Eve is next Tuesday, and Jeanne definitely needs all the stuff by then."

"No, I mean you'd better hurry the romance. Once you deliver up the goods, you may be kicked out of the nest."

Ron glared at him. "I might be tempted to make a romantic call if you felt the compulsion to shave or something."

Emmett laboriously got to his feet and shuffled off agreeably. What he didn't know was that Ron had been putting off this call for a couple of hours. If Jeanne was regretting their fantasy evening he was in no hurry to find out.

"Closing the bathroom door now!" Emmett called out.

"That's the last progress report I want to hear out that bathroom, Romeo!" Taking a bolstering breath, he picked up the receiver pressed Jeanne's number and waited anxiously as her phone rang.

"MOMM-E-E-E, Ronny wants to talk to you."

Jeanne sat up straight in the bathtub. "Is he at the door?"

"On the phone, Mommy." The doorknob jiggled. "You locked you in."

She smiled wryly. "Oh, sorry, champ."

There was a faint thumping sound near the floor. "Phone won't fit under, Mommy."

"Toby, where is Angie?"

"Right here" came her sister's muffled response.

"Hang on, I'm coming out."

Jeanne whisked open the door seconds later, wrapped in a bulky pink fleece robe. She stared anxiously at Angie's empty hands. "Where is the telephone?"

The normally confident big sister was looking altogether frazzled and embarrassed. ''Toby ran away with it.''

''Oh, Angie!''

''He doesn't listen to anything I say,'' Angie complained loudly.

With a huff of disgust, Jeanne flounced down the hallway. ''How can you let that child outfox you all the time?''

Angie trailed after her sister. ''I can't help it. I tried to make cleaning out your refrigerator a game.''

Jeanne stopped in the foyer, and spun around in amazement. ''Cleaning out my what?''

''It was a real disaster,'' Angie claimed. ''Tossing in a box of baking soda every six months isn't a cure-all.''

Jeanne raised a finger to defend her fridge, but decided against a tongue-lashing. She'd save her energy to deal with Ron's smooth tongue. The things it said, the places it went. Her damp body shivered beneath her robe.

Angie noticed her condition, and promptly misjudged the cause. ''You're going to catch a cold, half wet, half dressed.''

''Oh, go—'' Jeanne sputtered in frustration. ''Go clean out the freezer section!''

Angie saluted with glee. ''Yes, ma'am!'' With a click of her heels she was off to the kitchen.

Toby was clearly visible from the foyer. He was standing in the living room near the Christmas tree in his Disney-print pajamas, clutching the cordless phone, his blond head bobbing as he told Ron all about Jason's tree and how the Trent's was so much better. Jeanne listened from the doorway for a few minutes, convinced that Toby was in heaven.

It seemed only fair, since she'd been there for hours last night.

Finally, when Toby seemed to be repeating himself, she stepped up to take the instrument from him. ''Hi, Ron.''

''Hi, yourself.''

''Did I catch you at a bad time?''

''No—yes. I mean, well, I have a grueling day ahead.'' She closed her eyes, knowing how clipped she sounded. But it was the circumstances, not the company. ''After playing yesterday, I really have to keep the old nose to the grindstone today.''

''Oh.''

She paced round the room, biting her lip. ''I'm sorry. I just get like this under pressure.''

''Been there, done that,'' he said with forced cheer.

''So, you understand?'' she asked hopefully.

''Of course. Any chance of a break later? I'd like to come over, spend some time with Toby, finish off that scavenger hunt.''

''Not today, Ron. I just won't have a single minute today.''

''Tonight, then.''

''Even worse!'' she lamented, rubbing her forehead.

''I suppose I could finish up my article for the newspaper,'' he said grumpily.

''Sounds like a good idea,'' she enthused. ''Keep you busy.''

''About last night, Jeanne. Doesn't it seem like—''

''A million miles away?'' she finished, as she reached for a stray sock wedged between two sofa cushions.

''I was going to call it magic.''

She squeezed the receiver, her voice dropping to a whisper. ''It was really special for me, too. But you know how—''

''Know what!''

She winced at the thunder in his voice. ''That I have so much on my mind in the upcoming days. Obligations.''

''Well, if you're really busy—''

''I am. Look, I have to go. Toby's carrying a five-quart bucket of ice cream around the house. Toby, it's breakfast time!'' she shouted. Then on a note of regret she closed with a simple, '''Bye, Ron.''

"Ice cream?" Ron slammed down the telephone with force. "Why the kid couldn't begin to reach the freezer door handle. What a dumb excuse. What a dumb lie!"

Emmett, now freshly shaven and in his street clothes, peered into the kitchen. "Everybody going out for ice cream?"

"No, Pop. Nobody's going anywhere."

RON KEPT TELLING himself he was going no place. Lenora stopped by on her lunch hour to pick Emmett up for work, which gave Ron some badly needed peace and quiet. And in a rush of inspiration he finished his article for the *Clarion*.

Suddenly he had all the time in the world to think about Jeanne, to mull over their quick and unexpected courtship.

With nothing better to do, he decided to transcribe his handwritten journal to a computer disk. Edit it, condense it, and at the same time review, decide if this was where he wanted to be headed. It would be like taking a journey without ever leaving the high-rise.

He spent the afternoon typing, sorting, thinking. And it made him all the more certain of his feelings for Jeanne. But the exercise had its downside. As dusk set in, he wasn't sure he could get through the night without seeing her. Passion and irritation welled inside him as he packed up his computer and papers. He stuffed the works haphazardly on the top of Emmett's bookshelf.

If only she were free.

She couldn't help it if she was working.

He'd only be in the way.

If she was really working and not simply hiding from him.

She had enjoyed the intimacy.

But had she been as ready as she seemed?

She'd never lie to him, never just dump him.

By six o'clock he was behind the wheel of the Plymouth.

If she'd lost the magic, he'd just have to help her find it again.

THE LAST THING Ron expected was a traffic jam on Jeanne's small, suburban street. Cars flanked the curbs, wedged into the tightest spots imaginable.

It appeared that somebody was having one hell of a Christmas bash.

Ron crawled along the street at a snail's pace, planning how he'd pull up in her driveway and park off to the side in case she had a customer or two who needed a spot.

His plan was short-lived. The Trent driveway was already crammed with cars, and was the only one on the street in that condition. Apparently Jeanne was the one having the Christmas bash!

Ron's foot hovered over the accelerator. He was tempted to zoom off, nurse his wounds at an old familiar bar someplace—where the women would be happy to see him, and no doubt cooperative.

But he just couldn't do it. He couldn't let this go. He'd introduced her to his friends, and listened sympathetically to the story that she didn't see many of her old friends because of her widowhood.

Well, somebody was hanging around. Every light blazed in the house and music rocked the foundations. It seemed everyone was there but the cops—and him. He hung a left at the corner and slipped into the first available space.

He stalked down the sidewalk, barrelled around the corner and almost collided with a little man walking his dog. He apologized and kept on moving.

Was a pattern forming? he wondered as he jabbed the doorbell. Again, he was standing on this stoop, hopping mad. This time she wouldn't smooth things over with a limpid look. Nosirree.

Nobody answered the bell. As he was jabbing it for the fifth time the inside door opened. A young man of eighteen or twenty stared suspiciously at Ron. Then the storm door creaked open a crack.

"Where's Jeanne?"

"You sellin' something, buddy?"

Ron bared his white teeth. "No, buddy."

"You the brother?"

"No!"

Ron gritted his teeth in disappointment. Obviously this wasn't Jeanne's little brother Andrew. So, who was the young whip who seemed so overly protective of Jeanne? The kid edged his head and shoulders into view and Ron's eyes widened. He was wearing a tuxedo!

Young, but old enough, Ron surmised.

"She expecting you, or what?"

"Or what." Ron pushed past the kid, charged into the foyer and came to a quick halt. The place was crawling with couples in formal wear. He was out of place in his forest-green sweater, black jeans and blue ski jacket. What was going on here? He felt ancient. The kid who answered the door was on the threshold of manhood, but the majority of these other males were still battling acne!

He didn't notice Jeanne until she was right beside him.

"Good evening."

"Uh, good evening." Ron's eyes roved over her figure. She was dressed more casually than he was, in a mint sweatshirt and faded denims. But she looked every bit as harassed.

"You're upsetting the flow," she told him with a toss of her head.

Ron's brows jumped a mile. "Huh?"

"Oh, come on."

As she tugged him along by the elbow, Ron was vaguely aware of the teenage girls in candy-colored gowns staring at him. In a hungry, dreamy-eyed way that added to his embarrassment.

"This is Ron," Jeanne called out above the racket.

A very pretty Oriental girl dressed in rose taffeta inspected him from the studio doorway. "Is he yours, Jeanne?"

Jeanne blushed. "Well, yes, Jaclyn, I guess so. Wild-eyed and shaggy-haired and all."

"I would've come in black tie had I known," Ron announced evenly.

Jaclyn's slanted dark eyes danced merrily. "Never mind. You're way cool as you are!" She swished off to spread the news. Widow Jeanne was back in circulation. And had landed a hunk.

"Just look what you've done!" Jeanne chided, throwing her hands up in the air as she flew into her studio.

Ron followed. Amazingly, this room was empty. But it was obvious that a photo shoot was planned. An ice-castle backdrop covered the back wall, and a camera was set up on the tripod, ready for action. Jeanne closed the door behind them with a firm shove.

"What did I do?" he repeated. "I think what I did was polish up your image."

To his surprise she laughed. "Yes, along with disrupting my well-tuned schedule. The least you can do is explain why you've come in the first place."

"Would you believe I happened to be in the neighborhood?"

Her small mouth twitched. "Maybe..."

"And couldn't resist stopping by?"

She squinted at him. "You looked ready to beat somebody up."

He balled his fists. "Okay, okay, I was ticked and anxious about your brush-off and decided to come over. And subsequently went nuts when I figured you were having a party without me. Satisfied?"

With a throaty chuckle she cuddled up close, and eased her arms around his middle underneath his ski jacket.

''Happy, grateful, but not at all satisfied.'' She stood on tiptoe to give him a long, luxurious kiss. ''Oh, Ron, this is the nicest gift you could've given me right now. Caring enough to be jealous.''

Ron's hands skimmed her hourglass waistline and the base of her spine, and gently pushed her belly into his. ''We've been all through this, honey. I'm hooked.''

''I know. Still...''

''I do understand,'' he crooned in her ear. ''Last night we were tipsy and needy.'' He hugged her fiercely. ''But it's all the more real to me today. And I simply needed to hear the same from you. In person.''

''That's exactly right, darling.'' She rested her head on his chest, the rhythm of his hammering heart the sweetest music imaginable. ''Exactly how I feel, too.''

''So why didn't you want me around today?''

She raised her head to look at him. ''Because you're just too distracting!''

''What is going on here?'' he asked hoarsely. ''And how can we make them go away?''

''We can't,'' she said with a heartfelt sigh. ''This happens to be my biggest money-maker of the year. ''Pictures for Rigby High's Snowflake Dance.''

''Like prom pictures?''

''Yes. Another gold-mine event for area photographers. I'm hoping, with time, I'll garner some contracts for proms from area schools. But right now, all I have is Rigby's Snowflake. It's my third year at it.''

Ron looked around again. ''You herd the couples in here one by one and shoot them? Must take forever.''

She glanced at the clock on the wall. ''Yes, and it's time I got started.''

The door opened suddenly and Toby raced in, a cherub-faced terror in tennis shoes, dungaree coveralls and a festive candy-stripe T-shirt. ''Where's my hat? I need the hat to be the helper.'' His eyes grew round as he spotted Ron. ''Hey, Ronny! You come!''

''Sure, sport.''

The boy scampered over to wedge himself between the adults. Ron picked him up and gave a twirl in the air. Toby squealed in delight.

Jeanne reached for her spare camera on the desk and took some quick shots of the pair, then struggled to look stern. ''Now, boys, it's time for work.''

Toby's hazel eyes were huge as Ron set him down. ''My hat!''

''Is this it?'' Ron moved to the desk where he'd spotted a red-velvet Santa's hat trimmed with fur. Toby nodded, so Ron bent over and placed it on the child's crown of fluffy blond hair. The tip of the hat had a bell that tinkled every time Toby bobbed his head.

Jeanne clapped her hands. ''You, Toby, go tell the kids to line up. You, Ronny, go into the kitchen for Angie.''

''She's here to help? I'm not, but she is?''

Jeanne gestured toward the bathroom. ''Do you know anything about hair and makeup?''

Ron gazed into the brightly lit room and realized that it was set up like a beauty salon. ''Not a thing.''

''Then move out. Sit in the kitchen and have a glass of wine.''

Ron obeyed. Halfway down the hall he collided with Angie, a purple streak in sweats. ''You're needed,'' he informed her merrily. ''Like right now.''

''You're needed yourself, Ron Coleman,'' she returned candidly. ''Like today and tomorrow and forever.''

He gave her arm a pat. ''Just try and get rid of me.''

''I just want you to understand how fragile Jeanne is.''

''I know,'' he said solemnly.

''Angie, get your hiney in here!'' Jeanne appeared in the studio doorway, fists clenched, screeching at the top of her lungs.

''Fragile as crystal underneath,'' Angie mouthed hurriedly before dashing off.

Ron was still smiling as he sauntered into the kitchen, pleasantly lost in his thoughts. The idea of finding peace over a solitary glass of some fine vintage was a foolishly shortsighted one. He was confronted with a tidal wave of season's greetings. From all the Potters! Catherine and Martin, and a man promptly introduced as Angie's husband, Brad, were seated around the table with a huge bottle of cheap wine and platters of snacks.

No wonder the schoolboy had mistaken him for brother Andrew. He was the only missing link!

''Oh, Ron, you felt you should be here in support, too.'' Catherine gushed, steering him to an empty chair.

Here in support? He could see why Jeanne was so nervous. Not only did she have a job to do, she had all her overprotective guardian angels hovering by. ''Busy place tonight,'' he said simply, reaching for a large brownie.

''You must be hungry,'' Martin observed. ''Get him a plate, Cat.''

''Of course.'' Catherine bustled to the cupboard. ''Did you have dinner, Ron? Bet you didn't. I can tell. Try some of the veggie dip. And those ham slices are fresh from the deli.''

''Wonder if Jeanne is ready for a plate,'' Brad mused. ''Something without a lot of sugar to harm her teeth.''

''No, I don't think so,'' Ron said quickly as he loaded his own plate.

Martin poured him a glass of wine, which Ron gratefully accepted.

''Been busy today?'' Catherine asked solicitously. ''You and your charming grandfather?''

If only he could continue to steer her away from Emmett. He took a large gulp of wine. ''I've been writing all day,'' he told them. ''That article for the Minneapolis *Clarion*.''

"But we live in St. Paul!" Martin thundered. "So does Emmett."

Ron chuckled, familiar with the rivalry between the cities. "I grew up in Minneapolis, though. Know a guy on the paper."

"Tell us about the article," Catherine urged, leaning over the table.

He did so between bites. He explained that it was about returning to one's hometown, and seeing its qualities through wiser eyes. "It's scheduled for the Monday edition."

"We will buy a dozen copies," Martin bellowed in delight. "Maybe two dozen."

Ron, soaking up their interest and admission, decided he just might enjoy being a Potter by proxy more than he'd thought.

Jeanne appeared in the kitchen ninety minutes later, looking weary but relieved. "I can use some help now, with the picking up."

A round of groans filled the air.

"Like always, there are some dirt stains on the carpet and smudges on the walls. And, heaven only knows, why all my decorative pillows are stuffed in the oddest places!"

Angie appeared behind her baby sister, clapping her hands. "C'mon, people, you can't expect me to do it all."

Grumbles that she was more than capable followed. But everyone rose and marched to the battle areas.

Ron and Jeanne lingered behind.

"Sorry you came?" she asked.

"Not at all." With a deep groan, he gathered her close. "I like your family."

"And they adore you." She stood on tiptoe to lick some sugar from the side of his mouth. The act soon turned into a deep, heady kiss, a swift stolen moment that both knew would have to last them the night.

Toby bounced into view, his hat ajingle. ‘‘Hey, everybody, they’re stealin’ smooches again!’’

‘‘Hey, everybody,’’ Ron growled against her mouth. ‘‘I’m collecting my candy-cane kisses.’’

12

"SEEMS IT WAS your turn to sleep in," Emmett observed dryly as Ron stumbled into the kitchen bleary-eyed, dressed only in his underwear.

"It *is* Sunday," Ron said, mimicking the excuse Emmett had used the day before.

Emmett poured him coffee, then settled down in his favorite easy chair before the television set. Ron smirked when he realized *It's A Wonderful Life* was on the air. Emmett had always coveted the Jimmy Stewart role and attempted to critique the actor's fine performance year after year. The Potters weren't the only ones with Christmas spirit and tradition!

"Have a nice evening, Ron?"

"Yes, even got another gift item out of Toby. A bulldozer for his sandbox."

Emmett toasted him with his mug. "Well done."

"Wasn't due to my skills, really," Ron admitted, sinking into the *Hamlet* chair. "I was tucking him into bed, and he was rambling on about his new best friend Jason, and it just popped out that they'd both be moving piles of dirt around this spring. Thought I'd pick it up at Grace Brothers this afternoon when I drop you off."

Emmett nodded. "Did you speak to Jeanne about the photo?"

"Yes, and she said the copies would be ready today."

"Splendid, splendid!"

"You're welcome, Pop," Ron teased.

Emmett lifted his shoulders in a way that made his emerald robe shimmer. "As usual, we do favors for each other."

Ron arched a brow. "Meaning?"

"Meaning that Burt from the newspaper sent a messenger for your story."

"You should've gotten me up!"

"I didn't have the heart. You looked so peaceful. Anyway, the disk was right there on the shelf."

Ron jumped up, sloshing coffee on his bare thigh, and raced to the bookshelf. Sure enough, the disk he'd set atop his stuff was missing. "You gave him the red disk, not the yellow one."

"Yes, the one marked, *Clarion*."

"Good work. The other one's my journal. I was condensing it for fun."

Emmett rolled his eyes. "Sounds like a real gas."

"It was very satisfying," Ron insisted. "I've never been so in love and I enjoyed thinking and writing about all the things that have happened, and the way they all happened."

Emmett snorted and returned to his movie, and Ron went for a second cup of coffee. Both were startled by a sharp rap on the high-rise's entry door.

"Now who could that be?" Emmett rose slowly and ambled over to the peephole.

Ron, in no condition to greet callers in his skivvies, peered out of the kitchen, ready to dash to the bedroom. "So who is it?"

"Why, it's her!" Emmett rejoiced, admiration in his tone.

Ron scowled and hissed. "Her who?"

"The cheeky one. Cat."

Ron was a streak of tanned skin as he escaped to his room.

He reappeared minutes later dressed in the first thing he could put his hands on, his gray workout sweats. Catherine had taken far greater care with her appearance. Her flaxen hair was done up in a neat little knot, there was a dash of color on her high cheekbones, and her turquoise blouse and dark trousers were pressed to perfection. She was still a fine-looking woman. It was like looking at Jeanne twenty-five years from now.

His Christmas future. It warmed Ron to think of it. He wouldn't be a crusty old bachelor, after all. He'd be a doddering old husband, still foolishly in love.

"There you are, sleepyhead!" Catherine nodded at him from the dinnette area, a pair of scissors in her hand and rolls of snowman-figured paper piled on the table. It was clear she'd come to wrap Toby's presents.

"Morning, Cat."

Catherine looked around at her helper. "Get my tote, Emmer, over on the chair. There's ribbon, and tape, and lord only knows what else inside!"

Ron sidled over to nudge Emmett with his elbow. *Emmer?* he mouthed out of Catherine's vision.

The old man brushed him off like a pesky fly. "We're busy as blazes here. Help or get lost."

Ron gathered up Toby's gifts in the guest room, and hauled them to the dinette. Catherine eyed the remote-control car box, then unrolled some wrap. "Oh, yes, Emmer, there's a brown envelope in the tote for you from Jeanne."

Ron and Emmett exchanged a horrified look, and raced each other to the bag. Jeanne had sent along the photos of Emmett as Santa? Emmett's withered hand dipped into the tote and produced the eight-by-ten envelope. The men's expressions grew relieved. It was closed and crisscrossed with masking tape, impervious to snoops.

Catherine watched them curiously. "Seems rather large for a Christmas card. It's about the size of an eight-by-ten glossy."

"Maybe it's one of the photos she took of me with Toby," Ron improvised. "A holiday thing."

"We had a photo taken of Toby with Santa, you know," Catherine confided huffily. "But after all the fuss, Jeanne simply put it aside, won't even let me see it again."

"Jeanne knows best, I'm sure," Ron said. "Did I tell you I'm going to get that bulldozer this afternoon?"

"Yes, you told me last night." Catherine snapped her fingers, and pointed to the envelope. "Well, let's have a look."

"When we have all this work to do?" Emmett squared his shoulders and the deep voice that thrilled audiences filled the room.

Catherine's pretty blue eyes clouded. "You know, there's something about the way you lift your chin, and your voice when you speak out like that." She shook her head. "I'm sure I know you."

The men mumbled and turned away. Catherine shrugged and got back to work.

"So what is Jeanne up to today?" Ron asked. He'd moved to the table to hold corners as Catherine efficiently taped them.

"Oh, she and Toby are over at our place. Andrew's home from college—arrived at about six this morning. We had every minute of these days planned before you appeared, Ron. We wanted to keep Jeanne as cheery and busy as possible." She sighed, pressing a hand to her chest. "Jeanne is such a loyal kind of person. The type to make a commitment and stick to it. We had recommended that she play the field a bit before falling so hard for one man again. But here are the two of you, all locked up, heart and soul. I mean, you do love her back, don't you?"

"Yes, Catherine, I most sincerely do."

"Yes. Well, then it's all right then, isn't it?"

"It's all right," he assured her with twinkling eyes. "It's never been more all right."

''Oh, oh, what a merry Christmas for all of us!'' Emmett bellowed, bouncing Ron the basketball.

Catherine's back arched and her scissors stopped on the paper in midsnip. Ever so slowly she stood up to her full height, and turned to Emmett. ''Repeat what you said,'' she requested crisply.

''Whatever do you mean, Cat?'' Emmett asked guilelessly, still the first-class stage performer.

''Change those oh-ohs to ho-hos, if you please.''

''Rather not strain my voice, dear lady.''

''Go ahead, anyway. Make my day.'' Squinting meanly she raised the hand holding the shears and advanced toward the old man. Ron gently caught her wrist and disarmed her. ''I'll wrap the basketball.''

She forged on, her fingers now pointing accusingly. ''You!''

''Me?'' Emmett's tone was a silken bedroom baritone.

''I thought Jeanne was trying to keep us apart, and now I'm beginning to understand why. And I'll just bet that whatever's in that envelope proves my point.''

''Point?'' Ron croaked. The ball slipped from his fingers, and bounced to the kitchen, making a plopping sound in the electrified silence.

''Jeanne was behaving very strangely about that envelope. Didn't want me to see inside it.'' Before either male could stop her, she had snatched it from the coffee table, and was tearing away the layers of tape. Glossy eight-by-tens spilled out on the carpet. Images of Ron and Toby with the red-velvet hat were unfortunately followed by snaps of Emmett in all his jolly glory, holding tight to a startled Lenora. Catherine wasted no time snatching up a copy of the latter. ''Ah-ha! It's true!''

''Now, Catherine,'' Ron began slowly, putting out his hands.

An agonized sound erupted from the depths of her throat.

"Do you know what you've done to us, making Toby those promises?"

Ron stepped in front of his grandfather, whose facade was crumbling. "We've already settled this with Jeanne."

"Have you really!" It was more an exclamation of disgust than a query. "Jeanne said she was taking care of it—but—but this is how?" Catherine shook a fist at Emmett.

"You know I'm doing my level best to get the answers out of the child," Ron said reasonably.

"But it's the old man here who has the power to fix things to make a retraction!"

"Santa does not renege," Emmett said loftily from behind Ron's solid shoulder.

Ron stifled a laugh. "Catherine, everything is under control, honestly."

"Is it? What's the last scribble mean? You have all the others, but not the last one. The one that Toby's least likely to talk about."

Ron sobered. "I'll find out. I promise!"

"No, you won't," she spat furiously. Grabbing her tote, she shoveled all her supplies inside. "I'm taking these gifts along as planned. And don't you dare try and stop me. Don't you dare!"

The men carried the stuff into the hallway for her. She went off on the first of the two necessary trips to her car.

"Maybe you should try and stop her," Emmett suggested, sagging against the corridor wall. "From leaving altogether."

"Stop a Potter?" Ron raked his hands through his shaggy hair. "If I tried she'd probably gleefully add forcible confinement to our crimes."

"Very well." With a regal sniff he disappeared into the apartment.

Ron paced the floor for the next two hours. He called Jeanne's house several times, but there was no answer. Of course she was at the family compound, whooping it up with her brother and the rest. At least they would have been whooping it up until Catherine burst in on the scene. She'd probably be furious with Jeanne because Jeanne had kept Emmett's identity secret to protect Ron. The Potters wouldn't appreciate that kind of insubordination.

If only Ron could fix the situation. What would be the wisest next move? He paused at the window, overlooking Como Avenue, watching the snow fall ever so gently to the ancient trees below. For a moment he relived the chilly glory of their sleigh ride, the laughter, the carols, the second sleigh ride. They'd created their own Christmas card that night. Romantic perfection.

But all in all he should have known better than to expect an idyllic repeat of Christmas Past, of days as carefree as those of childhood. Christmas might very well be just for youngsters, after all.

The telephone rang during his musings. He picked up on the second ring.

"Oh, Ron! Thank goodness you're there!"

"Jeanne. Thank goodness you called." His voice cracked with relief. "I tried your house. Believe me, I'm so sorry for what happened."

"I'm sure you are," she crooned in sympathy.

"And rest assured, I'm here for you."

There was a pause on the line. "What I want to say, Ron, is that you're best off right where you are."

"Huh?"

"I mean, I'm glad you had the sense not to go to my folks', or come to my house."

His lean features darkened. "Jeanne, you can't mean it."

"The family's in an uproar. Everything's a mess."

"Is Catherine angry with you for shielding Emmett?" he asked tightly.

"Yes, a little. But they're busier plotting damage control, fuming over you and Emmett," she finished in a small voice.

''Oh.'' The single word response sounded flat and discouraged.

''You can't be surprised, Ron,'' she said almost accusingly.

''If only you'd stopped her from coming here, Jeanne.''

''I tried. But she's impossible. You know firsthand how impossible.''

''I can't help but be a little angry myself,'' he said hotly. ''I've run myself ragged trying to set this right for Toby, and court you, and it all blows up in my face right before Christmas.''

''I think you're being selfish here,'' she snapped.

''No, I'm not,'' he countered, his voice rising. ''A little more time and I'd have been the hero. I'd have found the last thing on Toby's list. All I needed was another day.''

''You don't know that, Ron! Nobody but Toby knows what that last wish is. Nobody knows if you could've made it come true.''

He hooted in disbelief. ''But just yesterday you were satisfied with my efforts. Thought I could do anything and everything!''

Her voice caught in a small sob. ''I'm so sorry, Ron. This is a lot my own fault, for sure. Maybe I was wrong to let myself fall in love again so soon.''

''That isn't wrong!''

''It hasn't worked out at all, though. My family's a wreck. They're trying to question Toby and he doesn't understand. He thinks they're crazy.''

''He understands very well then, in my opinion!''

''How dare you! With a loony grandfather who believes he's Santa Claus!''

''Oh, Jeanne. Let's not—''

''You know what I'm leading up to,'' she cut in sharply. ''We simply have to end things here. Before we get in too deep.''

"Before—" He was already drowning in his passions, his dreams. "But we love each other!" he roared.

"We hardly know each other."

"Not so," he insisted.

"A little corner of my mind still is unsure," she admitted. "About a future with a man so different."

"Different from David?"

"Well, yes!"

Ron felt his very soul was on fire. How could he compete with a memory? "How would he have handled all of this?"

"He would've throttled his grandfather into submission for starters," she readily replied.

"I just couldn't, Jeanne. It isn't our way."

"I know. David's from no-nonsense stock. And you, Ron, you're from—from summer stock!"

"Has it occurred to you that we come from the same kind of stubborn, high-spirited people?"

"Of course it has! And it spells dynamite dynamics. All the more reason to make sure the feelings are lasting, before we incinerate each other."

"I can't replace the even-keeled David, Jeanne," he replied tersely. "I won't try to whip Emmett into shape, either. All I can do is offer to settle down with a woman I adore and light her fire in my own unique way. If, all things considered, you're looking for a David Trent replacement, you're out of luck. It's your decision."

She made it, too. She hung up.

Realizing it was time for Emmett to get to the store, Ron quickly changed into a shirt and slacks, then tracked the old man down in his bedroom. To his amazement, Emmett was back in bed, the covers crowded up around his throat as though he had a chill.

"I just can't go in today, son," he said feebly.

Ron clenched his fists. "The last thing I need is another crisis!"

"I know, I heard your side of the battle." Emmett's head

lolled on the pillows. "I'm dreadfully sorry, but I've decided my portrayal of jolly old St. Nick is completely unappreciated. The Potters hate me and Stanley Bickel would prefer to replace me with an unprofessional hack. All in all, I have lost the will to do the part justice."

Ron circled the bed like an anxious physician. "You said yourself that Jeanne's complaint was the only one. That should give you the confidence to fulfill your contract."

"No, the spark is gone. Go to the store and explain, will you?"

"I'll call Stanley," Ron suggested.

"No, son. Go in and speak to him in person." He pursed his dry and trembling lips. "Don't want him to sue."

"Oh, all right." Ron turned to leave, but Emmett grasped his hand. "The family circus is clouding the issue. I feel that Jeanne's biggest problem is her fear that you're not the marrying kind. That you'd grow tired of her and Toby. If only you'd concentrate on that angle. Try to convince her."

Ron's gaze was hooded, his voice curt. "I gave it my best. She has no excuse for doubts. She's seen me at my most sincere and that is that." With that parting shot, he fled the room.

"Yeah, yeah, just as I figured," Emmett grumbled to himself. "A chip off the old block. In communications, but communicating like mud." Emmett waited until he heard the front door slam, then sat up, fully clothed and full of vigor. "Blundering kid." He swung his legs off the bed like a man half his age and scrambled around the apartment, to the phone to call a cab, to the full-length mirror to smooth any wrinkles in his sweater and trousers. In all his haste he almost forgot the two keys to everything. That wouldn't do. Wouldn't do at all!

RON RETURNED to the apartment hours later, beet-red and seething. He stalked up to Emmett, who was calmly seated in his *Death of a Salesman* rocker, reading a book.

"You knew it was going to happen! Knew!"

Emmett carefully slipped a bookmark between the pages he was reading. "What are you going on about?"

"Santa Claus! You knew I'd have to take your place at the Pole."

"Really!" Emmett savored the image. "How'd you do?"

His interest threw Ron off balance. He sank down on the arm of his grandfather's chair. "I don't know. Nobody threw tomatoes."

"Splendid. Thanks so much."

"You knew, though, Pop. That was a dirty trick."

"Stanley Bickel's cousin is standing by—"

"Not anymore," Ron cut in rudely. "He's in jail on some kind of traffic offense."

Emmett raised his eyes. "Oh, my stars."

"Lenora admitted that the whole store knows about it."

Emmett's chest heaved. "Very well. I did know about the bad-seed Bickel. But I really couldn't go in today, and my contract makes me responsible for the position—"

"Bickel explained all of that as he threw the suit on me."

"Well, in any case, I'll be more than happy to return on the morrow."

Ron exhaled. "No, you're fired."

"Fired!"

"Sacked, terminated, history. Bickel insisted. Said if we caused trouble he would sue."

Emmett made a cackling sound. "Oh well, just let him try to find a replacement, with two more shopping days till Christmas."

Ron released another breath, and patted the old man's shoulder. "He won't have to. It's me. For the duration."

"You! Ronny!"

''I'm sorry, Pop. But it's the only terms he'd agree to. He said the line moved quicker, and Lenora's production at the service desk was way up.''

''Oh, I see.'' Emmett bit his lip thoughtfully.

''Are you mad?'' Ron asked in concern.

''No, I understand you were trapped. And I had a long and satisfying run up there at the Pole.'' He smiled broadly then. ''Told you you had what it takes to shine in the footlights. It'll be kind of nice, having glossy photos of each of us in action. Santa and son.'' He gestured to the wall behind the television. ''I'll hang them both there.''

Ron's eyes crinkled at the corners. ''Yeah, sure. A couple of mad troopers.''

Emmett beamed approvingly. ''Even though you're my grandson, you've always been just like a son to me. The son I never had.''

''I know, Pop. Just the way...''

''The way what?''

''Never mind.'' Ron left the room quickly as his eyes moistened. He'd so foolishly begun to view Toby as the son he'd never had. Ron and Toby, father and son. The idea that Jeanne could just cut him off, because she'd been influenced by her parents' anger and their doubts, split his heart in two.

13

JEANNE'S PHONE RANG early on Christmas Eve morning. Just after six. Thinking it was the alarm on her clock radio, she gave the snooze button several vicious stabs with her index finger. When that didn't work, she felt her way across the nightstand to her telephone, snagged the receiver and drew it down into her warm cocoon.

"Merry, Merry Christmas," she mumbled into the mouthpiece.

"This is Elaine, Jeanne. Elaine Rosetti."

"Oh, Elaine." Jeanne blinked rapidly and struggled to sit up. Damn that Ron. Had he told his pals their problems?

"Just called to say that of course we get the *Clarion* delivered to our doorstep here in Minneapolis—"

"I don't follow you, Elaine."

"Oh, my gosh. I bet it's a surprise from Ron."

"What?" Jeanne knew her voice was sharp, but she couldn't help it. She'd had enough surprises.

"His article."

"Oh, I know about that—"

"The picture of him and Toby is precious. Adorable."

"There's a picture of the two of them?"

"Yes, Ron's putting the red hat on him. Didn't you know?"

"Not about the picture," Jeanne hedged, gathering her groggy wits as quickly as she could. Wasn't that article supposed to be about returning home and recapturing the lost spirit of Christmas or something?

"It's so precious and so revealing," Elaine went on. "I mean, the way it tells about Ron's return, his romance with you, the reawakening of family values inside him." She sniffed. "Oh, gosh, I just started to cry."

"And he named names," Jeanne said incredulously.

"Of course. You're a celebrity!"

Jeanne let her ramble on, and ultimately thanked her again for the wonderful party up north. She just had to see that paper. Right away.

"But where are we goin', Mommy?" Toby whined as Jeanne eased him out of his pajamas and into his clothes.

Jeanne released a harried sigh. "It won't take long. I just have to go buy a newspaper."

"We get one every day. On the step. I'll show you, Mommy."

"No, this is a different paper. From Minneapolis."

"Is it better?"

"Your picture's in there. With Ron."

"Me and Ronny!" His hazel eyes grew. "Gravy dam!"

The front bell rang just as she was helping Toby with his boots. She whisked open the door to find Emmett standing on the other side in a black felt hat and topcoat, a stack of papers in his arms.

"Wouldn't dare kill the messenger, would you?"

She grinned wryly. "Not on Christmas, Emmett. Please, come in."

Toby took the papers, raced into the living room, and plopped down on the floor. Jeanne went to retrieve one copy and guided Emmett back to the kitchen. "I'm afraid all I have to drink is grape juice," she announced. "Haven't had time to make coffee."

Emmett set his hat on the table. "Then grape juice it shall it be. Never had it before, but I'm game."

Jeanne brought a small glass to the table, her fingers itching to get hold of the paper.

"I feel there's something I should explain first," Emmett began.

"Elaine Rosetti already called with the details," she informed him. "As did several Potter relatives once removed. And an old grade-school teacher who never liked my handwriting. I know full well that Ron wrote about me, about us."

"Well, I just couldn't help feeling that you didn't have enough faith in Ron's sentiments."

"You felt? What do you mean, Emmett?"

"I'm here, because again I'm responsible for this situation." The old man studied his veined hands. "This article, as it stands, isn't as Ron meant it to be. It includes excerpts from his private journal."

With a horrified gasp, Jeanne fumbled with the paper.

"He submitted a much more superficial version to Burt Waters, the editor. I later delivered the second, more personal, disk, as well as the photo to Burt, claiming that Ron wanted him to blend it all together if he could."

"Ron must be ready to kill you!"

Emmett cleared his throat, fumbling with his tie. "No, I don't think so..."

"No?"

"He's still sleeping at the moment and hasn't a clue. I unplugged the telephone and closed his door."

She regarded him in exasperation. "Oh, Emmett."

"Thought if you spoke to him posthaste, patched things up, he would find the invasion of privacy worth it."

"You are so bad. So very very bad."

"Indeed." He sipped his grape juice docilely. "But I am right, am I not? You backed out because he suddenly was a Potter pariah and perhaps not a sure thing, not worth the fight?"

She hung her head. "Yes, it's true."

He tapped his finger on the paper. "You read this carefully. That's all I ask. If you decide you wish to reach Ron today, he'll be at Grace Brothers all afternoon."

"But why?"

"He's the new Santa there, of course!" He shook his head pityingly. "See what you miss when you slack off for even a day or two?"

She laughed, squeezing his hand. "I guess. Thanks for coming...and everything."

He drained his juice and stood up. "Oh, by the way, I must say I think you Potters owe me an apology."

Her forehead furrowed. "Now Emmett..."

"Well, it's partly my fault for refusing to have a look at your boy in the first place."

"What are you driving at?"

"Well, I didn't think I could recall his wishes. And understandably, because I did see hundreds upon hundreds of little monkeys."

Elaine thought she'd explode. "Emmett! The point. What is it?"

"I do remember Toby quite clearly. Not because of the toys he wanted, naturally. Not because of your lovely mother. But because of his last wish, so surprising, so delightful, so...splendid."

Jeanne peeled off her blue parka, joyously listening to Emmett's explanation. "Say, would you like another glass of grape juice?"

He nodded. "I believe I would. Good stuff, isn't it?"

GRACIE'S CURRENT SANTA couldn't help stealing a look at his watch that afternoon around two-fifty. Christmas Eve traffic in the store was thinning. Closing was scheduled for three.

It had been a slow day at the North Pole. Which was not surprising as it was a little late for the red man to make dreams come true. Or to have his own realized, for that matter.

How ironic that Jeanne should show up in the final minutes, wearing the same kind of determined expression she'd worn the first time they met in this place.

This time he watched her approach in her light blue jacket from behind his snowy white beard. His heart thundered in his chest, causing an alarming ringing in his ears. What could she possibly want now?

Jeanne slowed up near the gingerbread entrance to the Pole. Then, as though propelled by a burst of courage, she moved past the elves and photographer, climbed up the glittery staircase to the throne, and perched herself upon Santa's knee!

Ron cleared his throat. "I'm only the stand-in," he told her in his own personalized St. Nick bellow.

She searched his face frantically. "Don't you think I know who you are?"

"Do you know? Really know?" Ron stared her down with steely control. He was too hurt to assume anything, or to even hope for anything.

"As it happens," she went on, "I've already spoken to your predecessor. It's how I tracked you down."

"I don't understand, Jeanne," he said plaintively. It was sexual agony having her on his knee.

"Emmett came over to the house. With a copy of the article—"

"How did it turn out?"

She gasped in dismay. "Haven't you seen it *yet?*"

"No. Slept in. Came right over here. No one outside of Stanley Bickel and a few others even know who I am or where I am."

"Oh, Ron." She tipped her head against his soft white collar.

"People will talk, Jeanne—"

"You may as well know they're already talking."

"Meaning?"

She lifted her head and fingered his beard. ''Don't blow your stack, but Emmett tampered with your article.''

Ron's jaw slackened in disbelief. ''How? He wouldn't know the first thing about it.''

''He took your personal journal disk and the photo of you and Toby to the *Clarion* the other day—''

''Oh, no...''

''It isn't all that bad,'' she assured him. ''It's what made me rush over here.''

He lifted a bushy brow. ''Yeah?''

''Yeah,'' she confirmed with a nod. ''You were right and I was wrong, Ron. We do belong together. And the depth of your feelings for me and Toby—well, once I saw it in black and white, I melted into mush.''

His voice was husky. ''Tried to tell you.''

''I know. But I was married a long time to a different kind of man. It worked. I was happy. Then you came along and scared me clear to my toenails, Ron. What we shared was so sudden and intense, so—so different.''

''Maybe I just seemed too damn good to be true,'' he teased.

Her eyes twinkled. ''Gravy dam, you did.''

He asked cautiously, ''How about that family of yours? Is there a hangman's noose waiting?''

''No, not at all,'' she said happily. ''Why, once I called the Potters over to my place for an emergency meeting with Emmett—''

''You did what!''

Her blue eyes grew misty. ''Oh, Ron.'' She sniffed. ''Emmett did remember Toby once he saw him.''

''You're joking!''

''No. And do you know why?''

''Can't begin to guess.''

Her lower lip trembled. ''Because he wanted a new man around the house. Our house! Apparently he was tired of playing my little soldier—and baseball—all by himself.''

''Then Emmett was right, wasn't he?'' he marveled slowly. ''All Toby's dreams are within easy reach.''

''If you'll still have us!'' Throwing caution to the winds, she gave him a fierce hug.

Ron raised his hand to the redheaded photographer, ready and waiting at the tripod. But she didn't need the cue. The moment Jeanne pressed her lips to his, the bulb flashed. Why, anyone could plainly see the shot was picture-perfect.